ONCE A KING

ONE SECRET CORRUPTS A REALM

ONCE A KING

HOUGHTON MIFFLIN HARCOURT
BOSTON NEW YORK

ERIN SUMMERILL

hmhco.com

The text was set in ITC Legacy Serif Std.

Library of Congress Cataloging-in-Publication Data

Names: Summerill, Erin, 1978- author.

Title: Once a king / Erin Summerill.

Description: Boston ; New York : HMH Books for Young Readers, 2018 . |

Summary: Told in two voices, young King Aodren works with Lirra, a Channeler, to
dismantle his father's dark legacy and end the divide between Channelers—women
with a magical ability—and people without magic.

Identifiers: LCCN 2018034237 | ISBN 9781328949974 (hardback)

Subjects: | CYAC: Kings, queens, rulers, etc.—Fiction. | Magic—Fiction. | Fantasy.

Classification: LCC PZ7.1.S853 On 2018 | DDC [Fic]—dc23

LC record available at https://lccn.loc.gov/2018034237

Manufactured in the United States of America

DOC 10 9 8 7 6 5 4 3 2 1

4500739425

For Ma,
who showed me that the best partner of creativity is perseverance

CELIZE

Summer Castle

TOURNAMENT FIELD

Cathedral on the Cliff

Kingdoms' Market

Visitors' Camp

Orli's Home

Blacksmith Elementary

Lirra's Home

Shops

PORT OF CELIZE

Bakery

Tavern

FARMLAND

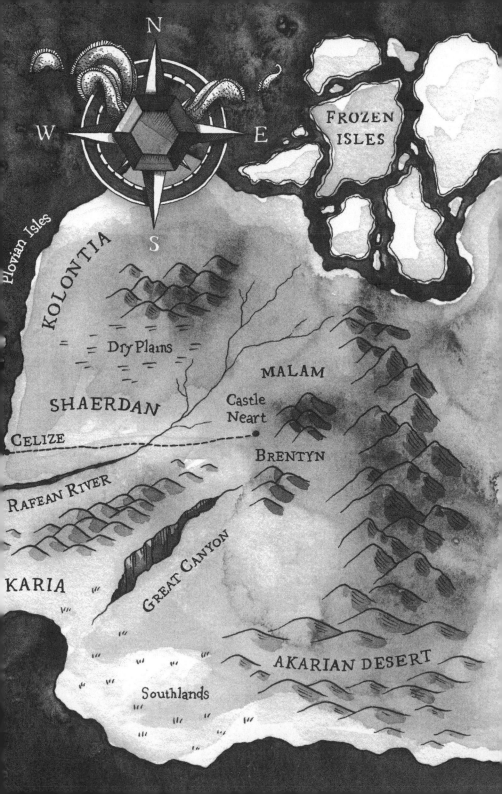

ONCE A KING

Hullo Beetle,

I'll not be returning in time for the summit.

CHAPTER

1

LIRRA

I LEAN AGAINST THE DUSTY ELEMENTIARY SHELF crammed with books and jars of animal bits, and stare at my father's letter. His nearly indecipherable scratch strikes me with swift disappointment. *Gods,* the All Kingdoms' Summit happens only every five years. It's not as if Da hasn't had time enough to arrange his schedule. The remainder of Da's message is blocked by another letter. It's sealed in my father's wax and addressed to someone named AC.

My heartbeat slogs through my ears, muting the chatter of mismatched accents and clatter of carriage wheels outside the Elementiary. What a fool I am for thinking this time Da's priorities would include something other than business. Having worked for my father for five years, I know better than to be hurt by this news. Just as I know, without reading further, Da needs me to deliver the letter to AC.

I suppose it also shouldn't be surprising that there's no note here for the littleuns or Eugenia, my stepmother and worrier extraordinaire. Overwhelmed by black-market trade and valuable secrets, Da tends to forget all else.

"Lirra, you done?" Orli's clipped tone echoes from the other side of the shelf.

I fold Da's letter, intending to finish it later, and squeeze my fingers along the parchment seam. One, two, three sharp slides.

"Almost," I call out, and shove the now-empty box back into concealment behind a jar of rat tails. To maintain our family's anonymity and safety, Da sends correspondences here for me to retrieve in secret. He trusts few people more than Astoria, the Elementiary owner and my former magic teacher.

"What'd he write?" Orli asks when I come into view.

My best friend is standing by the door, trapped in a stream of dusty light, right hand strangling the doorknob, the usual tawny tone leached from her knuckles. Despite her unease with Channeler magic, she's accompanied me here every week since Da left.

"He won't be returning for a while." I pick at the broken seal.

"You mean he'll miss the start of the tournament, right? He'll return for the jubilee and the other summit festivities."

I shake my head.

Raven brows shoot up. "He's going to miss your jubilee performance?"

My nail wedges under the last bit of red wax and frees it from the parchment. "Aye."

Astoria has one hand on her cane and the other clutching a pile of books, going about business as she usually does whenever I slip inside the Elementiary to pick up Da's mail. She ambles out of the backroom to her desk, where she deposits the stack. I'm not entirely sure she's noticed me until she lifts an age-spotted finger to shove her spectacles higher and then points to the letter in my hand. "Not what you were hoping?"

I slip it into my satchel and force a smile. "That's the way it is with Da's business."

"Oh, dear girl." She frowns. "And it's your first year entering the jubilee."

The sadness magnified in her watery blue eyes sours my mood.

My gaze drops to the ring of dirt darkening the hem of my day dress.

There's a shuffle thump of steps on the wood floors, and then Astoria's arms come around me, squeezing me to her wonderfully round body.

"Your da knows it's important to you." The love she radiates makes me feel like a cat basking in the sun. "He'd be there if he could."

Astoria has been Da's friend and closest confidant since

before my birth. She offered us a safe place to hide at her home in Shaerdan after we escaped Malam's Purge — the Channeler eradication that would have seen me killed for my magic ability. We have lived near her ever since. She understands Da better than anyone, but I don't want to hear her talk him up right now.

"She knows," Orli says. "All set to go, Lirra?" Her desperation to leave the Channeler school is as potent as the scent of lavender here.

"You don't have to leave so soon." Astoria returns to her desk. "Come away from that door and sit down."

"We need to run by the docks. Getting through all the visitors' carriages will take time." Orli points to the blown-glass windows. Outside, a rainbow of fabric has assaulted Shaerdan's capital city of Celize. Passersby wear their kingdoms' colors like a shield. Usually, the northern edge of town, where the cliffs climb up from the docks, sees little traffic. Travelers have invaded all of my hometown, even the quiet roads stretching east into farmlands and forests. Scores of people from the four neighboring kingdoms have been arriving for days in anticipation of the All Kingdoms' Summit and festivities — the Channeler Jubilee, the Tournament of Champions, and the Kingdoms' Market.

"Orli is right," I say. "We need extra time to look at the crowds." I have things to pick up for my jubilee exhibit that can't wait until tomorrow.

Astoria fiddles with the wrist button of her dress sleeve. "See you next week?"

I nod, even though it's uncertain if she's referring to the jubilee showcase or my next mail visit. My head is stuck on a memory from five years ago. At the last jubilee, Da and I watched from the sidelines. Channelers from across the kingdoms showed displays of magic. Breathless and awed, I confessed my dream to perform at the next jubilee.

Next week's jubilee.

Da said he wouldn't miss it for all the world.

Silence is the sweetest sound in the Barrett home, and such a rare thing to be had. It's alarming how loud the boards creak underfoot as Orli and I sneak inside the back door, both of us carrying packages from the dock market. Packages that could be easily snapped in half by my younger brothers' grubby fingers.

"Where is everyone?" Orli mouths.

I shake my head. The kitchen is filled with the usual mess, minus my family. Dirty dishrags lie heaped in a pile on Grandmother's table beside a discarded, half-finished drawing of a pig—or an owl. I cannot tell. A stale odor lingers in the air like a haunt of last night's leek-and-carrot soup. And then there's the crock of Eugenia's morning pottage, still sitting on the sooty hearth.

"Eugenia?" Never one to miss a Monday service, my

stepmother drags the littleuns to the cathedral on the cliff each week as penance for Da's profession.

No one answers.

I abandon my protective crouch around the wrapped wooden dowels. "The carriages on the road must've slowed her travel."

"Do you think it's odd that Eugenia will make peace over Millner's sins and then spend his earnings the next day?" Orli asks as we head down the hall toward the attic ladder that hangs in a permanent lowered position.

"When you talk about my da's business like that, it sounds wicked."

"It's not exactly saintly. Your father sells *secrets* to the highest bidder. Not produce or pelts."

"He's an information trader." I shrug off her comment, not eager to discuss my father.

Orli's head falls back, and she explodes with laughter. "That's a new one. Though a bit much for Millner Barrett. Maybe something like high ruler of the black market would be more accurate."

I laugh. At least she didn't call him *Archtraitor,* the infamous title he earned for defying the Malamian regent, evading capture, and building a secretive life in Shaerdan. It gets under my skin.

"My point is, she repents one day and spends his money the next." Orli follows me up to the attic room. She flops on my bed while I sit on the floor and arrange the dowels from largest to smallest. "It doesn't make sense."

Was that a note of irritation? I leave the packages lined up like soldiers before their captain. "What's this about?"

Gone is the easy smile she wore after leaving the Elementiary. Was today too much for her? Were the crowds overwhelming?

"I know what you're thinking, and that's not it." Orli slides her dark braids out of her face. "It's nothing. Forget I said anything."

"Nothing is nothing."

"That makes no sense."

I pinch her toe. "It means if something's important to you, it's important to me. No secrets."

She points to the packages. "Don't you want to finish unwrapping those before your brothers get home?"

I don't even glance down. "Subject change? Beginner's move. You know I have more self-control than that."

She guffaws. "A fox in a henhouse has more self-control than you."

"Exaggeration."

"Is it?" A little light brightens her stormy eyes. "I'm sore over Eugenia's soil order, is all. Satisfied?"

"The one for cabbage?" Wasn't that weeks ago?

"You know how the growing season is. Mum hasn't been able to enhance the soil." Late spring to summer means increased hours on Orli's family farm. Especially for her mum, who earns extra money by selling magic-infused soil for growing vibrant, pest-resistant plants. Altering the soil drains her energy, a cost all Channelers pay, which slows production.

"Has Eugenia been pestering her?" Even though Eugenia isn't a Channeler, she knows Channelers need time to restore energy.

I tear the packaging off the dowels to feel their notched ends, all sanded to a silken texture. The largest dowel, balanced on my open palm, is impossibly light. Almost weightless. The wood's scent is balsa and musk. A humid summer day and freedom.

"It's my mum." Orli's tiptoe-quiet response brings me back to the room. "She wants me to fill Eugenia's order. She thinks I'm ready."

"What do you think?"

She doesn't answer. A year ago, Orli was kidnapped as part of an attempted coup in Malam. The former regent was intent on siphoning magic from Channelers and combining the stolen energy into the ultimate weapon to use against the young king. I was part of the effort to rescue her, and ever since, Orli has been plagued with nightmarish memories and constant fears. It took months before she was able to leave her farm and venture into public. But she has yet to use her Channeler magic.

"I would help, but all I'm good for is blowing dirt around your farm." I nudge her knee.

Channelers have influence over one energy—land, air, fire, water, or spirit. Orli and her mother have the ability to manipulate the land, while I can harness the wind.

"That's all you're good for?" Orli rolls her eyes.

"It'd have to be a small pile. Dirt's heavy."

"You're full of hot air, you know that?"

"Better than dirt in the ears."

We both laugh, never too old for Channeler puns.

"Truthfully," Orli says, more serious. "All you've done this year is impressive."

Does she realize she's come far this year too? I open my mouth to tell her as much, but she cuts me off. "Don't be modest. I wasn't even referring to what you did for me." Her voice cracks with emotion.

My throat burns too. Dammit.

"I'd do it again," I whisper, knowing exactly how hard it was to find her. To free her.

Orli rubs her eyes, and then shoves me in the leg and adds an annoyed look. "Don't make me teary. I'd do the same for you, fool."

I know she would.

She scoots off the bed and sits cross-legged on the floor. "What I'm trying to say is what you've done with your gliders is a big deal. You use your magic in a different way than we grew up learning. Everything we created was from our energy. Like my mum and the soil. She has to sacrifice herself for every batch of stupid dirt. But your gliders are different."

"I use my magic to make them," I say, confused.

"No, you use magic to test them. To see if they'll fly."

This much is true. I wanted to build a contraption that would allow my brothers to glide in the sky without me having to conjure wind.

"Anyone, Channeler or giftless, can follow your pattern and make their own glider. You're going to show people a new way of looking at Channelers. Maybe they'll even see that we shouldn't be feared."

She's exaggerating. But . . .

"Maybe, hopefully, it'll inspire a few people," I say, though the possibility makes me feel like I've ingested a swarm of lightning bugs.

A door slams in the house, and a herd of elk rumbles through the hallway below. Eugenia shouts, "Not inside!"

"Sorry, Mum!" I hear my brothers say before the stampede alters course.

I rush to rewrap the dowels and hide them under my bed. "Do you want me to talk to her about the soil? Or are you ready?" I hate pressuring Orli, but she has to use her magic again one day. May as well be helping her mum and Eugenia.

"I'll figure something out. I'll be fine." Her expression shutters closed.

She thinks my winged inventions will change how people see Channelers. Maybe she's right. But what will it take to inspire her? To prove that her magic isn't to be feared?

I go downstairs to greet Eugenia in the kitchen and find her plucking dirty rags off the table.

"Any word from your da?" she asks.

"No." It's better not to mention he wrote me about business. When Da is working, Eugenia likes to pretend he's just taking a trip to visit friends. She won't acknowledge his methods of collecting and profiting off secrets if she can help it.

"Do you think he's all right?"

"He's been gone for longer stretches, and he always returns safely." I've become adept at managing Eugenia's worry.

Her hands knot in a dishrag. "Right. Of course. I'm sure he'll return for the festiv—"

The rear door smacks against the wall, startling us both. The twins race inside, skidding into their mother's feet.

Eugenia drops the rag, and screeches. "Boys!"

Despite her runny emotions, she lunges for them as they try to scramble away. Loren bangs into the table and upends a chair. Kiefer hunkers beside the hutch.

"What has gotten into you two?"

"Sorry, Mum," the boys chant.

"We don't run in the home. Look at this dirt. I just swept the floor, and now I'll have to do it again."

Loren rubs his hip. "Wasn't running, Mum. Just some quick moving."

"Save your quick movement for outdoors. Hear me?"

"But what of Lirra?"

"What about me?" I ask.

Loren's smile switches into something sly, like a youthful image of Da, all dimpled tanned cheeks, stocky frame, and windblown curls the color of wet driftwood. I've always longed to look more like them instead of a reminder of my mum, with nearly black hair so thick it could be roof thatching.

"Lirra does whatever she pleases." Loren turns pathetic cow eyes on Eugenia. "She don't follow rules."

If only that were true.

"And I've seen her run in the house."

Little toad. "You have not."

"Have too."

I turn to Eugenia for support. Working for Da requires living by another set of rules, something Eugenia knows even if she doesn't like it.

"You don't go to church." Loren points at me. "You sneak out at night. And sometimes you go around with mud on your face. Mum always makes us wash our faces. Doesn't she, Kief?"

Kiefer, the more silent twin, peeks around the hutch. "I seen mud on Lirra."

"Get back in your hiding spot," I growl at him before spinning to face Loren. "Don't pull me into this. You were foolish enough to get caught, so say you're sorry already."

He starts to complain, and Eugenia silences him with a look. The boys rush toward freedom in the shape of the back door. That's when I notice the specks.

Specks coating their trousers.

Specks on Loren's boots.

Specks that look an awful lot like *wood shavings?*

"Stop! Where have you two been?"

"Outside." Loren smirks over his shoulder.

"Where outside?"

"The shed."

"Which. Shed." My nostrils flare.

Kiefer cringes.

"Lirra, let them go," Eugenia says.

My glider wings are in that shed. If the boys touched them . . . "Tell me. Or this week at the summit festivities, I'll find the she-pirate, Song the Red, and pay her to sail you to Kolontia. The north is terribly cold. So cold that men and boys lose toes and feet and even legs. How fast will you run without legs, hmm, Loren? Tell me now—woodshed or my shed?"

"Yours," Kiefer blurts. His cherry cheeks turn pale pear green. "We only wanted a peek."

"We didn't touch nothing, promise." Loren presses his hands together in a prayer. "Spare me legs, Lir."

I hold in a smile. "Keep your stubby limbs for now, Loren. But if you—"

Eugenia scoots them out the door. "Don't be hard on them."

"They need to keep their dirty hands off my things."

"What do you expect, Lirra? They look up to you, and you run around breaking rules as if you've no responsibilities."

"No responsibilities?" Anger twists through me faster than

the twin tornados could destroy my stuff. "My responsibilities force me to break rules. My *job* for Da requires it."

She yanks a pin out of her bun, and her hair topples like a bird's nest breaking apart. "Don't pretend to be dedicated to your da's work when you spend all your time on gliders."

I gape at her, wounded by the insinuation. My family matters most. If Da asked me to pay more attention to his business, I'd do it. But he doesn't ask. He doesn't include me in every deal. He doesn't share all his secrets, as much as I'd like him to.

"What of your dedication?" I stomp to the window and point at the carriage parked inside the barrier of trees concealing our home. "Every week you visit the cathedral and make penance. Maybe instead of praying so much, you should notice how hard Da works for you. For the family."

Eyes widen over a stone expression. "Nonsense. You're angry because the boys were curious. I understand that, but you cannot blame them. Your contraptions look like children's toys."

Children's toys? Will the jubilee organizers think my glider is child's play too?

My fingernails dig crescents into my palms. "Was it curiosity when they broke your Plovian vase? The vase you insisted Da buy with his black-market money? Don't be a hypocrite." It comes out like spat venom.

Last year the twins knocked over the vase. Eugenia was

shattered. That same colorless devastation overtakes her expression now.

A baby's cry peals from the hallway.

I bite my vindictive lip. "I — I shouldn't have said that."

"Julisa's awake." Eugenia gives me a look of defeat and leaves.

I return to where Orli is waiting for me in the attic, my chest stuffy and hot with frustration. And shame.

It's not her fault that Da is gone. Or that he takes on too much work and doesn't allow me to help manage the load. He has me deliver messages to informants, listen to private conversations, and track people's habits, but he never asks for more. He tries to manage most of the work alone.

Loren and Kiefer are too young to help, and I doubt Eugenia would let them get involved in Da's business even if they were older. I'm the only one he can lean on. It's up to me to help him. Eugenia is right. I should be focusing on Da's letter, not my gliders.

"Whoa, what happened?" Orli watches me climb the ladder. "You look ready to practice dagger throwing on a live target."

I dig through my satchel for the letter. I peel it open and remove the letter to AC.

Hullo Beetle,
    I'll not be returning in time for the summit.

The rest of the page is blank.

"This cannot be all there is." I flip it over. Da would never use this much parchment for so short a note, or ask me to deliver a letter with no instructions. His message must be here, hidden.

Orli peers over my shoulder and hums to herself.

I trace the blank page. "I wonder if he used a blood charm. Da's never used one before. Blood charms are illegal, and even if they weren't, they're hard to come by," I say, remembering what Astoria taught us. "But it would explain why there are no words."

She releases a shuddery breath and taps the letter. "Right. And we are talking about Millner."

"I guess there's only one way to find out." I pull a dagger from my boot.

Orli sits on the bed, trembling fingers sliding under her thighs. "Go on."

I hate that magic makes her uncomfortable. But I have to know what Da wrote. I sink the blade's tip into the fleshy pad of my finger. A crimson drop bubbles from my skin and drips onto the ivory parchment, fanning out as it seeps into the surface.

Hullo Beetle,
    I'll not be returning in time for the summit.
    If you're reading this, you figured out the blood charm. The

following job must be completed immediately and privately. As you can tell, secrecy is of greatest importance.

To fulfill an agreement I've made with the king of Malam, you must deliver the enclosed letter to him. Don't curse. I know this assignment will displease you, but it must be done.

The king's letter has also been sealed with a blood charm. You'll find nothing there if you attempt to peek. Please explain to King Aodren how these types of charms are activated. The man's Channeler knowledge is in the budding stage.

Deliver the letter before the summit is underway. It cannot be late. Tell no one and go unseen.

Give my love to Eugenia, the boys, and Julisa.
Love, Da

"Bloody stars."

I'm not displeased. I'm furious.

What deal has my father made? King Aodren cares nothing for Channelers. Hell, his kingdom has encouraged the hunting of Channelers for the last twenty years. This is why my father and I were forced to flee Malam and live in Shaerdan. King Aodren may have ended the Purge Proclamation, the horrific law that was responsible for the deaths of countless Channelers in Malam for the last twenty years, but he did so out of desperation. Last year, King Aodren needed the Channelers Guild, the governing women who oversee all

Channelers in the five kingdoms, to save his life and help stop a plot to usurp the throne.

My efforts to save Orli caused my path to cross Aodren's. I was the one who introduced him to the Guild, and I even saved his life in battle. But has he ever expressed his gratitude for either?

No. Not at all. Ungrateful lout of a king.

King Aodren cares only about himself.

Da has all sorts of unsavory business associates, and though I dislike it, it's not so shocking to discover King Aodren is a new one. Royal coin is as good as commoner coin. What I don't understand, however, is why the king of Malam needs help from Da, ruler of the underground.

I press my fist to the sudden bloom of ache in my belly. I want to forget this request and finish my glider. But Eugenia's comment earlier nags me. Da needs me. And maybe this is the way to finally prove he can rely on me.

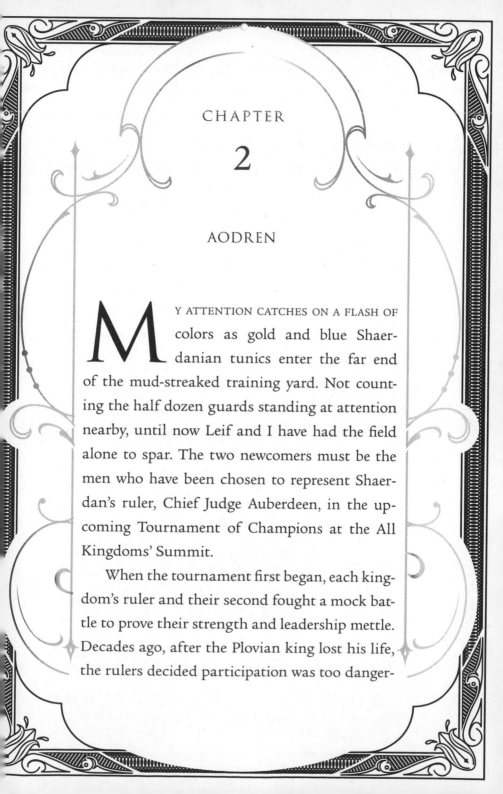

CHAPTER

2

AODREN

M Y ATTENTION CATCHES ON A FLASH OF colors as gold and blue Shaerdanian tunics enter the far end of the mud-streaked training yard. Not counting the half dozen guards standing at attention nearby, until now Leif and I have had the field alone to spar. The two newcomers must be the men who have been chosen to represent Shaerdan's ruler, Chief Judge Auberdeen, in the upcoming Tournament of Champions at the All Kingdoms' Summit.

When the tournament first began, each kingdom's ruler and their second fought a mock battle to prove their strength and leadership mettle. Decades ago, after the Plovian king lost his life, the rulers decided participation was too dangerous, and tradition changed. Now the most skilled warriors in the land vie to fight in place of their leader.

Leif, the first of my chosen competitors, swings his practice sword through the air. I thrust upward to block. It's too late. His waster slams my left arm. Bone-rattling pain lances from elbow to shoulder, and my weapon hits the ground.

Godstars! "Solid strike." I suck a breath between my teeth to temper the pain.

"Are you whistling, sir?" Leif chuckles.

Glaring, I straighten my posture, regain some of the dignity he knocked away, and switch to breathing through my nose, despite the moisture that clings to my nostrils. Shaerdan's humidity is also out to kill me today.

"I shouldn't have landed that," Leif says in a low voice. In my periphery, I notice one of the ever-present guards avert his gaze, and I wonder if he heard Leif's comment. It's too sympathetic for the captain of the royal guard—the elite force of the most skilled combatants in Malam. He needs to control that emotion if he and Baltroit, the other Malamian competitor, are to prove they're the best fighters in the five kingdoms. Grit wins tournaments, not sympathy.

The last All Kingdoms' Summit was five years ago, and I didn't attend. It's more important than ever that we have a good showing during the tournament. We must prove to the other leaders, my late father's peers, and to Malamians that Malam is worthy of being here. That I am worthy of being here.

I roll out my bruised shoulder. "I shouldn't have let you. On the battlefield, distraction means death."

Leif watches the Shaerdanians through the slits in his helmet. "Lucky there's no risk here." He reaches for the fallen practice waster and swings it in an arc. "Not with this blunted sword."

I move into position. "Enough talk."

"Oh, you're recovered? Ready to get beat?" Exhaustion helps Leif forget himself, a benefit of our sparring sessions. Too often, he lapses into the formality he feels the captain of the royal guard should maintain around the king. He forgets I am just a man and he is my closest, if not only, friend.

Chuckling, I switch grips to take the sword in my dominant right hand. "Captain and court jester, let's see how you fare now."

He snorts and swings his waster. I've spent the last six months training with Leif. I've studied his movement. He is quick, but I'm faster. I block his blade and push my weight into his. He stumbles. A vulnerable space opens between his elbow and ribs, and I strike. Leif grunts against the pain.

The rhythm of our clanks and curses echoes across the yard. This rigorous sparring session keeps Leif competition-ready for the Tournament of Champions. And it tempers the uneasiness that came on earlier today when my traveling retinue exited the forest and first beheld Shaerdan's summer castle. The stone fortress is designated for all leaders and dignitaries during the summit and sits north of Celize like a solemn gray throne.

My absence from the last summit sparked rumors that spread like a scourge. *King Aodren's too young. Soon he'll be just like his hateful father and the blood-spilling regent. Malam's people are divided, and the kingdom is weak. Under King Aodren, only time remains until the kingdom falls.*

Malam's history has more shameful spots than the sky has stars.

My father was a prejudiced man, whose fear of Channelers spread to his advisers and led to the Purge—a kingdom-wide Channeler eradication spanning nearly two decades. The feverish hunt for magic users turned neighbor on neighbor. After my father died when I was a child, a regent ruled until I came of age. He closed the Malamian borders so no one could leave or enter Malam. Trade halted and our economy suffered. This dark time was further blackened when, a year ago, the regent didn't want to relinquish power. He led a coup, killing hundreds of citizens and half of Malam's nobility.

The rumors hold some truth—I am the youngest ruler at the summit, my people are divided between support and opposition for Channelers, and Malam has been weakened.

But I won't be my father.

I won't allow Malam to fall.

When Leif and I are both aching and bruised, we stop fighting. I lean on my sword, breath sawing through my lungs. Leif tugs off his helmet. He swipes sweat from his beard and shakes out his hair. The usual amber color is now a slick mud-brown. "I could sleep till the first night of the tournament."

My thoughts as well. However, "It wouldn't do well to miss dinner."

Leif mutters an unenthused agreement.

Once our gear is stored in the yard house, two guards follow me and Leif off the field.

"See how in sync they are?" Leif glances at the Shaerdanians before they're out of sight. "If Baltroit would practice here, we'd have a better chance of winning the cup."

I scratch the day's stubble on my jaw. The summit, the tournament, and the jubilee are key factors in turning Malam's tide. We must do well in all three. When Lord Segrande insisted his son be chosen as the second competitor, I complied. Segrande was integral in the negotiations to reopen trade with Shaerdan, and going forward, his support is necessary to boost Malam's economy. While Segrande and I form alliances and trade agreements during summit meetings, Baltroit and Leif will be fighting in the Tournament of Champions.

Thousands of Malamians have traveled to Shaerdan to attend the events. A tournament win will inspire pride. It'll give Malamians a reason to rally together. A reason to set aside their differences. And hopefully, later, a reason to spread unity back in Malam.

Baltroit is a fierce fighter, but he's arrogant and refuses to train with Leif. While I could order Baltroit to the practice yard, it may offend Segrande, who has spent as much time training his son as I have with Leif.

"He won't let us down," I say, determined. "The two of you will do well."

Leif shoots me a look that argues otherwise.

The castle's grand hall is a clamor of voices, thuds, and scrapes, all under the aroma of rosemary and bread. As we pass through, conversation dims and everyone in sight bows. Our boots clack loudly against the stone stairs leading to the third floor, where Malam's private rooms are assigned. The two guards who followed us from the practice field take up posts at our closed corridor, while Leif enters my chambers.

He points to the stack of letters on the desk. "The courier delivered these to the castle. Also, the welcome meal will begin in two hours."

Half of Malam's fiefs have new leadership, and the repeal of the Purge Proclamation has made it possible for Channelers to return to Malam. A difficult transition, to say the least. To stay abreast of brewing tension, each lord reports on his fiefdom. Even during the summit.

"Inform Lord Segrande and tell him to come to my chambers at a quarter till." I start toward the washroom.

Leif lingers. "Your Highness, one more thing."

Your Highness. Few dare meet my eye, let alone speak to me directly. Some decorum is expected, but Leif's slip back into formality is aggravating. And isolating. "I'm scarcely six months older than you, and not a quarter-hour ago, you were trying to hit me with a practice sword. Call me by my given name."

"You're the king." He coughs into his fist.

"I'm aware. Trust me, rigid formality isn't always requisite. Understood?"

"Aye." His gaze shifts to the door. "At tonight's dinner, though, it'll be formal. Yes?"

"Yes. But you may talk with the other dignitaries."

"I—I'm not sure I can." A maroon tint stains his neck. He yanks his beard. It's hard to reconcile the man before me with the bear from the practice field. "Thing is, talking is not my strength."

Leif has notable battle experience, good rapport with the royal guard, and is unfailingly loyal, but he is also new to nobility. Too busy trying to bring Malam out of the darkness, I've overlooked his greenness.

"Talk about the tournament," I suggest. "King Gorenza will no doubt have much to say, since his youngest son is competing."

"Could work." He focuses on the floor stones for a long minute. "I won't be skilled like Captain Omar was with conversation. But I'll try."

I laugh, loud and irreverent. The long day is bringing out Leif's wit and humor.

But he doesn't join in, his mouth is pressed into a grim line.

Oh gods. Is he serious? My previous captain spoke in monosyllabic sentences.

"Leif." I restrain my laughter. Composure has been drilled into me since birth. "Omar used to say it's the message that matters. Remember that. Treat this dinner like those at Castle Neart."

"I mostly talk to Britta at Castle Neart. She's not here."

The comment comes unexpectedly.

The words settle over me like a scratchy wool throw. Britta and her husband are on their wedding trip instead of attending the summit. It's odd to consider her married, since I once hoped she would share my life. But . . . Britta is on my council. We will continue to work together. She will still be a friend.

"You'll do fine," I say, tone clipped.

Silence, and then, "Certainly, sir." Leif bows and leaves my chambers.

So much for convincing him to use my name. I walk to the desk and study the letters, though it's a fight to focus on any one of them. Perhaps Leif is right to remind me that friendships should be the furthest thing from my mind right now.

My focus must be Malam.

Correspondence to Aodren Lothar Cross, King of Malam:

March 25
  To the King our Most Sovereign Lord,
  By dictate of your wise council, I begin my monthly report of the affairs concerning my humble fiefdom. The abolishment

of the Purge Proclamation has been posted in the markets and common areas, and all countrymen have received notice of the new law sealed by your great hand. May the news be received well. Or perhaps I should write, may the news be received better than it has been thus far. I'm certain those displeased with the return of Channelers will soon welcome the newcomers.

Last, Sir Chilton, who inherited the bordering fiefdom after Lord Chamberlain was killed in the tragic attack on the castle, has struggled to manage his lands. The poor lad. If he needs to be relieved of his land, I offer my guardianship.

Your servant,
Lord Wynne of Jonespur

April 19

To the King, Lord of Malam,

This past month, four Channeler families returned from Shaerdan to reclaim lost lands. Unfortunately, their return was met with opposition—one barn fire, three travel carts destroyed, and numerous fights in the market square. I wish I could report these numbers amounted to less than last month.

In addition, the ore mine can no longer keep men employed until trade demand increases. The line of needy outside the church has doubled. And yet traders continue to come from Shaerdan. Considering Malamians have no coin to buy Shaerdanian goods, the traders must be foolishly optimistic.

Regardless, I hope the bordering kingdoms will welcome our trade soon. They cannot turn us away forever.

Your loyal man,
Lord Xavier Variant

April 24

To King Aodren Lothar Cross of Malam,

Difficulties have arisen as returning Channelers have declared ownership and sought possession of land that has been in another's hand for nearly two decades. Last week, a disagreement led to the destruction of two alfalfa fields, a Channeler booth in the marketplace, and a clergyman's entire cart of bread for the needy. It's impossible to say if these actions were meant to harm. I believe they were intended to scare.

Scribe for the Lord of Tahr,

Sir Ian Casper

May 5

To the King our Most Sovereign Lord,

Though your wise changes in the law dictated that the market be open to all, the appearance of Channelers has caused disturbances. Truly, I do all I can to keep peace. Channelers have been so bold as to ask friends and family to boycott the merchants that have refused business to persons of magic.

However, not all merchants have excluded Channelers. A new trader in the market square has been selling Channeler-made healing balms. A portion of townspeople have shown interest in his goods. One remedy gaining popularity is called Sanguine. It is a healing oil, and quite effective from what I've heard. Perhaps it could be a boon to our economy.

As always, I am humbly dedicated to overseeing my fief's needs, just as I could be with any additional land you might wish to grant upon me.

Your servant,

Lord Wynne of Jonespur

May 22

To King Aodren,

Calvin Bariston of Fennit passed on from injuries sustained in a tavern fight. It's uncertain who stabbed him, since he first stabbed two other men and one woman. Calvin was acting erratic, and was, we believe, possessed by a devil.

Rumors started that the cause was the Channelers. Those rumors were quickly proved unfounded.

Scribe for the Lord of Tahr,

Sir Ian Casper

June 1

To the King of Malam,

Rumors about the Channeler oil have spread after an occurrence last week. Onlookers reported that Mr. Erik Bayles met a passing trader in the market square to purchase Sanguine. For unknown reasons, Mr. Bayles became angry and struck the trader, who then hit back, punching Mr. Bayles once and killing him. The trader left town before he was questioned. I've sent men after him.

Without answers, many blame Channeler magic. Either Sanguine gave the trader unnatural strength, or it caused Mr. Bayles's death. Those who knew Mr. Bayles best have insisted he was a hard man to kill. I did not inquire how many times they tried.

The dispute has divided the town. Some businesses have refused service to anyone associated with Channelers. While I could force businesses to open their doors to all, I fear it will not end the division.

I must know, is Sanguine truly harmful? Please advise on how to restore order to my fief.

Your loyal man,

Lord Xavier Variant

After I dress for dinner and Leif returns with Lord Segrande, I scan the letters I received over the last few months and compare them to the newest batch.

"Anything promising, Your Highness?" Segrande surveys

the letters. His salt-and-sandy hair has taken a severe combing, unlike his untamed beard that twists and curls over the starched collar of his dinner coat. The mismatch suits Segrande, who is known for earning as many calluses as the people working the fields of his fief.

"More reports of division and opposition. Poverty in the ore fiefs. Destroyed property, disturbances in the market. More rumors that feed wariness of Channelers." The chair scrapes the floor as I push back from the desk and pace away.

Our retinue spent two weeks traveling through Malam. Two weeks of passing through towns and farmlands and seeing firsthand the chasm between countrymen that should've been mended by the Purge's abolishment.

Those two weeks confirmed that decrees don't assuage distrust.

We are a gray, threadbare tapestry in desperate need of new threads to strengthen us. But my people have spent two decades fearing the very color we need now. Regardless of the abolished Purge, our factionalism leaves us weak.

Ignoring the powerlessness dragging through my veins, I stalk across the room, drop down on a bench, and fasten the buckles of my boots tighter.

I remind myself that this is why I'm here. The summit, the tournament, the jubilee — they will be the start of change for Malam.

"What of this one? Sir Casper mentioned Sanguine, the Channeler oil. That's a pebble of good news." Segrande leans over the desk. His dinner coat bulges around his buttons. "More people buying the oil means more people are trusting Channelers."

"Look at Jonespur's letter. Or Variant's." I stand and scrutinize my shirt for lint, finding none. "Two men have died, and rumors link them to Channelers and the oil. People believe the oil is dangerous."

"Fools," Leif grouses from where he sits on the hearth's edge. "If they knew anything about Channelers, they'd know there's no danger. They're not going around killing anybody."

Segrande abandons the desk to wait at the door. "Some ideas are hard to bury. Those people have feared Channelers all their lives. That rock won't be turned over easily."

It's always rocks with Segrande. In this case, he's greatly underestimated the size of the problem. The prejudices dividing Malam are mountains. I look out the window at the city of tents stretching across the land to the southeast where thousands of foreigners have come for the Tournament of Champions and the jubilee.

"Has the Archtraitor reported anything?" Segrande asks.

"Millner." Leif mutters something more about unturned rocks.

"Slip of the tongue." Segrande chuckles. "We're the only three Malamians who refer to Millner by his given name. Most still consider him an enemy of Malam."

Irritation hardens Leif's face. I hadn't realized he had an opinion about Millner. He said nothing weeks ago when

I mentioned my choice to hire the man. But perhaps Leif's insistence on respect is because he and Millner share a commonality. Millner was once captain of the royal guard. Years ago, he protested the Purge. Because he was nobility, his defiance was considered traitorous. Guards burned his home, killing his wife. In retaliation, Millner ended those men's lives and became a fugitive in Shaerdan. Over the years, rumors have twisted the story, marking him as Malam's enemy—the Archtraitor.

But I know better than to put much weight in rumors. I've always admired Millner for standing up for what was right.

"He's sent no word yet," I admit, albeit reluctantly. I hoped his information would shed light on Sanguine and give me something positive to report to the Channelers Guild. It would be remiss of me to put off informing them. I tug on my dinner coat and turn to Segrande. "Draft a letter to Seeva. Explain the situation."

A cough sputters out of him. "The entire situation? The men who died? The rumors?"

I understand his apprehension. As a member of both the Channelers Guild and my advisory circle, Seeva Soliel won't be pleased to hear the rumors. And even less pleased to discover I waited to tell her. The Guild was reluctant to pledge their support to Malam, and though Seeva serves me, her loyalties still lie with Channelers first.

"Tell her everything," I command as we exit the chambers.

The guards escort us through the winding halls of the castle to the dining hall, where the other delegations are already seated around a mammoth oval table. The chief judge of Shaerdan, the queen of the Plovian Isles, the king of Kolontia, and their dignitaries sit on the far side, while I take a place beside Ku Toa of Akaria and her dignitaries, with Leif and Segrande at my right. Our guards remain in the room, their five different types of armor matching the flags hanging behind them. The mesh of kingdom colors serves as a reminder that not so long ago, Malam was headed to war with Shaerdan.

And now Shaerdan is the hosting kingdom and Chief Judge Auberdeen is the summit officiant. He makes formal introductions and then speaks about the upcoming summit meeting schedule, the Kingdoms' Market, the jubilee, and the tournament.

When the latter is mentioned, Leif shifts forward, eager and ready. The motion doesn't escape notice. King Gorenza scowls at my captain, likely because Leif will be competing against his son.

"All competitors fighting in your name must be declared at the March of Champions tomorrow." Auberdeen sets down a leather tome, thick with a hundred years of rules.

A murmured agreement rolls through the room, and then the meal is served.

The other leaders launch into a conversation, showing

their familiarity with one another. Auberdeen boasts about a new ship design that will make it possible to double the size of a trade shipment.

"A ship that large will give you freedom to introduce new imports," says an Akarian dignitary.

"True." Auberdeen nods to the Plovian queen. "Like silks from the isles."

"How fortunate for Malam that we've reestablished trade with Shaerdan." Segrande thumps the table, drawing light laughter. "In fact, we're already seeing the benefits." He turns to me.

"Yes." I lower my fork and seize the transition to discuss Sanguine. "I've heard word of a new import in our markets."

"You've snared our attention, Young King Aodren. Tell us more."

Young king? King Gorenza's booming delivery in a brisk Kolontian accent doesn't lighten the dig at my age. He sits languidly on the other side of the table, a head shorter than me, shoulders twice my width, nose like a hawk's. He has one arm draped on the chair's back and the other resting on the table. A casual domination of space.

"What item of trade, specifically, are you talking about?" he asks.

"Channeler oil," Leif answers.

"Oil for Channelers?" Auberdeen's confusion is mirrored by others around the table. He takes spectacles from his pocket and holds them beneath his unkempt eyebrow hedges. "Is that the new import?"

"Yes. No . . . I mean, no." Leif's face is the same color as the beets on his plate.

"Captain O'Floinn is referring to Sanguine," I explain. "It's said to be a Channeler-made healing remedy. Have you any experience with the oil?"

"Sounds familiar," murmurs a Plovian dignitary.

"The oil comes from Akaria, no?" King Gorenza focuses on the Ku, who is sitting to my left. "What do you know of it?'

Ku Toa is older than me by four or five decades, small in stature, and has a shorn head—as is the custom for the southern kingdoms' leaders. I turn to her, curious about her answer. But her dignitary, Olema, answers. "We have an oil in our land called Sanguine."

"Are they not the same, Fa Olema?" Gorenza props both arms on the table.

Olema is an ancient man, older than the Ku, with a face mapped in wrinkles. He exchanges a look with the Ku. "I cannot say."

"It's the most potent of all Channeler healing aids. Is it not?" asks Judge Soma, second in command to Auberdeen.

Everyone turns to the thin, lanky man.

"That so?" Gorenza stabs a roll with his knife.

Soma nods. "It's similar to Beannach water, but more potent. Are you familiar with Beannach?"

Earlier this year, Judge Auberdeen sent Soma to Malam to draft a treaty between our kingdoms. Soma was earnest and well informed. His contradicting opinion on Sanguine confirms that the rumors were fueled by prejudices. I know I should be pleased that Sanguine isn't hurting my people, but the hatred that must exist in my kingdom to start such a vicious rumor gnaws at me.

"*Beannach* means 'blessed,'" says Leif, jumping in when he can. "It replenishes."

A flicker of a smile twitches on the Ku's face.

"I know what it does." Gorenza shoves pieces of the impaled roll into his mouth, chewing viciously before adding, "Even if we don't use Channeler magic up north."

"And yet," says Soma, "at every summit, a Channeler from your kingdom performs in the jubilee."

"We don't use their magic, but they live among us." Gorenza yanks his knife free. He swings the point to face me. "Kolontia hasn't outlawed and hunted Channelers as Malam has."

Lord Segrande develops rigor mortis.

Queen Isadora's fork clatters on the table.

"Now that the stone's been thrown, we can move on," I say, having anticipated this reaction from the other leaders. "After all, Malam has. There isn't one of us whose kingdom has a spotless history. My people's shame is merely more recent."

Judge Auberdeen and Ku Toa's eyes slant to me, assessing.

Gorenza scoffs. "Will we actually see Channelers representing Malam at the jubilee this year?"

"Of course," I say. They think Malam will have no representative in the Channeler show, like the last four summits. They're wrong. The jubilee is one event in which I can rest easy. "Katallia of the Channelers Guild will wear Malam's colors. I'm honored that she calls Malam home."

Katallia became an ally when she fought alongside me to defeat Lord Jamis. When she performs in the name of Malam, she'll inspire pride in all Malamians.

"I'm sure it would've been difficult to find another willing Channeler," Gorenza says, oddly quiet. "How fortunate for you that Katallia's life was spared during your kingdom's extermination, which you did nothing to stop when you first came into power."

The room goes silent.

If a rat scuttled across the floor, its steps would register louder than a drumroll.

The pommel of my sword digs into my hip. A call to arms against such an appalling insult to my honor. I drag a breath through my teeth, tempering the wave of intense loathing, and bridling the urge to cut Gorenza down.

The smallest movement catches in my periphery. A Malamian guard has edged forward. Gorenza stares at him, nostrils flared in a look of daring that says he's primed to shed blood. Any guard in this room wouldn't hesitate to kill a person for caustic remarks made against their leader, but because Gorenza is the king, my guard waits. As does everyone else, sitting with bated breath.

I'm not here to start a war. I'm here for Malam, I remind myself.

For allegiances. For unity. For my people's future.

I flick out my hand, low to the side in a staying motion.

Auberdeen bangs the table with his fist, though he keeps an eye on me. "Enough talk of trade. King Gorenza, you have a grandchild on the way, do you not? Let me tell you about what my granddaughter said to me just this morning."

The single lamp illuminating my chambers is not enough to give shape to the clothing chest or prevent me from slamming my shin into the corner. I hop back, cursing, and yank off my coat. My boots come off next. One tumbles beneath the desk. The other hits the curtain. For a half second, I swear it's followed by an *oomph*. I pull the tunic over my head and let it drop, welcoming the cool evening air.

A shadow moves from behind the curtains. An intruder.

Pulse ricocheting through my veins, I snatch the sword at my hip.

The man grabs for something behind him. I lunge, thrusting the blade's point at the intruder's chest. He lets out a squawk. Hands hang at his sides, frozen.

"Don't move or I'll kill you."

A blast of wind slams into me, knocking me to the ground. I manage to keep a hand on my blade. I jump to my feet, but the distraction has given the intruder the advantage.

"I'd apologize for using a wind gust to knock you down," he—no, she says. A woman? A Channeler. Shock has me frozen in place. How did she get in here? "But you had a blade digging into my heart."

She shakes out her hands and steps into the lamplight. Blue eyes rimmed with stripes of black lashes stare at me from under a boy's cap. She looks like a scrawny stable boy. "You don't recognize me?"

The scrawny-stable-boy disguise throws me off. But a memory emerges of her on the same battlefield as me. Last year, she came to Malam seeking her friend, and she ended up fighting beside me to stop the army of traitors from taking Malam.

When I don't answer immediately, she huffs. "Figures." And then she tugs off her hat, releasing a coil of raven hair. "It's Lirra Barrett. I saved your life earlier this year."

She mutters under her breath about me not remembering, and then adds something that sounds like "arrogant arse."

Any shock still chilling my veins quickly heats with anger. Regardless of our past, how dare she be so brazen as to sneak into my room, use her Channeler magic on me, and then disrespect me?

"You've trespassed in my chamber. State your purpose." My tone is terse and cold.

She blinks at me. Her mouth pinches like she's tasted something bitter, and then she withdraws a letter from her pocket. "This is from my father."

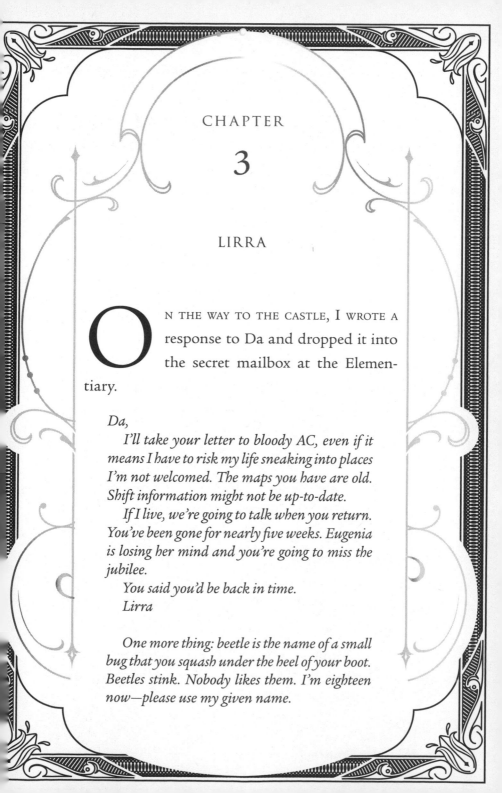

CHAPTER
3

LIRRA

O N THE WAY TO THE CASTLE, I WROTE A response to Da and dropped it into the secret mailbox at the Elementiary.

Da,

I'll take your letter to bloody AC, even if it means I have to risk my life sneaking into places I'm not welcomed. The maps you have are old. Shift information might not be up-to-date.

If I live, we're going to talk when you return. You've been gone for nearly five weeks. Eugenia is losing her mind and you're going to miss the jubilee.

You said you'd be back in time.
Lirra

One more thing: beetle is the name of a small bug that you squash under the heel of your boot. Beetles stink. Nobody likes them. I'm eighteen now—please use my given name.

Considering how many foreigners have swarmed Celize, clogging the roads and packing the camp set up by the tournament field, there's no telling when my letter will be delivered. But having jotted down my frustrations makes being in the room with the king of Malam infinitesimally more manageable.

King Aodren hasn't given me more than a second glance since I had to conjure wind to knock him down. His lips form a colorless circle around his thumb, the one he nicked to produce a drop of blood, as he peruses Da's letter. He reads at a snail's pace, with no care for his tunic still in a puddle on the floor.

Having snuck past a dozen guards already, my nerves are pulled taut. So standing here in the open, waiting for this man to tell me what Da has written, makes me even jumpier. The irritation I feel toward him doesn't help. He's not my king, and his kingdom isn't my kingdom. Once he tells me what Da has written, I'm out of here. Away from this ungrateful man who cares so little for Channelers that he cannot remember those who help him. The rumors about him using Channelers for his gain must be true.

I glance to the window, assessing other routes if a quick escape is needed. While I know the guards' schedules, I don't know when one of King Aodren's retinue will enter.

His thumb is no longer bleeding. He shakes out his hand and then pinches the bridge of his nose. A straight, never-been-broken nose. So unlike the other men to whom I've de-livered messages, whose rough lives have earned them equally rough exteriors. King Aodren is too straight. Too smooth. A sharp patrician profile, fine jaw, light bronzed skin too flaw-less to be real—a trick of the lamplight. It's impractical. A man who holds a kingdom's worth of power should be gritty and fearsome. Not fine. His face doesn't suit his title. This man is Aodren without *King* affixed.

It's unfair that he's so handsome. All gold hair and golden skin and a jaw like a wooden carving. Someone who wields his power so poorly and unjustly should have boils. Everywhere.

"Did you need anything else?"

His question startles me. I shift my weight and pluck at my tunic. "Pardon?"

"Are you in need of anything?"

"No. I mean, yes." I snatch my cap off the rug. "I'm waiting to hear what's in the letter."

Golden brows lift. "Is it any of your business?"

I'm already on edge from the sheer effort expended to break into this fortress and from being forced to interact with Aodren at all. I flick the parchment, and his gaze snaps to mine. "I'm the person who risked her life to sneak inside a highly guarded castle to bring you that. I'd say it's my busi-ness."

Those studious eyes slide into slits. "And what would your father say?"

"I don't think he'd say anything."

"Really? Why is that?"

"He isn't here."

He barks out a laugh. But just as abruptly as it came, it fades behind a bored expression. He scoops his tunic off the floor and slips it over his head. "When he returns, you can discuss with him the contents of his letter. For now, they are a private matter."

"Private?" I repeat, confused.

"The letter is addressed to me, the king of Malam."

"I know who you are." It's bad enough that Da is never home and I have to deal with Eugenia's constant state of worry that leads to fights like the one this morning. It's worse when I know it's because Da is doing favors for this pompous arse. "Could you please just tell me where he is?"

Wherever Da is will clue me in to what he's doing. And then maybe I can figure out how to help Da finish this job quickly. Or I could complete the job for him, then he'll see that he can rely on me as his business partner.

Aodren creases the parchment's folds. "I cannot."

"Cannot? Or will not?" Does he realize the effort it took to get here? Or the risks I faced?

Aodren crosses to the door, pulls it open, and strides into the hall. I watch him go, my jaw unhinged. Apparently if you're a king, you can make an exit in the middle of a conversation. The bludger. I want to pickpocket the letter right from under his perfect nose. But he may have left to alert the guards.

I shove my hair under my cap and climb up on the desk. Without knowing what the king is planning, the window will do as an alternate exit. I am in the opened window frame when he returns with Leif in tow.

"Where'd she go?" Leif scans the chambers.

The sight of my cousin makes me stop and smile. He doesn't notice me, but Aodren does. The king points out my location, and Leif throws his head back and laughs. "Lirra, what are you doing there?"

"It's nice that someone remembered me," I say, and Aodren's mouth puckers like he licked a lemon. "I was leaving."

"There are doors for that," Aodren drawls.

The night breeze slips through the window and blows past me. "A clever observation, Your Highness. But there are also guards with swords for killing intruders."

"Leif will escort you home." The finality in Aodren's tone is cool and crisp, the first bite of an October apple. It draws a shiver through my limbs, and I know I have no choice but to obey. I glare at the letter, captive in his hand. So help me, if Da asks me to deliver another one to this man, I'll leave a fish in his royal bed.

I follow Leif into the dim corridor, never once looking back at the king.

. . .

"I can make it home on my own," I tell Leif once we've left the castle grounds and we're traversing the main road that cuts through the camps. All around us groups gather at fire pits, telling stories over cups of tea and ale. Though clouds hide most of the stars, the full moon brightens the sky behind the ragged gaps.

"I gave him my word." The moonlight washes out his already sunless Malamian skin. "Also, it's nice to escape the castle."

Very few know the true location of my home. Safety, and all that. But I let my protest go, sensing Leif truly needs a break from the castle. When we met last year, we learned we were cousins, our families separated during the Purge. We spent a great deal of time together and became friends. Leif used to smile more. Sadness marks him now.

We approach the round fountain marking the heart of the camp. A center post rises in the shape of a tree trunk, and a dozen spigots branch off, spitting water into the pool below. Children run on the stone bench rimming the fountain, their paths winding around, their giggles and shrieks acting as music to their dance. A woman stands at the fountain's edge. She moves her hands and the water in the spigot closest to her, guided by her Channeler energy, sprays outward, hitting the children from head to toe. They squeal and run the loop again. Eugenia would have forced the twins to bed by now. But with the camp abuzz with conversation and anticipation,

I doubt anyone's going to fall asleep anytime soon. Maybe the woman is trying to tire the kids out.

"How's Gillian?" I ask about the handmaiden in Malam who had captured Leif's eye.

His deep frown is punctuated by the crunching of gravel underfoot.

"Was that too brash?" I nudge him with my shoulder. "It's a problem of mine."

A weak flicker of movement lifts the corners of his mouth. "I'm aware. She decided we . . ." He blows out a loud exhale. "We weren't a good fit."

That's a lie if I've ever heard one. They were completely inseparable, igniting rumors of marriage.

He must recognize the disbelief on my face, because he adds, "There was someone else." It's quiet, brimming with rejection.

Oh, Leif.

It's difficult to imagine Gillian passing Leif over for another. She and I weren't close friends; however, we lived together for a short while. She never struck me as someone who shuffled beaus like cards at a gambling table.

Leif's boot hits a rock, sending it skidding along the road ahead of us. "She's with a lord now, if you can believe it."

I gape. "She traded up?"

He winces, shoulders tightening.

All the time spent around Da and his rough informants

is showing. "Sorry. I didn't mean to suggest that you're not as valuable as a lord. I only meant, well, there are levels of nobility." In another life, courting a nobleman would've been expected of me so I could make an advantageous marriage. Though I'm not that girl anymore, I understand a lord outranks a captain and the pressure a girl might face to choose rank over the goodness of a man like Leif. Gillian . . . she was a kind girl, but she was in love with the ideas of romance and nobility. And all their nice things.

"Don't think badly of her," says Leif. Sweet Leif. "She knew him before. In the shuffle after the coup, he came for her. They were meant for each other."

Though we're family, I cannot imagine how anyone would not want this man. I reach around his wide shoulders to give him a friendly squeeze.

A shout echoes into the night.

Ahead, three men are near the far side of the fountain, facing the Channeler woman. The man nearest her stands with his feet wide, back taut, reminding me of a wild dog on the verge of attack. "We won't let you spread your poison," he says in the distinct blunt accent specific to Malamians.

If the ignorant Malamians knew anything about Channelers, they'd know she wasn't poisoning the fountain. It would go against the Channeler code — never use magic to do harm.

"Then don't use this fountain." The Channeler woman

pulls two children into her skirts as two men arrive at her side. The rest of the kids scatter.

"Your devil magic isn't allowed outside of the jubilee." The Malamian's voice grows louder and sharper. I notice the men are holding water jugs. Upon seeing the woman Channeling the water, they must've assumed—as ignorant, bigoted Malamians would—that she was tainting the fountain.

The argument gains volume and onlookers. I recognize one: Baz, a dockworker who's been flirting with me for months. His persistence would be annoying if he weren't so playful. He helped me order the dowels for my glider.

A Malamian yells a slur, and Baz's calm ignites into fury so swiftly, it's like watching lightning hit a forest during the dry season.

Baz punches the Malamian.

Shocked, I watch a fight break out.

Leif's moving, sword ready, rushing forward, shouting a command to stop in the name of the king. But no one's listening. No Shaerdanian cares for Malam's ruler. They think Aodren is a tyrant like the regent before him. The Malamians are in such a frenzy, I doubt they'd stop for anything, even King Aodren himself.

Fists smack against flesh. The fight spreads, a hungry fire consuming anyone on the path. Thuds and grunts and shouts rise like smoke above the frenzy. I rush forward, unsure where to go, or how to help. Channeler slurs fuel the blaze, and soon more than a dozen people are engulfed in the chaotic brawl that's grown too fast for Leif to stop.

Someone will die if it doesn't end soon.

Leif needs help. More than I can give. He needs the guards from the summer castle.

That's when I hear a child's wail and spot the two boys who had been hiding in the Channeler woman's skirts. Two little boys huddling together, years younger than my brothers, caught between the fountain's edge and the fury. An arrow of panic shoots straight through my chest. I search frantically for their mother among the men, who are fighting like beasts, feral and more violent than the typical tavern brawl. No one hears the boys' cries. No one will notice if the nose crunching beneath his fist belongs to a man or a child.

The fighters move, blocking my view of the boys.

Suddenly, I'm sprinting, dodging knees and elbows and clawed hands, weaving closer to the fountain. A thin, childlike wail spurs me faster. Faster.

Someone slams into me. The impact throws my body sideways against the fountain. I hit hard, the stone edge like a blunt blade, knocking the breath from me. Pain tears across my ribs. I try to inhale to get my bearings, but my lungs won't respond. Whoever did the damage has already moved on, either finished with me or so enthralled by beating another that he's oblivious.

Weight on my hands, I push myself up. *Find the boys. Find the boys.*

Agony stitches my left side, chopping my efforts to breathe into short gasps. I hear the clang of blade hitting blade. More than a few have graduated from fists to weapons. This fight won't last much longer.

I force air into my lungs and, breaking camp rules, hop into the fountain pool and slog across to where the boys huddle. Water courses down my legs as I tuck each little boy under an arm and rush around bodies and fists to the haven of the nearest tent.

I drop to my knees in front of them, my ribs ablaze. "Stay here, all right?"

The boys hunker down against the canvas, nodding, eyes like moons.

"I'll find your mother. You stay. Got it?"

Their trembling chins dip down and up.

I scurry back to the fountain, scanning the pandemonium for the woman. A groan rents the air, raw, anguished. The hairs on my neck stand.

Abandoning my search for the boys' mother, I look for Leif. Which is Eugenia-level ridiculous since he's Malam's tournament competitor, one of the most skilled fighters in Malam and fully capable of holding his own in a brawl. Still, my gaze ricochets between bloodied and bruised faces. I exhale a breath of relief when it's evident Leif isn't among them.

He must have gone to get the guards from the summer castle while I saved the boys.

But then a shock of rich auburn hair drags my eyes to the ground.

There, amidst the fallen, unconscious men, is Leif, with a blade's handle protruding from his chest.

CHAPTER

4

AODREN

I TOUCH THE PARCHMENT TO THE LAMP'S FLAME and watch the words burn away until all that remains of Millner's letter are flakes of ash. Even if he hadn't specified to keep his report secret from his daughter, I wouldn't have shared anything because it might compromise the situation in Malam. Besides, it was a brazen request. Those eyes glinted with anger like sharpened chips of slate.

Shouts sound in the distance.

I flick the last bits of the letter off my trousers and move to the window. Lanterns approach the castle gates, cats' eyes bobbing in the late evening. The yellow cast renders the holders' uniforms indistinguishable at first. But as they draw nearer, Shaerdan's blue and gold colors identify the men as castle guards. They're carrying something between them and shouting for the gate to be lifted.

Unexplained unease worms through me as it did the night of the coup. Memories of the past flash through my head in a haze of blood.

I bolt from my room, and rush through the corridors, startling the castle guards posted outside Malam's hall. They follow me down the stairs and through the inner keep, to where five wings branch away from a grand hall. The summer castle is a misshapen stone spider.

Doors near the base of the stairs screech open; wood slams against stone. Guards hustle inside, their movement awkward, their shuffling steps compensating for whatever they're carrying. A disheveled girl, wearing stable clothes follows behind.

Lirra? She couldn't have left my chambers more than half an hour past. Why has she returned? And with so many guards?

"What happened?" I cross the foyer to meet her, parting the crowd of castle workers and dignitaries, who all at once take in my presence and bow. Lirra doesn't move. She's slackened, haunted, unfocused, not reacting to anything, so I repeat myself, my voice sharp and demanding. "Lirra, what happened? Why are you here?"

A wince tightens her unfocused eyes and her ashen face.

"A fight broke out in the camp, Your Highness," the nearest guard answers for her. "Your captain happened upon it."

Leif was in a fight? What does this mean for the tournament? A low buzzing starts at the base of my skull. Judge Auberdeen and King Gorenza move closer to the group of guards. Out of the corner of my sight, I catch the red-and-gold robes of Ku Toa and her dignitaries standing near the Plovians.

"Explain," I demand.

"Y-Your . . . Your Highness." She struggles to push out the moniker. "I—I didn't know what was happening." Lirra wrings her hands. "And then there were the boys, and they were going to get hurt. Their mother wasn't around. I looked, but—" She sucks in a slice of air, her features bunching up, and then she tucks an elbow into her side. "I was so worried that I ran—"

"Can you start at the beginning?" I step closer to force eye contact.

But Lirra keeps babbling, her sentences tumbling over each other.

"Lirra," I say. Then, harsher, "Lirra, stop."

Her teeth dig into her bottom lip, stopping the flow of words. Wet, inky lashes sweep down to rest against her cheek. The sight pierces me with worry. I wasn't patient or agreeable with her earlier. I regret that now. But those thoughts escape me the moment the guards move position, opening their protective cocoon around a man lying motionless on a board. *Leif.*

"He was stabbed," Lirra whispers.

"No." My pulse roars though my ears. I rush forward, not believing my own eyes.

He has a seeping wound, high on the left side. He should be dead. But his chest rises and falls in quick, shallow jerks. He's fighting fate. Shock pelts me like shards of ice, freezing and piercing me with grief.

"How?"

The question is intended for everyone, yet no one answers.

Confusion rolls into fury as I stare at my fallen captain. "How did this happen?"

A heavy hand falls on my shoulder. "Come, Aodren. Let the guards carry him to the healer's room."

I turn to find Auberdeen, the man who, a little over a year ago, would've met me on the battlefield. Wariness and distrust remain between us; that much is evident by his somber set eyes that don't quite meet mine. But my concern for Leif eclipses all else. In a daze, I follow as the men carry Leif on a board and walk to a branching hallway. An exchange of voices starts up behind me. Orders are issued. Someone calls for all involved to be captured and held in the lower level of the keep. I tune them out and walk with the guards to the healer's room.

Leif is laid on a cot in the middle of the room. Fluids seep from his tunic into the linens, staining them bright red. Then even more blood flows as the healer removes the blade. She is a thick, robust woman in a tidy frock and veil, with movements that appear practiced and efficient as she pulls back Leif's drenched clothing. All I see is the blood, running like small rivers of crimson from his wound, trailing down his lifeless arm, and puddling on the stone floor.

I squeeze my eyes shut, but the dull, wet thwacks and scrapes of the healer's work fill my ears.

I pace away from the cot, walking the square prison of the healer's room while she issues commands like an army general, telling all the guards but one to stand watch outside. She orders the remaining man to supply her with clean white rags from a supply table, bottled remedies from the shelved wall, and thick stinking paste from a stone mortar. Time crawls as she cleans the wound, treats it, and sews it closed.

"I'll leave you with him," she says eventually.

I cross the distance to the cot in two long strides, hoping for a miracle that isn't there.

Leif is too still. Too gray.

"Is that all you can do?" I choke out.

"Yes, Your Highness." She stands with hands folded, eyes downcast, and mouth pulled into a pucker on her square face. "I've washed him with Beannach water and stitched him closed. But it was a grave injury," she says, tonelessly as if reading a town decree instead of discussing a man's life. Leif's life.

"But he will live. Yes?" I rake my hand across my brow. "I know men who have been stabbed and lived. Hell, I've been stabbed, and here I am."

Her gaze flicks to Leif. The buttonhole of her mouth cinches tighter. "I'm sorry, Your Highness. I cannot say. I've done all I can."

An airless breath wheezes out of me.

This woman has no soft lines. No pity. Like the rest of the

four kingdoms, she cares nothing for me or my people. She sees the mistakes of my kingdom's past. Anger unfurls inside me. Who is she to deny me? I want to break something. To destroy all the bottles lined up like an army on the wall behind her. To use the power of my crown to force her hand.

I lost so many people during the coup, from loyal lords who were murdered to my former captain, who was my closest adviser and friend. Now I trust few, to say the least. But one man I know I can trust with my life is Leif. I cannot lose him now.

Desperation claws through me like a rabid animal.

But I silence it. I will not be the tyrant the world expects me to be.

"Please," I say, and the guard stiffens, probably never having heard a king beg. "This man has saved countless innocent lives. He is good and honorable. I saw the Channelers Guild heal a fellow. The four of them worked together. If there is anything else that can be done for him, if you will summon Channelers to save him . . . I am pleading with you. Please save him."

The nurse looks up and studies me for a long moment and then nods. "I will return shortly, sir."

She bows and rushes from the room. I turn back to Leif and focus on him with the intensity of one poring over philosophy and history books. Small jerks rattle his torso. His lips are cracked and gray. His face slack. I've seen this before.

I've watched other men take agonized breaths before death swooped down and snatched their souls.

Breathe. Keep breathing, I urge Leif.

"Your captain was young, but a true, loyal servant." Judge Auberdeen's low gravelly tone breaks the quiet.

I look and find him in the doorway. I think he's been waiting outside, allowing me time alone, and I'm not sure what to make of it. Auberdeen is a difficult man to read, but then, the history of war between our kingdoms gives us both reason to be guarded.

Stopping a few paces from the cot, he views Leif. "Some deaths are destined, and we can do nothing to stop a man from crossing the infinite river."

"My captain hasn't passed." The words come out like a wintry gust.

"No, not yet," a quiet female voice interrupts.

Auberdeen and I turn to greet the newcomer. Ku Toa walks into view, her robes scuffing like whispers over the stones. In spite of the crimson wrap looped around her head, my attention is drawn to her eyes. Round, wise eyes.

"You are right." She nods a greeting to the chief judge. "Sometimes we cannot stop others from leaving this life. We can, however, try to influence a friend away from the edge."

"This situation is dire," says Auberdeen. "Perhaps too late for attempts that might give false hope to our young king."

If this is support, it might as well be a thrown dagger. "Hope or despair for my captain need not be your concern, Judge."

"My apologies," he says, his tone unguarded and genuine. "I'll leave you to say goodbye to your friend." As he exits the room, I wonder if perhaps I've misjudged the man.

Now it is only me, Leif, and the Ku.

She moves through the healer's room and comes to stand beside me. "The last year has held too many trials for one person to bear. Has it not?"

"There have been many, but not so many that I have given up hope." I choose my answer carefully, wondering what she thinks about me and my land.

The unfettered attention of her owlish eyes is unnerving, as if this woman, who is ancient and ageless all at once, can see into my darkest thoughts. When I consider there is still much to learn about her and Akaria, the imbalance bothers me.

"Hope you must always have." She extends her hand, where upon her palm is a thumb-size bottle. Burgundy liquid clings to the glass, the consistency thick like oil. "Perhaps I can help. Something to aid your man. To spare you another loss. *Sanguine*. It means 'the fluid of life.'"

A shadow moves in the room, and I glance over my shoulder to see the healer woman. She must've sought out the Ku.

I consider asking for more information on Sanguine.

What was shared at dinner isn't enough to provide a full understanding of the oil's uses, or how it works, or if there is a chance it could make Leif's condition worse. Though worse would mean death.

But Ku Toa presses the bottle into my palm; its warmth, from being held in her hand, spreads to mine. "You can save him."

Can I trust her?

I turn to Leif and feel myself crumbling inside. The rubble is covered with anger. I want to scream at the turn of the night's events. Nothing is fair. Leif should've never gotten hurt.

From what I know, Ku Toa has no motive to harm Leif or me. But I've been fooled before. When you rule a kingdom, few who cross your path are truly trustworthy. The summit has barely begun, and already there is tension among the leaders. I am leery of trusting anyone. My gaze drops to the bottle. What other choice do I have?

Leif will die regardless. Ignoring the overwhelming feeling of uncertainty, I force myself to make a choice. I open the bottle and, at her direction, tip the Sanguine to his mouth. A drop of deep burgundy rolls down his cheek, but most of the oil makes it between his lips, staining them the color of life.

When the bottle is empty, we wait.

How long does it take for Sanguine to work?

Seconds turn into years. Years to eons.

Leif shudders, a violent racking heaves his chest. His breath becomes staccato gasps, and then leaves as quickly as it came. His chest does not rise again.

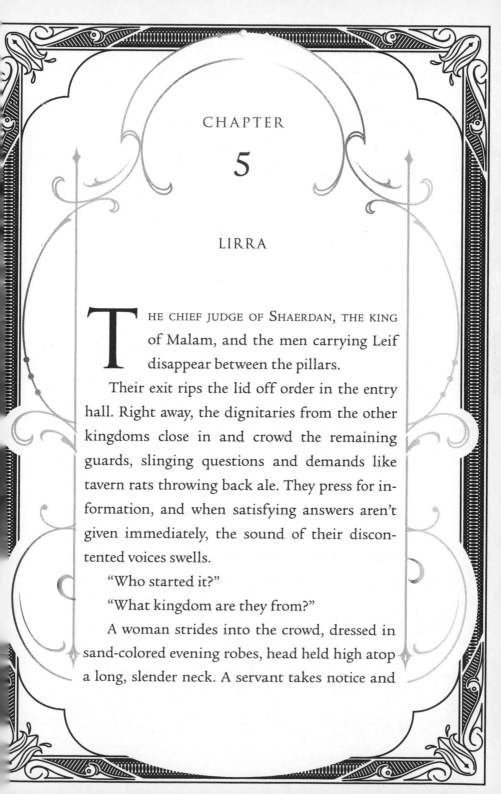

CHAPTER

5

LIRRA

THE CHIEF JUDGE OF SHAERDAN, THE KING of Malam, and the men carrying Leif disappear between the pillars.

Their exit rips the lid off order in the entry hall. Right away, the dignitaries from the other kingdoms close in and crowd the remaining guards, slinging questions and demands like tavern rats throwing back ale. They press for information, and when satisfying answers aren't given immediately, the sound of their discontented voices swells.

"Who started it?"

"What kingdom are they from?"

A woman strides into the crowd, dressed in sand-colored evening robes, head held high atop a long, slender neck. A servant takes notice and bows, whispering her name to the others. She is Queen Isadora of Plovia.

"Why did this happen?" she asks, but her words are lost in the loud conversation.

Her assessing gaze homes in on King Gorenza. Her nostrils flare, so slightly I doubt anyone but me has noticed. The lanterns' glow barely touches her rich, black hair, so dark in fact, it seems to absorb the light as she strides across the foyer to greet the northern king.

I trail a few paces behind her, needing to know the answer to her question. Grief knots my throat. I cannot let go of how quickly the fight escalated. Baz's shift into rage was lightning swift, which is nothing like the dockworker who's been flirting with me for months. So, *why did this happen?*

"It was the Malamians," says a guard in the thick of the group. "They were harassing a Channeler."

That much is true. But Malamians harassing Channelers is nothing new. And it's never resulted in a brawl like the one tonight. Could it be Shaerdanians have finally hit their tolerance limit?

Disdain for Malam's prejudices spurs another round of murmurs from the Shaerdanian guards. Someone brings up the Purge. Another claims Channeler treatment hasn't changed much in spite of the abolishment of the Purge.

"Hate never listens to new laws," says one of the Plovians.

"Those Malamians cornered the woman at the well. She's

alive only 'cause a kinsman jumped in," a guard near me shouts. "Shaerdanians take care of their own."

True, the people of Shaerdan look out for Channelers. Whereas, in Malam, they were hunted for nearly two decades.

"Course they do. But let's not overlook that it was Leif O'Floinn from Malam who risked his life to help the Channeler woman." This comes from an older man. He looks as though he's skinned a bear and is proudly displaying the spoils on his face.

Before sneaking into the summer castle, I read Da's notes on who would be traveling in Aodren's retinue. The grizzly bearded man is Benjamin Bromier, the Lord of Segrande.

"Maybe he jumped in to take down the Channeler," a guard argues.

Lord Segrande's casual demeanor is gone in a flash. "Watch it, boy. That's the captain of Malam's royal guard you're talking about. He's a supporter of the Channelers, as is the rest of Malam. He's known as the Channeler Defender."

"Leif might be a supporter of Channelers, but he's not like other Malamians." The Shaerdanian guard's argument is ballsy, considering Lord Segrande looks primed to tear him apart.

The only person in this room who actually saw the start of the incident is me.

It's true, men with Malamian accents were suspicious of the Channeler woman's water play. Their actions were unsavory, but they didn't corner a woman who was alone. She was joined by other Shaerdanians before things spiraled. It was the Malamians who were outnumbered and a Shaerdanian man who threw the first punch. I consider clarifying, though I'm not sure it'll matter.

"They're hurting our women."

"Bunch of feebs."

"Watch it." Lord Segrande's threat thunders over the crowd as he searches for the speakers.

I cringe. The guard's slur for giftless people isn't fit for a royal audience. The phrase might be intended for the Malamians, but at best, it's a tasteless smear spoken by a moron, because the cut includes himself. Men do not have Channeler abilities.

"Their people should've never been allowed near the tournament or market."

Someone chuckles darkly. "You know they won't come to the Channeler Jubilee."

"String the bludgers up."

"Enough!" King Gorenza's shout conquers the others. The stocky man, a couple decades older than me, with shoulders wider than a door, is nothing if not imposing. "This insolence would never happen in my country. Gather all involved," he commands the guards. "Return immediately to the fountain and track everyone down."

Everyone?

Surely, he doesn't mean me. I had nothing to do with the fight.

My neck crawls. I'm in a crowd of guards who have just been ordered to capture me. Better get scarce. I move to the perimeter of the room. The shadows near the corridor where Leif was taken provide decent concealment. Everything in me calls me down the hall to Leif, to see how my cousin is faring. But I know his room will be surrounded by guards.

"This is not your kingdom to command, Gorenza." The soft rebuke comes from a man standing just inside the pillars. He's a walking artifact in red robes. Compared to Lord Segrande and King Gorenza, the man is ancient. White-peppered brows sit above eyes that might've been black once, but now are the color of morning mist against a canvas of brown, papery skin.

"I demand order." King Gorenza's voice grinds like a millstone. "Ku Toa should too, Fa Olema."

The second man, Olema, hums a brief, noncommittal tune.

"I wasn't aware that Kolontia had developed a liking for Channelers," says Queen Isadora.

King Gorenza eyes her. "My concern is for safety during the summit," he says coolly.

"Of course. But, might I ask, whose safety?"

"All of ours."

I don't want to leave Leif, but I cannot stay here and allow them to catch me. How can I get out of here without someone noticing me? My cap flew off at the fountain. Most of the pins have popped out of my hair. Aside from a few pieces trapped on top of my head, the rest hangs around my shoulders in tangles. Dirt covers the stable hand clothing, and two tears, darkened with dried blood, show my injured knees. I may as well be a princess walking into a tavern.

I take the first few steps toward the door and then pause. What if Leif doesn't make it through the night? *Seeds.* The thought sinks a dagger into my heart. Chief Judge Auberdeen and King Aodren are with the healer, seeing to Leif. They'll be heavily guarded and impossible to sneak past.

I could wait in King Aodren's room for word. Then I won't be far from Leif. And while the king is at Leif's side, I could busy myself by searching for Da's letter. The idea is tempting because it'll let me be here for Leif. But with all the guards around, I might get caught. Also, considering His Majesty's earlier refusal, I know if he catches me trying to steal the letter, he won't be a font of information about Leif or my da. Better to leave and return tomorrow when the furor surrounding the fight has died down.

Leif will survive. He'll be fine. The healer here at the summer castle is one of the best. She'll keep him alive.

I sneak around the pillars and slip out the door.

I've barely made it into the courtyard when a man peels out of the shadows, flanked by two guards. "Lirra Barrett, stop right there."

"Judge Soma." I jolt.

The frown he wears sharpens his nose and cheekbones into blades made colorless by the moonlight. A chill slips over me, lifting the fine hairs on my arms.

Da has one hard-and-fast rule when it comes to business. *Don't get involved with anyone or anything too big.* Our business deals aren't connected to or part of anything that would bring about government- or kingdom-wide consequences. For this reason, we do not interact with members of the chief judge's counsel. However, Judge Soma used to be a kinsman intent on building a name in shipping. Before he worked his way into the ruling authority, he had transactions with Da.

"Hullo, Judge." My best cheery smile lifts my cheeks. Hopefully it'll detract from my odd dress.

"Where are you going?" His commanding stance, coupled with the way his nose sniffs the sky when he speaks, is nobility born, nothing like his common upbringing.

"Home," I say as if I'm not uneasy. "It's late, and I've chores in the morning. No doubt you'll have a long day of summit meetings tomorrow."

His expression warms a tad. "That I do."

"Well, I must go before my stepmother worries. Good night, sir." I start to curtsy, remembering a second too late my lack of skirts. The result is an awkward bob.

"I'm sorry, but I cannot let you leave." Judge Soma motions to the guards.

I lunge in the direction of the gates, but the guards move quickly. Their hands seize my arms, digging into my skin when I try to twist away.

They force me to turn toward the keep. Images of being trapped in the castle's prison flash through my mind. The thought sucks the air away. I slump so I'm dead weight and suck in enough breath to bellow at them to release me.

"Let me go!"

Their ears are garbage. My shouts don't work. I yank to free myself, and the man on my left sinks his fingers into my shoulder, immobilizing me with pain.

"That'll do, Lirra." Judge Soma's boots click on the cobblestones. His fingers shoot out and take my chin like an angry parent might force their child's attention. With the moon and castle lanterns behind him, he's cast in shadow. His brown hair is an inkblot attached to a stick figure. Fury kindles in my belly. I squirm and consider biting him. He has no right to handle me.

I want to sink my teeth into his hand, but I resist the temptation. He has two guards helping him. Three against one aren't good odds. Best I'd get is blood in my mouth and a backhand to the face.

"What do you want from me?" I ask, but his grip on my chin is too tight, so it comes out as "Waddyawanfrome?"

Judge Soma releases his hold and smooths the sleeves of his shirt over each wrist, then runs his hands down his velvet vest. "I saw you in the castle entry. You heard the Kolontian king. You were involved this evening. Until it's sorted out, you will be detained."

Vines made of ice twist around my lungs. "But I had nothing to do with it!"

"You were seen at the fountain."

"I was helping two boys. They were caught. If I hadn't run in, they might've been seriously hurt."

His gaze shifts to my knees and then to the dirt on my tunic and trousers. Does he think I was fighting too?

"I didn't hit anyone, I promise. Look at my hands."

The guards' grip on my arms doesn't loosen, so at best all I can do is wiggle my fingers.

Judge Soma shakes his head. "The command has been given. By a king, no less. I'm sorry, Lirra. I have to follow orders, and you were there."

Inside the lower levels of the keep, beneath the kitchen and far below the armory, there is a room with no windows, barely breathable air, and temperatures that make me think they've imported the gray sky from Kolontia. Bars separate a dozen cells in this cave, touched by the flickering light of a single lantern.

This is where they take me, tossing me in one of the cells without a second look. The lock clicks as it latches, and the guards walk away. The second they're out of sight, my heart turns frantic and tries to punch free of my chest.

I can handle darkness. I can manage the cold. But the cells

are tight, barely room to lie down. The bars are closing in on me, and I can't breathe. The feeling of suffocating has me leaping off the bench and tugging at the bars.

"They'll be back soon," a woman says, and I stumble over her legs. Moving a step to my left allows the solitary lantern's light to fill the tight space in our cell. The woman who spoke is the Channeler from the fountain. Discomfort has dammed my throat, so I nod and turn to pace the few pitiful steps that the cell will allow.

Across a walkway, in the cells opposite mine, I spy the shapes of several men. One lies on the bench; another takes the floor. A few sit along the back wall, deep enough in the darkness to prevent me from being able to see them well. I keep staring, though, because eventually my eyes will adjust.

Even here, Da's training kicks in. I'm looking for details, searching the scene for information that might come in handy someday in the future. After a minute or so, I can make out the two kinsmen who came to the fountain.

"Baz," I whisper. "Is that you?"

His head jerks up so more of the yellowish lantern light shines on his rakish features. The uneven cast adds a kink to his already-crooked nose. It'd be ugly on some men, but it's charming on him.

"Of all the places to run into you, Lirra." I think a smile lifts his cheeks.

His jest eases some of my anxiety. I tell myself to be grateful that I'm trapped with Baz, someone I know, because it makes the confinement almost bearable. At the very least, it helps me to stop focusing on the crush of the bars.

"They're bringing in everyone involved in the fight," I say.

His brows stretch upward, and his mouth pops open. In the shadows, he could be mistaken for a ghoul. "You were out there too?"

"I wasn't throwing punches, but yes."

He rubs his forehead. "How did I not notice you?"

I'm wondering that too. Anytime I get within a stone's throw of the docks, Baz appears at my side, slinging out ridiculously flirtatious comments and trying to convince me to go dancing with him. I've declined his offer at least a dozen times, knowing he chases a dozen other girls. His persistence was flattering, then it was annoying. Now it's incriminating. I'm not so full of myself to think I turn every man's head, but Baz always seems to know when I'm around.

"I'm not surprised. You were so . . . angry. Beyond angry," I say, straight to the point. "It didn't seem like you."

He scrubs his eyes. "What do you mean?"

Brawls are rare on the docks, but the few times one has broken out, Baz was never involved. He's not the violent type. "Baz. You broke a man's face. With your knee."

He murmurs something to the fellow beside him. It's too quiet to distinguish, but the man sits up straighter. They share another whisper, and then both Baz and his friend face me, attention unwavering and taut with agitation. His change in demeanor confuses me.

Earlier, I thought their rage was spurred by other events that might've happened before they entered the fray. Now I'm left to wonder . . .

"I haven't seen that side of you, is all." I conclude with a shrug, as if their reaction isn't suspect.

Our conversation has garnered interest from the adjacent cell of Malamians. From what I can see in the dim light, the foreigners' faces are mottled and bloody. One man's profile is disfigured from swelling. He's the one whose face Baz broke.

That's when I realize Baz and his friend are barely bruised. In comparison to the foreigners, they're practically as fresh and flawless as spring daisies. There's something very wrong here. Who knew Baz was such a skilled fighter?

"Baz." I consider my words, looking for the right ones to go digging for whatever he's hiding without putting the two men even more on edge. "Is everything all right?"

"Keep yer nose outta his business," says Baz's friend.

All right. So I'm not a master at this yet. They're hiding something, and not the *too embarrassing to share* kind of something. From Baz's hunch and the other man's threatening posture, it's a secret they'll fight to keep. Probably more dangerous than anything I should scout, but I'm too angry to tuck the blunt side of my personality into hiding.

Squaring my stance, I meet the other man's hard stare. "You made it everyone's business when you started a fight in a public square. It could've been settled with words. People could've walked away. Not everyone did. And now we're *all* stuck down here. I want to know why."

CHAPTER

6

AODREN

LEIF'S BODY IS LIFELESS. HAD KU TOA NOT reached for me, her frail grip spreading unexpected warmth through my sleeve, I would've left, unable to swallow the death of yet another friend. At least an hour has passed while the Ku has remained steadfast, stoically determined to see Leif rise. My eyes refuse to focus on Leif's slackened features and his pale skin. As if the refusal will push life into my friend. I clutch my stomach, but the pain of his loss is everywhere. It strips my strength. It knots my throat and stings my eyes.

"We should go." The words are dry as ashes.

She squeezes my hand. "Where is your hope?"

"Hope failed me a quarter-hour past when the healer came to mop the floor." My gaze sinks to the stones, clean now. How many times has she scrubbed blood off these floors for them to gleam so smooth, the stones' texture gone?

A gasp slices the silence.

My gaze flies to Ku Toa. She smiles and looks at Leif.

He couldn't have made that sound. His eyes are still closed. His face slack. Body fluid no longer oozes from the blood-stained stitches. Not even when his ribs expand. With a start, I realize he's breathing. He lives!

Relief crash over me, and a mountain-size weight slides off my chest. Leif is alive.

"He'll make it?" Judge Auberdeen's voice comes from behind me.

Too focused on Leif to say anything, I simply nod. Leif's chest rises and falls, subtly, slowly, filling me with gratitude to see him breathing.

"Sanguine takes time to fully spread through the body," the Ku whispers. "Tomorrow, he may wake."

She could've mentioned this before. Staying true to her enigmatic manner, she says no more, and leaves as quickly and mysteriously as she came. There's so much I don't know about Sanguine, and even more I don't know about Ku Toa. But what's certain is my people have it wrong about the oil. Until they're better educated about Channeler magic, there will be a division in my kingdom.

In the morning, the castle bustles with activity. I skirt around the crisscrossing paths of servants, some with arms full of linens and others with baskets of food, and sneak into the healer's room. With an hour before the first summit meeting begins, I visit Leif to find he is still asleep.

He doesn't respond when his name is called or his arm is jostled. I have to remind myself that Sanguine requires time.

Time we do not have.

Lord Segrande walks through the doorway. He bows before moving to the foot of Leif's bed. "Still sleeping, I see."

"He hasn't stirred since my arrival."

A worried noise rumbles in Segrande's throat. "Didn't you say he got some Sanguine oil?"

"It's not instantaneous. Ku Toa said it takes time."

"Hours or days?"

"I wish I knew." Pressure increases between my temples at his subtle reminder of tonight's event, the March of Champions.

Feeling worried over the event is ridiculous, considering how close Leif came to death last night. But I haven't forgotten my goals for the summit and the tournament. Now that Leif is going to make it, my focus must return to Malam. Tonight, the men and women representing each kingdom's leader in the Tournament of Champions will be announced. Tomorrow, youth will show off their combat skills, and Friday, the competitors take the field for the first event, the melee.

"Having only one champion could impair Malam," Segrande says, as if I've not already considered the impact.

I rake a hand through my hair. "If we don't score well in the melee, we may as well be out of the competition." It's callous to consider the ramifications of Leif's injury in this way, but that is my duty to Malam. I'm grateful my captain, my friend, is alive. And yet I'm frustrated that all my plans for uniting Malam behind its champions are coming unraveled.

In the last year, Leif has become legendary among Channelers and the giftless. Stories have circulated, tales of how he pled for the Purge's abolishment and convinced the Channelers Guild to fight at my side during the coup. How he fought heroically to restore order to the kingdom and avenge those who lost their lives in a senseless bid for power that benefited only a few. People believe in Leif. They call him Channeler Defender and Defender of Malam alike. They idolize him for his large stature and undefeated fight record. He is the only one who can unite all Malamians behind his banner. His role as champion is crucial to bridging the divide.

"I'm sure Baltroit will manage. He's well trained in all areas of combat, and he already fights like two men. We'll still have a chance to take the cup." Segrande's pride in his son downplays the problem. It's not just about fighting and winning. It's about giving people hope.

Segrande's comment also reminds me of something my own father once said. He wasn't a good king or even a good man, but his words ring true.

Pride unites.

My country has forgotten that kind of pride. Pride to be Malamian, Channeler or giftless, common or noble. I need Leif and Baltroit to win an event flag, or — dare I dream? — the All Kingdoms' Cup. Then we will start to regain our pride. Differences aside, we might remember how to be a people united.

The melee calls for all competitors to take the field in a mock war. With only one competitor, we'll have no chance of winning the melee flag, let alone the tournament cup.

Regardless of Segrande's faith in his son, Baltroit needs Leif as much as Malam does.

I just don't know what to do about it.

Shouts and cheers echo from every corner of the field as the royal carriages roll to a stop. An announcer declares the name of a kingdom, and the corresponding leader emerges, followed by two dignitaries — or in my case, only Segrande. A bold trumpet plays as we walk on a path of carpet to an elevated platform. For the March of Champions, all the leaders will be seated together. During the subsequent nights of the tournament, four other platforms constructed around the field will accommodate each kingdom's visiting nobility.

Once we've all been introduced and the crowd has quieted, the announcer launches into a speech about past tournaments. Applause thunders across the field as the man recognizes the kingdoms that earned banners in years past.

I clap with the others, but out of the corner of my eye, I notice Segrande is not cheering. He's nervous for his son. On the ride to the tournament field, he talked of nothing else. His attention is set on the eastern gate, where the champions wait in a house-size tent. It's been erected as a place where the fighters may prepare for their bouts and where healers will see to the competitors' injuries.

Eventually, the time comes for the announcer to introduce the champions. Yelling through a cone to project his voice, he reveals the first fighter, Hemmet, a champion from Kolontia. He rides a snowy stallion covered in ribbons of black and silver onto the field. Some people hold up the Kolontian banner with a wolf's head in the center of a rose. Hemmet pauses in the center and waves. The man's hair is pulled back and separated into a dozen raven braids that bounce as his horse circles the field, bringing Hemmet closer to the spectators. The crowd's approval soars to screams.

"He'll destroy your men." The comment slithers over my shoulder.

I turn to find King Gorenza behind me, lip curled into a smug sneer partially hidden behind his facial hair. "Battle is in my son's blood. His great-grandfather was the last royal competitor to win the tournament cup."

"It was your grandfather who killed the king of Plovia?"

"Indeed, it was." He looks at the Akarian warriors who have just taken the field. I feel a chill wash over me at the pride in his admission.

Flags of red and yellow are hoisted into the sky and the mark of the desert serpent coils around the colors. The crowd's approval rattles the stand for the two female fighters. "In this tournament, fortune doesn't favor the weak or less-skilled warrior, even if he is a king." Gorenza smiles.

"Luck matters not. It will be skill, stamina, and heart."

His laugh is condescending. "Your men have heart. Mine have undefeated records. Hemmet has won every bout in Kolontia."

Two competitors ride onto the field with the green and brown Plovian flag held high.

I clamp my teeth together and calm myself before responding. "And outside of Kolontia?"

Gorenza's nostrils flare. "Are you insinuating he'll not do well?"

"Not at all. I'm merely eager to see how he'll fare." Hemmet was Kolontia's champion at the last tournament and Kolontia won no banners, but I don't mention this because neither did Malam.

His gruff chuckle grates against my back. "Soon, boy king. You will see soon enough."

The crowd cheers for Shaerdan's men. Blue and gold flags are hoisted into the air.

My fingers grip the platform's rail, knuckles going colorless. I pray for Gorenza to suffer a sudden infliction of vocal paralysis. Unfortunately, the gods aren't listening, and for each person who walks onto the field, Gorenza issues an endless catalog of weaknesses and ways in which his champion son will conquer.

Peace in Malam means peace between kingdoms, I remind myself, repeating the words like a mantra.

The announcer cries, "Baltroit Bromier and Leif O'Floinn of Malam."

Baltroit rides out alone on a black horse, a contrast to his pale-wheat-colored hair and trimmed beard. He has Malam's maroon-and-gray flag, marked with the royal stag affixed to his shoulders. Both of his hands are extended, as if to receive the crowd's praise. Some applause rolls through the crowd, though heavily littered with jeers and a collective disapproving groan.

"Poor Leif, fell to the Channelers before he could compete," shouts someone with a distinctly Malamian accent.

Rumors have already spread? I lean toward the side of the royal booth and listen to the conversation below.

"It's a sign. He got hurt because he's a Channeler lover."

I feel like I've been hit on the head with a poleax. Word has spread faster than I anticipated, but what's worse is that people, Malamians, have connected Leif's injuries to Channelers. I'm on my feet, angry and ready to correct them, when a hand lands on my forearm.

"You have only one champion?" Gorenza's question rolls into a growling chuckle.

I stare over his head, not wanting to give him the satisfaction of my answer. "They announced Leif. He will be our other competitor."

"If he can walk."

I don't entertain his response with one of my own.

Gorenza's smile slowly grows, showing too many teeth. "My men will devour your champion in one minute instead of two." He opens his mouth and bites together in a hard clack. The snap ignites rage inside me, fierce and fiery in a way that goads me to be reckless. In the wake of Leif's injury, decorum would dictate that he would extend his sympathies. But Gorenza cares nothing for propriety, and that lack of respect fuels me more to prove him wrong. To show him how mighty Malam can be.

Baltroit will not fight alone.

If Leif cannot fight, we will have another competitor.

CHAPTER

7

LIRRA

I WAKE UP, AND THE WORLD IS BLACK, AS IF A thief has stolen the shape and color of my surroundings. Disoriented, I blink and rub my eyes. Grit on my fingers grates my cheek. I pull my hands down and hold them over my pounding heart. *Where am I?* My nose wrinkles at the putrid smell of old water and sour bodies. I've woken in strange places before, but this darkness is different, impermeable and suffocating, dank and disquieting. And my memories, solid as smoke, are useless.

I roll to my side and push off the ground. Dirt, hay, stones. Tender sharpness ripples down my left side, and I sit still, knees tucked to my chest. The airy scrape and scuttle of someone's snore echoes nearby, and last night shutters back in bursts...the fountain and Leif...Judge Soma...the guards...a holding chamber in the lowest recesses of the castle. Stars, how could I forget? I squeeze my eyes shut and pray for six lanterns to light every corner and cranny in this horrible place, but when I look around, the darkness is unmoved. And though I cannot see the cell's bars, I feel the iron trapping me, closing in, stealing the air.

Breathe.

I draw in a slow, slow breath. I'm not alone. Others are here.

Last night, the guards brought everyone connected with the fight at the fountain down here, and after providing us with a measly meal of stale bread and bone broth, they left, carrying out the only lantern. I watched the stream of light through the cracks around the door, as if it were reaching back toward me. Until it faded completely. I lost myself then, consumed in the *whoosh, whoosh* of each inhale. But all that air had nowhere to go. My lungs were pinholes. The shadows spun, until a soothing hand landed, warm and firm, on my back, and a woman's whispers promised me all would be fine, until I finally fell asleep.

Now I prop my head on my knees, and my ribs twinge with ache. Leif is probably lying in the healer's bed right now, laughing with the other guards. At least, I hope he is.

"Are you all right?" A woman's whisper comes from somewhere to my right.

"I—I'm good," I say, embarrassed. She's the one who sat

beside me through last night's attack. She must think me mad. "Thank you . . . for your help yesterday. I—I'm not normally . . . I wasn't myself."

"No need for thanks. A little mothering comes naturally to me. I've got two littleuns and a third on the way. Besides, I owe you my gratitude. You're the one who saved my boys from being crushed. I am in your debt."

Seeds. She's stuck in this stale chamber, where the stench is unfit for rats to breathe, let alone for an expectant woman.

"You shouldn't be down here. Have you told them?"

"About the baby? Aye, it didn't matter."

I like to think Malam has sole ownership of the inhumane treatment of its people, but I know that's not true. Her confessions sickens me. It challenges my support and faith in Judge Auberdeen, since he must've allowed the guards to throw her in here.

"Where are your boys now?" I ask.

"With my husband. He tried to stop the guards and earned a nasty thump for his trouble. It gave my boys a fright to see the guards handling their da that way, but I cannot say it was any worse to witness than the scene at the fountain." She pauses and takes a gathering breath. "My boys will be all right," she tacks on in a thin, reedy voice.

"I'm sure they will be." I could tell her about my brothers and their resilience, but those stories are about scraped knees and frights in the woods. My brothers have never seen a scuffle like the one at the fountain. Da and Eugenia do all they can to keep the littleuns protected. Whereas, I'm an outlier in my family, having witnessed the world's underbelly from my crib the night my mother was killed and my life forever changed.

Nearby, a snore ends with an abrupt snort. At least, I hope it's a snort.

I wonder if Baz and his friend have woken yet. Last night, after I demanded to know what happened at the fountain, Baz admitted his actions were spurred by the loss of an aunt during the Purge. We all suffered at the hand of the Malamians during the Channeler eradication. Baz's quick rage seemed uncharacteristic, but then, we all have conflict inside.

"My name is Donella," the woman says.

"I'm Lirra. I'd shake your hand, except mine's dirty and I cannot see well enough to do it."

Her quiet laugh tiptoes though the darkness. "I tell my boys that the dark is nothing to fret over. It's just the light wearing a thick cloak."

"It's not the dark so much as the confinement," I confess.

"Oh? You don't like tight spaces?"

I fight off a shiver. The pale stretch of warped skin that wraps around my back and left side is sore after yesterday's fall. Despite what Eugenia and Da have repeated for years, the old burn scar proves my fear of being trapped isn't unfounded. "Something like that. But we won't be in here for long. I hope."

"Well, let's be glad they didn't throw us in the oubliette."

Yes, the death hole would've been worse. Then I think of Leif again. *He'll make it,* I tell myself.

Sometime later two guards bring food and a lantern to light the holding chamber. I start to speak to the man who opens our cell, but he shoves a tin bowl of food into my hands and ignores me. The food is tasteless, lumpy gruel. I hold my breath and eat, because it certainly isn't odorless.

"I'll find a way to get us out," I tell Donella after forcing down another bite.

"I believe you. If you can swallow that, you can do anything."

I laugh and then gag on a chunk caught in my throat.

A pained grunt comes from another cell, drawing our attention. Baz's mouth opens, and a shuddery moan echoes into the chamber. He holds his head in his hands, fingers woven through the dark strands, and his body trembles. What's wrong with him?

"Morning meal?" Donella mouths, pointing at her untouched gruel.

Gods, I hope not. I clutch my stomach, rethinking my choice to eat.

In another cell, the Malamians scrape their dishes clean and drop them on the floor. I watch them, but not a single one shows any sickness. In fact, their lackluster delivery of a few belches is followed by a shout to the guard to bring more food.

Baz lurches up off the bench, his face pasty and beaded with sweat. Could he have caught the ague?

With little warning, he throws himself at his friend, earning some yells from his cellmates. He mumbles something unintelligible and then starts clawing the other man, searching like a rabid animal.

"Get off!"

The yell from his friend seems to only enrage Baz.

"You stole it from me," Baz says, menacing in a way that prickles my skin. He lurches up and spins, eyes wild and sweat flinging from his brow. This isn't the Baz I know. This is the man from the fountain. He turns back to his friend, and they wrestle. They roll on the floor. One kicks a bench into the privy pot. Luckily it doesn't tip over.

Their fight draws attention, and soon men in the other cells are shouting them on.

Baz grabs something from his friend's pocket and then an elbow smashes his nose. His hands fly up to clutch the run of blood. A small apothecary bottle drops to the floor with a *tink*. I try to figure out what it is, but the men shuffle around and one kicks the bottle into the shadows.

The guards enter and threaten the men with the oubliette. In a flurry of movement, Baz's cell is straightened and the bottle hidden. I haven't forgotten, though, even if I don't know what it means.

That evening, hours after the dinner meal is served and choked down, the chamber door opens. Judge Auberdeen enters, followed by Judge Soma, King Aodren, and Lord Segrande. I never thought of relief as an emotion that could follow intense dislike. For as much as I thought I loathed Aodren, seeing him beside the chief judge fills me with the hope that they've conversed as leaders and decided to let us go. I push off the floor to stand, and grimace against the burn in my ribs.

Aodren's gaze skates over the prisoners and halts when it meets mine. His lips part. He must not have known about my arrest. He nudges Lord Segrande and subtly directs the older man's attention to me. Though I'm not sure why. Would Aodren have told his dignitary about my role in delivering Da's letter?

I should've been kinder to him when I snuck into his room. I should let go of the past and how he didn't remember me.

"We're still not sure what escalated the argument into a fight," Judge Soma is saying. I cling to their conversation, hoping to hear word of Leif. He must be on the mend. "Until that can be determined, allowing these men to go free would be a risk for all attending the festivities."

Aodren sputters and coughs.

"It's the air down here." Judge Auberdeen smacks him on the back.

"Thank you, I'm quite all right." Aodren stands straighter. "Did you say the entire summit? Two weeks is excessive."

Lord Segrande nods his agreement after glancing around the dank chamber, nose twitching.

"They've been fed, and the lanterns are snuffed at night for privacy. These cells are nothing like your deathtraps in Malam." Soma sweeps his arm out, like we're lounging in luxury. I want to lock him up and see what he thinks then. "They'll be more than comfortable until the summit's end."

"Have you spent much time in Malam's *deathtraps*?" Aodren asks, and I silently cheer him on, surprising myself, considering how he treated me when I delivered the letter. But anyone who needles Soma gets my support. I'll never forgive the judge for throwing me in here with the brawlers, even if that means siding with the arrogant king of Malam. "Any dungeon time is excessive for some of the people you have detained here."

A murmur of approval comes from the Malamians' cell.

"You forget your place." Judge Auberdeen tips his nose up. I'm not sure if he's disgusted by the smells of his dungeon or galled by Aodren's show of backbone. "Everyone in this holding chamber was part of the fight at the fountain. It happened on Shaerdanian soil, so perhaps we should allow Judge Soma to deal with them as he sees fit."

It's shocking to hear the chief judge agree with Soma. I always believed the leader of Shaerdan to be a just man.

"Everyone?" Aodren nods to me.

"Everyone," repeats Soma.

Aodren's fist flexes. It's so subtle that I doubt the others notice. "Half the men detained in here are Malamians. And while the summit is in session, the treaty states that my countrymen fall under my purview."

"Of course." Soma moves between both men. "Judge Auberdeen only wishes to ensure safety for all attendees. The recent unfortunate events in Malam have made us more cautious. Perhaps your people made mistakes that we can avoid."

Soma's comment hits the target. Even in the weak light I can see how Aodren's face blanches.

He has the power to set us free. I stare at him, willing him to show more of that edge he just displayed.

Aodren glances from Soma to me, then to the ragged bunch of Malamians.

Come on. Speak up.

Soma walks between the cells. "The guards tell me there was a fight in the cells earlier. They started a fight at the fountain, and now this? If these people cannot maintain a level head in here, think how they'll act when they're unrestricted." He pauses and turns back to face the other men. "With daily meals, they'll be better off in here than in their camps anyway."

The man is shoveling dung.

I grip the bars. If I thought it might help our case, I'd interrupt, but drawing attention to myself will remind them of the stable hand clothes I'm wearing. And that might garner more questions. The last thing I want is for them to discover that I snuck into the castle before the incident at the fountain.

"What about the women?" Aodren motions to me and

Donella. "Didn't your men say the Channeler was harassed? Isn't that why the fight started? That would mean this woman was the victim. And I was told the girl was only involved because she rescued two boys."

Chief Judge Auberdeen murmurs something like an agreement.

An urge to say something to help my cause beats through me, but uttering the wrong words will make my situation worse. The guards threatened Baz and his friend with the oubliette, a pit somewhere in the castle's dungeon. The threat of it keeps me silent.

"The Channelers Guild will be unhappy to hear that two of their sisterhood have been confined," says Aodren.

"True." Soma walks back toward the exit. "Though they'll surely understand our need for safety. We don't want any other Channelers being targeted by" — he turns and lifts his nose in the directions of the bruised Malamians — "more of them. By keeping all involved imprisoned, we're sending a message to the other festival attendees. The camps are a safe place, free of fights and intolerance."

A muscle along Aodren's jaw ticks. "Locking up Channeler women to keep other Channelers safe makes little sense."

"I agree," Judge Soma says. "Their confinement down here is unfortunate. It won't be for long. I'll gladly step aside and place the women in the Guild's custody when they arrive at the festival. But we must maintain order."

The Channelers Guild won't arrive until later this week.

Four more nights.

Soma turns to Judge Auberdeen and lowers his voice, but I can still pick out what he's saying: "There are thousands of foreigners in Shaerdan. If another fight like the one at the fountain occurs, there may be lost lives. Wars have been started on less."

To my dismay, Judge Auberdeen nods, seeming to accept Judge Soma's extreme reasoning. I stare up at the black ceiling, feeling it press down on me. I have to get out of here. My fingers whiten on the bars. Panic bubbles in my chest. I urge Aodren to argue, since he seems to be the only one speaking sense, but it's as if Soma's words have snaked around Aodren, trapping him like a field mouse. Have both men fallen under Judge Soma's spell?

"Let's continue this conversation elsewhere." Judge Auberdeen extends his hands, ushering the men toward the door, confirming my nightmare is nowhere near ending. They're leaving, and I'm not. I'm trapped in this cell.

"Wait," I call out. "Please, wait."

They stop and turn back. Hope sparks inside me.

"Me—me and Donella weren't part of any fight. We got trapped in it all. It wasn't our fault. It was the wrong place, wrong time, when the men lost all shreds of sense they never had in the first place." I release the bars, hiding my shaking hands behind my back, and try to show my most sincere, pleading smile.

Aodren steps toward my cell, his expression pained.

"No." Judge Soma's response comes down like an ax. Then he points to me. "You'll be let go with the rest of them or when the Channelers Guild requests your release."

My gasp is sharper than a slap. I scramble along the bars to the corner of the cell, getting as close as I can to Soma and Aodren. An ache flares and stretches across my left side. "You cannot keep us in here. We—we haven't done anything wrong." My breath stutters, and tears burn the backs of my eyes. I blink them away as I unravel before these men. There's nothing I can do about it. Panic seizes hold. "P-p-please don't leave. I—I cannot . . ."

Aodren's attention lingers on me.

"Please . . . King Aodren." The words scrape out in a rough whisper. I hate that he was going to leave me here and follow those men out the door, and yet, he's my best hope right now. "Please let us go. Donella is with child. It's not safe for her in here."

His eyes flare.

Lord Segrande says something I cannot hear, and then both men turn away and wait for the guard to open the chamber door.

Bloody king of Malam.

"Let us go." I rattle the bars. "Do you hear me? She's pregnant. We weren't part of the fight. I'm the one who alerted the guards. You cannot leave us in here."

As long and loud as I shout, none of it makes a difference. They do not return.

CHAPTER

8

AODREN

I N THE PAST, WHEN TREATIES WERE FORGED BE-tween our kingdoms, Judge Soma proved reliable and wise. Tonight, however, he's proven it's time to reevaluate my opinion.

His strict edict to imprison those involved, turn them into public examples in order to sway others from similar harmful activity, might make sense for the people who actually were fighting. Extreme, merciless sense. No reason stands for two women, who were bystanders and threw no punches, to be detained. Nothing can be gained, no added measures of security, in jailing innocents. His actions don't make sense.

She looked nothing like the ballsy girl who broke into my room. Shoulders curled forward, elbows tucked tight to her body, it was as if she wanted to make herself smaller. Admittedly, the sight pricked me with guilt. If I'd allowed her to leave the castle the way she wanted to, she wouldn't have been caught in the fight at the fountain. For that matter, neither would Leif have been there. It wasn't until after the March of Champions that I vaguely recalled hearing an order for all people involved in the fight to be detained. Ironically, it was Gorenza who reminded me when he gloated about catching Leif's attacker.

I knew that challenging Soma more than I already had, in front of the prisoners, would've been detrimental. I followed him out to show respect, respect that will hopefully be returned during the summit as Malam seeks favorable alliances.

But my plan from the moment I set eyes on Lirra and Donella was to set them free. This is why, after parting ways with Soma and checking on Leif, I go to meet Judge Auberdeen.

In his study, we talk ruler to ruler.

"They are innocent bystanders. They should not be held," I say, fighting to keep my voice level. I don't want him to see how furious I am about Lirra and Donella's imprisonment.

He resets his spectacles on the bridge of his aquiline nose and looks through them, as if studying me in meticulous measure, like a swordsmith might inspect a newly forged weapon for flaws. "How can I overturn Soma's decision?"

A ruler's command, given in a time when all kingdoms have gathered to seek peaceful agreements, outweighs a dignitary's intolerant decision. He knows this.

When I remind him, he says, "Flexing your leadership may ruffle some feathers."

"True, but you are a just and fair man, who will do the rightful thing," I say, and then launch into a discussion pertaining to stewardship over the citizens of our kingdoms. I may not have been a ruler for as long as Chief Judge Auberdeen, but I have spent years studying law books and histories of our kingdoms. Innocent Channeler women and their families have suffered at the hand of my kingdom for far too long. Knowing how they've suffered fills me with fury.

I must see justice served.

Our conversation goes on until Auberdeen yawns, removes his spectacles, and rubs his eyes. "It appears you understand the laws as well as I do," he says, and I detect a hint of respect. "You understand the ramifications of having the prisoners released in your name?"

"I do. Now release them."

Lirra is sleeping fitfully, tucked next to the slightly older woman. Her breath puffs from the gap of space between her chapped lips. Dirt darkens her high, rounded cheeks. I steal a moment to study the girl. Even in sleep she looks scared. It adds to my guilt for not managing to free them sooner.

The guard unlocks the door and swings it open. The rattling causes others to stir. Lirra's eyes blink open. At first, she seems stupefied by my appearance. Then a glare darkens her face like a thunderhead moving in front of the moon.

"You," she croaks, her voice roughened as if she shouted for hours. "You left us."

"I came back," I point out.

Her scowl sharpens. I admire her fight.

"Lirra," the other woman, Donella, whispers a scolding. In the darkness, her widened eyes track over me before she lowers her head.

"You can sit there and be angry, or you can leave with me," I tell Lirra. "If the latter is your choice, we should go now, before the others wake."

"What of Donella? I won't leave her."

"Of course. She's coming too." When she revealed the woman's condition, I thought it would be enough to stop Soma. Not so. Instead, after we stepped outside of the chamber, Soma indicated Lirra, daughter of the Archtraitor, had inherited her father's gift for lying. Even if Lirra had lied, hearing that a pregnant woman was in a cell should've given him pause. At the very least, he should've verified the story.

I help Donella stand, and the woman's shocked eyes fall on me once more.

"Thank you," she whispers, and I guide them out.

Lirra sits across from me in my traveling coach, head canted to the side as she openly studies me. After we left the holding chamber, the carriage driver and my guard took us directly to Donella's family. When Lirra said goodbye, she embraced the woman and her boys like long-lost family.

"I didn't think you were coming back," Lirra admits now

that we're alone. The wheels sink into a rut, and her body jostles against the seat.

"I gathered as much."

The frown she unleashes hits me like the crack of a schoolmarm's switch. "I thought you were going to leave us there to wait for the Guild."

I would've never waited that long. I almost tell her that I didn't want to make an enemy of Judge Soma before trade negotiations get underway, but in my head, the explanation sounds calculated and harsh. Lirra's opinion, for some reason, matters.

"Negotiating with Judge Auberdeen is best without an audience," I say instead.

She watches me. "That's probably the wisest choice."

There's no hint of sarcasm in her comment. I'm not sure why that pleases me.

"You can leave me here," she says once the carriage nears the crossroad dividing the camps. One way leads to the summer castle, the other to Celize.

"In the middle of the road?" We're a long walk from Celize, where I assume she lives.

"Really, I don't need a ride." She smiles. Had I not witnessed the carefree beam she blasted at Leif yesterday, I might think the expression genuine. Instead I recognize it for what it is: an attempt to disarm me.

Lirra is an attractive girl. Even with filthy clothes, matted hair, a grime-streaked face, and a foul smell from the prison that clogs the air around her. But more than that, she's clever. I didn't see it before, but I can now.

"Did you not wish to visit Leif?" I ask, oddly curious about the Archtraitor's daughter, though I know she must want to go home after spending a night and a day in the cells.

"Oh, Leif." She sets her hand over her heart and her eyes grow distant. "I . . . I must be more tired than I thought. Time in that cell was . . . well, exhausting. Of course I want to see him. He's doing well?"

"Better than I thought possible," I admit.

She agrees to return to the castle, and an unexpected smile lifts my lips, though she doesn't notice, as she is staring out the carriage window. The moonlight breaks from the clouds and paints the tents we pass bluish-gray. All the kingdom flags are united under the colors of night. If only it were that easy for Malam. Earlier in the evening, when Baltroit took the field, shouts of approval clashed with jeers. We need a victory to convince Malamians to unite, and once they do, maybe their unity will continue when they return to Malam.

For a victory to be possible, we need a competitor. Tournament rules state that competitors fighting in the name of their ruler must be declared by the March of Champions. Leif was named as Malam's competitor, with the note that he's been injured. No one else can take his place. Except me, the ruler for whom he was going to fight.

The carriage rolls over the gravel road. The closer we come

to the summer castle, the more time I have to consider the hazards of competing in the melee.

Just as sabotage was a risk in the past, it will be the same now if people discover I'm going to fight in my own name. No one can know of this plan until the tournament begins. Not even Segrande and my guards, who would surely stop me from taking such a risk. And it would be best if no competitor know until I walk onto the field. I'll have to sneak out of the castle and make my way to the competitors' tent unseen. An impossible task. Unless . . .

Lirra sways with the lulling movement of the carriage. Her stable boy disguise, now grimier from the fight and time in the cells, would fool anyone into thinking she was a young lad. The only thing that gives her away is the matted lock of dark hair hanging in her eyes. What she said the first night is true — she saved my life when she helped during the coup. It was shock at finding her in my rooms that kept me silent. In recent months, her father has become an unlikely confidant. If I can trust him to keep my secrets, I should be able to trust her.

"Why are you staring at me like that?" Her eyes dip to her tunic. She touches the blackish stain that might be blood. Her nose scrunches, and she abandons the shirt to run a hand through her hair, fingers catching in the dark knots. "King or not, it's impolite to gape. In case you forgot, I was jailed in a stench hole with a dozen other people for the last twenty-four hours. You wouldn't look much better."

She has no compunction about treating me as her equal.

So much of dealing with nobility is talking around what you intend to say so as not to cause offense. Lirra doesn't care.

I'm not sure why that's so intriguing.

"I would." I struggle to keep the corners of my mouth from lifting. I raise my hand and circle a finger around my hair, showing how much shorter it is than hers. "I have less to keep clean." When she stiffens, I know my joke as gone awry. "I meant your hair, not your clothing."

She turns back to the window.

"I went before Judge Auberdeen tonight to secure your freedom," I say. "In exchange, I'd like a favor from you."

Her head whips in my direction. Her eyes, sharper than two daggers, drop down, inspecting me from my boots to my face. She lunges, catching me off-guard, and grasps the opening of my surcoat in one hand. "Are you planning on throwing me in the holding chamber if I refuse?" Contempt salts her words.

"We've gotten off to a rough start." I gently pry her fingers from my coat. It crosses my mind that she might've seized my dagger with her other hand. But I don't look down, and I try not to appear startled. "I want to begin again."

Wary eyes stare from a dirt-streaked face. "What does that mean?" She settles on the other side of the carriage, and I'm pleased to see she hasn't divested me of my blade. The wheels roll to a stop, rumbling over the gravel, and moments later, the driver opens the door. I dismiss the man and the guard who is beside him to wait near the castle entrance so Lirra and I can finish our conversation. The men bow and leave.

I give my attention back to Lirra, trying to find the best way to explain what help I need from her and why.

"Now that Leif's been injured, Malam is down a competitor," I explain, going for a straightforward approach. "Without two fighters on the field, our kingdom is sure to come in last. A team cannot come back from that deficit. The only man who can fight in his place is me."

She leans back against the carriage seat. "What does that have to do with me?" Then her sooty lashes lower into midnight slits. "Why exactly did you free me?"

Because it was the right thing to do. Instead, I say, "I need your help."

Her skeptical expression doesn't change as she listens to me explain that I want to travel from the castle to the tournament field in disguise. No one can find out, not even my advisers, who would try to stop me before I have a chance to enter. From firsthand experience and knowing her history of working for her da, I know Lirra is the master of disguises. She's the key to making this plan work.

"You need a disguise?" She stares at me incredulously. "What of the risks? Someone could kill you, and it wouldn't be considered treason or an act of war. It would be a hazard of the tournament."

"If no one knows I'll be fighting, no one will have time to

plot my assassination. As for the fight that happens on the field, they won't be able to take me down." The second night is less of a concern. Depending on how fast Sanguine works, Leif could recover by then. Since his name was called out at the march, he should be able to return to the field.

Her arms cross. "That confident, are you? Have you been training?"

I cannot help but smile. "Yes."

She dusts off her pants, fingers skating gently over her exposed, scabbed knees. "You really want to win." She tilts her head. Her gaze is shrewd. Assessing. "You hope to take the tournament cup?"

She sees too much.

"Doesn't everyone?" I ask casually, as if I'm not desperate for the win. Her dislike of me was blatant in my room last night. I doubt she'd understand my driving need to give Malam back some of the pride and unity that was lost under my father and the regent.

I push the door open and step out. She hops out of the carriage behind me. A cool ocean breeze cuts through the day's heat, blowing between us.

"Would you like me to speak to the healer about tending to your wounds?"

I swear her hand flickers toward her left side. She glances at the castle and frowns before turning to face me. "I'm good."

We're the only two people in the yard. At this hour, the castle is quieter than a mausoleum. Everyone is sleeping. I look her over, trying to assess if she can truly be trusted.

"Lirra, I also need you to guide me out of the summer castle."

Her body locks up, chin jerking in my direction. "I haven't agreed to help you. And yet you assume I'll get you a costume *and* escort you out of there." She hitches a thumb toward the looming castle behind us.

"I need your help. You snuck in yesterday. Is sneaking back out so hard?"

Her head tips back, exposing her dirt-streaked neck as the night sky holds her focus. She mutters something to the stars and then looks at me. "Hard?" she repeats. "You have to know the tunnels. When the guards change station. Where they're positioned. There is risk involved. Not so much for you, but if I'm caught, Judge Soma won't hesitate to throw me back into that hellbox. You may be king of Malam, but you cannot grant me permission to enter tunnels that are secret."

"All right, there are risks. But . . . this plan of mine isn't possible without your help," I admit.

"Don't tell me that. Don't put this all on me." Lirra lets out a growl of frustration, but when she talks, her voice is softer than before. "The thing is, I have plans to enter the jubilee. And I've spent so long working on my—" She worries her dirty tunic with her dirtier hands and glances at the castle. "What you're asking of me is presumptuous. I know you freed me tonight, but Soma won't let you overrule him again if he catches me. And I'm not going to do anything that will get me sent back to that cell. Tell Leif I'm relieved he'll be okay."

She walks away. Lirra might as well have punched me in the face, for how her refusal flattens me. There is no one else with her know-how and access to disguises. No one who has the information about the guards' schedules and the secret tunnels. What will I do without her?

I need her help. There is too much risk involved if others find out I plan to fight in the tournament. My trip to the field must be made in secret.

What if I offer her information? She wanted Millner's letter. Using her father to force her hand coats my insides with brackish unease. I'm not the manipulative tyrant the regent before me was. But then, is it manipulative to propose a trade? She was furious when I didn't turn over the correspondence. I could offer the information in a simple exchange, Millner's command to keep Lirra out of it be damned.

She is nearly to the edge of the courtyard. I run to catch her, footsteps crunching the gravel. She glances over her shoulder. A grimace flashes on her face, and her left hand slides up to press on her ribs.

"Are you injured?"

Her nostrils flare. "I'm fine. But I meant what I said. You cannot change my mind."

"I thought you might be interested in a trade."

"I'm not. There's nothing you can offer me to convince me to take that risk. Good night, Your Highness."

She keeps walking. I doubt I've ever met anyone as tenacious and headstrong as Lirra.

"Lirra, do you want to know what your father wrote?"

She stops and swivels to face me, expelling a harsh breath like steam from a kettle. The threads constraining her annoyance are thin as commoner's cloth. Something inside me comes alive at the spark in her eyes. This conversation should fill me with worry over my outlandish plan, but instead this feels . . . fun.

"Apparently," she snaps, "I was wrong."

CHAPTER

9

LIRRA

A FEW HOURS BEFORE DAWN, I CREEP INTO MY home and upstairs into the attic. The image of Leif, unconscious and pallid, in the healer's room haunts me. While I wanted to choke the king of Malam, I appreciate that he kept his promise and escorted me through the castle to visit Leif. If only my cousin didn't look so haggard. A fresh wave of guilt hits.

I shuck off my clothes, unable to stand the filth any longer, and wipe down my body as best I can, using a rag and the bowl sitting on top of my chest of drawers. The porcelain washbowl doesn't match the rest of my room. Small, delicate roses painted along the rim contrast with the frayed cloth I soak in the water and press to the scratches on my limbs and face. It's too fanciful, reminding me of a life I'd rather know nothing about, but Da traded a large sum to have a few of my mother's belongings salvaged after the fire that stole her life. He smuggled them over the border so I might have a piece of her.

He's made many sacrifices on my behalf. Too many to ever repay.

Once the grime is wiped away, I inspect the yellow-and-purple patch that has bloomed in the scarred skin atop my ribs. My fingers prod the tender area. There are no broken bones, just bruises. I keep a few bottles of Beannach water hidden under my chest of drawers for times like this. I don't want my appearance to concern Eugenia or the littleuns. The Beannach water helps me regain my energy quickly. I guzzle it, hoping the aches will subside.

After sliding on a nightdress, I'm too tired to do anything more than sleep. My disgusting mess of hair will have to wait till tomorrow. But the second my head hits the pillow, I realize I won't be able to sleep despite my exhaustion.

Negotiation is a gambler's game, and knowing when to show each stake-raising card requires skill. Like a master, Aodren forced me to fold with his final reveal. We shook hands to seal the agreement—he'll turn over the details in Da's letter after I provide him with a disguise and escort him to the melee on the first night. I kick away the blanket and twist to my side, considering our deal, the precautions I'll have to take, the risk of getting caught. There's no way to wiggle out of the agreement and still have him deliver Da's letter.

I'm a hare caught in the hunter's trap, and the feeling keeps me awake until the sun peeks over the horizon.

Hours later, bangs and shouts and squeals — normal morning ruckus — wake me. Every muscle in my body groans. I pull the blanket over my head and attempt to fall back asleep, but hardly any time passes before someone pushes my shoulder, then pushes it again.

"Whaaaa?" I roll to face my intruder, pleased that my ribs are less tender.

"You awake?" A broken twig pokes out of Loren's curls, yet he peers down at me like I'm the odd one. I think he wants to ask where I was the night before. But we rarely discuss my absences because they're usually related to my work for Da.

"I am now," I grumble.

He beams, showing his big, crooked teeth. "I brought you something." The hand behind his back comes out of hiding. A rope hangs, loosely coiled, over his forearm.

I squint. "You brought me rope?"

"I thought you might want it back."

Sitting up, I straighten my nightdress. My head spins and I taste the nastiness of morning horse breath. "Uh . . . thank you for returning it."

Loren's mouth hitches to the side in an apologetic twist. "I, uh, I'm sorry for getting in your stuff. Is that why you didn't come home the night before last?"

When he isn't a hellion, Loren has a sweet side that softens all my hard spots. Before he can escape, I pull him into a hug and loosen the twig from his hair. "Lovable Loren, you came back! Don't let the beast take control of you again."

He squirms out of my grip and puts on affronted airs. "Stop it. I'm no beast."

I snort. "I was working," I say, instead of telling him where I really was for the last day.

He accepts my answer with an easy smile and digs his hands into his trouser pockets. "Thought so. I figure you need the rope for the jubilee. You're gonna get the glider done in time, right, Lirra? 'Cause my friends are all coming to see it. I been telling them about your flying inventions forever."

The first night of the jubilee starts after the melee. With less than a week to finish preparations, I don't know how I'm going to get through the list of things I need to do to complete the wings *and* help King Aodren.

"Orli's gonna come too, right?" Loren asks. "She'll wanna see them."

"I hope so," I say, though Orli won't attend in spite of how much work she has put into helping me sew the wings. I know she wants to see them take flight. But a night of magic displays will overwhelm her.

"When are you going to let me and Kiefer fly?"

I smile. "Soon. What time is it?" I ask, thinking there might be time to see Orli this morning before I have to meet Aodren with his disguise.

"Almost time to eat." Loren clutches his belly like hunger pains have gotten to him. I'm no fool. Loren is always eating.

"Breakfast?" I scratch my head and remember the vile state of my hair.

"No. You've slept all morning. It's the midday meal."

I leap out of bed, groaning, and rush around the attic, grabbing a clean dress, the pumice stone, and soap. Chances are the king will have to wait for me, but I'm not going anywhere in this state of ruin. Besides, if I have to put off seeing Orli and finishing my glider to do the man's errand, the least he can do is wait for me. I'll disguise him so completely his own mother wouldn't recognize him, then show him how to get in and out of the castle. After that, I'm done with His High and Mightiness.

AODREN

THE PALLOR OF LEIF'S SKIN HAS THE GRAYISH-green tint of an unripe melon, not the healthy color of recovery, as I was secretly hoping. There is no way he can fight in tonight's melee, which means the plan with Lirra Barrett is a go.

"You'll be getting back to your chambers soon, my dear." The healer, who I've learned is named Margeria, has taken a liking to Leif. She inspects his wound, touching around the stitches, prodding for signs of infection. To his credit, Leif doesn't so much as flinch.

"Wannafightem . . . bludgers . . . Wincup," he slurs, voice raspy and dry, eyelids too heavy for him to lift.

"All in due time, dearie." She swipes his forehead with a cloth and spends another minute neatly tucking the linens around his body. He kicks them loose a second later.

"Gimme . . . biscuit?" Leif attempts a smile, only to have exhaustion foil the plan. Biscuits are a bizarre request.

The woman chuckles, surprising me, because she's barely given me more than a pinch-mouthed curtsy. "Rest up, and when you wake, I'll have two waiting for you."

She crosses the room and sets the cloth over the edge of an empty bowl. "Your Highness, I've given him something to ease the pain. He won't be quite himself," she says. At best, her tone is formal, unlike the warmth she showered on Leif. I cannot tell if it's due to my title or the history of my kingdom. Regardless, I'm grateful to her for fetching Ku Toa the night of Leif's stabbing. Had she not done so, he wouldn't be groggily fighting to watch us now.

"Thank you," I tell her. "For all you've done to help him."

Margeria dips in a customary bow and leaves.

Now that we're alone, I'm not sure what to say. My guards are waiting for me outside the healer's room so I can have a private moment to discuss the tournament with Leif. Taking his place tonight hasn't bothered me, until now. Which is why the words fail me. The eager anticipation and the dedication he showed in training these last few months will be for naught.

Leif's eyelids slog downward. The sleep concoction the healer gave him must be working. Perhaps now isn't the best time to discuss the tournament after all. I walk to the door, ignoring the relief that comes.

"Ya going?" Leif croaks.

I turn back to face him. "Do not let me keep you up. I came to see how you're faring. However, you need your rest. I will return later."

He yawns. "Who'sformal . . . now?"

The mumbled question loosens me up enough to abandon the wooden-soldier stance and return to his bedside.

"Yer betterwhenya . . . forget being king," Leif says, entertaining with his candidness.

"I'll keep that in mind." I smile inwardly. How much of this conversation will he remember later?

Leif wriggles to try to loosen the cocooning blankets, but gives up quickly and frowns. "Cannafight . . . tonight . . . no-fight."

"I know." I try hard not to cringe. It serves me right for trying to sneak out. He deserves to hear from me what is the plan for the melee. "I'm going to fight in my own name."

His eyebrows crawl up like slow, sluggish caterpillars, but they make it up his forehead. A little of the exhaustion clears from his eyes. "You . . . in the melee?"

I nod.

"Baltroit know?"

"No one knows but you and Lirra. She's going to help me." I explain her role this evening, though Leif probably won't remember half of what's being said.

When I'm done, he stares glassy-eyed at the closed door. "Better watch Hemmet," he says after a beat, talking about Gorenza's son. "Man's . . . crafty."

"I will."

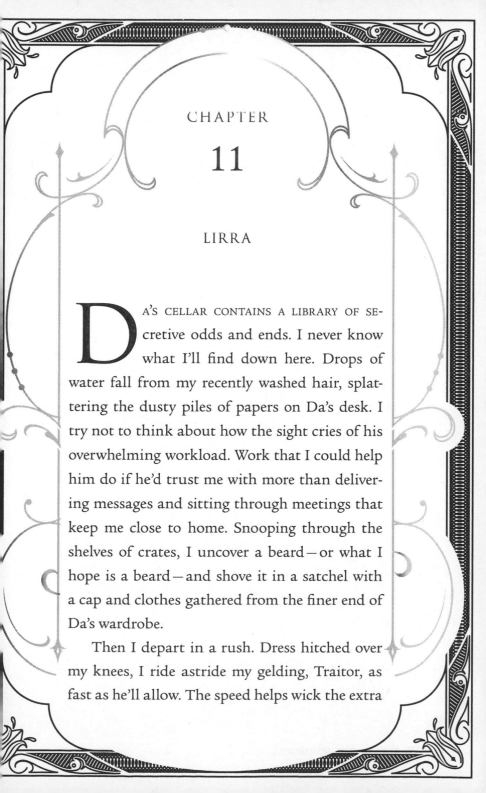

CHAPTER

11

LIRRA

D A'S CELLAR CONTAINS A LIBRARY OF SE-
cretive odds and ends. I never know
what I'll find down here. Drops of
water fall from my recently washed hair, splat-
tering the dusty piles of papers on Da's desk. I
try not to think about how the sight cries of his
overwhelming workload. Work that I could help
him do if he'd trust me with more than delivering messages and sitting through meetings that
keep me close to home. Snooping through the
shelves of crates, I uncover a beard — or what I
hope is a beard — and shove it in a satchel with
a cap and clothes gathered from the finer end of
Da's wardrobe.

Then I depart in a rush. Dress hitched over
my knees, I ride astride my gelding, Traitor, as
fast as he'll allow. The speed helps wick the extra

water from my hair, so by the time I reach my destination, my braid is dry.

The street leading to the Elementiary is surprisingly less crowded than the rest of Celize. A fancy carriage with the seal of Malam's royal stag is parked in front of the smithy, just to the east of Astoria's Channeler school. A handful of guards wait outside the door.

When Aodren mentioned he was going to stop at the Elementiary, I didn't think about how Astoria would react. Perhaps I should've warned her.

I dismount Traitor and rush into the shop.

Astoria is standing beside her desk, stiff as a creature preserved in one of her jars of lavender liquid. Her uncharacteristic glare is fixed on a point to the right of the Elementiary door. I twist and find Aodren, in a maroon surcoat, perfectly shined buttons, perfectly coifed hair, perfectly noble king.

A smile softens his face.

Seeds, what other king smiles like that?

"You're here," I say, breathless from the ride.

A nod. "I am."

Astoria sputters, the muscle under her left eye twitching. To say she dislikes Malamians is an understatement. Astoria rarely utters an unkind word about anyone. But last year, when she discovered the king of Malam sought help from the Channelers Guild during the coup, she cursed Aodren's name more than a dozen times. Like most Shaerdanians, she believes he abolished the Purge to get access to the Channelers Guild. To use their abilities for his gain.

"Why is he here?" Astoria's mouth puckers.

"He came to learn about how you run an Elementiary," I say, and then look to him.

"I explained as much," he says. "Twice now."

"Why are you here at the same time as him?" Astoria clarifies.

I give her a sheepish shrug. "He was already planning on coming here, and we needed someplace private to meet, so I figured this was a good place. I should've warned you beforehand." I check the door latch behind me and glance through the rows of bottle-lined shelves for other people.

"We're alone?" I ask, to be certain.

"Aye. His men cleared the Elementiary. Except they left him." She says the last bit like she's spitting. She ambles around her desk and sits.

"I didn't mean to catch you off-guard."

"Pish, that doesn't matter. What concerns me is why you'd meet with him in the first place."

"Astoria," I say, pleading for her to stop. He's *right* here. Even if she doesn't like the man, her blatant and brazen disrespect could land her in prison. I know she hates his country and him, but she knows when to feign respect. Considering his guards are mere steps outside the door, she should be cautious.

"Were you forced? Surely, you're not so foolish a girl to trust this—"

"No need to condemn me." I cross my arms. "Da started business with the man. I'm just trying to finish it."

In the corner of my eye, I catch the movement of Aodren's hands fisting. I pray for him to have patience with her, in spite of her disrespect. He could have her killed, but I'm starting to understand him better, and I don't think he'd do that to Astoria. Besides, he's the ruler of a kingdom that spent twenty years hunting our kind. He must understand that he has no right to expect the trust of Channelers.

Astoria sniffs, twisting her head to the side. "I thought you knew better, Lirra. Nothing good comes from Malam."

I roll my eyes. Has she forgotten we're both originally from Malam? Her reservations have some validity; however, it's obvious Aodren is nothing like the cold-blooded regent who ruled before him. Can she not see that? If he hated Channelers, he wouldn't have fought so hard to get two of us out of prison last night.

"Son of a scrant," hisses Astoria.

To his credit, he doesn't shout for his guards. If she said the same of Judge Soma, she'd be hanged, and he's not even the ruler of a country.

"Astoria," I scold, and she studies a book on her desk.

I decide it's time to move this meeting along, so I step closer to Aodren to size him up. "You were right to want a disguise. You'll definitely have to lose those clothes if you don't want to draw attention."

The edges of his face relax. Was he worried that Astoria would convince me to back out of our deal? His fingers move to his surcoat's buttons, deftly unfastening them.

"Wait, not now," I cry. "Don't you have to return to the castle for the remainder of the day's meetings?"

"Don't you need to fit the disguise to me?"

"Me? I'm not a tailor."

"What else can the Channelers do for him? Polish his boots?" Astoria's interruption is the last one. I spin to face her, the fabric of my dress smacking the nearest shelf, and swipe my hand across my neck in a cease-action motion. The mocking and cruel things she's said are so unlike her typical kindness.

I turn back to find a shade of rose creeping up Aodren's face.

"Here." I ignore his embarrassment and shrug the satchel off my back, thrusting it into his hands. "Everything you need is in there. You can check out what I brought, and I'll show you how to apply the beard." Then, turning to Astoria, "He's going to use the backroom."

She purses her lips, probably mentally cursing Aodren a thousand different ways as he walks to the rear of the Elementiary.

"What was that?" I throw my hands up once he's out of

sight. "You cannot talk to the king of Malam that way. Not if you want to live much longer."

"I—I know. Seeing him riled me so. His men came in and pushed everyone out." Gone is the plucky woman who gave Aodren a dressing-down. Moisture blurs her Channeler blues. She kicks up her trembling chin. "Nothing good comes from Malam."

She's thinking of things and people other than us, like the darkness that shadowed the country's past. It bothers me, though, that she cannot see Aodren's done some good.

"He overturned the Purge," I say.

"He might've banned hunting our sisters, but that doesn't mean he's remedied the problem. That kingdom has sown prejudice and hate for decades."

"You mean since he was a child with no say in the matter? He's made a start. He deserves credit for that. We shouldn't judge him for the actions of the rulers before him."

Astoria rubs her eyes dry. "Bah! That man ended the Purge to save his rump. He needed the Channelers Guild to fight his battle. He is no different from the men before him."

It's the same harsh assessment she's argued for the last six months, and yes, there might be truth to her claim. But while he's in the next room, I'd rather not discuss it. Astoria shuffles away from the desk to resume her daily work. She plucks items from different nooks that hold an array of Channeler supplies —herbs, plants, powders, oils, animal parts, and books.

"I'm sorry," I say.

She glances over her shoulder, a sad smile on her face. "You're not at fault, my dear."

"You won't tell anyone that I'm helping him?"

"You know I won't." And I do. Astoria may be cantankerous to Malamians, but she's dependable and true. She doesn't pry further into my business or question why the king of Malam needs to alter his appearance. All she does is offer a gentle reprimand, a *tsk* of her tongue against her teeth. "Remember, Lirra, charm and good looks only serve to mask a man's true character. Don't fall for his act."

"You know me. I know all about disguises."

A true smile shines on her face, and I'm relieved to see the Astoria I know and love once more.

I go to the backroom to check on Aodren, hoping he didn't hear much. When I enter, he turns away from a table covered in a dozen ancient Channeler books.

"Interesting reading?"

He crosses his arms. "She doesn't like me much."

I've no argument for that, nor does it seem like he expects one. Astoria lost a sister to the Purge. It was years before Aodren's rule, but her scars of enmity and grief are no less real than the burn mark on my left side—a token of the night Malamian guards took my mother's life.

I cross the room to where Aodren has placed the satchel and withdraw a tunic. "It isn't as fancy as the clothes you're used to, but it's nicer than commoner clothing. I thought it would be less shocking if you resembled a lesser nobleman.

They tend to blend into the crowd, not drawing attention like the noble elite."

"Thank you," he says, eyeing the tunic with flagrant approval.

"Well, I said I'd bring you a disguise."

"No, I mean, thank you for what you said out there." His eyes lift to meet mine. "You didn't have to defend me. But you did. I appreciate that you can see my actions are different from the regent's or my father's."

It's strange how the small compliment softens my frustration. "Well, I wasn't saying you were perfect."

Aodren's mouth twitches, and for a moment I think he might smile.

"Noted," he says, and then lifts the triangular swatch of hair, his long fingers turning it over. "A beard?"

"Only a king would keep such a clean shave. You need to hide some of that beauty." I laugh, and his hand rises to the strong line of his jaw. The reaction catches me off-guard, because surely he's not bashful. The man has flaws, but his appearance is definitely not one of them. His irritatingly perfect face may as well have been carved from an artist's marble.

"Hmm, do you have something to cover my hair?"

"Look in the bag. I packed a cap."

Aodren sifts through the items, withdrawing the clothes and turning them over. He surprises me by neatly folding each piece. "You put thought into this."

His words wash me with warmth. "It was nothing," I say,

because that's the truth. "It's not as if I had a choice. You did say I had to bring a costume if I want that letter."

"True. Though you could've brought something terrible."

I shrug, as if he hasn't made me feel a little taller, a little lighter, and a little off-kilter. He gathers up the items, putting them back in the bag, and heads for the door. The man trapped me into sneaking him out of the castle, so I shouldn't want to help him more than what was agreed upon. But my conscience is a mule. It won't allow me to walk away without sharing a few necessary tips.

"If you don't want people to notice you before the first melee fight, you need more than the clothes," I blurt out.

He turns around. "Go on."

"Well . . ." I chew my lip. "You stand like a king."

A small smile quirks at his mouth. "I am one."

"Yes, but your posture gives you away."

He looks down at his feet. "How should I stand differently?"

"Less stately."

He stares at me blankly.

I extend my hands. "May I?"

Aodren edges closer and positions himself as he would for a tailor.

I walk behind him and touch his shoulders, and the hard planes lower a fraction. Then, I flatten both hands against his broad upper back, ignoring how his muscles leap under my fingertips, and push gently until he reacts, curling into a believable slump. I circle to his front. The tilt of his head is off. His chin sits too high.

We stand so close that I can faintly detect his skin's scent of soap and clean linens. I try not to breathe too deeply or think of how good he smells. I focus on cupping his jaw in my hands and gently drawing his face down. But when the warm brush of his exhale touches my cheek, and his green, green eyes land on mine, I realize a beat late he may have personal boundaries. My heart gives a hard kick, and I suck a breath through clenched teeth. I expect him to pull back. But . . . he doesn't. His eyes drop to my lips, pausing before lifting to meet my gaze.

The patter of my pulse picks up speed, crashing and crescendoing in my ears. My hands drop, flitting over the folds of my dress, while I feel overheated and lightheaded. I edge back, putting space between us.

"Any more advice?" Aodren asks.

I force a smile that is normal and unaffected. "Remember to act the part. You're impersonating a lesser noble. Until you step on the tournament field, you must be someone else. Forget you were once a king."

"Once? I still am king."

"Yes, but you don't want others to notice. You have to pretend your crown-wearing days were in another life. You must act less haughty and privileged."

"Haughty?"

I cringe. "Try to act less royal."

"I'm going to need more specific instruction." His finger taps over lips that twitch like he's struggling to hold back a smile. "How does one act 'less royal'?"

Is he toying with me?

Those eyes glow greener.

Seeds, he is. I shove the items back into the satchel and toss it at him. "Start by saying a dozen prayers to the gods."

His throaty laugh follows me out of the Elementiary.

I spend the rest of the afternoon working on components of my wings.

When dusk falls over Celize, I set out toward the summer castle. Dread for what might happen tonight twists me tighter than the line knots I should be tying on the glider rope to give a pilot more control. But I'm eager to see Leif and read Da's letter to Aodren.

Entering through the main gate is quicker than sneaking in. And infinitely more stressful. Lanterns are ablaze everywhere, so anyone in the shadows can watch me approach. Each step closer to the main doors kicks my heart rate up a notch, and not in an *I have Aodren's face in my hands* way.

Aodren assured me my entrance would go unquestioned, explaining my visitations are approved, since I am partly responsible for saving Leif's life.

The guard at the main door greets me and guides me to Malam's corridor, where Leif has been brought to recuperate. I'm on edge, unconvinced that Judge Soma won't materialize and drag me back to the holding chamber hell. Even though Aodren says he has jurisdiction over me and Soma has no power to put me in jail, I have a hard time believing it. But I keep reminding myself that soon I'll know what's in Da's letter. Hopefully it'll tell me what he's working on and where he is, so I can jump in and help finish the job. I wonder what Da would think if he knew the lengths I'm willing to go through to prove myself to him.

A welcoming croak comes from my cousin when I enter his private room. I rush closer, grinning, suddenly weightless with relief to be free of the guard, and even more relieved to see Leif alert. My fingers skate over his matted hair. "You're all right?"

"Aye."

I'm so pleased by the simplicity of his answer that I settle in the seat beside him, my hand on his arm, needing to feel his pulse, to know he'll survive. "I — I was so worried . . . You didn't look good. I thought . . . Well, I'm just glad you made it."

"My thoughts exactly." Aodren's confident, clear tenor echoes behind me. "Are you ready for me?"

What an absurd question. I twist around to give him a tart response and . . . gape.

He is so handsome.

In a tailored coat and close-fitting breeches . . . *stars* . . . he's the refined picture of royalty. The outfit accents his strong, muscled frame that narrows at the hips and spreads wide through his shoulders in an imposing way.

I'm tongue-tied. I realize there's nothing at all absurd about his question. Not after the varying reactions he's inspired in me over the last few days.

Seeds and stars, who could ever be ready for the chaos of the Malamian king?

CHAPTER
12

AODREN

S NEAKING OUT OF THE CASTLE IS EASIER THAN sneaking in," she says after we've dodged a chambermaid, kitchen help, and two guards on our descent to reach the tunnels under the castle. Since I am not familiar with these halls, it's difficult to keep up. I try to guess which way she's going to turn next, and fail.

It seems everything she does keeps me guessing. For example, her appearance tonight. It's more befitting a court gathering than an evening of covert activity. Her arms are full of her dress, hefting it up high enough that her ankles are displayed as we race through the depths of the castle. I cannot fathom why she would've worn it.

"Is that the least conspicuous outfit you own?"

She rolls her eyes. Did she not chide me at the Elementiary about my appearance drawing attention?

"Less noise," she whispers, and hoists the gown so it cannot scuff on the stairs.

Lirra pulls me into an alcove. The echo of a guard's footsteps comes closer and then continues on, until it's out of earshot. She then explains that the guards patrol the castle, walking the same routes each night. How easy it is to sneak in and out when you know the pattern. Lirra would make an excellent security adviser.

When we reach the lower levels of the castle, she smooths her full skirts down and gestures for me to stop. To my confusion, her hands disappear in the green folds of fabric. An instant later she withdraws a . . . Is that a map?

Her clever pockets are impressive. She unfolds the aged parchment, presenting a well-worn sketch of the castle's layout, and consults the map. After a few moments, she refolds it like an accordion and slips it into her hidden dress pocket.

"That way," she says.

We wind through the castle's belly, where the maze of halls would be impossible to navigate without her leading the way. And then without warning, she stops beside a low wooden door that nearly blends into the surrounding rock.

Lirra digs through her dress's pockets, this time producing a hand-size waterskin. After taking a sip, she offers it to me. I decline but watch, enrapt, as it disappears back into the material. Waves of her black hair fall over her shoulder as she starts twisting side to side and slipping her hands into her skirts. The urge comes to tuck the curls behind her ear to see what else she'll unearth. Her hair is blocking my view.

Lirra glances up and catches me staring at her.

A coy smile replaces the look of concentration, her thick, sooty lashes batting twice and then open wide. "Your attention flatters me, Your Highness."

I step back. "I wanted to see what else you have in there."

All signs of flirtation vanish. "Your gaping makes me itchy. Stop it."

"It's your dress," I say, not wanting to admit the true course of my thoughts. "It confused me at first, but now I can see its utility."

She rolls two small metal sticks in her palms. "Did you think I wore it for you?"

"No." I shift my weight. "It appeared too restrictive for the night's activity. But its functionality is impressive."

"Thank you." She curtsies, a smooth motion worthy of any highborn lady and not something I'd expect of the Archtraitor's daughter. Until I remember that before he was the Archtraitor, Millner was a member of the Malamian nobility, making Lirra a highborn lady. Though she wasn't raised that way. "At the tournament, ladies will be dressed in their finest. This gown helps me blend in. Also, dressed like this, no one would ever think I'm hiding six sets of throwing daggers."

Godstars. "You are?"

She laughs and inserts the sticks into the lock. "Only one set. But I could carry six sets if I wanted to."

I cannot decide if I find her candidness aggravating or refreshing. But she has me smiling and intrigued to know what she'll say or do next. It's a refreshing change from how others treat me.

A few twists and the door unlocks, swinging open to a wide hole of pitch-black.

"This path runs in a straight shot from the summer castle's keep to the cathedral on the cliff," she says.

I maintain my neutral expression, ignoring the cloaking darkness ahead.

"If you reach out with both hands, you could touch either side of the tunnel. If you stand to your full height, you'll probably bang your head. Remember that. Ready?"

"Yes." Though I am not. The space is tight and close, giving too much freedom to my dark imagination.

After we enter, Lirra closes the door behind us.

We have gone a few steps when a *hic, hic, hic* of her jerking breath echoes in the pitch-black. I am not the only one uneasy. Something has spooked her.

"Lirra?" I ask, forgetting my own discomfort.

"I'm fine," she says. I don't know her well, but I can tell she's lying.

Her steps echo, indicating she's moving forward, so I follow close enough behind that I can feel the hem of her dress connect with the toe of my boot. The musty tunnel is cooler than the castle halls, but the temperature hasn't dropped enough to be the cause of her shivery breath.

"Lirra," I say again, and then nearly knock her down when I run into her back.

My fingers seek her arm in the darkness and then trail down to her hand. Lirra allows me to sandwich her hand between both of mine. Hers is made of ice. My palm covers hers, sliding up to her wrist and back down. She releases a breath. Neither of us breaks the silence, but the tension in her arm eases and stays that way as we continue forward until eventually entering the cathedral's catacombs.

The light is too strong at first. But after blinking a handful of times, my eyes adjust. We've emerged in a dusty cavern. Lirra lets go of me and slides her hands over her arms.

"They always have one lantern lit," she whispers, not quite meeting my gaze. I want to know what rattled her, or at the very least, know how to help her. But I doubt this headstrong girl will admit anything to me.

She points to the satchel on my shoulder, and mouths, "Hurry."

That single word returns my attention to the night's purpose. I step into an adjacent burial chamber and switch outfits. All I have to do is travel unnoticed to the tent where the champions wait in preparation for the first event. Once there, I'll have no more than a few minutes to gather armor and Leif's sparring swords before the event begins. It's not too great a challenge. I've already passed the hardest part — keeping the plan from the other leaders and sneaking out of the castle.

When I emerge, Lirra inspects my work, adjusting the cap over my hair. "You're ready," she pronounces.

Less than a quarter-league from the cathedral, makeshift merchant shops and small bonfires surround the tournament field. Voices rumble from gathering crowds while more people approach, their wooden carriage wheels crackling on the gravel road. Anticipation is as vivid as the dozens of torchlights made to shine directional light, illuminating the tournament field by Channeler magic.

I stand outside the champions' tent, my stomach high in my throat. Lirra disappeared as soon as this part of the bargain was filled. I was disappointed, though not surprised. She is helping me only in order to gain information about her father. And yet, for a moment in the tunnel, with the sound of her fearful breaths and the touch of her small, chilled hand, I felt useful. Needed by another person.

Despite the servants and nobility who move through the halls of Malam's Castle Neart, the life of a king is one of solitude. In my twenty-two years, I can hardly remember a time when someone has *needed* me for me and not just for the power of my crown. Perhaps that is why the moment her fingers left mine, I felt the absence down in my core. I'll not soon forget the touch of her hand, nor what it felt like for her to lean on me.

It felt like trust and belief.

If only my people felt this way about Malam. I'm here tonight for this very reason.

Everything I've prepared runs through my head—the request for Leif's weapons to be brought to the tent along with my practice armor, which bears the colors of Malam, but no specific royal marks. My nerves are frayed, hoping it will all come together.

Around the field, the crowd buzzes like a sentient thing. A loud hum of banter comes from the people streaming by. I see clothing in blue and gold for Shaerdan, black and silver for Kolontia, red and yellow for Akaria, and green and brown for the Plovian Isles. They talk about their kingdoms' competitors, chanting and cheering the fighters' names. I cannot help but notice few wear Malam's maroon and gray. And those who do are quieter, more subdued.

I stand outside the champions' tent, waiting as the fighters stroll out and gather at the edge of the tournament field.

"Bloody Malamians, I hope they're destroyed on the field," I hear someone say from a crowd of Kolontians and Shaerdanians passing by.

"On the field? Soon enough that kingdom will fall."

I bite my tongue and push through the tent's flaps. Inside, rows of benches and curtains separate the expansive staging area into six sections. If the respective flags are any indication, the competitors from each kingdom have been allotted private space to prepare. The remaining area, where the curtain is open for all to view, is a healer's station. No one is there. They've all left for the start of the tournament.

Keeping my head ducked, I hurry forward and push through the curtain leading into Malam's section of the tent.

Baltroit Bromier pushes his long sandy hair out of his face and glances up. I halt, pulse kicking through my ears. I thought the space was empty. I've sparred with him many times on Castle Neart's training grounds. He's sure to recognize me in spite of the borrowed lesser-noble clothes and false beard. I haven't even confessed my plan to Segrande, but perhaps now is a good time to tell Baltroit. We can use the next few minutes to discuss a joint attack for the melee.

"You got something to say? Or you mute?" His animosity is unexpected. Shocking. "Figures they'd give me the lame one."

He thinks I'm a page.

Baltroit starts sharpening his blade. *Sharpening his blade?*

"Only practice swords are allowed," I say, remembering to moderate my voice halfway through my comment. I sound like a lad in the throes of puberty. What am I doing?

"That's right. This is for later. In case I need it."

What would he need it for? Baltroit has always been a little erratic. The bitter violence he's harboring is new. Or, at least, a side I've not seen before. "What would you need it for?"

His stone zips along the blade. "You a Malamian? You sound like one."

I nod.

"You hear what they're saying about us. No respect. If yer not given it, you take it."

My eyes narrow. "You mean to start a—"

"I'm starting nothing. But I'll finish it." He rubs his beard just like his father does and scowls. "Yer a nosy filly. Get outta here and tell them I'm coming." He sheaths the sword and stands, grabbing his helmet.

Outside, the sounds of the tournament grow to a loud drone. It's soon to start. I step out of the curtained area, stunned by Baltroit's malice. He's not acting like himself. It must be adrenaline for the fight. But I can't worry about that now. I'm running out of time to get ready.

"Hailing from Kolontia, fighting in the name of their king, are Hemmet Vonk and Zane Marza."

I rush out of the tent as I tug on a helmet. After Baltroit left the champions' tent late, I had mere minutes to pull on chain mail and hardened leather body plates. I reach the field as the roar from spectators rises to a deafening pitch.

Hemmet and Zane cross the field.

Another spark of cheers ignites when Hemmet pumps his broadsword in the air.

I hide behind a healer's cart where Baltroit stands waiting for his name to be called. Here I can keep an eye on him and watch the tournament field.

The noise dies down, and the speaker calls on the next two

champions, Io and Fehana Caloi, sisters from Akaria. Whispers of awe rush into the night, sounding like a wind in the trees. Feet hammer the ground to welcome the two women warriors. Dressed in black from head to toe and each carrying two thin swords, they're a fearsome pair. The seams of their clothing show sewn-in armor, pieces of hardened leather to protect all their vital areas.

"Easy prey," I hear Baltroit say.

He's wrong. If he studied their movement, he'd recognize the tell of agility. They're alert and light on their feet.

Baltroit is a fool to think these women are any less lethal than the eight male champions that will be fighting this evening. I shift my grip on Leif's sword. It's heavier than my own sparring weapon, a fact I hadn't accounted for. But I have my short sparring sword fixed at my waist as a secondary blade.

The announcer yells for Malam's fighters, and my heart jumps into a gallop. I give Baltroit a half-dozen strides before I move away from the cart and walk onto the field. Baltroit crosses to the center, where the other competitors have lined up. I head to the announcer's stand. The man finishes his introduction of Baltroit before taking notice of me.

I've nearly reached the stand when the man leans away from the cone he's been shouting into. "Look, not just anyone can take a champ's place. Only King Aodren himself can compete. You can't just walk on for Malam. If you wanted to fight—"

I pull off my helmet.

He blanches. Nearest us, sounds of confusion replace the

chatter and cheers, while farther out, voices still yell for champions and cry for the tournament to begin.

"As you know, my captain, Leif O'Floinn cannot fight tonight." I draw my shoulders back and pull on every bit of kingly propriety, wearing confidence like a fake beard. "Therefore, I'll fight in my own name."

The announcer's gaze darts from me to the platforms around the field, where the other leaders sit, to the spectators who still have no idea what's happening. "Yes, yes of course, Your Highness. But the, ah, risks, sir. Have you considered those? It's why proxies fight for their ruler."

"Yes."

His mouth stutters open and closed. Word of my appearance moves on waves of whispers through the crowd. Their loud chatter drops into low tones, and the weight of a thousand eyes falls on me. It doesn't take long for people to remember their voices. At first it's a murmur, then chatter, and now a roar. I cannot hear what they're saying, but the message is clear. They're not pleased.

"I'll take my place on the field." I pull on the helmet and go stand with the other competitors.

Baltroit's confusion morphs into embarrassment. "Your Highness, I—I didn't know—"

"The final champion," the announcer's voice booms, though many cannot hear it. "Hailing from Malam . . ."

Applause is swallowed by jeers.

"Fighting in his own name . . ."

Hurrahs buried under hisses.

"Aodren Lothar Cross, King of Malam."

Eventually a hush settles over the crowd, silence, bloated with uneasiness and hesitancy, so the announcer can declare the rules. I cannot see the other competitors' expressions. But I feel the weight of their stares.

The melee will take place over two nights, with one day of rest and other festivities in between. The battles will run until one man is left standing or until the judges sound the horn for time. Each hit is recorded, and the team that lands the most hits will win. No one may strike a fallen champion. Anyone who falls must stand within ten seconds or be eliminated for the remainder of that night's battle. At the end of the second melee night, hits will be tallied, and the kingdom with the most will be declared the winner. The winner takes home the coveted melee banner and earns twenty points toward the All Kingdoms' Cup. Second place takes fourteen points. Third place — ten, fourth place — eight, and fifth place — four.

A short song rings from trumpets, tearing my focus from the crowd.

I can do this. I flex my hand on the pommel of my sword and unsheathe the weapon. My head clears of everything beyond the men and women around me. *For Malam.*

The trumpets cease, and the fight begins.

Baltroit immediately runs forward, poleax in both hands.

His approach is more aggressive than mine. In the frenzied beginning moments, I assess the others around me. Some men cut across to the nearest champions, vicious in their attack to rack up points. Others exercise caution.

A ring of steel against steel releases jeers from the audience. I move in, Leif's broadsword at the ready, its extra weight throwing me slightly off-balance.

One of the Plovians rushes in my direction, raising his club. I sidestep and twist, narrowly avoiding a blow, then swing my sword down and catch his leg.

He grunts, topples forward. I strike again, but miss when he rolls and pops off the ground.

He's fast, blocking my next slash with his club. I land another hit to his core, but then he manages to hook his club against Leif's sword. His movement rips the weapon from my grip. I'm fumbling to take it back when the man's heel lands against my knee. His club hits my back. I buckle, sharp pain zinging through my leg and between my shoulder blades.

A gasp and a curse fly from my mouth. I shake off the pain, the ten-second rule in mind, and scramble to my feet. The man has moved to take on another opponent when he notices that I'm standing again. He changes direction and charges. I seize the short sword from my belt, barely managing to block his club. There wasn't time to locate my first weapon.

The echo of the crowd starts to edge back in. I hadn't noticed it before. Embarrassment over the terrible start sweeps over me, but I push the feeling away. *Focus. Fight for Malam.*

I don't think about the disadvantages of the short sword. Instead I use the closer proximity and the weapon's lower weight to pick up my speed. Years of training sharpen my movements. Swing, block, parry, strike. I advance on the man, my precision scoring point after point until he falls.

I stumble back, pulling gulps of air, and look around. Champions are paired off. As soon as one falls, the victor moves on to another. Points. I must keep landing hits if I want to rack up points.

Grabbing the discarded broadsword, I run toward an unoccupied Shaerdanian. Whoever he fought before me dented his helmet and bloodied his face. He carries one end of a broken pole and a short sword. Our duel of blades begins. We circle, and when his sword dips a fraction, I lunge and strike. Leaping in and out, dropping low and twisting away, I manage to avoid all but two hits from him, while my blade scores a dozen more points before I manage to divest him of his sword.

I go after the Shaerdanian's broken pole. Baltroit suddenly appears behind him. My co-champion slams the butt of his weapon against the man's head, his features twisted with hate and rage.

What was that?

Anger rushes through me, but there's no time to process his action before I'm pulling up my sword to parry a strike from one of the Akarians, Io, I think. Her swings are stealthy and quick, her face impassive, her focus sharper than her true battle sword.

I push Baltroit out of my head and match Io. Strike after strike, she's relentless. But I block and swing. When she lands a hit, I come back to score an equal point on her. We take over the field, dodging other champions, leaping over fallen weapons, dueling with waning energy. I stop thinking of winning points. Instinct guides my movements. The world fades, and with it, the crowds, the tournament field, even the strain in my limbs.

Our speed increases, our blades clanging, crashing, snapping.

And then a horn bellows.

The first night of the melee is over.

CHAPTER

13

LIRRA

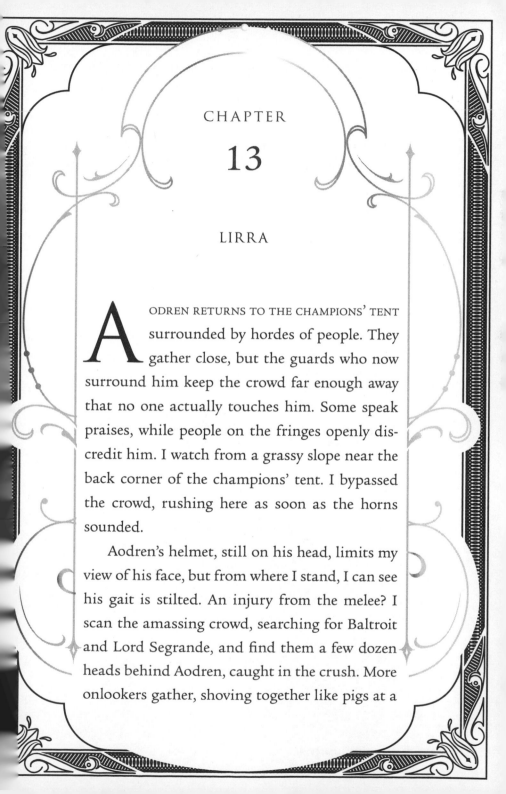

ODREN RETURNS TO THE CHAMPIONS' TENT
surrounded by hordes of people. They
gather close, but the guards who now
surround him keep the crowd far enough away
that no one actually touches him. Some speak
praises, while people on the fringes openly discredit him. I watch from a grassy slope near the
back corner of the champions' tent. I bypassed
the crowd, rushing here as soon as the horns
sounded.

Aodren's helmet, still on his head, limits my
view of his face, but from where I stand, I can see
his gait is stilted. An injury from the melee? I
scan the amassing crowd, searching for Baltroit
and Lord Segrande, and find them a few dozen
heads behind Aodren, caught in the crush. More
onlookers gather, shoving together like pigs at a

trough, trying to catch a glimpse of the king of Malam even after he's made it to the tent. Baltroit and Lord Segrande follow him inside.

A leader competing in his own name is unusual. The surprise of it must be the reason for the press of people and why they don't leave. More champions follow, and with them, the numbers grow. The chatter is nearly as loud as the cheers during the melee.

Minutes go by. Then a quarter-hour. Then a half.

The crowd doesn't disperse. If Aodren's waiting for them to leave, he'll be here all night. And so will I. It's a frustrating thought. But the wait is manageable. Besides, after he hands over Da's letter, we'll have no reason to meet again. This is what I wanted. And yet the thought doesn't please me like it should.

I listen to the chatter about the champions, most of which is focused on Aodren. Some good, most not. There's a lot of speculation and negative opinions being shared. But for all their criticisms, no one says a word about his sword fighting skill. He was an impressive sight to behold tonight.

"Make way, make way!"

The shout comes from a driver. Four horses pull a carriage, painted maroon and etched with the symbol of a stag, through the reluctantly parting onlookers. It comes to a stop outside the champions' tent, and moments later, Lord Segrande appears. He demands the people move back, and when they do,

Aodren steps out of the tent. Still dressed in armor and a helmet, he now wears an identifiable formal cloak pinned to his shoulders. Most people drop their eyes to the ground, while people in maroon and gray lower themselves to a knee.

Aodren stalks forward, paying the crowd no heed, like an angry bull might charge across a field of daisies. There's no longer hesitation or stiffness in his walk, but his back is slightly hunched, so unlike his typical kingly posture and more like the man he pretended to be in his disguise. Something isn't right, so I look closer. The man entering the carriage has a heavier step. He moves with purpose, but not the confidence that comes with a lifetime under a crown.

That man is not Aodren.

The crowd has fallen for the ruse, however, and as the carriage attempts to roll away, many follow, impeding the convoy's movement.

So what's Aodren's plan now?

I move closer to the back side of the tent to peek in. Voices filter from within, hushed, but not close enough to hear. I duck behind the nearest barrel, sinking to the shadowed ground just as the flaps of the tent open. Two people exit and pass near my hiding spot.

"What's the count?" The barrel beside me creaks. The man talking must be leaning against it.

"The Plovians are last. Our score is shy above theirs. You fought like a sorry scrant tonight." Irritation whittles the second man's words to sharp points. I hear no noticeable accent, and realize they're Shaerdan's champions, Otto Ellar and Folger Falk.

A huff. "You saw the size of the Kolontians."

"Nah, what I saw was the king of Malam score so many points off you, you may as well have lain down and played dead." It must be Folger who says this, since Otto was the one who fought Aodren and lost. What a sight that was.

"It won't happen again," Otto says.

"That so? You got some kind of remedy for being pathetic?" A soft scuffle follows. Then, a sharp inhale. "Where'd you get it?"

Otto's voice is a scratch lower than a whisper, and I can't hear his response.

"How much?"

"Enough for tonight, and twice more for the final melee."

Their conversation continues in quieter tones, dropping more words than I manage to hear. The blade in one of my pockets is poking my thigh, but I don't dare move. I hold still and listen. I catch *Channeler, stronger, oil*—which seem nonsensical when strung together. From what I gather, they're going to try a Channeler remedy to help Otto fight better. I nearly snort at the idea, and have to clamp a hand over my mouth and nose. If such a remedy exists, I've never heard of it.

Are they talking about Beannach water? I doubt it.

All the champions have access to Beannach to help replenish their energy after tonight's fight, so drinking some wouldn't give Otto an edge over the other fighters. Although, maybe Otto thinks the Malamians and the Kolontians won't use the Channeler water since their kingdoms have always been afraid of Channeler magic.

A cramp is eating my right calf. I suck in a breath, ignoring the pain, and wait for Otto and Folger to clarify, but the men abandon their spot by the barrel and return inside.

I rise, shaking the ache out of my leg, when the tent flap slides open again, and I flatten myself to the ground.

The crunch of grass sounds.

I peek from my hiding spot and find Aodren walking toward the low hills in hurried, long strides. Wearing the clothes I gave him, he's nearly unrecognizable, with a slumped posture and a hat hanging down around his ears. Dressed like this, he will be able to avoid any unwanted attention from the crowds. The king of Malam is not well-loved and it is dangerous for him to go anywhere without his guards. I race after him, steps as noiseless as possible. He's impressively adapted my tips. I draw nearer and call out to tell him as much.

Aodren spins around, hand shifting to the blade on his belt. He realizes it's me and straightens, but not before I see his startled expression. More than surprised, it looks haunted.

"No one but me," I say, hands out at my sides.

"Will you always sneak up on me?" He teases, though his tone's edge is sharp and his gaze skits to the shadows around us. There is a scant scattering of a crowd near the front of the champions' tent. The field is mostly darkened now, and fewer than half the merchants' lanterns remain lit. Is he worried about someone noticing him now? Or is there something more?

I close the distance between us. "You are a king, and since every eye in the five kingdoms is on you, there are few opportunities for a commoner girl like me to get close without a little sneaking."

"You are hardly common."

Spoken with such certainty. It paints a blush on my cheeks. Does he know that a lifetime ago, before my father brought me to Malam, that statement was true? "You, on the other hand, have taken up the commoner act quite impressively."

"You've taught me well," he says, and then plucks a piece of grass from the end of my hair. "I thought you might've left."

He continues walking, and I fall into step beside him. "Same here. You almost had me fooled with the royal carriage."

"Was that wishful thinking?"

I laugh. "It seems to be a theme when I'm around you."

His smile sparks, spreads, and illuminates his entire face beneath the shadow of his cap. Stars, he could put out an eye. "Is that so, Lirra? What do you wish for?"

My pulse skitters erratically.

I tip my head, hiding my grin behind a length of hair. If any other boy and girl were alone under the same indigo sky speckled with stars, sharing our same smiles, same laughs, same words, I'd think they were flirting. But reality shakes that thought. A king would never show interest in me, a Channeler from Shaerdan, the daughter of his kingdom's most infamous traitor.

He must have loads of admirers. He doesn't need one more. Besides, all I want from him is information about my da. Once I have that, my life will return to normal, managing Da's deal and sneaking in time for my gliders.

"Tonight, I wished for you to hurry along," I say, with a forced yawn. "I'd like to return home sometime before dawn."

"Right," he says after a beat. "Let's pick up the pace."

He strides toward the cathedral, each of his steps requiring two of mine, quietness hovering between us like an obstinate gray storm cloud. I'm annoyed with myself for ruining the playful banter.

Eventually, he slows so jogging isn't necessary.

"Baltroit took my place," he says. "I wasn't prepared for the rush . . . after the melee . . ."

"Me either." I glance over, catching a glimpse of distress on his face, and I suddenly want to ease that burden and see his smile again. "Some people aren't comfortable in crowds," I say, thinking of how Orli was months ago. It's something she's mostly overcome. "Even if you didn't mind crowds, tonight would've been nerve-racking."

"It shouldn't have been. My entire life has been in front of a crowd."

In front. Not a part of the group, but an outsider looking in. I suppose in this way we are similar.

"Baltroit didn't put up a fight about letting you return to the castle alone?" I ask, wondering what became of the champion. "Isn't the royal guard supposed to provide you protection?"

"He did, just not in a traditional sense." He grimaces. "His diversion gave the crowd reason to disperse. All I had to do was wait. I bathed in the meantime." He slides the hat off his head, so his mussed hair, darkened and damp, falls in chunks against his light golden skin.

I remember the subtle roughness of his jaw in spite of his clean shave when I touched him at the Elementiary. My hands twist the material of my dress. "Why aren't you wearing the beard?"

"It was cumbersome."

My palms face him. My body's energy pulls the breeze toward me and, along with it, a whiff of Aodren's masculine, soap-scrubbed skin. And then my wits snap together, realizing what I've done with my Channeler magic.

Bloody seeds. I stumble to a stop. What is wrong with me?

"Everything all right?" Aodren asks.

Thank the gods for the quarter-moon that doesn't put off enough light to show the mortification burning from my earlobes to my toes.

"Fine," I say. "I'm fine."

His brows arch up.

I brush past him, annoyed at myself, though more so at him. The king of Malam comes to town, and I start acting erratically, saying things I wouldn't usually say and feeling generally unsettled.

Nothing could be clearer—as soon as I have the information my da gave him, this arrangement will come to an end.

CHAPTER

14

LIRRA

ENTERING THE CASTLE IS EASIER THAN I'D anticipated, but then, that could be because Baltroit has notified the guards of the king's unconventional return. I hope that's not the case, because I don't want them to be aware that someone has snuck in and out of the castle recently.

After Aodren changes back into his regal clothing, we pass through the tunnel into the lower levels of the keep. We climb the stairs and find most of the castle halls empty. Twice, we sneak past a guard, but our movement draws no attention. I wonder if our actions are ridiculous. The guards may have heard word of Aodren's performance in the melee. If they are smart, they will have pieced together my arrival and Aodren's appearance tonight. They will know we're sneaking around the halls. But I'm not sure they're that clever, and sneaking around with Aodren is more fun than I've had in a while.

We reach Malam's corridor, and Aodren leads me into Leif's room. Baltroit is sitting beside the captain. He swings his untied sandy hair over his shoulder and turns to face us.

"How'd it go?" Leif's voice croaks. It's good to see him more alert than he was earlier. Whatever the healer has given him has worked well.

"Sneaking around? Or the tournament?" Aodren approaches Leif's side, and Baltroit stands. The champion wears an oddly sheepish expression as he bows to the king and then steps to the side so Aodren can use the vacated chair.

"Yes," Leif says.

Aodren drops into the seat. "Yes to both questions? I'd say it went fairly well on both accounts."

"Fairly well?" I cry, sidling up to Aodren and nudging him in the shoulder. "Hardly. He was *impressive* on both accounts, but his skill with the sword was unparalleled."

Baltroit crosses his arms.

"Of course, both Malamian champions fought well," I add, and the guard's eyes flick to mine, his chest lifting a fraction. "Baltroit started with a poleax, cutting a path right across the field."

"Truly? I would've liked to see that." Leif switches his attention between Aodren and Baltroit. "Of course, there would've been no contest if I was there." Leif's grin is laced with pain, but it's nice to see his gentle, lighthearted side returning.

"Now, that would've made the night more interesting." A soft chuckle floats from Aodren. "I'm sorry you couldn't compete." The comment rings true. Aodren's respect for his captain runs deeper than I thought. I'm slowly learning that everything I thought I knew about the king of Malam is wrong. "Do you think you'll be ready in two days for the second night of melee?"

"Hope so." Leif winces. "I don't want to miss it."

"I'd rather you didn't either. Tonight worked well because no one was prepared for my appearance," Aodren says. His eyes darken, and I wonder if he's thinking of the crowd's reaction after the tournament. "It would be best if you could return."

Leif scratches his chest around the wound. "I'll do my best."

Aodren provides a humble version of the first melee night. I don't hesitate to add details to spruce up the story, and even Baltroit jumps in to explain how he pretended to be Aodren so the king could escape out the back to avoid the crush of the crowd.

"Your Highness," Baltroit says, dropping his chin to his chest, as Aodren stands to leave some time later, "if I had known that was you in the tent . . . I wouldn't have spoken so harshly to you. Please forgive my foolishness."

Aodren considers his comment for a moment. I don't know exactly what happened, it seems like Baltroit said something inappropriate to the king before the match. "I accept your apology. However, I caution you to keep the same standards no matter who you may be around. A man should be consistent and true to himself."

Baltroit bows as Aodren exits the room. I follow him to his private chamber.

"Thank you for your help today," he says once the door is closed.

I shrug, deciding not to point out that I wouldn't be here if he'd given me Da's information when first requested. But now that the night is nearly over, I appreciate the new perspective I've gained of the king of Malam. I'm glad I decided to help him.

A yawn stretches my mouth. "It's been a long day. I should go. Can I see Da's letter?"

"Right, it's late." He walks to the desk and pulls out a stack of missives. "I must, um, explain something first."

Confused, I walk to where he sits, figuring Da must've written about something truly strange. "I would really rather you just let me read it. I know my father and his subtle context."

"I—I don't have the letter."

"What are those?"

A frown carves a canyon between his golden brows. "These are correspondences from noblemen in my kingdom." He taps the folded parchments into a neat pile and lays them flat, his fingers resting on top. "I burned your father's note."

He what?

"You. Lit. It. On. Fire?" I punch out each word.

He nods, and my jaw comes unhinged. I didn't take Aodren for the type to renege on a deal. But then I realize, as all our conversations flash through my mind, he hasn't reneged at all. Never did he specify handing over the actual letter.

Seeds, did he play me for a fool?

This oversight would never have happened with anyone else. I'm usually dagger-sharp in negotiations. In Da's underground trading world, I cannot be anything less. And yet I've allowed Aodren's presence to dull my wits. That ship of realization sinks to the bottom of my gut.

"Well done, King Aodren." I want to blast him with an icy breeze that knocks him flat on his arse. "I hadn't realized your gift for trickery."

He looks gutted by my words, as if he's truly sorry for not being honest with me. "That was not my intention, Lirra."

I scoop up the sides of my dress, lifting the hem off the floor, and stride to the door. Any response is swallowed by my embarrassment at how easily I've succumbed to his charm.

"Don't you want to know what he wrote?" Aodren asks. There's a hint of desperation in his voice. "I'll tell you everything."

He does sound sincere, but do I trust him to share the truth?

"Lirra." His tone is pleading, softening my rigid back. "I meant no deception. This misunderstanding is my fault."

No, it's mine. I know better.

"Your father's last line directed me to immediately destroy the note. I followed his order."

Sounds like something Da would say. Would Aodren know that?

I'm frustrated with the entire miscommunication, knowing Aodren must think me mercurial. In my defense, a small line of missed information can change the course of an entire deal. Can I blame him for not being upfront with me? I never would have helped had I known the letter was burned.

"I should've pushed until all the details of our agreement were clarified," I concede. Anyone in my business knows that. "Is it too late to accept your offer?"

"It's not too late," he says softly, picking up the stack of letters. "A few months ago, I received word of a new item being traded in Malam, a healing oil called Sanguine. I hadn't heard about it before. I thought it would be a boon to Malam, something the giftless would benefit from. And in turn, it would be a catalyst in changing people's opinions about Channelers." There is pain and need in his voice. I can hear it as clearly as I can see his desire to bring change to Malam. It makes sense now, why he stepped up to fill Leif's position in the tournament. He will do anything to unite Malam and move his people past the anger and hatred of the Purge.

Aodren tosses the missives on the desk. "I thought it would be best to find out more. If the rumors proved true, what better staple for healers throughout Malam than this Channeler oil? I commissioned your father to find the creator. I hoped to bring her to Malam, or meet her before the summit."

Da's urgency to deliver the letter makes sense now. He's never one to miss a deadline.

Aodren's eyes linger on the desk. "But more recently, rumors have spread that the oil is harmful. That it causes illness."

I walk to the edge of the plush rug, where chairs are situated around an unlit fireplace. There is a hazy memory in the back of my mind that tells me I've heard of Sanguine before, but it's not solid enough that I can place it. "Do you think the oil is dangerous?"

"No." His long legs carry him from the desk to the fireplace. Aodren stands with his back to me, his palms scraping the growth of stubble on his jaw. "There were a couple of deaths that had some ties to Sanguine. So then people in my country started rumors." He turns around, expression grim. "People who are resistant to accepting Channelers and their remedies. The night Leif was brought in, he should've died. I pleaded with the healer to find someone to help him. She sent Ku Toa."

"Truly?" I move to the tall chair and rest my arms on its velvet back. Ku Toa is a mystery, even to Da and his unlimited web of informants. "Rumor has it she's rarely seen in public. She almost never speaks and is the most powerful Channeler in the kingdoms, though I don't know what her gift is. You say she healed Leif? Is she a Spiriter?"

"That much I don't know. She compared Sanguine to a Spiriter's healing and then had me use it to heal Leif."

"Stars, the oil must be powerful." More so than Beannach water, which reinvigorates an exhausted person or helps ease aches and pains after a fight. If Sanguine heals like a Spiriter, it can bring a man from the brink of death.

"I have a foggy memory of something Astoria once told me," I admit. "Something about the Akarian Channelers and how they collectively pull their power together to create a healing remedy. The Channelers of Akaria are not taught and governed under the Channelers Guild. In Shaerdan, Channeler magic is like a religious club, and Channelers are part-time priestesses. We are revered for our gifts and celebrated during holidays and festivals, like the upcoming jubilee. During the rest of the year, our magic remains mostly unseen except by Elementiary owners and the girls they're teaching.

"In the southern kingdom, Channeler women serve Ku Toa like soldiers to a king. Their abilities are tools, used daily by the kingdom. Is Sanguine made by the Akarians?"

"Yes. The Ku didn't give me details, but she admitted ownership."

I move around the chair and flop down in the seat, giving way to my exhaustion.

Aodren turns his back on the fireplace and kneads his thumb into the other hand's palm. "I'd like to eliminate any more misunderstandings between us. I know we don't know each other well, but I want you to trust me, so you have no reason to disbelieve what I say next."

I'm here. The moment in the tunnel when Aodren was not the king of Malam, but a friend. I want that again.

He switches hands, massaging the other palm. I think he's nervous.

"Go on," I say.

He takes a seat, resting his elbows on his knees. "I already mentioned that your father was going to track down the maker of Sanguine for me. In his letter, his findings were the same as Ku Toa's information—the oil comes from the south and is used for healing. But he also wrote that he'd met a few traders selling the oil by claiming it gives Channeler magic to the giftless. He was going to figure out who was supplying the oil so we might stop the spread of the false information."

It's impossible for giftless to develop Channeler powers. No magic-laced oil will change that. I snort. "If people have purchased Sanguine thinking they're going to have Channeler magic, they'll probably be angry when they realize it's false. Seems like a good enough reason to spread rumors."

"My thoughts as well. Your father mentioned that his inquiries about traders had drawn unwanted attention."

"*Unwanted attention?* From who?" I lurch up, shifting to the edge of my chair. Da didn't tell me he was in danger. Why would he keep this from me?

"Your father didn't say; however, he did urge me to find

another informant because he no longer felt Sanguine was in his realm of business."

Sounds like Da. Meddling in the treatment of Channelers in Malam already cost him a wife and a home, so I understand why he wouldn't want to risk Eugenia and the littleuns by continuing down this path. But hiding out and suggesting Aodren find another informant are red flags, hinting at a greater threat than dishonest traders.

"That's all?"

He nods. "That's all."

Considering the treachery in Aodren's kingdom, he has reason to distrust others. But if he trusted Da with this, then he should have known he could trust me. "I know we don't know each other well," I say using his words. "But was I not trustworthy enough for you to tell me this before?"

An apology flashes in his eyes. "Your father forbade it."

I cross my arms. "He wouldn't—"

"He wrote, *Don't tell Lirra. She cannot stop herself from getting involved.*"

My hands fly into the air with an outraged groan. I've heard that line from Da too many times to accuse Aodren of lying. Out of spite and worry, I want to go this very moment, retrace my father's steps, and get so involved in this business of Sanguine, I'm rolling in it. My head feels as if I've gorged on a holiday feast of information. As I digest what he's said, the silence between us stretches so long, it's a wonder Aodren doesn't ask me to leave.

Da's spent a lifetime risking himself for others and escaping perilous situations. But luck doesn't last forever. If there are hazards, I'm the one who must be there for him, just as he's done for me. Our business of trading and dealing secrets is run by the two of us. No one else will come to his aid. If there is a way to help him and stop rumors from spreading and harming Channelers, then Da's right: I cannot stop myself.

CHAPTER

15

AODREN

L IRRA KEEPS HER ATTENTION ON THE FIRE-place while her teeth rake against her bottom lip, making the blood rise up so her mouth looks like a summer rose.

I force my gaze away. "You're thinking about finding him."

"Am I that transparent?"

"Not always." *Not enough.*

She yawns behind her hand and then smiles. "You say the oil has no negative effects?"

"That's what I've gathered. But there are many who do think it's harmful."

"I don't understand why Da thinks he's in danger. But maybe the person Da angered is a territorial trader, and they suspect Da is try-ing to steal their business." Lirra yawns again and stands to leave, smoothing out her skirts. "I guess, thank you?" A hollow laugh. "I'm not sure that's the right thing to say, so maybe I'll just part with *Good luck in the tournament and the summit.*" Her hands flit around, gesturing to the silent castle. Everyone is asleep. The only sound is her dress *swish-swish*ing on the floor. It feels like we're alone in the world.

"Thank you," I say.

The moon beyond my window shines down on a countryside filled with a city of tents, a tournament field, and the makeshift shops for the Kingdoms' Market. She cannot be close to home. The idea of her alone in the night coils uncomfortably through me. I cannot forget the fight at the fountain.

"Stay," I say suddenly.

Lirra turns around, her brilliant blue eyes unable to disguise how my request has startled her.

"We do not know each other well, but we're not enemies," I quickly say. It's improper for her to sleep here in this room, but it's been a tiring evening and she has a long way to travel.

She nods slowly. "Friends?"

"Yes, friends." I blow out a breath. "I don't want to tarnish your reputation. But offering you a place to sleep is the least I can do after all you've done."

"Reputation," she mouths, and then smiles to herself.

"I wouldn't do anything to —"

"I know," she says, her smile turning shy.

"And it's late and you're tired. I would offer a ride. However, opening the stable would draw more attention than either one of us wants right now. There are no homes anywhere within an hour's walk. Unless you're staying in the camp. Are you?"

Her head shakes a negative, and my feeling that she should remain here grows stronger.

"You know, I'm capable of caring for myself," she says. "I've faced dangers far worse than walking home alone at night."

"I'm aware. You saved my life, remember?"

A real smile bursts onto her face. It infuses me with a second wind of energy I shouldn't have after an eternally long and taxing day.

Lirra is fully capable of wielding the dagger hidden in her dress. I tell her as much. What goes unsaid is how crippled I am by the thought of her needing it on her way home. It shouldn't matter to me. But when I consider, too, that she would have to face the tunnel once more, I repeat my request. "Stay, Lirra. It's been a long day."

I cross the room to the wardrobe to withdraw nightclothes, and hold up one set. My offer for her to stay rattles through my head. I'm a king throwing propriety to the wind. And I don't really care. My hands shake, so I grip the fabric tighter. "Yours to use. That is, if you don't have a change tucked into your functional pockets."

She chuckles softly. "I'm fresh out."

Lirra takes the offering and moves to the far side of the room, where a partition separates a small washbasin and the entry to the garderobe from view. When she's done, my shirt hangs off her narrow shoulders and swallows her arms. It's impossible to stop cataloging how the garment falls loosely on her . . . and where it doesn't.

I break my gaze and look away.

By the time I've shucked off all my formal layers, pulled on trousers and a shirt, and returned to the open area of the room, my blood is running a few degrees hotter. I tug the collar from my neck, cursing the sweltering Shaerdanian weather.

The bed, an island in the middle of the chamber, is untouched. There's no sign of Lirra. Did she change her mind? I stalk the room from end to end, my tired steps more like stomps.

"Toooloud." The slurred groan comes from the opposite side of the bed.

Lirra lies curled on her side, nestled on a pouf of green material. Amused, I note her dress has yet another function.

"You don't have to sleep on the floor. Take the bed."

Her breath flows between her parted lips, a soft, slow scrape. She's fast asleep.

The urge to move her somewhere more comfortable tenses through my hands. Only, I don't act on it. Lirra probably wouldn't appreciate being touched while she sleeps. I settle for sliding a pillow under her head and covering her with a blanket.

· · ·

She's gone in the morning.

Instead of wondering when she left, if she had to sneak past servants and guards, or how long it took her to trek home, I focus on the leaders, who would rather discuss the tournament than trade. Judge Auberdeen announces the ranking for each kingdom based on the first night's point tally. "In last place, Plovia. Then Shaerdan. Malam is tied for second alongside Kolontia. Akaria leads."

Malam is in second place? We fared better than I imagined. We likely won't win the melee banner, but second-place points will give us a solid start. If we do well in the following events, we could still win the cup.

"Is that the tally, including the young king's points?" Gorenza asks. Since the meeting started, this is the third time he's insinuated that I should not have been able to compete.

Queen Isadora rests her hands on the sides of her chair, a long braid of ebony hair snaking over her shoulder. "And why wouldn't King Aodren's points be included? He's done nothing to merit disqualification. Or are you raising opposition to him merely because you dislike competition for your boy?"

Gorenza's lip twitches into a sneer. "Nothing wrong? The man was deceptive. Why was it none of us knew of his intentions until the moment the tournament began?"

A few dignitaries add their murmurs. It worries me that we are starting the meeting discussing the tournament, instead of getting right to the meat of trade discussion. I don't want this conversation to affect opinions or willingness to trade. But then, I should've considered my participation in the melee would garner interest and opinions.

"How did you get from the castle to the tournament unseen?" Judge Soma asks. "None of the guards noticed you leave."

"I think the guards might've been too busy betting on champions to notice King Aodren's exit. Clearly, the man walked right out of the castle." Segrande catches my eye. He wasn't pleased to find out my plan after the tournament, but he'll be nothing but loyal and supportive in public.

It wouldn't bode well for Lirra if Auberdeen and Soma were to discover her involvement. They wouldn't like to know she has a secret way in and out of the castle. Segrande and Baltroit are the only two privy to that information, but I have sworn them to secrecy under the threat of losing their titles. I would've told all this to Lirra, but she left before I had a chance.

"That's an interesting maneuver you pulled." Gorenza stares at me from across the massive mahogany table. "I didn't think you were capable."

"Are we discussing my sword skill? Or my ability to make undisclosed choices?" I ask, my voice unintentionally sharp. Between Gorenza's comments and my thoughts of Lirra, it's a struggle to keep a lid on my irritation.

He flicks his mustache. "The fight was passable. I meant your deception."

"Now, there wasn't deception, per se," Segrande pipes up beside me. "King Aodren exercised his right to fight in his own name, and he did so by the rules of the tournament. He is under no obligation to reveal his plans to you before he is ready to do so."

Gorenza chuckles. "So you agree, he hid the truth?"

"What is the point of this query, Gorenza?" the Plovian queen asks.

"The point, Isadora, is that all champions must be announced before the melee. He didn't make it known beforehand that he would be fighting in his own name."

She leans back in her chair, appearing bored. "Is that a rule? Or a custom?"

Gorenza repeats her questions to Judge Auberdeen, who sits at the end of the table, head tipped toward Judge Soma in a whispered conversation.

Judge Auberdeen straightens in his seat. He props his elbows on the table and steeples his hands under the curtain of his brown beard. "It is a rule that proxies are announced before the tournament begins. There is nothing specific to rulers who choose to join the fray at the last moment." His spectacled gaze shifts to me, displeasure writ across his face.

"My choice was one made in haste due to the unexpected affliction suffered by my captain." How can they dispute that?

Gorenza slides his chair away from the table. He brings his hands up behind his head, as if he's sunning himself on a rock while sneering at the sky. "If a man is declared a king's proxy, do the rules state that the king himself may come back and steal the man's place?"

Steal? I flatten my hands on the table, drawing resolve from thin air.

"Your wording is harsh, no?" says Fa Olema.

"Perhaps," concedes Gorenza. "But this situation is unprecedented. It wouldn't be right for us to allow rules to be broken simply because we're not able to have a direct and, yes, harshly honest conversation."

"Privacy isn't against the rules," Judge Soma says in my defense, surprising me. Even Judge Auberdeen, who sits beside him, appears shocked. "Technically, in a mere matter of moments, King Aodren declared himself as a participant, and his name was clearly announced as a competitor in the melee."

Gorenza's palm lands on the table with a resounding thud. His mouth curls into the curtain of his mustache. He looks to me and then to Soma. Fury under a placid expression, like a calm ocean, hiding churning, deadly waters beneath.

"Shall we move on to matters of trade?" Segrande attempts to guide the conversation.

Nobody responds.

"Not ready to turn that rock over?" Segrande forces a chuckle. "All right, what else did you think of the tournament? We've said enough about King Aodren. Let's discuss the other competitors."

"I found your warriors impressive. I am not surprised they've earned the most points," Judge Soma tells Ku Toa.

Since learning that he imprisoned those involved in the foun-tain fight, I've judged him harshly. His engagement with the Ku shows the side of the judge that I was expecting to meet at the summit.

"It is a lifelong discipline for them—their mothers and fathers before them were warriors," says Fa Olema. "But they were no more impressive than King Aodren." He tips his head in a small bow to me. "You show unique training."

"Thank you. Though if we're discussing work ethic, Bal-troit Bromier must be mentioned. Mastering the poleax de-mands extensive training that can last years."

Segrande's chest expands a notch in pride.

Queen Isadora pushes her braid over her shoulder. "Yes, he was a sight to behold. But might I add, your sword skill far ex-ceeds anything I've seen from Kolontia in decades."

Her castigating snub draws King Gorenza's anger. "A good thing," he drawls, "that you'll have another chance to watch King Aodren."

"No, I'm afraid she won't," I say, thinking my comment will be all that's needed to release the tension in the room con-cerning my participation. "Leif isn't here right now because I encouraged him to rest. But he's on the mend, and"—I glance at Ku Toa—"thanks to the healer and the remedies he's been given, he'll be ready to step back into the champion role to-morrow night."

Gorenza looks to Auberdeen, expecting something.

Judge Auberdeen adjusts his spectacles on his nose. He

drags out the tome that he'd placed on the table the first night we met as leaders. "Yes, well, the rules state that King Aodren can fight in his own name, but there is no rule that allows competitors to change places with one another once the event has begun."

"What does that mean?" Isadora looks back and forth between Gorenza and Auberdeen.

"It means," Gorenza says with relish, "that our little boy king must finish the tournament."

"No." Segrande's response comes out as a bark. "There is no time for him to do both. How will we be able to continue the summit?"

"Perhaps he should have considered that before."

The room erupts in a clash of opinions.

For a moment, I sit frozen in shock. I thought Gorenza wanted me out of the competition and would do all he could to make that so. I didn't think for one moment that he would argue for me to stay in. If what he's proposed is declared the rule by Judge Auberdeen, many of my plans for the summit will be thwarted. I trust Segrande, but not so much that I'd turn over executive power to make decisions on all trade. Malam has been at odds with the other kingdoms since my father's reign. We need to make the most advantageous deals possible if we're to have a hope of turning around Malam's fortune. How will that happen if I cannot be a part of all summit meetings?

Soon everyone in the room is expressing an opinion except for Ku Toa and her quiet, watchful dignitaries. Most of the other men and women around the table reject Gorenza's suggestion because they can see that kingdom agreements and policy meetings benefitting them would also be thwarted. Chief Judge Auberdeen stands and calls the room to order, his rough voice rolling over the arguments until everyone falls silent.

He places the large volume on the mahogany table. His fingers rest on the open pages. "It says here that champions must finish an event or withdraw, but once an event begins, substitutions cannot be made." He turns to me. "Only you and Baltroit may compete in the second night of melee. After that, your captain may fight in your name in the remaining events."

Gorenza crosses his arms and leans back in his chair, clearly displeased.

"Now that it's settled," Judge Soma interrupts, "let's save talk of the melee for after the final round. Then our time won't be wasted on the losers."

We return to trade discussion. The leaders vote to close a mountain route, opting for trade to continue through the seaports, with the only opposition coming from Gorenza. He claims pirates make the ocean too dangerous for trade. When Isadora contradicts him, Gorenza accuses her of protecting her family's livelihood. A family relation he outlandishly claims to be Song the Red, a young ruthless pirate.

Their argument eventually runs its course, and we adjourn for a midday meal.

Once seats are taken and plates are dished, talk returns to the melee. Segrande nudges me. "One more night. Then your focus can shift entirely to the summit."

Gorenza spears a piece of cabbage with his knife. "That is, if he makes it. Anything can happen in the melee."

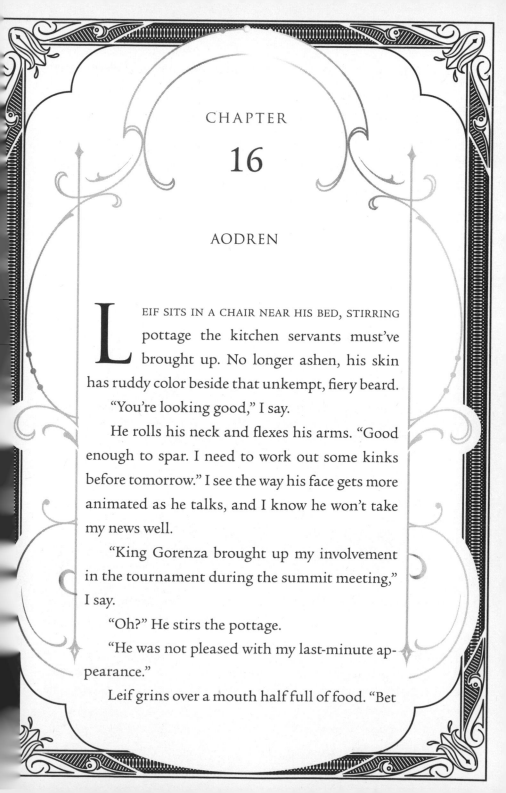

CHAPTER

16

AODREN

L EIF SITS IN A CHAIR NEAR HIS BED, STIRRING pottage the kitchen servants must've brought up. No longer ashen, his skin has ruddy color beside that unkempt, fiery beard.

"You're looking good," I say.

He rolls his neck and flexes his arms. "Good enough to spar. I need to work out some kinks before tomorrow." I see the way his face gets more animated as he talks, and I know he won't take my news well.

"King Gorenza brought up my involvement in the tournament during the summit meeting," I say.

"Oh?" He stirs the pottage.

"He was not pleased with my last-minute appearance."

Leif grins over a mouth half full of food. "Bet

not. I haven't been around him much because of the stabbing and all, but Baltroit stopped by today. He had some things to say about King Gorenza. Sounds like the man has it out for Malam."

"Yes, it seems that way." Segrande must be filling his son in on the summit. I wonder if he's already told Baltroit about the melee.

"Might be trouble for setting up trade over the northern pass."

I murmur my agreement.

Leif digs out another scoop and shoves it into his mouth. He chews and then looks at me with a tilted, sheepish smile. "I'm more excited to get back on the field tomorrow than I am to start attending the summit meetings."

I do not want to deliver this news. "About the melee . . . you will not be competing tomorrow night."

His hand pauses midlift. "What's that?" Pottage slips off the edge of the silver spoon and plops into his bowl.

It doesn't matter that the decision wasn't mine. Sitting here before Leif, seeing how his face loses all animation, stabs me with guilt. "King Gorenza insisted the rules be enforced," I say. "Once a champion has begun an event, that same champion must finish the event. This means you cannot compete. Only I may return for the second night, or choose to forfeit my position and allow Baltroit to finish alone."

Leif grunts and takes another bite, jaw grinding as he

slowly chews. "Yer—yer not going to do that, bow out, are ya?" His speech is tight, frustrated.

There are risks associated with the melee, which is the reason leaders stopped participating in the event so many years ago. King Gorenza made sure to remind me of that. But even if he hadn't, I'm already aware of how vulnerable a position it is to be on that field. It doesn't matter that we're using blunted weapons; a hit to the neck, or the head, could be permanently damaging.

On the one hand, I feel like it would be irresponsible of me to compete. But then, if I don't, Malam will fall to fourth or last position. We wouldn't have a chance at the cup.

Segrande would caution me to forfeit my position for my own safety. I'm grateful Leif hasn't done that. He understands why I would feel compelled to compete.

"I will fight," I say to Leif, making the choice in spite of the hazards. I have fought for my life and my kingdom in real battle. I can fight a mock battle, if it means the possibility of uniting my kingdom in pride and hope.

Leif's forehead wrinkles, his auburn brows pulling together as he stares down at his pottage. He curses under his breath and mutters something about training six months. I let him stew, because this decision must be difficult to hear. After a beat he says, "Keep your eye on Hemmet. He's formidable, and guaranteed, his father will make sure he's got a trick or two saved for you."

"Good advice," I say. "I'll keep that in mind."

"This is good. It'll give me more time to recover," he says, but it sounds like he's trying to convince himself.

Missing the tournament is more galling than he wants to admit, and I suspect missing the melee will bother him more once he regains his strength. Six months of anticipation and training cannot be abandoned lightly.

"It should've been you on the field," I tell him.

He stares hard at the bowl in his hands. "You're the better swordsman, and the king. That makes you the rightful competitor."

That's debatable. Perhaps this is why he doesn't look up to meet my eye.

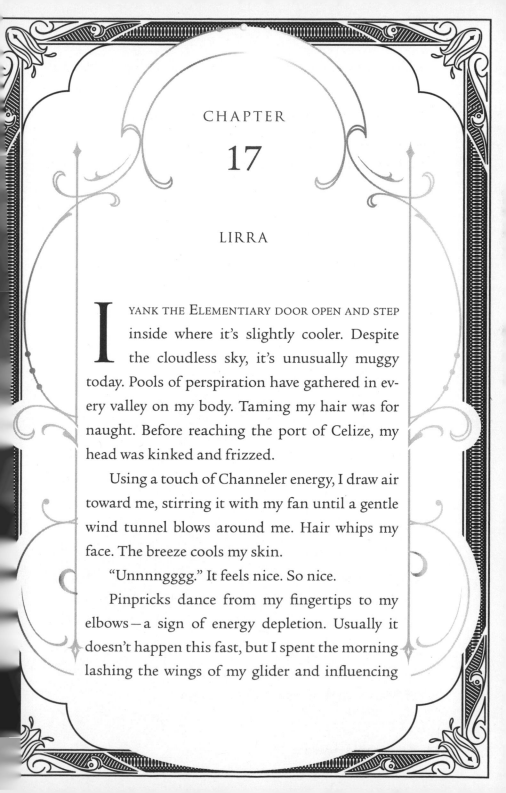

CHAPTER

17

LIRRA

I YANK THE ELEMENTIARY DOOR OPEN AND STEP inside where it's slightly cooler. Despite the cloudless sky, it's unusually muggy today. Pools of perspiration have gathered in every valley on my body. Taming my hair was for naught. Before reaching the port of Celize, my head was kinked and frizzed.

Using a touch of Channeler energy, I draw air toward me, stirring it with my fan until a gentle wind tunnel blows around me. Hair whips my face. The breeze cools my skin.

"Unnnngggg." It feels nice. So nice.

Pinpricks dance from my fingertips to my elbows—a sign of energy depletion. Usually it doesn't happen this fast, but I spent the morning lashing the wings of my glider and influencing the wind to give them lift. A short nap and a few steamed buns from the baker weren't enough for full replenishment. With an unsatisfied grunt, I stop toying around. My hair flops. The air falls stagnant.

"Where did the breeze go?" Astoria's voice comes from somewhere in the Elementiary.

Her distinctive *shuffle scuff thump*s nearby. I glance around the shelves and nearly jump out of my skin when I spot a warped view of her face. She's standing on the other side of the closest shelf, peering through a jar of talons in petrification juice. Last time I saw her, she was enraged over Aodren's presence. I feel bad about that. To answer her question, I vigorously shake my tingling hand.

"Ah, what have I told you about wasting your Channeler energy on frivolous matters?" she scolds, and moves out of sight.

Frivolous is this fan. I sigh and wave the fancy, frilly piece harder. It's a whisper compared to a Channeler-coaxed breeze, but then, I don't normally use the fan for actual fanning. It's a prop for obscurity.

Ever since I woke on the king's floor, his pillow under my head, his blanket over my shoulders, and a hint of dawn on the horizon, my mind has been buzzing. I haven't been able to stop thinking about last night's conversation about Da and Sanguine. Everything Aodren said made sense, except for the reason Da would go into hiding. Why would an oil as beneficial as Beannach draw that kind of danger?

Then I remembered all of the odd things I'd seen over the last few days — the scene at the fountain, the struggle between Baz and his friend in the cell, the dropped bottle, the champions' conversation — and the strangest notion occurred to me. What if they're all pieces of the same tapestry? What if the connecting thread is Sanguine?

Of course, I have nothing substantial to back up the idea. This is why I've come to visit Astoria. Few people have as much Channeler knowledge as she does. If anyone knows about Sanguine, it'll be her.

"First, I came to apologize for yesterday," I say, throwing my arms around her though her hands are full, and squeezing.

"You're a lovely girl, my dear. Thank you, but no apology necessary."

I step back and trail her toward her worktable. "Second, I was hoping for information."

"Oh, Lirra." Astoria sets a book down between a few dozen small bottles of liquid and three mounds of dried herbs. Her sympathy-filled eyes gaze at me. I glance around, confused.

"I still haven't heard from your father," she says, misunderstanding. "Though Duff Baron is in town, and he mentioned he'd seen your father recently."

I tuck that information away, relieved to hear Da's been in contact with someone, which means he's not in as much danger as I'd thought.

"Actually," I say, "I came to ask something else."

"My goodness. I jumped ahead, didn't I?" A chuckle shakes her shoulders. She ambles around the table and sits down. "Go on, then."

I watch as her aged hands gather herbs from different piles and deftly bind them together with twine. Long before Astoria ran the Elementiary, she grew up on an herb farm in Malam.

"Have you heard anything about Sanguine oil?" I ask.

A frown wrinkles her mouth. "Why do you ask?"

"Someone mentioned it recently. And I think a sailor friend of mine has some," I say, not lying. When Da ran from Malam with little more than the clothes on his back and a baby tucked under his arm, Astoria gave him refuge. We trust her implicitly. Which is why I hate withholding any details. But with the summit in progress, and visiting Malamians reminding her of her sister's death, Astoria is on edge. I don't want to draw her into this mess any more than I have to, especially if Da didn't even want me involved.

"Are you talking about that ruffian who has been attempting to court you?" She finishes knotting up one set of herbs and moves to grab another.

"The very one."

"Figures," she mutters. "He's the type to go after Sanguine."

"Because it's a healing aid?" Sitting down in the chair across from her, I pick up some herbs and copy her process.

"Yes, and it's a valuable, sacred oil. Sanguine is known to

be the only Channeler remedy that can actually heal someone. Because it's made by Channelers in Akaria, it's harder to
come by."

Her answer still doesn't explain why someone would want
to silence Da's questions. Aodren said people in Malam wrote
letters recently claiming the oil was harmful. He thinks it's
only rumors sparked by people who fear Channelers. But what
if there is some truth there? I know I'm reaching for answers,
but I cannot seem to see an obvious danger facing Da. And
if I cannot see the danger, then I'll never be able to figure out
how to help him or the Channelers who are being blamed for
the oil.

"Does the oil have any side effects?"

Astoria tilts her head, studying me. "True Sanguine is a
gift that the Channelers of the southern kingdom create as
an aid for the kingdom's elite warriors, should they ever fall
in battle. It is something that rarely is sold in other kingdoms
because Akaria is unwilling to let their stores of Sanguine go.
It does not have any side effects other than complete healing."

"I've never heard of anything so powerful."

"Aye, it's extremely rare, and can take years to make."

"You said *true* Sanguine."

"Aye." Her hands get busy again sorting them. She pauses,
brings it to her nose, and sniffs.

"Astoria," I say, and when she doesn't explain, a groan tears
out of me. "You're torturing me. What do you mean by that? Is

there another Sanguine oil?" She still doesn't respond. "Fine. You just said Sanguine is sacred to Akaria and valuable and rare. It cannot be that sacred or rare if it's being produced to sell in Malam."

She gives me an approving nod, a gesture that also means I should continue.

"Right, so I've heard some conflicting rumors that it gives Channeler powers to the giftless. But then I also heard it causes illness. Is it possible that there is an imposter oil out there, being sold as Sanguine, that doesn't have healing power?" I ask, throwing in a wildcard idea.

"Aye."

I stop bundling herbs and stare at her. "What do you know of the imposter oil?"

"I know nothing good comes from that oil."

She knows much more than she's letting on. "What else?"

Her mouth pinches, and it transports me to years past when I was a young girl in the Elementiary. Astoria made me work for everything I learned.

"I saw Baz and a friend arguing over it," I tell her, leaving out my short stint in the chamber of damnation under the summer castle. "They were acting different. Angrier than normal." Angry enough to nearly kill a man.

"Fools," she says with a huff, before reaching for the twine to bind the herbs.

"Did their behavior have something to do with the oil?"

She rolls some herbs between her fingers, breaking them into a dozen tiny pieces that flutter onto the table. "I'll only tell you this, so you'll know to be cautious," she says. "I'd never want any harm to come to you."

I squeeze her hand. "I know."

"There is a Sanguine being sold, but it doesn't heal. It gives a burst of strength to the user that can take hours and sometimes days to fade."

This must be what the Shaerdanian competitors were talking about outside the tent last night. "There is an oil that gives people increased strength? I didn't think it was possible."

"In addition to the surge of strength, this new Sanguine quickens reflexes and dulls sensitivity to pain. That's a heady effect that people seem quite taken with."

"Does the oil also bring on bouts of rage?" I ask, certain now that Baz and his friend ingested the newer oil.

She glances up and flicks a finger in my direction, a silent command to keep working. I pinch some herbs from each pile and grab the spool of twine.

"Imagine giving a spoiled child a bite of the most delicious dessert," Astoria says, the teaching tone in her voice transporting me back to when I was her Elementiary pupil. "What happens when you take it away?"

Her silly analogy almost makes me snort. "They want more?"

"Yes, to the point of having a conniption. Then imagine what would happen if you allowed the child to have their fill."

I'm sure it'd be like the time Loren and Kiefer snuck out of bed, found the iced cakes Eugenia made for the Merryluna Festival, and devoured all but two. In the wee hours of the morning, a horrendous moan woke the house. What came after was a cacophony of heaving, retching, and Eugenia's hollering.

I suck in an *ahhh*, understanding Astoria's comparison. "I see what you're saying, take away the oil, and there will be withdrawals. Too much oil, and the buildup can make them sick. What kind of sick?"

She stares back at me like I already know the answer.

"Rage?"

She nods and gathers the completed herb bundles to place them in a basket. "That is the first sign of over-consumption."

Baz must have had too much of the oil. That's why he started the fight at the fountain. Seeing the Malamians threatening a Channeler would have pushed him over the edge.

"And the signs? What will happen if Baz keeps taking the oil?"

"In everything, there needs to be order," she says. I've heard these words a hundred times. They are the code Channelers live by. "The giftless weren't born with Channeler energy. So it isn't natural for their bodies."

"But what of Beannach water?" Giftless can consume that Channeler remedy with no negative side effects.

"Like most Channeler remedies, Beannach water contains minimal amounts of our energy," Astoria says. "When it's ingested, the water flushes through the body and exits, causing no harm. The new Sanguine oil does not work the same. When consumed repeatedly, it stores up in a person's body. For the giftless, that much Channeler energy twists a person's mind. Rage, confusion, illusions — are all side effects."

"Are there more?"

Her expression tightens and she nods. "I suppose, if someone kept taking the oil, their body would become over-burdened by the Channeler magic, and they would die."

I hold a hand to my neck. The herbs, having fallen from my fingers, lie scattered across my lap. "That makes no sense. The original Sanguine saves lives. And yet you're telling me the new Sanguine, if taken in excess, will kill a person?"

"That is the balance of our world."

I shake my head, wishing Astoria would leave the riddles and parallel thoughts out of our conversation. "Does balance apply to Spiriters? If they heal someone who is giftless, will that person eventually die from the Channeler energy in them that has saved their life?"

"There are other factors involved when a Spiriter heals someone. The transferred energy links to the Spiriter. This link is why the giftless person doesn't go mad and doesn't lose their life eventually."

The comment settles in my stomach like sour milk. I think of all the tomes I've read in the Elementiary, and I know she's right. "People cannot keep taking this imposter Sanguine. They have to be warned."

Astoria lets out a bitter sigh. "You say that as if the effects are not known. Assuming your friend hasn't lost his mind yet, he's aware of what's happening. He simply does not care. Like other giftless people, he wants power that he should not have, regardless of the cost."

Sometimes Astoria can be too callous when it comes to the giftless. I don't have a stomach for her harsh outlook right now. I push away from the table, arms shaking as I snatch my fan.

"I've answered your questions. Now you'll let this topic rest?" she asks.

The hazards of Sanguine affect more than the user. Da, Leif, and even Aodren are proof. In all the years I've known Astoria, deception has never tainted our relationship. A thread of guilt whispers through me because I know this is not a conversation she would want me to share with Aodren, the king she loathes. And yet, if people can truly get hurt and die from the new Sanguine, I need to warn him. Things in Malam are already bad for Channelers, and if the giftless start dying from a Channeler remedy, tensions will only worsen and even more people will die. If I deliver this information, maybe the king will return the favor. I don't know how much danger Da faces, but now I'm certain he could use my help to finish this job.

"I will," I say, and when her pleased, relaxed smile shines back at me, I duck behind my fan and leave her behind.

CHAPTER

18

AODREN

IN THE AFTERNOON, THE SUMMIT MEETING ADjourns so we all may travel to the port of Celize, the hub of Shaerdan's sea trade. A road runs southward from the summer castle over a few low hills and past the flat grassy stretch where the camps, merchants' tents, and the tournament field are located. Patches of forest break up farmlands. And beyond, Celize's whitepainted buildings ascend the ocean-side cliff like tight rows of soldiers. Shoulder to shoulder, and at varying heights, they stand proudly beneath orange roofs.

The carriages roll through town to where the cliffs level into a wide bay. Seagulls squawk at our arrival.

Once we all disembark from the carriages,

Judge Soma guides the group onto Shaerdan's newest ship. His tour takes us through the berth, where he points out passages from the sleeping quarters to the cargo storage below.

"After her maiden voyage, she'll be the largest vessel on the open waters," Soma states proudly when we return to the main deck. Salty winds temper the day's heat.

Gorenza squints out at the calm blue. "And an easier target for pirates."

"A fair wind abaft her beams, and no one will catch her." Soma sweeps his arm upward to the rigging and the masts. "Not even your pirates."

I've heard Judge Soma's roots are in cargo ships and trading. Based on the sailing and sea trade knowledge he uses to counteract Gorenza's barbs, it's likely true. While their conversation carries on, leaders and dignitaries wander off the boat, some in favor of shade, others drawn to the shops lining the port. The guards who traveled with us from the summer castle split up, two men to each leader. Soon townspeople notice us and gather around, slowing our ability to separate.

"There goes the bloody king o' Malam," I hear someone say.

The guard at my right side draws his sword and searches for the guilty party, but it's impossible in the amassing crowd that's gathered. "Back up," he calls to them. "Or we'll have you arrested."

The surrounding crowd obeys, though the barbs keep coming. "A right bludger he is," someone shouts.

"Channeler user!" a woman shouts.

I cringe and consider returning to the boat, but wherever I go, disfavor tends to follow.

The man protecting my left lunges for her, his sword drawn. I shout for him to stop, and the crowd goes silent. The guard's baffled expression at my insistence spreads to the others. The men cannot understand why I would allow disrespectful comments to be uttered in my presence. In truth, a small voice inside me wonders the same.

Punishing this woman won't earn the respect I desire for Malam. Nor will it inspire my people to change. The royal decree to end the Purge Proclamation starts with *A kingdom ruled by fear is destined to fall*. I believed those words when I wrote them, and I believe them now.

"What are you doing?" Segrande presses through the crowd and comes to my side.

"The only thing the blade can force is fear," I tell him. "Respect must be earned. And I suppose I have not done enough to earn it yet."

He pulls his lips in tight, and I wonder if he's reserving judgment until we're alone.

"Let us cheer the champions who did well last night," I shout out to the crowd, hoping to redirect conversations. Then I continue up the hill away from the crowds. The guards are silent, stoic sidepieces to me and Segrande, who has fallen back a step, disapproval creating a barrier between us.

I used to think the custom of respect for royalty erected

walls of solitude around me. Now I see how fear, disapproval, and animosity have the same power.

The farther we walk, the more the crowd thins until we're almost alone. My back aches from yesterday. After the long hours in meetings, the tightness has increased. Ahead, a shopkeeper sweeps the cobblestones. Two sailors emerge from a doorway, only to change direction when they notice me and the guards at my rear.

"Seclusion prefers a nobleman's company best," Segrande says.

"You mean a nobleman prefers seclusion?"

"Do I? I hadn't thought so." He looks pointedly at the retreating men who scurried away. He is right. Few people dare approach me, let alone meet my eye. The seclusion is sometimes like a prison sentence for high nobility.

"What of the nobleman's preference?" I ask.

He shrugs. "For some, it would be wealth and power, but I think that you and I would rather smile at faces that will smile back, instead of those etched into coins."

"You are right. If only there were more willing to smile." Though Segrande often seems like a watchdog more than an ally, people are important to him. Malam is important to him. And I think, perhaps, I am too. The thought is comforting.

Ahead, a door swings open. A bawdy song filters out, and a man stumbles forward before the door slams closed behind him.

Segrande stiffens. The man ahead is Baltroit, and he's

fallen too far into his cups to walk straight. He crashes into two women stepping out of a bakery, and Segrande curses.

"The day of rest between fights was wise," I say, to ease his distress. "It gives champions time to celebrate their victories."

"Or drown their sorrows," he grouses.

I wave toward Baltroit. "See to him. He has tonight to catch up on rest."

Now that the crowd is gone, one of the guards follows after Segrande. The other remains behind me.

The bakery door flies open as we pass, and a woman rushes out, tripping into me. Her arms flail, and I'm forced to grasp her so we both don't fall. She smells of sea breeze and honeysuckle and warm bread. When I move away, the guard lunges toward her, as if he might detain her for accidentally crashing into me, but I put out my hand.

"It was an accident," I say, and he retreats, giving me space to help the woman.

The familiar blue eyes that stare back at me above a pink lace fan are a pleasant surprise. Her hair, partially drawn away from her face, falls around her shoulders in shiny curls that have always looked black to me, though I see now strands of deep brown woven into her raven hair. Against her yellow dress, the contrast is striking. Beautiful.

"Lir—"

"Your Highness," she says with reverence. Did she intentionally cut me off?

The fan flutters in front of her face, and her lashes sweep down, as if she's chagrined. The Lirra I've come to know is near impossible to ruffle, let alone embarrass. Her free hand flattens to the skin above her sweeping neckline. I force my gaze to the top of her head as she dips in a wobbly bow to the cobblestones.

"I b-b-beg your forgiveness. I didn't see you there." Her eyes flit everywhere but at me and sink behind the fluttering pink lace.

Is she nervous? How is that possible?

"Accidents happen. No apology necessary," I say uncertainly.

She squeaks or giggles, I cannot tell. This version of Lirra, painfully shy and simpering, throws me. I cannot make sense of her behavior in contrast to the girl who slept in my room last night.

She apologizes profusely again, and then adopts a frightened-rabbit expression when the guard tells her to move along.

It's a ruse. It must be. And yet, even when she's playacting, this girl manages to render me speechless. I watch her go, questions building, but the moment she's out of sight, I shut them down, remembering Segrande's comment about solitude. Curiosity over Lirra is unimportant in comparison to the summit and the tournament. Whether I like it or not, my business with her is done.

. . .

Back at the pier, the other leaders are still busily exploring the wide array of shops. I climb into an empty carriage, thankful for a moment to finally rest. I collapse forward to loosen the bunched muscles in my back. That is when a crunch sounds.

I straighten and pat my chest, feeling a crinkle under my palm.

A folded piece of parchment has been stuffed into my jacket. I smile to myself. I should've expected there was more to the run-in with Lirra.

AC,

Meet me just before sunrise. Cathedral on the cliff. Remember to take two rights, two lefts, a right, left, right, and right. Come alone.

LB

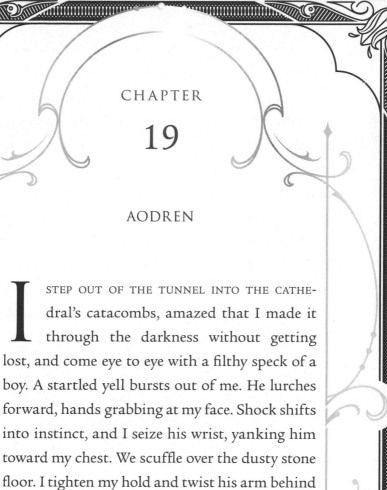

CHAPTER

19

AODREN

I STEP OUT OF THE TUNNEL INTO THE CATHE-
dral's catacombs, amazed that I made it
through the darkness without getting
lost, and come eye to eye with a filthy speck of a
boy. A startled yell bursts out of me. He lurches
forward, hands grabbing at my face. Shock shifts
into instinct, and I seize his wrist, yanking him
toward my chest. We scuffle over the dusty stone
floor. I tighten my hold and twist his arm behind
his back.

"Yeoooow!" the little cud screeches.

"What are you doing here?" I demand, pulse
galloping in my veins. Lirra told me before no
one comes down to the catacombs. Did he follow
Lirra? "What do you want?"

"Aodren, let go!"

I blink. The boy's voice belongs to Lirra.

My hands fly upward, instantly releasing her. She called me by my name. That's the first time I've heard it on her lips. It's as unexpected as her disguise and . . . nice.

She shuffles back and rubs her wrist, a flesh-melting glare directed at me.

"I didn't recognize you. Why did you attack me?" I ask.

"I wasn't trying to attack you, you fool. I was trying to silence you."

Lirra's disguise is so well-crafted it would've fooled her own family. Extraordinary. She's a dirt-encrusted chameleon. Not a speck of her smooth, tan skin is distinguishable beneath the muck. Her dust-covered hair is roughly drawn back, held in a band, and braided in the style many sailors and street merchants wear. Each trouser hem is frayed. Rips show her slender, filthy knees, and mud stains a shabby shirt that could fit two people her size. So large, in fact, the excess material drapes her shoulders in the same way my shirt hung on her two nights ago.

No. It cannot be. "Is that my—"

"Shirt? Yes." She grins. Dirt flakes off her face and dusts her—*my*—shirt.

"You turned it into a dirty cabin boy's disguise?"

She frowns. "You think I'm a sailor?"

"A miscreant, then?"

"You're calling me a criminal?"

"You did steal my shirt."

She laughs. "I'm a beggar." To show me her disguise, she plucks the shoulders of the shirt, and holds the fabric away from her body.

I knew this already. Lirra's outfit impressed me the second I realized who hid beneath the muck. No one will question her presence at the cathedral, where vagabonds often gather for meals and coins the clergy provide.

The stiff decorum required throughout yesterday's summit meetings that stretched well into the evening still clings to me. But it takes only a moment in Lirra's company to feel the bindings of constant correctness and royal dignity loosen. Before we get to the business of why she asked me to meet her, I lean closer and, in an uncharacteristically and intentionally riling way, ask, "Perhaps some advice?"

Her brows quirk upward.

"If you want to fool others—" I lower my nose near her dirty neck and sniff. Despite the disguise, her skin holds the scent of the ocean breeze. I step back before I can do something monumentally stupid. "You have to smell the part."

Lirra's back snaps straight. "You stole my words. That was my advice to you."

"I believe, Miss Beggar Barrett, you said 'act.' *You have to act the part.*"

Lirra's lips fall open.

I swipe a hand over my face to hide my smile. "Feel free to add my tip to your arsenal of impersonations."

Her head drops back, and a laugh erupts, carefree and unguarded. "You're horrible," she says and then pauses to recover from her laughter. "And surprisingly clever."

"Is it so surprising?"

She assesses me from head to toe. "No. Now, come on. It would be a shame to miss the sunrise."

"The sunrise?" Does she simply want to spend time with me? The thought pleases me, even though my goals for Malam don't allow for dalliances. My focus should be on the summit meetings. The tournament melee. The lack of Channeler support for Malam at the upcoming jubilee.

And yet I follow her up the stairs.

Lirra doesn't stop at the main level of the cathedral. She rushes between the pews to the bell tower stairwell. I should stop her before we reach the top. I should insist she immediately divulge the purpose for this meeting. And I definitely should remember my days allow no time for unnecessary diversions.

And yet I follow her to the bell tower.

There isn't much walking space around the ropes and beams affixed to the bell. Lirra shimmies against the wall to reach the gaping eastern-facing window. She climbs onto the wide ledge, sits with her legs crossed, and pats the space beside her, as if this time between us is completely natural. As if we are friends. As if I am not a king and she's not daughter to the Archtraitor of Malam.

And yet I follow her onto the ledge.

My leg presses against hers. I look out. To my disappointment, the view is a gray sky with streaks of dark, brooding
clouds. She won't be able to see the sunrise today. For her sake,
I am disappointed that she'll miss it. But if seeing the sunrise
is the only reason she brought me here, then this is a waste of
time.

"We should discuss the reason for this meeting," I say,
irked when the delivery has the stiffness of my patrician upbringing.

A finger lifts and presses to her lips.

A glow from the east suddenly paints her face in rose hues.
Her finger leaves her mouth and points to the tree-topped
horizon. There, the sun crawls over the evergreens' edge and
pushes life into the stubborn clouds in vibrant yellow, coral,
and glorious purple.

"It's always the loveliest before a storm," she says.

The soft warmth in her words cuts right through my
thoughts. She makes me forget my responsibilities.

My gaze dips to her smile. A madman's desire to wipe her
lips clean, to see them full and pink, shudders through me.
Gravity pulls me closer, and when she turns, her eyes flare at
our proximity. I want to know what her mouth would feel like
against mine.

She blinks and returns to staring at the sky.

I clench my fist and tap it against the stone ledge. What
am I doing? This curiosity isn't anything new. A year ago, I
thought I felt something for another, but I came to realize

it was our time spent together that made me think we were sharing something more than friendship. These last few days I've had time alone with Lirra. My spark of interest in her isn't anything I should heed. If anything, it's a mark of my inexperience around others. I cannot let myself get caught by Lirra's free-spirited lure.

"Tell me why you wanted to meet," I cut to the point.

The carefree expression vanishes from her face. "You were right to worry about Sanguine."

"You have new information?" This is unexpected. She made no indication that she was going to continue looking into Sanguine. Did she go out of her way to help me?

"I spoke with Astoria yesterday." Lirra recounts her conversation about a new strain of Sanguine oil that has the kind of draw that keeps taverns afloat with men deep in their cups. She details how those who drink the oil will feel less pain, fewer aches, and at the same time, they'll have increased strength.

"You're saying this new oil would make it so people could lift more weight? Or wield a sword with more force?" I ask, though it sounds implausible.

"I think so."

Astoria is no fan of mine. Is it possible she concocted this story? What would be her motive?

"Increased strength would be a lure to many," I say, unconvinced, but also unsettled. That kind of promise preys on deep insecurities, especially in a kingdom of people who have been weakened. "If this is true, it might explain how rumors started about Sanguine giving a person Channeler powers. Magical vigor? Sounds similar to lore about Spiriters."

She leans against the side of the window opening. "That isn't all. This new Sanguine is dangerous. When taken repetitively, the hazards are rage, confusion, illusions, and even death."

"Did she have proof? I know you're saying there are two different oils. But it makes no sense they would have the same name and opposite outcomes. The Sanguine Ku Toa used saved Leif's life. Even Judge Soma mentioned it at the first summit dinner. He didn't indicate any dangers."

Lirra sits up straighter and frowns. "Why would I lie?"

"You are not the one I'm doubting."

"Astoria might not like you or your kingdom, but she has no cause to lie. Besides, she didn't know I was going to pass this information on," she admits with a guilty grimace. "Astoria mentioned the risks, but she wouldn't say more because she's too worried about me getting involved. And rightfully so, considering Da's current status. But I have my own proof," she says, explaining the rage preceding the fountain fight, a struggle between prisoners in the cells, and the conversation she overheard outside the champions' tent.

I climb off the ledge, needing to stand to think this through. "Why would someone name the oils the same thing?"

"Astoria said the original oil is sacred to Akaria and valuable. Maybe someone created a second oil to capitalize on the real oil's value. Do you think the Ku might know something?"

Akaria is the origin of Sanguine. There is reasonable cause to speculate that the Ku would have knowledge of a counterfeit oil. The Akarian leader strikes me as guileless. I doubt she'd mislead me if I talked to her privately.

"I don't know," I admit. "It's possible."

Lirra puts her feet flat on the window ledge and pulls her knees up to her chest. Her face turns toward the horizon, though she doesn't appear to focus on anything in particular.

"Someone doesn't want the new Sanguine trade to stop. That person is hurting Channelers and is the reason my da isn't home with his family," she says, and then wipes the morose expression off her face. "Whomever we're dealing with is powerful and dangerous. Da is out there trying to uncover information about Sanguine. I wonder if he's come to the same conclusion we have. If he hasn't, I cannot sit by and let him puzzle this out alone."

"He did say he wanted you to stay away." I remind her of Millner's letter—*She cannot stop herself from getting involved.*

"When Channelers aren't at risk and he's home where he belongs, I'll sort out his grievances. This choice is mine to make. He needs to see he can trust me. I'm going to figure this out for him."

Fair enough. I'm glad to have her on my side.

She thrusts her hand out for me to shake. "I propose we work together to figure out who is heading the new Sanguine trade."

"Work together how?"

"Continue seeking information in your royal circles, and I'll keep my ear to the underground. In a couple days, let's meet and exchange notes. You'll relay everything you've heard, and then I'll do the same."

"I'll go first?"

Her raven brows arch up. I suppose it's fair.

I start to ask where we'll meet, but she gives me a look that says, *Leave it to me.*

My hand grasps hers in a firm shake. "Agreed."

After the summit meetings adjourn in the afternoon, I meet with Ku Toa and her dignitaries. Thus far, Akaria and Malam have had no disputes. Despite my purpose for coming, I hope to maintain that peace, but from the moment I bring up Sanguine, Fa Olema is standoffish.

"It sounds like more rumors," he says. Unlike his usual placid self, his mouth twitches in distaste.

"I have reason to believe there may be another Sanguine. One that poses a danger," I say, compelled to defend myself and, at the same time, annoyed that Olema's small show of judgment has such a strong effect on me. "Those who ruled before me made grievous mistakes. I want to bring change to Malam so my people can thrive. That is why I must know more about this oil."

Olema edges forward a fraction, his grip on the tall back

of the Ku's chair. I think he might respond, but Ku Toa's hand peeks from her robe and flattens in a staying action. "Tell us more about what you've heard."

I'll not break Lirra's trust, but in order to gain answers, I must give them some details. I explain the men's rage preceding the fountain fight, and then, without sharing names, explain Astoria's understanding of the new Sanguine and the perilous effects of its overusage.

"Who you choose to believe has no bearing on actual facts," says Olema disdainfully.

"Of course." My jaw clicks. "However, as I said before, my concern is my people. All of them. Which means I need to know what Malam is dealing with, preferably before more people are hurt and blame is cast on Channelers."

The elder dignitary looks away, seemingly mollified by my answer and yet still displeased.

"The Sanguine in Akaria does not affect the giftless as you've indicated," says Ku Toa.

"But is it possible there is another Sanguine being made in Akaria?" I press. "Or is it possible to duplicate your Sanguine?"

Olema and Ku Toa exchange a look before Olema says, "Anything is possible. Though it's more likely you are chasing rumors instead of accepting that sometimes discord runs too deep to be settled."

A frustrated sigh slips out. This oil has turned me into a dog chasing its damned tail.

"You said Sanguine is valuable in Akaria." I turn to the Ku, thinking about my talk with Lirra and why she thought someone would want to replicate the oil and sell it. "Is it costly because it provides miraculous healing? Or is the value linked to the supply and demand of the oil?"

"You think we would extort money from our people for a healing remedy?" Olema's judgment tremors through his wrinkles.

"I mean no offense," I say quickly.

He turns away from me, shifting in his seat, his taut body a clear sign he no longer wishes the conversation to continue.

"Sanguine heals my people. That is why we value it," Ku Toa answers. "But we must safeguard it as well, because we can produce less than a barrel a year, which yields one hundred bottles."

When each decision I make can affect an entire kingdom, and misjudgments could have devastating consequences, I've learned to be meticulous about inferring more than what's been said. In this case, three important points register.

First, Sanguine isn't merely a limited commodity. No, it's as rare as the jewels affixed to my coronation crown. Just considering the lives that might've been saved last year in Malam renders the oil invaluable, let alone how many lives it could save in the world at large.

Second, Ku Toa sacrificed a bottle for Leif, a man she has no responsibility for. Her action proves her character. I will not doubt her again or forget her sacrifice for him.

Third, I'm certain whoever is making and distributing the imposter oil in Shaerdan and Malam knows the real oil's value and is intentionally using the same name to fool buyers, regardless of the hazards.

Only one thing is certain: the mastermind of the trade must stopped.

CHAPTER

20

LIRRA

W E'RE SITTING IN ORLI'S BEDROOM.
When Orli was kidnapped,
her mum painted all the furni-
ture in this room the color of clouds on a perfect
summer day. Even the linens were replaced to
brighten the room and fill her family with hope.
It's beautiful, pristine, and sterile.

"I won't let anything lead back to you," I tell
Orli, who will be playing the role of my coachman tonight.

I cannot see her responding expression. The
afternoon light, pouring through the curtains,
causes too much of a glare. In the driver's costume, she's a smudge of maroon against the
colorless background.

"You've already said that, and I believe you."
She steps away from the window and plucks the

carriage driver's cap off the bed. Dust tumbles off, a hazard of taking things from Da's cellar, and a light coating falls to her bed linens.

I start to conjure a small wind to blow it clean, and then remember where I am.

"Smack it out," I tell her. "I didn't realize it was so dirty."

"You're worrying over nothing. No one will notice that tonight." She twists the cap in her hands, around and around again. "It's fine."

"You're sure you're not nervous?"

"Maybe a little." She studies the hat in her hands. "But aren't you? Isn't King Aodren? With crowds from every kingdom, it's only natural to feel some nerves."

I peer into the oval mirror over the dresser, and pin a curl to my head. "He's quite impressive with a sword. Mesmerizing even," I say, unable to hide my wonder. "He doesn't seem to be nervous when he fights, but that's because he's so focused."

She moves to stand behind me so I can see her reflection in the mirror. Her skin is a shade darker than mine, though her eyes are two shades lighter. Orli is beautiful.

Until she shoots me an annoying, all-knowing expression. "He seems to have your thoughts completely arrested."

I frown. "That's not true."

"Oh? You haven't brought up your glider once since arriving an hour ago."

I haven't? I think back over our conversation, and it's all been about Aodren. "Well, that's because I'm almost done."

Her lips purse to the side. "Weren't you almost done three days ago?"

"Aye, but then I was imprisoned and all that."

She laughs. Smug Orli.

I shove another hairpin in my hair. "Look, I only brought him up because I didn't want you to feel pressured. I can make other arrangements."

She snags a pin off the dresser and pushes it into a spot on the back of my head. "Really? You have another plan in mind?"

"No. But—"

"You're ridiculous." In the reflection, Orli gestures to her outfit, a horseman's coat, tailored trousers, boots, a cap, and, poking from my satchel beside her bed, a dust cover for her face. "No one is going to recognize me. I'll be hidden in plain sight."

"Tie on the dust cover, at least. Make sure it fits with the cap," I tell her, and when she complies, I turn around to face her, my head tipped to the side, scrutinizing the scene. The curls from the unpinned side of my head sweep over my shoulder.

Dressed from head to toe in a driver's outfit, complete with a dust cover for her mouth, the only part of Orli that can be viewed is the slash of deep skin around black lashes and pale-blue eyes.

"You're right. I don't recognize you, and I brought the outfit."

She grins. Like me, she understands that it's often easier to face a crowd when pretending to be someone else.

I finish pinning my hair into the perfect coiffure befitting a noblewoman. After I step into the sapphire dress with a wide-spread skirt and gold fastenings, Orli helps me cinch the ties. With each tug, the size of my waist, in relation to other curves, seems to shrink.

This gown is my least favorite disguise because it lacks utility. Unlike my other dresses, stitched with a dozen clever pockets intended to hide things, this gown was made to enhance "certain womanly features," as Eugenia would say. In it, I feel stripped down and bare. Once belonging to my mother, this gown is a fanciful reminder of what life might've been if the Purge had never happened, if she hadn't been killed, if Da hadn't fled Malam to save me, leaving his noble title and land behind.

I do not miss the life I never knew, especially if it meant wearing dresses like this every day. I wish my fleeting curiosity about that life would end. It makes the one I'm happily living now feel like a lie.

"You're sure about the crowds?" While Orli has been out in public loads of times, she hasn't been to an event that has brought together people from all five kingdoms. I fear seeing all the Malamian maroon will trigger her memories of the past. But I don't say this.

She rolls her eyes. "Stop acting as if I haven't been around people before. Stop treating me like my mum does."

"I just want you to be comfortable."

She sweeps her arms around at the bright white room. "And do you really think this is where I'm comfortable? I'll find my place. For now, I'm going with you where I can be of help."

Truth is, I don't need her help. Aodren does.

Asking this of her, and knowing that her last association with him was in Malam, riddles me with guilt. But she's taken the mention of him in stride. Perhaps she's right. I need to stop worrying about her so much.

When we're finished readying our appearances for the evening, we load up in my father's carriage.

Aodren mentioned that he wanted to sneak into the tournament, for fear that if he were to show up in all his royal glory, he'd be besieged by spectators. A reasonable fear considering he's received a lukewarm, if not chilling, reception from the other kingdoms. He has many enemies. And to avoid embarrassing the guards again, he's going to exit the castle as himself, riding with his dignitaries, who will then deposit him at my chosen location.

Orli drives the carriage to a tree-lined back road that runs south of the cathedral on the cliff. To the northeast, rolling fields crawl away from the ocean and the cliff, and stretch out to meet the summer castle. Going farther east, the hills flatten to make way for the tournament field. But here, where the stretch of forest marches past the church to tumble down the cliffside, we won't be noticed.

A scant league to the northwest, the sun sets behind the cathedral's spires, its rays wrapping the towers like a mammoth gilded crown. Appropriate, since we're waiting on a king.

It isn't long before a plume of dust lifts from the gravel road, announcing his arrival. In contrast to the approaching carriage's royal seal and shiny maroon paint, the carriage in which I wait is dull gray, lacking all adornments. Da, who prizes invisibility and anonymity above all else, had it specifically designed to be nondescript.

The royal ride slows to a stop a dozen paces away. The horses paw the gravel, huffing out their annoyance at having been stopped. The door swings open to a view of a midnight-blue tufted-velvet coach. Lord Segrande, Leif, and Aodren exit. Baltroit stays behind.

I'm thrilled to see more color has returned to Leif since two nights ago. He's recovering fast.

I wrap a silk lady's veil over part of my hair and around the lower half of my face so only my eyes are visible. With my skirts bundled in my arms, I step out into the dewy evening.

"Milord." My fingers trill a dainty wave. In my best Malamian lilt, I say, "Might I have an audience with you?"

Aodren stops midstep and frowns in my direction, an adorable line creasing his forehead. "Lirra?"

I lower the veil of hair, and recognition dawns on Leif's face. But it is Aodren who takes long strides to cut the distance between us.

He yanks off his glove and seizes my hand. This wasn't part of the ruse I envisioned.

Even so, the contact of his skin sends a zing of excitement through me as he draws my fingers upward. The end-of-day stubble on his chin scrapes the top of my hand. I laugh awkwardly, and start to pull away from this silly charade. But then his warm, intoxicating breath whispers against my skin. The barest press of his mouth follows, and I'm done. Thoughts vanquished. Done.

"A fine carriage, my lady." He withdraws and takes in the rig. He looks to Orli, where she's seated on the driver's bench. The budding thrill I feel must be for her tonight. It will be good for her to see some of the tournament. It's certainly not because Aodren just kissed my hand.

"Complete with a coachman?" Aodren says.

"A friend. Orli." I manage to wrangle two thoughts together.

"Hullo, Your Highness," whispers Orli. She bends into an awkward bow from where she's perched.

"It's a pleasure. Thank you for your help this evening."

And with that, the timid expression slides off her face. She beams at him. Aodren's kind words are so at odds with the man I thought he was a week ago.

Lord Segrande calls out across the distance, "All well?"

Aodren gives them a sign and waves them away. Leif shouts his approval for my appearance, which makes me blush, and then they're off.

I sweep out my arm, gesturing to the open carriage door. "If you wouldn't mind, Your Highness."

"Please, a lovely lady must always enter first."

Right. Ladies first.

Because he is himself, Aodren takes my hand to assist me into the carriage. For my part, I pretend his touch does not send thrills through me. My ridiculously rioting heart and I swoop into the carriage.

We roll up to the champions' tent, and as expected, crowds press around the royal carriages. People chant the names of their favored competitors. No one pays attention to the gray carriage that parks around the side of the tent.

Nearby, a cheer rends the air. I exit and see some people cheering for Baltroit. Some booing.

While attention is diverted, Aodren steps out, expresses a quick thank-you, and escapes into the safety of the tent.

Orli's gaze homes in on the amassing crowd. All around us, sounds of the tournament swell. Lanterns gleam, lighting the way to the field. It's a cacophony of talk and laughter, shouts and applause. She sits stiller than death, her focus on the floating Channeler lights that help illuminate the field.

"Orli, are you all right?"

She doesn't blink as she nods.

"Take the rig home," I insist. "I'll get back on my own."

Her hands tighten on the reins, the deep tone of her skin taking on a gray hue. "I'll wait."

I know she wanted to see Aodren fight, but it's obvious she's overwhelmed. The post-melee celebration will be worse if it's anything like years past, when it was more confrontation than actual celebration. It's not uncommon for heated debates to escalate into brawls. And if some of those people have taken the imposter Sanguine . . . Orli cannot wait here.

"I think I made a mistake by pushing you to come," I admit. "You should drive back."

"You didn't push me," she says, her spark returning. "Sorry, I was caught off-guard by the lights. I'm fine now. I'll watch from up here, and after King Aodren fights, I'll head to the cathedral."

I bite back a groan. I know she's capable of making her own decisions, but I can't help the urge to protect her. "Yes, good plan."

We part ways. Near the elevated platform where a few of Shaerdan's judges have gathered with their families, I spy a familiar face, a tall sailor friend of Baz's. He stands a head above most people around him. Would he know something about the oil?

Keeping the veil over my cheeks and mouth, I wiggle through the growing crowd, until I secure a spot directly behind him. Then I wait. The best crumbs are gathered by the patient mouse.

Melee-goers fill the extra spaces around us, until we're all fish in a barrel. Baz's sailor friend peers over his shoulder. My dress has grazed the backs of his legs. I pretend I need to get by, which he allows. I climb up the steps of the platform and move to the edge to keep him in my sight. The height gives me a view that I hadn't seen before.

Another fellow moves in so I can no longer see the tall man; however, they appear to be talking. Do they know each other? The second fellow is wearing a pouch in front of his left hip. The lid sticking out of the pouch looks connected to a bottle. Sanguine?

When the second man abandons the sailor, I follow.

The man weaves through the crowd and leaves the tournament field. He passes the area where lines of tents have been set up in preparation for the Kingdoms' Market that begins directly after the tournament and will go until the end of the summit. Market traders from near and far have come to sell wares. If my search tonight turns over nothing new, the Kingdoms' Market will surely provide answers. All the prominent traders will be gathered together. One of Da's men, Duff Baron, will have a booth. He or his stepdaughter, Prudence, might know something about Sanguine. Prudence is a friend and just as involved in her stepfather's business as I am in Da's.

The man makes his way toward the competitors' tent. Lingering by a cart, I keep myself in the shadows.

The back flap of the tent moves. Someone from inside is conversing with the man. I'm not close enough to see who it is, but then the person inside the tent reaches out into the incriminating moonlight and takes an offered bottle.

It's Otto, Shaerdan's champion. I overheard him the first night of melee.

He uncaps the bottle and tips it to his lips. Alarm blasts through me. My mind jumps to Leif with a dagger protruding from his chest.

I wait for the man to leave and then I sneak around the back side of the tent. I have to let Aodren know.

A crowd rushing by the tent slows my path. Then the guard refuses to let me past, forcing me to go the other direction. When I finally reach the opening, a healer stands as gatekeeper for anyone going in and out.

"Please, may I speak with King Aodren?" I say as polite and patient as an anxiety-ridden girl can be.

"I'm sorry." The woman glances past my shoulder and then with confusion says, "He's already gone."

At my back, the crowd bellows to life. Chants fill the tournament arena. It's a war cry. Feet stomp, shaking the ground. Drums beat. Trumpets rend the night.

The competitors have already taken the field. The melee has started.

No, it cannot be too late.

I haul my skirts up and run toward the field, unsure what can be done now, but knowing there must be a way to warn Aodren. If it weren't for the wide reach of my skirts, maneuvering through the crush would be easier. I'm a chorus of "pardon me, excuse me, if you wouldn't mind . . ."

The crowd is impassable.

Too many have gathered shoulder to shoulder, hungry, wide-eyed carrion birds, gleeful at the possibility of carnage. I duck under a raised arm, slip around a father holding his boy atop his shoulders. Shouting, jeering, laughing, loud faces blind me to what's happening on the field. The distance between me and Malam's platform might as well be leagues for how impossible it is to maneuver around everyone.

The crowd releases a collective "Ooooohhh," followed by gasps and cringes.

Anxious, I push forward and wade more aggressively through the sea of people.

Part of the field comes into view. An Akarian warrior fights the fierce Kolontian, Hemmet. Both of the champions from Plovia have already fallen. Aodren and Baltroit and the Shaerdanians aren't visible. Too many people taller than me block my view. I need to get past them to see the entire field.

A man's hand hooks my elbow and tugs me back. His gaze dips to the scooped neckline of my dress. "I could use some pretty company."

I slam my heel into his instep. "That kind?"

The bloody arse hops back, spitting out slurs and curses, which, if I were truly a noble kinswoman, would make me faint from shock. People around us yell for him to be quiet. His disruption frees up enough room for me to wedge past another couple of men.

And then the field comes into view.

Baltroit's poleax clashes with the same weapon held by

Folger Falk from Shaerdan. In a quick sweep, Baltroit crashes a blunted ax against Folger's helmet. The second man spins. He swings to block. No bursts of energy or fueling rage come from Folger. In fact, he's barely managing to keep up with Baltroit's powerful blows. Folger must not have taken the oil like his co-competitor, Otto.

Their attack and retreat move them down the field, opening a clear line of sight to Aodren. Thank the gods, he isn't one of the fallen. His sword meets the blade of an Akarian warrior. He is masterful. Around me the crowd gasps and claps as Aodren seizes control. He advances. His strike drives the warrior back.

A ruckus of cheers echoes through the crowd. I glance around, first seeing the many lanterns like gold splotches of light against the dark sky. Then, nearby, the faces of spectators. They cheer and clap for Aodren, giving support to the unexpected competitor. Pride bubbles in my chest.

Aodren's blade swings down, striking the warrior. She falls, knocked unconscious. And when she doesn't stand after a few seconds, the crowd roars, their chants counting out the seconds until time is up. She has been disqualified.

Aodren reaches out, extending a hand to help her up, and tips his head. The move honors her and at the same time shows a chivalrous side that speaks of his regal upbringing. People applaud her as she rushes off the field, while all the ladies gathered around the tournament field let out a collective sigh. Silly hens.

I realize I'm smiling in a smug sort of way. Knowing Aodren makes me feel like I have pieces of him that no one else has. A ridiculous notion, but still, one that flutters inside.

The melee grinds on. Baltroit slams Folger down. The vicious hit lands so hard, it echoes across the field. Folger doesn't get back up.

Otto beats one of the Kolontians.

One by one, the champions fall out of the running.

Some are too injured to continue. Some are unconscious.

Baltroit has positioned himself closer to Hemmet, the Kolontian favored to win, and the remaining Akarian. Everyone senses what's about to happen, because the noise dims a second before Baltroit thrusts his poleax at the woman warrior. She's too busy defending herself from Hemmet's flail to block Baltroit's incoming attack.

The hit sends her to her knees.

But since she's not completely down, Hemmet or Baltroit can land another strike and earn another point.

Hisses and boos fill the air.

Hemmet doesn't swing his flail at the Akarian, though. He aims the metal ball at Baltroit's helmet. The *thunk* of impact echoes across the field. The Malamian champion crumples.

Aodren rushes to his co-competitor's side as applause crackles through the spectators and a chorus of unified voices chant the ten-second countdown. Baltroit is eliminated.

The Akarian warrior lurches to unsteady feet. But she lifts

her blade, pointing it toward Hemmet, in a show of determination. It draws cheers from the crowd.

Nobody seems to notice Otto charging toward the other three competitors. Not Hemmet and the warrior woman, who have both taken fighting positions. Not Aodren, who has been checking on his co-competitor.

No one sees Otto until he's paces away from the action, sword raised. I cringe in that final split second, anticipating how Otto's strike will land. First, he'll eliminate the closest and most injured of the three, the Akarian.

But he shocks us all, leaping past her to slam his blade down on Aodren's right shoulder. The lead arm.

A cry breaks from Aodren's mouth, the sound of his pain tears across the field. His blade tumbles to the ground. His body spasms. And then it's as if my Channeler ability has influence over time and not wind. Everything slows down.

Hemmet steps away from the warrior woman. He swings. The ball of his flail arcs through the air, and crashes into Aodren's helmet.

The king of Malam falls.

I feel the impact, in my head, in my chest, in my heart. *Get up,* I urge him. But he does not move.

Ten . . . The crowd's count reverberates in my skull.

Nine . . . Aodren lies partially on his side and stomach, so still. Deathly still.

Eight . . . Otto spins to Hemmet, slicing the Kolontian man at the neck.

Seven . . . Hemmet stumbles.

Six . . . Otto strikes again, and Hemmet falls.

Five . . . The Akarian warrior lifts her sword and turns to Aodren.

I cannot look anymore.

CHAPTER

21

AODREN

A THOUSAND HAMMERS CHIP AT MY BRAIN. Fire spreads from my right shoulder to my fingertips, over my body, through my lungs, and into my skull. Spots blur my vision as I try to make sense of the blurry, slanted horizon.

Gods, the pain.

Breath grinds through my lungs and whooshes in my ears over the shapeless background noise. And then, all at once, the muffled din sharpens into one booming word. *Ten.* It ricochets between my ears. Realization comes instantly—they shout the seconds remaining before I'm disqualified from the melee. Before Malam is out.

Nine. I try to lift my head. Agony lances up my neck.

"Eight," the crowd cries.

Seven. I try to move my right hand under me and push. Nothing happens. My fingers are numb.

Six. A tree falls, or a man. A blurry giant crashes nearby, his helmet tumbling off. Is that Hemmet?

Five. Get up, that's all I have to do. I curl my knees inward.

Four.

"Stand," a woman says, and warm pressure lands on my good shoulder, tugging until I have my upper body off the ground. I balance on my good arm. The Akarian warrior stares at me.

Three.

I grip her arm, needing the help up to my knees.

Two.

Standing is a precarious affair. My foot slides forward. Leaning most of my weight against the woman as I rise, shakier than a newborn colt. Why is she helping me?

Silence descends, blanketing the raging animal that is the crowd. The final number doesn't come. Even Otto, with his crazed eyes, remains motionless other than his twitching fingers on the sword and his heaving armored torso. He stands over Hemmet's fallen body.

The warrior slides out from under my arm, leaving me to struggle for balance. Her sword lifts to a ready position. But I'm not sure what is happening. Have I been eliminated?

"The king of Malam is still in the fight," the announcer's voice blares from the tower. It opens the beast's gate, drawing out its roar. The spectators' riotous shouts and stomps quake the ground beneath my feet. The melee is not over.

To my left, the warrior lunges, sword crashing against Otto's. He growls, and his eyes flare, showing too much white, like a rabid dog's. He's enraged. I've not seen this version of Otto before. He's nothing like the man I dueled the first night of melee.

Understanding splits through the painful haze of my head. He's taken Sanguine.

The oil's boost of strength and rage combined with its ability to decrease sensitivity to pain gives Otto the advantage. The Akarian will not last and she knows it. Pain flares in her dark eyes each time their weapons connect.

My right arm hangs useless at my side. I pluck my sword off the ground with my left hand, suddenly grateful for all the left-handed dueling practice I've had with Leif.

I swing around Otto's side, distracting him so the Akarian can land two hits. I am paying her back for the mercy she showed me. The Shaerdanian scuttles back to put us both at his front. He tries to take us both on, but, regardless of the oil's added effects, Otto proves no match for our combined sword skill.

An arc of my blade divests him of his weapon. The warrior woman's sword slices against Otto's helmet, and the man drops, another tree felled.

From every side, noise in the arena rises to a fever pitch. Cheers, shouts, wails, shrieks. It's impossible to take in everything. All I know is my fight is done. Had it not been for the Akarian's help, any chance Malam had to win a banner would've been lost before now. It's honor enough to be standing here with her — two final champions.

I lift my sword, though I'm too weak to put up much fight. But I want to give her as many chances as possible to earn points for her kingdom. My continued fight honors her.

She swings, and I can barely keep up. She lands three hits, and then we hear the horn.

The trumpet's bright, resonant sound ends the melee.

I lower my sword, touch my hand to my chest, and bow.

My attention sweeps from the crowd to the fallen champions. A few have risen to their feet and lean heavily against their poles and swords. Others have been carted off the field. A couple remain prone on the muddy, matted grass.

While the points are tallied, the ragged, dazed fighters return to the field, moving toward their comrades. Baltroit trudges to stand beside me.

The announcer calls all to attention. A hush descends. The sound of my own breathing seems too loud for the sheer noiseless anticipation.

"For the first time in twenty-five years," the announcer's voice booms, "by total number of points earned from hits —" He pauses.

"Malam wins the melee!"

I blink. Pain ripples through my body. Baltroit is gripping my left arm, leaping around and shouting and whooping along with hundreds of other voices. Malamians flood the field to celebrate the victory, their disdain for me forgotten if only for this moment.

The Akarian appears before me. She sheathes her sword and repeats my bow. "Well deserved."

People swarm us from all sides, maroon and gray flags flap in the breeze, and songs of Malam echo into the night.

Stars. We won.

Baltroit and I ride on top of shoulders with a banner hanging between us. A wave of people carry us to the row of traders' tents where a makeshift tavern is packed with Malamians dressed in the colors of our flag. Our escorts lower us to the ground, and mugs of ale are pressed into our hands. Around the tavern tent, mugs are lifted and cheers follow. I shake a dozen hands and happily endure two dozen back slaps. Excitement has muted the pain. Leif, Lord Segrande, and a couple of royal guards who have come to Shaerdan for the All Kingdoms' Festivities gather nearby, keeping watch. But I don't feel the suffocating press of the crowd that I experienced after the first night of melee. Being around the Malamians' gleeful faces and boisterous chatter is exhilarating.

I pull off my helmet and thrust it in the air. "Hearts, blood, lives for Malam!"

A chorus repeats Malam's credo thrice more; each time

the volume rises until it's near deafening. The emotion coursing through me is as proud and resounding as their voices. It vanquishes any doubts I may have had about fighting in the tournament.

When more drinks start flowing, I move through the group, shaking hands and mirroring cheers as if this is who I've always been. It takes more time than I would've ever imagined to make my way to where Leif sits on a stool, half-slumped over the table.

"Feller's had one too many," says the barkeep.

I study Leif's lined face and squinty eyes. He looks pained, not drunk.

"A good fight you put up, sir," he says.

"Thank you. Are you ready to return to the castle?"

His brows rise, looking like brownish-red checkmarks. "The night is young, sir."

"Yes, but I've had a beating, and you look like you've had one recently as well."

"That is true." He chuckles. "But don't you want to enjoy your moment? Celebrate until dawn."

The celebration is wonderful indeed, but while friends gather together, recounting stories of the melee, the one man in this tent I consider a friend is in desperate need of returning to bed. He'll be competing in another few days. He needs all the rest he can muster. I point to the empty rows of shops beyond the tavern tent. "Other than Malamians, the crowd has cleared out. I've reveled in the moment. But should I need more celebration, a victory can be appreciated from any location as long as friends are nearby. Let's return to the castle."

"Good plan," he says on a groan.

I inform Segrande that we're leaving and help Leif to the champions' tent. As soon as we part from the crowd, it's obvious Leif isn't inebriated. He's in pain. He folds forward and winces as he walks. For the first time, I think that Gorenza might have done us a favor by insisting that I fight tonight. There is no way Leif would have been ready to compete.

Once we are inside the tent, Leif takes a seat.

Some of the competitors are still around. As they exit, the Plovians mutter lackluster congratulations while the Kolontians sneer. The person I want to find is Otto. He might be resistant to sharing his oil source, but I will do what it takes to pull a name out of him. But he's already left, and soon the only people who remain are the healers. They give me Beannach water, which I throw back; I request the same for Leif. Then while he sits in the care of the healers, I wash up and change as quickly as my injuries will allow.

Leif and I exit the tent, and I scan for the simple carriage that brought me to the tournament. I'm not surprised when I cannot find it anywhere in the vicinity. A lot of time has passed since the melee ended. It would be ridiculous to expect Lirra to wait, since I had planned to ride to the castle with my fellow Malamians. I shove my disappointment down and help Leif into the royal carriage.

A gentle breeze sweeps through the summer night. I

glance back and see that we're alone now. Near the setup for the Kingdoms' Market, the tavern tent is alive and bustling. But everyone else is gone.

A snore rumbles from inside the carriage. Leif is already asleep.

I tell the driver to take Leif back, and I inform him I'll make my way to the castle alone. He starts to argue, but I shut the carriage door, give the side a solid smack, and send the driver on his way.

I walk fifty paces toward the cathedral and realize I'm acting like a fool. I'd hoped to catch up and thank her for helping me. Now that the summit meetings will be consuming my time, I may not have a chance to tell her later.

And yet even as I think this, I know it's ridiculous. The truth is, I'd hoped to see her once more for no other reason than to be near her.

I've made a poor choice. Fatigue sets in as I continue walking. My shoulder burns with each step. I should've had two cups of Beannach water. After coming off the first rise, the shadows shift ahead.

I pause.

Lirra steps out from behind one of the lone trees that's strayed from the forest. Her fingers clutch a swatch of silk, the piece used earlier to obscure her face. The sight of her cuts something loose in me.

I walk down the slope to meet her. "You're here."

She glances over her shoulder in the direction of the cathedral. "I saw you were celebrating, so I went to check on Orli. I thought I'd make it back before you needed to return to the castle. I didn't mean to keep you waiting."

"You were walking back?"

She nods.

This girl. The distance Lirra has trekked to the cathedral and back for Orli... for me... Her selflessness squeezes a place under my ribs. Since the first night she brought the letter to my chambers, she's been resilient and unbreakable in all the tasks I've needed her to do. She should be tired of me by now. But she looks up at me with hope and kindness, tightening the spot in my chest until I feel breathless from it.

"You were brilliant tonight," she continues, unaware of where my thoughts have gone. "But then you gave me such a fright. Are you well enough? How is your arm?" She lets out a little entrancing laugh, full of unabashed sincerity. "You were quite impressive."

"Did you think so?" I close the remaining distance.

A shy smile is punctuated by an eye roll. "Of course, then you had to go and sweep all the ladies off their feet with your chivalry. Had you intended on winning hearts along with the flag?"

My aches forgotten, I'm suddenly mindful of one heart in particular, one I have no claim to but want desperately to win.

"And that fight you put up," she goes on. "It was . . . well, it was magnificent and vexing." Her hand flicks, sweeping the scrap of material through the air. "Then Otto struck you . . . I—I was worried."

The catch in her voice. The candid, guileless words.

How did I ever think Lirra was merely pretty?

She is stunning, and at the same time, clever, fearless, and bold. Nothing about her makes sense in my world. But despite my attempts to stifle any interest in her, she's bewitched me nonetheless. Lirra's refreshing candidness seizes my attention. I see the beauty in her wit, her compassion, the risks she takes for friends, the risks she's taken for me.

"Aodren?" Her soft, dusky lips wrap around my name.

This is not wise, a warning blares in my head. But I step closer, no doubt looking like a starved bear with sights on wounded prey.

My hand lifts to cup her bronzed cheek, all logic fading under the furor in my veins as I tilt my head down. With my last shred of sanity, I pause, nose near her temple, breathing in the fresh scent on her skin, sea breeze and sunshine. Every nerve in my body stands at attention.

"Lirra," I say in return. I should be embarrassed about how hoarse and needy it sounds.

She tips her face up. "Were you going to kiss me?"

Gods, that question on those lips. My mouth presses against them, and the hiss of her breath slides into mine. I wrap an arm around her waist to drag her closer. Pain rips through my shoulder and forces a gasp out of me.

"Oh," she pulls back, "I didn't mean to—"

For all I care, my arm could fall off right now. Nothing will stop me from kissing Lirra. I silence her worry with my mouth. Thank the gods she allows me to coax her honeyed lips open and drag my tongue against hers as her body molds to mine, fitting perfectly in my arms. Her hands climb up my neck and twine into my hair, her touch better than anything I've ever felt. Lirra's kiss steals my mind, my heart, my desire to be anywhere but here.

CHAPTER

22

LIRRA

Aodren's hands slide from my waist up my back, leaving a trail of heat as the press of his lips switches from soft and inviting to hard and demanding. I've been kissed before, but the sweep of his mouth belies any experience I might think I've had. I have never been kissed. Not if kissing is like this.

My fingers wind into his hair, needing to muss it up, to mark him. Aodren tugs me closer, and I, too willing, fall into him, the scent of his soap-scrubbed skin washing over me. He tastes of mint leaves, rain, and freedom.

It sets my mind spinning when he drops a kiss beside my mouth, across my jaw, to the edge of my ear, and down the hollow of my neck. I'm weightless and heavy all at once. I'm one of my gliders, wings spread, soaring high.

The wind picks up and whips my hair into our faces. Aodren pulls back, and his fingers graze across my cheek, moving the strands away. The wind has always had a way of clearing my head. It must be part of my ability. I can speak to the wind and, in turn, it talks to me. It reasons. It reminds me that perhaps kissing the king of Malam isn't a good idea. The man I once thought of as my opposite, my enemy, is sinking under my skin and wrapping himself around my heart.

His hands slide down my back and over my scars. The brush of contact clears my head like someone has slammed two pots together. I jolt back, remembering who I am. *Daughter of the Archtraitor, a Channeler, a Shaerdanian.* What am I doing? I cannot lose my heart to the king of Malam. If I know anything about him, it's that his country comes first.

Aodren blinks hazy dark eyes and presses his kiss-reddened lips together, holding in a smile.

A voice from the corner of my mind argues I'm not Shaerdanian, that I wasn't born a commoner. In another life, I may have been considered a good match for Aodren. But I wear the scars of the past, always a reminder that I'm not that Lirra Barrett. That life is not mine.

"We should go," I say.

"Right. It's late." His hands fall to his sides, and as if nothing happened, he begins walking beside me and talking about the upcoming jubilee and the remaining tournament events. The almost seamless transition would work if the taste of him weren't still on my lips. It makes me wonder if this thing between us means anything. Or if it's a dalliance that is entertaining for the time being. But then what?

A dark mood settles over me. I try to listen as Aodren explains the plan for Baltroit and Leif to enter the two smaller events, jousting and archery, before one of them will move on to the grand finale, the battle of swords. He updates me on his conversation about Sanguine with Ku Toa, and I explain what I witnessed before the tournament began.

Aodren rubs his shoulder, his brows dipping between a wince and a scowl. "I figured Otto had taken Sanguine," he says, recounting the difference in Otto's fight versus his performance on the first melee night. It reminds me that Aodren could've died tonight. This only deepens my desire to find the maker of the oil.

"There is someone I'm going to contact," I say.

"Who?"

"An informant of Da's should be in town this week for the Kingdoms' Market. He or his stepdaughter might be helpful."

"Is this someone you can trust?" He pushes a hand into his already skewed hair. I swallow a secret smile because this Aodren, a wee bit messy, is my favorite version of him.

"Yes, Prudence is a friend."

"And you're certain she isn't duplicitous? The supplier could be anyone." His wariness makes sense, considering all the subterfuge in his kingdom. However, I have years of instinct to rely on, instinct that's always proven reliable.

"Actually, the supplier cannot be just anyone," I say thinking out loud. "The oil contains Channeler energy, which means a Channeler must be involved."

"If someone is using dark magic to make the oil, won't there be obvious physical markings?" Aodren asks, thinking of the dark veins that stain a Channeler's skin when she dabbles in dark magic.

"If the oil is being made without the intention to harm, then there would be none of that."

"How would the maker not know it's harmful?"

I shrug. "It happens with herbal mixes. Earth Channelers make them for all different purposes. But if the tea made from the herb is used for something other than what the mix was intended for, it could hurt someone."

"Are we making the search for the supplier harder than it has to be? I will just talk to the Shaerdanian champions." Exhaustion pulls Aodren's shoulders low and slows his steps. The man is one gust of wind away from tipping over.

"You could try," I say, and then remember the way Baz and his friends reacted in the cells. "But I wouldn't do so alone."

His expression dawns with understanding. His arm hangs at his side. He needs something more to help him recover. Ahead, the carriage is parked just off the road leading to the cathedral. By the time we reach Orli, Aodren's speech has started to slur with exhaustion and pain. He should've taken an entire skin of Beannach water from the champions' tent.

"Get in." I pull the door open.

"Find a healer?" he asks, a different sort of haze in his eyes.

Perhaps it would be best to take him to the castle, but I don't think he would make it through the tunnel alone, and faced with the thought of riding up tonight and possibly encountering Judge Soma and the guards, I make a selfish choice.

"I'm taking you home."

After dropping Orli off, I turn the carriage onto a country road, winding through the farmlands that rim the thick woods covering the land south of Celize. We pass by fields broken up by patches of forest until reaching a cluster of trees broken up by an offshoot path that is mostly obscured by overgrown shrubs. I drive along the path to an abandoned, decrepit farmhouse. *Almost home.*

The horses know their way. They pull the carriage around the property to where signs of travel fade into another rise of woods full of exposed roots and gnarled trunks. Normally, I would leave the horses and carriage here, but tonight we wind through the woods to the other side.

Here, like a lone hibernating bear nestled in the glade, is the Barrett homestead.

I can only imagine how angry Da would be if he knew his years of carefully maintained secrecy were about to be compromised. For this one reason, I suppose it's good that he hasn't come home yet.

I'll make a tincture, give Aodren more Beannach, and when his energy starts to return, take him back to the cathedral.

He climbs out of the carriage, eyes reddened and sleep hungry, arms tucked around his torso, and legs stiff. He follows me around the side of the house and down to Da's cellar. Eugenia and the littleuns will be asleep by now. Somewhere in the array of boxes, bins, crates, and containers, I'll find everything needed to mend him. Da, a collector as much as he is a dealer of secrets, owns buckets of Channeler healing supplies. If only he were an organizer. Nothing has a set place, which hinders my search for Beannach water and herbs. By the time I've pulled everything together, Aodren is slumped in Da's chair.

He needs somewhere to rest while I make the tincture. I cross the room and push some crates off a rarely used mattress. It's stiff and lumpy, nothing a king would sleep on, but he won't be here long.

"Come rest here," I say, a little embarrassed. "It's not very nice, but it'll do for now."

"I couldn't imagine anything better." He peers at me from Da's chair with a gentle, sleep-soggy smile, and suddenly, warmth blossoms in my chest, sweeping away any misgivings. I don't wonder if he should be here, but rather how I will ever let him go?

Startled by the depth of my feelings, I occupy myself with finding herbs.

Astoria taught me to make a healing aid with a pinch of chiandra, a scrape of wormwood, two springs of elm berry, and a handful of dried clary sage. The mixture steeps in

Beannach water, and the outcome is a drink that eases pain and fades bruises. A trip out for wood and kindling takes longer than expected. Aodren is nearly asleep by the time I set the kettle on the fire.

A search around Da's cellar turns up a blanket. I use it to cover his legs, and then ladle the tincture tea into a mug.

"Aodren? Can you wake? You need to drink this if you don't want to be sore tomorrow."

His golden lashes lazily climb upward, and cozy green eyes blink at me. His "thank you, Lirra," comes out rumbly and warm, like a bite of cobbler right off the fire.

He sits up and blows on the drink. "Do you like working for him?"

"My da?" I shrug.

He drinks and then lowers the cup. "I know few people with your skill set. You're talented. Your father must be proud."

"Thank you." I duck my head. "I . . . I do enjoy the work."

He finishes the tincture and places the empty mug on the shelf. "But?" he asks, reading the slight hesitation in my words. "If you weren't working for him, what other things might you be interested in?"

I must be a fool, because my first instinct is to answer his question. I have to stop myself and remember that this isn't just a regular man. No matter how I like to pretend he's just another acquaintance of Da's, I cannot keep pretending he's not the king of Malam.

I worry my lip, wondering if perhaps I've made a mistake bringing him here.

"You're tired. We should head back to the castle." My fingers twist in the folds of my dress.

"I'm not tired anymore," he says. The liar.

But he grins, and it's disarming.

The next thing I know, we're leaving the cellar, him at my heels and my head in pieces. He waits outside the shed while I gather the components of my glider. He watches with blatant curiosity as I place each item in the grass.

For the jubilee, I've created two smaller gliders and one larger one, which isn't quite finished yet. I attach the components of the smaller one. Two wings span out from a slim oval disk. Attached below the disk is a basket, one that could be used to deliver items. Or, on a larger scale, it could carry people.

"Watch," I command, trying not to wonder if he'll like my gliders or find them childish.

My hands turn outward, facing the wood and fabric contraptions. I draw the night air to me and then take off running, releasing the glider into a gust. My energy encourages the wind to guide the glider higher and higher, searching for a warmer lift of air it can ride without my help. The night has cooled the land around us, but I finally find a balmy breeze for the glider to ride.

I pull back on my Channeler magic, letting the wind work its own magic, and only now and then using a nudge of energy to keep the glider afloat. Once the wings catch the air current, it takes almost no Channeler energy for the glider to stay skyward. After much time has passed, I guide my creation to the ground.

"You amaze me, Lirra," Aodren whispers, breaking the comfortable silence that has formed around us.

The compliment warms me.

Aodren walks beside me to the shed to put the glider away. "Could a person ride on one of these?"

"That's my goal."

"Would the person have to be a Channeler?"

"No," I tell him. "That's the beauty of my invention. In history books, I read about other people who wanted to fly like birds. But to make and test an invention that gives a man wings is too dangerous. The learning process could result in death. But because of my gift, I've been able to create different models and test them without fear of plummeting to my death."

He stares at me. "And after they've been tested, can anyone use them? Even someone giftless like me?"

I nod.

"You've taken your Channeler magic and used it to create something everyone could benefit from. Brilliant." He breathes out the word.

There it is again, the compliments that come unexpectedly and rattle me.

"Not brilliant, just born with a little extra magic." I pick up the glider.

"And modest."

I cannot help but smile. "I'm hoping to share my gliders at the jubilee."

"You and your aunt will be performing on the same field, but for different kingdoms."

He means Aunt Katallia, my father's sister, who remained in Malam during the Purge years because it was too risky to uproot her family. Somehow, she kept her Channeler ability a secret, though she's a longtime member of the Channelers Guild.

"Yes, except she'll be part of the jubilee grand finale." He follows me to the shed and helps me take apart the glider. "I'm going to audition for the smaller show, the showcase. Channelers of every ability level can enter. The grand finale at the end of the week is only for each kingdoms' most celebrated Channeler."

"It matters not if you're in the finale or the showcase. These gliders are brilliant. Anyone who has the privilege of watching you work your magic will be impressed," he says, and then gives me a sheepish look as we leave the shed.

"Thank you," I choke out.

He blows a breath into the night. "It's been difficult to convince Channelers to represent Malam. I overlooked the showcase because no one from Malam will be entering." The moonlight through the trees casts him in colorless hues.

I can imagine how difficult that would be. "You know, I was leery at first of your intentions. I didn't think you cared for Channelers beyond what they could do for you. But now I can see you want a better life for them, for everyone. What you're doing is admirable. You want to show your kingdom that Channelers aren't to be feared, but accepted. Give it time and others will see your vision."

I wish Astoria would give Aodren another chance. If she could hear him now and see that he's nothing like the Malamian leaders before him, surely she'd find no fault.

Aodren follows me back into the cellar. He sits while I stir up another concoction. The more he drinks tonight, the better he'll feel tomorrow.

We fall into a comfortable quiet as he sips from a mug.

"Lirra," he says as my eyelids are starting to droop.

I jerk upright in Da's desk chair. "Yes?"

"I keep thinking of how your glider could change the world."

"You and Orli," I mutter, even though his words thrill me.

"Your gliders can be used to benefit all sides of society. They can be appreciated by giftless or Channelers."

I nod. "I wanted to make something that could be used without a Channeler having to be drained of energy to keep it afloat. But Channelers are still needed in the process to create them. So it might open opportunities for Channelers to find a way to work in their towns and cities without having to drain themselves of energy constantly."

"It provides a way for Channelers to live openly with their

magic," he says, and shifts over, making an obvious spot for me next to him on the mattress. I squish closer to him, noting how good he always smells, like soap and man. "Using your magic as a tool to assist the bigger project will show Channelers a new way of approaching their ability. And in turn, maybe you'll inspire more Channelers to think of ways they can build and create with their magic."

He's so animated, his hands lifting to express what he's talking about. Tea sloshes out of his mug. "That's an entire economy that could open up. People to assemble the parts, Channelers to test the inventions, traders to sell the final product."

I'm mesmerized by his spark, his vision of what could be.

"Why don't you pursue this?" he asks.

I pluck the pilled lint off the blanket on the bed. "I want to," I admit. "What you said about showing Channelers other ways they can use their magic, that's what I want to do. I want us to be innovative and not beholden to jobs that just endlessly drain us of our energy."

His hand drops on top of mine, preventing me from picking at the blanket. "What's stopping you?"

"My da. Part of me is still waiting for his approval."

"Is that why you are working so hard on this Sanguine problem? For his approval?"

I shrug. "I care about him. I want to help him. I want him to trust me and recognize what I'm capable of doing on my own. Also, I cannot stand by knowing the oil has the potential to ruin so many lives. I can help, and to me that feels right. What about you? Would you do something else if you could?"

Aodren leans back until he's lying down on the mattress, his hands under his head and elbows out. "No, I don't think so. I feel like I'm meant to do this work, and in truth, there are many things I enjoy about being the king. Mostly I want to make a difference. I want to bring change to Malam that will positively affect the people." A sigh moves like a wave through his chest. "But I'm starting to wonder if that's possible."

"Of course it is. One man's voice can start change."

"But can it erase the destruction brought on by the former leaders? One voice cannot reach everyone."

"Maybe you're thinking about it all wrong. Instead of taking on all the work that needs to be done across Malam, maybe you just have to be the man who shouts at the snowy mountain until an avalanche starts."

He scrubs his face and laughs a little. "I'm not sure I'm following. Perhaps I'm more tired than I thought."

"I mean if there's a loud enough disturbance, it can loosen the snowpack and trigger an avalanche that will slide down the mountain."

Aodren's face scrunches. "You want me to wreak havoc and destruction?"

"It's a metaphor." I laugh. "If you want to bring about

change, all you need to be is a voice. A voice loud enough to start a storm."

"Start a storm," he repeats, with a smile, tired, weak, and shadowed by the darkness, that still makes the man look impossibly beautiful.

CHAPTER

23

AODREN

FAINT LIGHT SNEAKS IN THROUGH THE CEL-lar's vents, illuminating Lirra's dark hair. She is molded to the side of my body, and her head rests on my arm. I drink in the curves of her rested face and her full lips, and sharp longing pulls me forward. But then, with a jolt, I realize I've been asleep the whole night.

At the castle, someone could enter my chambers and discover my untouched bed. Didn't she say it takes only one voice to spark a storm? Talk will lead to questions, which will lead to Lirra . . . to whatever we're doing together. I can't expose her to that, even if my own reputation was sterling enough to take the vicious gossip that would follow.

I force myself off the mattress. Lirra mumbles, curling toward the empty spot, and I want nothing more than to return. Because she's warm and comfortable and serene.

I have to leave.

Quiet, to allow her rest, I pad out the door. Stairs lead up from the cellar to the grassy clearing around her quaint home. Beyond that, forest surrounds the property. Grayish light rolls through the trees on the morning fog. I'm relieved because it means the hour is early yet. My return to the castle could still go unnoticed. The question is, where do I go from here?

I edge away from the steps to figure out where to go, and two boys land in my path. I stumble back, barely managing to catch myself from tumbling into the cellar. They literally dropped from above. I glance up to the gables over two windows. They couldn't have jumped from there. Could they? The boys, identical copies of each other — same sable curly hair, rounded cheeks, muddy boots peeking beneath baggy trousers — are wearing capes tied around their necks.

"Are those bed linens?" I squint against the faded morning dawn and lean to the side to get a better view.

One boy picks up a rock and waves it at me. "We're asking the questions, stodger, not you. Who are ya? And what're you doing in there?"

Stodger?

He actually throws the rock, something I'm not expecting. I lunge to the left, dodging the blow. My shoulder and back strain from the flash movement, and pain lances through my muscles.

"I mean no harm." I clutch my bad arm and let out a low groan. "I'm a friend of Lirra's."

The little scrapper grabs another rock. "Yer a bloody Malamian." His hand moves up, ready to throw. At this rate, these two boys are going to undo all Lirra's healer work.

"Loren!" A slice of her voice comes from behind me, sleep-roughened, starchy, and stern. "You drop that rock right now."

"This stodger your friend, Lir?" the second boy asks.

"He is, so don't scare him off with rocks." She snaps her fingers at the one she called Loren. "Put the stick down!"

"You're saying he's stodgy?" He cackles and drops a small branch that could've done me major damage. When did he pick that up?

Lirra steps to my right side and sighs in exasperation, but the effect is garbled by what sounds like a chuckle. I glance at her and see she's holding a hand over her mouth to hide her grin. But still, I worry how her stepmother will react if she discovers I'm here.

"I'm a friend," I tell Loren, hoping it's enough of an explanation.

"That so? What's your name, then?"

"Aodren," I say at the same time Lirra says, "He doesn't have one."

Loren's eyes turn into slits, an expression his brother

shares. "Smells like fish guts to me. Lirra don't have male friends. What's your real name?"

A rush of pleasure at the fact these boys have confirmed Lirra is not involved with another, and they have no idea who I am is the last thing I should be feeling right now. Still, it's nice to lose the weight of the crown, if only for a moment. "Aodren is my birth name."

"Just like the bloody king o' Malam?"

"Loren," Lirra scolds. "You do not talk like that."

"I've heard you say it loads of times," he shoots back, and then turns to his brother. "Hasn't she, Kiefer?"

The less talkative one nods. Lirra's cheeks bloom red like two poppies in June.

Tamping down my amusement, I tell Loren and Kiefer, "You're right. People call me Aodren just like the bloody king o' Malam."

Both boys snort and hoot. A little laugh bubbles out of Lirra. She good-naturedly wraps an arm around their shoulders and proudly introduces them as her brothers. She pinches one and chides the other, love warming her tone. Then she sends them away. Anyone can see Lirra cares deeply for her twin brothers, and they feel the same. What would it be like to have a family like Lirra's? To be loved, in spite of your title? What a stark contrast Lirra's life is to the sterile, loveless environment of my youth, shuffled between tutors, the regent who tried to kill me, and my former captain.

"I should leave," I tell Lirra. The fog has slunk to the west and through the surrounding trees, more light breaks past the branches. If I wasn't late before, I certainly will be now.

Before Lirra leaves me at the cathedral, she reminds me of her plans to talk with one of her father's informants. I know she's as eager as I am to find the supplier and stop the trade. We agree to meet tomorrow before the joust by the champions' tent.

Parting from Lirra at the cathedral, I rush through the underground passages and into the keep's lower halls. Clanks, creaks, and chatter echo from the waking castle. I have almost reached Malam's corridor when steps scuff behind me. I spin around, feeling a sick sensation like my stomach is wedged under my breastbone, and find Segrande.

"It's you." My breath slides out.

A frown cuts into the forest of his beard. "Just the man I've been looking for. Late night?"

"You could say that."

"I didn't take you for a tavern-goer like my son." I hear the fatherly reproach in his words, and it amuses me.

"Good, because last night I wasn't in my cups."

"No? Where have you been?" He lowers his voice on the last part and follows me to my chambers. "I came to your room earlier, and it was clear no one had slept in your bed. Also, you look . . ." He scratches his facial hair as if seeking the right word. "You look rumpled."

We step into the privacy of my room. "I went to Lirra Barrett's home," I admit. "I ended up sleeping the night there."

Segrande drops into a chair, like a boulder plunks off a mountain, and taps his fingers to his lips. Usually he's boisterous and loud. This quieter version is disconcerting.

"Segrande?"

"You have disappointed me, sir."

"Excuse me?"

"To carouse with a young lady who is not your wife, or intended, or even one of your countrywomen. It is unseemly. May I remind you that you are the king? There is no higher power in the land. If you treat your position with negligence and laxity, you set a precedent."

I stare at him, dumbfounded. "Lord Segrande, what exactly do you think I've been doing?"

"The specifics of what you do with her or any other woman are none of my concern, but I think you should practice discretion while we're here at the summit."

"Segrande." I say his name like the crack of a whip. Anger brims under my skin. "I did not go to her home, woo her into ruin, and then drunkenly wander back to the castle after a night of bedding. I was injured last night and exhausted. She saw that I was in need of healing remedies and drove me to her home. Considering what happened the last time she was here, I'm sure you can understand her aversion to the summer castle. She repaired me as best she could. We talked about her Channeler gift and her plans for the jubilee. And then we fell asleep. Is that specific enough for you?"

He stands and folds his arms over his belly. His mouth guppies open and then closed. He unfolds his arms and sits on the edge of the chair. "Forgive me, Your Highness. I—I misunderstood."

"You're forgiven."

"Perhaps you could be more discreet when you visit Miss Barrett," he suggests gently.

I narrow my eyes on him.

"I accept what you're telling me. I meant what I said before—our lives tend toward seclusion. That is a heavy rock to bear. So knowing you've found a . . . friendship in the Archtraitor's daughter pleases me. But not everyone will be as understanding."

"Explain," I say, disliking the turn in the conversation.

"Many in Malam still see her father as the enemy. And if they don't, they expect their king to find companionship in Malam's noble circles. Perhaps that is something you should consider."

I cross the room and sit down in the chair opposite him, dropping my elbows on my knees. My head is too full of implications to voice a response. He's given me something to think about, whether I like it or not.

"You said Lirra's a Channeler?" Segrande asks a beat later,

tone completely different from before. "Wanting to enter the jubilee?"

I nod, uncertain where this is going and why the sudden mood change.

He steeples his fingers and taps them to his chin. "We may be in need of her services."

"How so?"

"Late last night, Judge Soma came to me. He said King Gorenza uncovered a rule in the tome for the Channeler Jubilee. It says members of the Guild cannot represent individual kingdoms."

"Are those rules still current?" I'm gripping the arm of the chair so tightly, holding in my anger, that the wood edges bruise my palm.

"Yes." He pushes out of the chair and crosses to the window, blocking the light. "We could petition for them to be changed; however, even if the leaders agree to amend the original rules, any changes wouldn't go into effect until the next summit."

Damn Gorenza. Before coming to Shaerdan, Segrande, Leif, and I focused on the tournament and the summit meetings because Katallia's performance at the jubilee was a sure thing. I knew it would be spectacular and awe-inspiring in all the ways Malam needs, because Katallia is a gifted, powerful wind Channeler.

The Channeler Jubilee is scheduled later in the summit

because it's the culminating event. It's bigger than the tournament. Though it isn't a competition, there is still talk of which kingdom's Channeler had the best performance, had the most skill, was the most powerful. If Malam is the only kingdom without a Channeler representative, the absence will send a damaging message to the other kingdoms as well as to the citizens of Malam.

It will confirm the prejudices that have plagued my people and define us in a terrible light.

It will appear that Malam hasn't progressed past the Purge.

Would Lirra consider representing Malam?

In the last few days, I've asked her to do a great deal. It would bother me to ask this as well. And yet, if she were truly a viable option, I would do it. I'd do anything to break my kingdom from the manacles of the past.

"Channelers representing each kingdom are supposed to be from that kingdom," I tell Segrande.

"Well, Lirra is, isn't she?"

I drop my head into my hands. "Originally, yes, but her father took her from the kingdom when she was a babe."

A torrent of stories about Lirra's father and Malam's past return in force. My father suffered an untimely death. His passing stirred people's suspicions. Convinced Shaerdan's Channelers were the cause, my father's advisers closed the border and drafted the Purge Proclamation. Millner Barrett was the only member of the inner court who disagreed. He spoke out against those who hunted Channelers. When guards went after Millner, Lirra's mother, a Channeler, was tortured and killed, and their home was set on fire. But Millner's escape and evasion of capture became legendary. He became the Archtraitor of Malam.

And Lirra? She was a girl whose mother, home, and land were ripped violently from her life.

I cannot imagine she would ever want to claim Malam again as her home. The thought is chilling, both for my hopes for the jubilee and my growing interest in Lirra.

"Find someone else," I tell Segrande.

"We will be hard pressed at this point to convince a Channeler to stand up for Malam. Most are still leery to admit they are one. They don't want their neighbors to know."

I shake my head. "It cannot be her."

After a morning meal, I cross Leif's path in the main hall.

"You're looking well," I say, noting a sheen of sweat coating skin that looks healthier than it did when I saw him last. The real Sanguine truly does work wonders. Last night he was hunched over in exhaustion and pain. Now he stands upright, full of energy. "Have you been out for a stroll?"

"Nah. I've been sparring."

"You convinced Baltroit to work out with you here?" I fall into step with him, crossing between the pillars to the stairs.

"I walked to the tournament field."

His admission surprises me. He was stabbed a week ago. Last night he could barely walk from the tavern tent to the carriage. Today he's walking to and from the tournament field?

"The Channeler oil makes me feel like a new man," he says, reading my expression. He rolls his head side to side and then moves his shoulders forward and back as if to demonstrate his returned limberness. "I'm sick of being cooped up in that drafty room."

I chuckle. "Well, I'm glad to hear it. Whenever you're ready, I'd be happy to return to training you."

"You up to that?" He tips his head toward my injured shoulder. "You took a nasty hit last night."

"It is a bit sore," I admit. We climb the stairs, and at the top I glance around to make sure we're alone. "Lirra prepared a tincture, which has taken most of my aches away."

His smile fades at the mention of her. "She's a girl of many talents," he says, looking at me with a watchful eye.

"That she is."

"You've been spending a lot of time around her," he says, and to my confusion, it sounds like there's a spark of irritation in his comment. Leif is definitely not acting like himself, which makes me think he shouldn't be sparring yet.

"You don't seem thrilled about that." I pause at the top of the stairs.

He tugs at his beard. "She's my cousin. I want to make sure she's being treated right."

I stare at Leif, wondering if he understands the cut in his words. Behind us, one of the guards approaches. I gesture for the man to stay back. I face Leif.

"I wouldn't treat her with anything but respect," I tell him, my tone a stern warning.

Leif's gaze widens, almost like he's coming to himself from a dream. "Of course, Your Highness. I meant nothing of it."

Even so, his comments have sawed jagged edges into the memory of last night's kiss.

"If you'll excuse me, Leif." I step back, needing space to gather my thoughts, and inform him that I'll see him at the summit meeting in an hour.

Around the mahogany table, we discuss tariffs, stolen goods, and security measures for trade routes. Because ore and other metals are plentiful in Malam, we're finally able to lock down a trade deal with all kingdoms except for Kolontia. I wonder if anything fruitful will come from conversations with King Gorenza, who attempts multiple times to goad me about the jubilee. In a moment that perhaps isn't my finest, I mention the melee flag hanging in Malam's corridor. After that, Gorenza keeps his growls to himself.

The guard posted outside Malam's corridor stops Leif, who then catches up to me and conveys the message. "The Channelers Guild has arrived. They're waiting in your chambers with news from Malam."

Two members of the Guild sit beside the unused fireplace

in my chambers. Seeva Soliel, the woman who is also a member of my inner advisory circle, and Katallia Barrett, Lirra's aunt.

"Is there any way around Gorenza's claim?" I walk to the fireplace to face them, hoping they have answers for who might represent Malam at the jubilee.

Seeva shakes her head. "Unfortunately, the rules haven't been officially changed since then. To maintain order, we have to abide by them."

"You will have to find another Channeler." Katallia leans back in the chair. How can she look relaxed right now?

"Easier said than done."

Lirra resembles her aunt. They both have similar features, big blue eyes, wide cheekbones, and a kind smile. But unlike Lirra's raven hair, Katallia has wild auburn curls that refuse to be tamed by her braid. Seeva Soliel has hair the same color as Lirra's, but the texture is curlier and thicker, worn closer to her head.

"I'm afraid we've only brought more bad news," Katallia says.

"We've received correspondence from our sisters in the south of Malam." Seeva stands. She's a tall, graceful woman, whose height is complemented by long, emerald robes that drape from her shoulders. She pulls a piece of parchment from her pocket and passes it to me. "One of ours was attacked by a man. He trespassed on her land and went after her with a blade. To defend herself, she used her ability to heat him."

"Pardon?" While I've come to learn more about Channeler magic, there is still much I don't know. *Heat him?*

Katallia explains that rare, gifted fire Channelers can heat someone's internal body temperature.

"Were there any fatalities?" I think of the impact this sort of altercation can make on the local townspeople, and how quickly one rumor can spread fear.

Seeva's nod is solemn. "The man."

"She killed him?" The question comes out, astonishment more than anything freeing my words. It's rare that Channelers ever cause harm, let alone end another's life.

Seeva perches at the edge of her chair. Her eyes narrow to slits. "She did not kill him. He killed himself." Her words come out clipped with contempt.

Katallia's hands flap at Seeva, gesturing for her to relax. "From what we understand, the man was acting erratically and violently. The Channeler subdued him, and he retreated. He started destroying her property, tearing out her fence with his bare hands, and then, suddenly, he just dropped dead."

I rub my temples and drop down onto the cool, unyielding hearth. *Could it be caused by the fake Sanguine?*

"The problem now is townsfolk believe our Channeler sister caused his death." Seeva smooths the green material out over her lap before folding her hands and looking directly at me. "They want answers."

Of course they do. When tragedy occurs, and death is the toll, people are more willing to believe an explanation that confirms their prejudices than the truth. News of this man's death couldn't come at a worse time. The division in Malam is growing wider.

Seeva rises. "Our sister Channelers who have tried to reclaim their former lives in Malam have not been welcomed. This rough transition has made other Channelers leery to return. The Guild has discussed this matter, and we have decided we can no longer support the movement of Channelers back into Malam."

I gape at the women. The transition has certainly been rocky; however, Malam needs the returning Channelers as much as those women who were chased away during the Purge deserve to reclaim all that they lost.

"What of their homes? The land they left twenty years ago?"

Seeva flicks her green robes behind her and comes to stand beside the chair. "We cannot continue to encourage them to return to a land where their lives will be at risk solely because they possess Channeler abilities. They do not exist to help you redeem Malam's reputation, King Aodren. It is better to have lands lost than lives."

"A month ago, you were willing to support my effort to bring Channelers back into Malam."

"A month ago, Katallia was representing Malam in the jubilee and Leif stood as the Channelers' champion. His role in Malam has encouraged others to openly accept our sisters and welcome them back. But he did not take the field, and rumors have circulated that a Channeler is to blame."

I want to growl my frustration. Why is the truth so difficult for people to accept? "Will you consider waiting? I'm . . . there is much we're doing at the summit and tournament that will help change the tide."

Katallia and Seeva exchange grim expressions.

"We see your effort. You've done well in the tournament, but you have no Channeler for the jubilee. When people hear of the discord in Malam, they will not believe your land is a safe place for them." Seeva walks to Katallia's side. "We will wait until the end of the All Kingdoms' Summit, but even then, having no Channeler in the jubilee will send a message louder than our pull of support."

The weight of her words hits me like a boulder. Who will stand up for Malam at the jubilee? Nothing could be bleaker than the lack of possibilities. But I cannot give up. I rise, standing to face the Channelers. "I'll find someone."

CHAPTER

24

LIRRA

Now that the Kingdoms' Market is officially open for business, it's a bustle of activity. Canvas shops fill the entire field adjacent to the tournament on the southeast side. The grass has all been flattened, covered in tables and tents holding a smorgasbord of exotic fruits and vegetables, spun silks, softened pelts, tools, weapons, and the chatter of bartering.

After Aodren left yesterday morning, I worked on my glider all day to ready it for the jubilee. This morning, I took a final test flight. It went perfectly.

Now I have everything ready to register for the showcase.

Orli and I look like our normal selves, two friends in plain, commoner dresses, hair braided like crowns, summer flowers tucked behind our ears. We wait in line at a booth on the edge of the Kingdoms' Market, where Channelers eighteen or older have come to register and demonstrate their abilities. After each Channeler has presented her showpiece to the organizers, they will plan the order of performances during the showcase. Today, almost everyone who signs up will be able to participate.

I've brought a small glider with me, unassembled, in the pack on my shoulder. I shift the weight as Orli and I step up to the table, and Astoria greets us with a proud smile. She's wearing a ruffled, long-sleeved dress. I recognize it as one of her favorites. But it's a warm day, and sweat drips down the side of her rounded cheeks. She's been out here for a while.

"Do you need something to drink?" I ask.

She waves the question away. "I'm fine. Just a long day. I wondered when I'd see you."

"Maybe I changed my mind," I tease. I set my pack on the ground and reach for the quill to sign my name.

Her ink-smudged fingers cover mine. "That's a terrible thing to tease about. This is your heritage, and you should be here, not running errands for your father."

My hand slips on the parchment, leaving an ugly black spot behind. Her words remind me that he's still gone. He'll miss the jubilee. He'll miss my gliders.

I'll find Duff today. His stepdaughter will know something about Sanguine.

Astoria points me toward the tournament field, where

Channelers are separated by ability. Orli squeezes my hand, wishing me luck, and then leaves to wait beyond the field's edge. I'm proud of her for coming this far.

I move to where the other wind Channelers are gathered. We're called forward, one at a time, to present our abilities. Each person tries to impress the show coordinators, wanting to win the coveted spot of the showcase. Some possessing the same ability as me call on gusts of wind that howl around the field. Others play with leaves and grass clippings, making the piles swirl up into minicyclones. When it's my turn, I hurry and lash together my glider.

"Can I start over there?" I point at one of the nobles' stands erected around the field. I had hoped to launch it from a higher point, so it swoops down before hitting a pocket of warm air.

"All performances have to be done from the center of the field," the coordinator tells me. She checks out the line of women behind me and then widens her eyes as if to say, *Hurry up.*

I set my glider down and step away. I try not to think about how, in my dreams, Da was always here with me, cheering me on. I'll find a way to get him back for the jubilee. My hands extend out at my sides, calling the wind forward. It takes a few tries. My focus is as skittish as my pulse. I feel twitchy. I cannot find my grounding. Spurts of wind whip around the field, making the glider hop like a frog. I push more energy out of my hands, trying for better control, and a gust blasts the glider off the ground.

It shoots up to the sky—

And plummets, hitting the ground with a terrible crack.

No!

I run to where my broken wings lie, a tangle of wood and rope and white fabric, on the bright green lawn.

"Is that all?" the coordinator asks.

Embarrassment burns across my face like Channeler heat. I lift the limp wings. Two dowels are broken. My eyes itch. "Yeah, that's all."

"It's all right," I hear Astoria say. She ambles over and tells the coordinator that she can vouch for me. That during the jubilee I won't choke.

Doubt twists the coordinator's face, but she doesn't argue.

After packing my broken glider into my satchel, I trudge off the field beside Astoria.

"You have too much going on up here," she says, pointing to her temple. "You need to clear your mind. Whatever's vexing you, take care of it, so come Saturday, you're ready to show the world how powerful you are."

I nod, accepting her advice. Between Da's absence and the Sanguine mystery, it's no wonder I can't concentrate.

Orli and I try to walk through the least crowded aisles of vendors. Still, droves of people are here. A discordant clash of five different accents mixes with the scent of fresh bread, ripe produce, and even riper people. For Orli, the scene must be overwhelming.

I need to find Duff.

We've barely turned down the second row when people on all sides smoosh us. Based on snippets of conversations, I realize they're trying to reach the stage at the end of the booths, where an earth Channeler will soon be performing. These small market performances, precursors to the jubilee, raise crowd interest and share information about Channeler magic.

When an arm's width of space opens to my right, Orli and I escape the crush and dart behind the tents. A small alley gives the traders a place to store their wares. We continue weaving through traders until we're in the walkway of the fourth row of textile merchants.

Orli's arm chokes mine. Buggy eyes and lips a tight colorless line.

"Too much?"

"It's busier than I anticipated," she says with a sheepish shrug.

"Let's go in a booth for a while," I say. "Maybe the crowd will thin."

She nods. It doesn't take long to find a tent that is filled with a rainbow of yarn. At least a hundred spools in every color cover the merchant's table. This is the perfect spot for Orli, who has become obsessed with bright colors. A stop here isn't on today's plan, but I know the diversion will soothe her anxiety.

"Have you ever seen so many colors?" We duck into the tent.

"Never," she says with reverence for the array of spools, the fear all but faded from her face.

A few people run their fingers over the strands of wool, saying things like, "This is too rough for my needs," and "Too much give in this one," but their eyes tell a different story. They want the yarn. They're hoping to haggle a better deal.

"Anything you could use?" I ask.

"What isn't there to use?" Orli laughs, a welcome sound. "I want it all."

While she is busy perusing the yarn, I scan the stretch of merchants for Duff Baron and his stepdaughter, Prudence. Duff, a currier by trade, has had many dealings with Da. If not for Da's letter warning that his informants aren't trustworthy, I'd ask Duff outright about Sanguine and where Da's been searching. Instead, I've decided to talk to Prudence. We've had enough interactions throughout the last few years to solidify my instincts about her. Besides, she's not necessarily an informant, since she isn't key to her father's business. But I know, like me, she's privy to almost all her father's dealings.

Orli chooses a spool the cheery shade of sunflower petals, then hands the merchant a few coins. He wraps up the item in paper and binds it with string before asking Orli what she'll make with the yarn.

While they're talking, I turn back to the market, and my gaze catches on a dress. It hangs from a vendor's tent. Dyed to the cerulean brilliance of a clear cove, the fabric is stunning. The sleeve of the garment is being examined by a girl with tawny braids and curls. Everything about her hair and commoner dress is nondescript. Much like my appearance. But I'd recognize Prudence Baron anywhere.

"I'll be back in a moment," I tell Orli. She is consumed in conversation with the merchant and barely spares me a nod in response. Perfect.

I shimmy past two men bartering over a pelt and walk behind the tents until I reach my destination. "Lovely dress, Prudence."

She startles, hand flying to her mouth, and when she realizes it's me, she cups her rosy cheeks. "You goose! You scared me."

"I'm sorry."

"No, you're not." A laugh follows, and Prudence's arms wrap me in a hug. "How are you? I haven't seen you in months."

I squeeze her in return and then untangle myself. "Doing well."

"And how is —"

"She's also well. Better than before." The last time Prudence and I talked was on my return from Malam, bringing home Orli, energy-drained, fragile, and broken. "She's here, isn't she?"

"Yes, that's a big improvement." Genuine relief spreads over Prudence's face. "That's what I hoped to hear. I said a dozen prayers to the gods for you both. Will you be preforming at the jubilee? Will she?"

"That's my plan. I just signed up for the showcase."

"To show the wings you were building?"

I smile. "Yes, my glider."

"Well, you should get this dress for your performance. It would highlight your eyes splendidly." Even though her grandmother was a known Channeler, Prudence is giftless, like Eugenia. That's the way with Channeler magic. Astoria taught me that Channeler magic was a gift from the gods, but because it's been abused and devalued in our society, the gods have allowed it to fade with each passing generation.

"I'll consider it," I tell her, though buying a dress isn't on my list of things to accomplish today. I turn away from the dress and lower my voice. "Has Duff mentioned my da lately?"

"Not in the last month or so," she says, easily and openly. She's telling the truth, a fact that overwhelms me with disappointment. "I'll ask Duff. Maybe he has heard something."

Da's warning rings in my ears. "No. Don't." I touch her arm. "It's nothing to bother him about." Only, my response comes out strung tighter than a clothesline.

"Lirra. What's going on? And don't make up a lie, because I'm on to you."

I consider my options. Do I really think Duff is a problem

for Da? No. But Da needs secrecy. But he also didn't include me in his plans. So I'm free to make my own choices. Besides, Prudence isn't one of Da's informants. She's one of mine, and I'm free to talk to her. "There's a new import in the markets, something called Sanguine. Have you heard of this?"

The subtlest stiffening of her posture answers the question.

"You have. Do you know who's supplying the trade?"

"Is this why you're asking about your da? Has he started selling it?"

I shake my head.

She lifts a pair of gloves from a vendor's table, inspecting them in a way that blocks our faces from anyone who might be watching. "Lirra, this oil is bad business. You don't want to get involved."

"I've heard that before."

Prudence swats me with the gloves and then places them on the table. "Well, maybe it's something you should listen to."

Near the front of the tent, two women squabble over a spool of crimson yarn. I slide a stray hair around my ear and tip my head toward the outside of the tent. She follows me to the less crowded back ally.

"Millner is somehow connected to the oil. That's why you want to know about him and Sanguine?"

I shrug.

"Oh, Lirra," she says, sweet and pleading. "You've got your feet in more shadowy business than anyone else I know. No way did I think you'd be tangled up in the oil. Though I suppose I should've."

Her comment spreads something dark in me. A tiptoeing traitor, lurking between my head and heart that wishes for a life with fewer secrets, fewer disguises, fewer conversations in back alleys. What my life would have been if Da had never become the Archtraitor and turned to the business of selling secrets, if he hadn't needed to train me in the family business.

He might see me as me and not as an assistant.

It's a slippery thought, one that leads to others. I tamp it down, shame coursing in to fill my empty spaces. The closest I'll come to that life will be when I spread my wings at the jubilee. Sharing my love of flight will expose the most honest, most vulnerable version of myself. And even if Da cannot be there, it will be enough for me. It will.

"I only need to find the maker of the oil," I tell her. "What do you know?"

Prudence glances to the right. Perched on a stool two tents away, a man smokes a pipe.

Shifting her back to the possible onlooker, she links her arm through mine and guides me in the opposite direction. "All I know is my father was asked to take a few crates into Malam a couple months ago." Her whisper is nearly noiseless. "He didn't know what was in them. Didn't think much about it until he heard word from the trader, wanting more. Whatever was in the crates sold quickly. Duff doesn't usually deliver trade goods. Bigger loads are too conspicuous."

I nod, understanding. Everything she's said is sound.

"But then a second round of crates turned up at one of Duff's pickup locations, and attached to it was a hefty bag of coins. Duff delivered the goods. The trader who accepted them confessed some interesting things."

If this story were coming from anyone else, I might raise questions at the fact her father made a habit of delivering packages for people he didn't know. But then, I've known for years how Duff operates. Like my da, Duff understands that sometimes it's best not to know all the details.

"What kind of things?" I ask.

"He told Duff that the crates were full of oil. And people couldn't get enough of it. He said the oil was supposed to give people Channeler powers, but he had witnessed other reactions. He said the oil made people erratic and angry. He said he knew of a man who died from it."

"Yet he kept selling it?"

"You know how traders are. Most would sell a used coffin and toss the corpse if they thought they'd make a profit."

A harsh opinion, but true.

"I've heard the oil does those things too." I pause as a merchant shuffles out of a nearby tent to sort through a few bags. He notices us and points to the other side of his booth, explaining that we're in the wrong area. Prudence quickly apologizes and turns around so we head back the way we came.

"I don't have much time." I glance between the booths at the main walkways, checking on Orli. "I don't know how much longer Orli can handle this crowd. But does Duff know who was leaving the crates?"

Prudence shakes her head. "He picked them up from the same place he would pick up secret correspondences. He didn't know who was dropping them off. But a month ago, he arrived earlier than usual, and there were two cloaked men at the drop spot. One short and round through the middle, one tall. I think Duff knows who he saw, but he won't say. It's his secrecy that worries me. Makes me think whoever it is has a great deal of power."

I frown. "It could be anyone."

"I'll ask him again, but I'm not promising anything."

"Thank you. I can come back tom—"

A woman's scream stops us midconversation like the fall of an ax. All the small hairs on my body stand on end. *Orli.*

I turn away from Prudence and duck between the tents. The steady stream of people has clogged the walkway next to the yarn vendor. Their shouts and jeers are at a near frenzy. I shove between them, until I break free of the crowd.

I don't realize what I'm seeing at first. A broken rainbow of a hundred scattered spools of yarn cover the ground. The table is broken, and the distraught vendor rapidly attempts to gather his goods.

I spin around to the people who are yelling and egging someone on. Another cry, high-pitched panic, rises above the jeers.

"Orli," I shout, and shove through where there is no path between the people.

Someone pushes me back, and an elbow connects with my cheek. The impact shoots dizzying pain through my face. I gain my bearings and duck low to press through the people. On the other side of the aisle, I find Orli tucked into a corner of the fur trader's tent, her normally dark skin the color of ash, her fingers clutched tightly around a package. She's penned into the booth by two men who are fistfighting where the fur trader's table used to be. Pelts and skins are strewn across the muddy grass.

"Stop!" My shout goes unheard, but Orli's head jerks up, and she sees me. I wedge into the booth and dodge their flailing arms. My hand grasps Orli's just as the crowd erupts in cheers. I turn to find the fight is over. One man has knocked the other out, and guards have flooded the area. They quickly break up the press of people and seize the fighters.

To my shock, I realize the last man standing in this fight is Baltroit, Malam's champion. His eyes are bloodshot, and the way his breath pants from his nose reminds me of an angry bull. He tries to throw off the guards, shouting obscenities at them. But five of them subdue him, shackle his wrists, and drag him away, no doubt headed to the holding cell I'm intimately acquainted with.

Only, they don't get very far. Baltroit collapses, his body tipping and thudding to the ground like a felled tree.

Seeds. Someone needs to talk to him about laying off the ale. I've heard how much time he spends in the tavern.

I wrap an arm around Orli, and wait as a guard kneels at the champion's side to help him up. The man touches Baltroit and waits, and waits, and waits —

Face colorless as a specter, the guard glances up. "He's dead."

CHAPTER

25

AODREN

THE SUMMIT MEETING ENDS IN THE EARLY afternoon, and a royal convoy takes the leaders and dignitaries directly to the tournament field for the first day of the joust.

Discovering Malam needs a Channeler for the jubilee was a blow yesterday, but our ranking in the tournament is promising, keeping me hopeful and eager for today's competition. The joust is an event in which Baltroit typically dominates. He will hold the lance first today. Leif will compete in the second round.

Our arrival draws a crowd that clogs the road. From the carriage window, I can see people clamoring to get closer to the convoy of royal carriages. Even with Leif and Segrande at my side, a sense of vulnerability comes from sitting in a conspicuously ornate carriage, emblazoned with

Malam's identifying stag. Sneaking around with Lirra has become too much the norm. The thought brings a smile to my lips.

Guards flank us as we exit. All around, people drop, lowering to a knee. A scattering of cheers and clapping comes unexpectedly from the crowd.

I look out at the sea of downcast eyes. Supposedly a show of respect, downcast gazes have always felt like a disconnection. I've accepted the norm of it, never having had anyone give me contrary advice on how a king should act. I wonder if change isn't needed simply in terms of Channeler prejudices. Perhaps I need it too.

The other leaders and their guards walk straight to the field, but I gesture to the men around me, indicating our group should stop at the champions' tent first.

A portion of the crowd follows the other leaders. But many stay. Some hold maroon-and-gray flags.

"Thank you for coming." I address the Malamians. "Your support matters. Together let us cheer on our champion. And like the melee, may we take home another flag, another reason to be proud of who we are and where we come from."

Flags are waved while many clap and holler.

"Three cheers for Malam," someone shouts, and my heart soars.

This is the spark of unity I've been hoping for. I need them to take this pride back to Malam. I pump a fist in the air. "Our hearts, our blood, our lives for Malam!"

The words are repeated back, and the applause swells.

Guards part the crowd and escort us to the champions' tent. There, I stop and scan the faces of those around me, hoping to see Lirra. She's not in the group of people who have followed me from the carriage.

"Shall we take our seats, Your Highness?" Lord Segrande is bouncing on his toes, excited to see his son compete.

After a moment longer, it appears she's not coming. Something must have held her up. Reluctantly, I nod and our group walks to Malam's box.

Leif sits beside me. He's dressed in a set of clothes that have been made to fit perfectly under his armor. He wanted to watch the first round to size up the competition. Segrande paces the small walkway in front of the chairs. I wonder if he was equally anxious before the melee.

An air of disquiet fills the field as people flock to the edges. Their conversations about the competitors' fighting skill swell until the sound is nearly deafening.

The announcer calls out the names of the starting competitors, but no one can hear him until the trumpets play the opening tune and the crowd quiets. After the horns blare, the man shouts the competitors' names again, and a round of cheers rumbles from every edge of the tournament field.

A Shaerdanian guard in the kingdom's blue-and-gold uniform rushes onto our platform. His sudden appearance has Leif leaping up and reaching for his sword. The guards behind me step forward.

But the newcomer takes a hasty knee, showing that he's not a threat.

"Rise," I tell the man, and he bobs upward, his flushed skin coated in a sheen of perspiration.

"I come bearing news, Your Highness." He stares at me with wide eyes. His hands twitch at his sides.

"Go on."

"There was a fight in the market." The man's breath bursts out. His gaze darts from me to Leif. "And your champion was involved. Baltroit Bromier."

Hearing Baltroit's name shoots dread through my system. I can only imagine the worst about the fight he's mentioned. Baltroit has likely been thrown in the cells and will remain there for the rest of the week. He won't be able to compete.

"Where's my son?" Segrande demands.

In the background, the thunder of hooves and the first crash of jousting poles echo across the field. The guard's mouth bobs open and closed, regret and sympathy fill his eyes, and I *know* what he has to say is worse than I've imagined.

"He — he — he collapsed, sir. He's dead."

First, there was disbelief, angry shouts of denial, and threats against the guard.

Then, after we return to the castle, to the quiet, dim room where Baltroit's body has been laid on snowy sheets, only then is the terrible truth impossible to deny.

Segrande rushes to his son's side while I wait by the door,

giving him space. The last stretches of daylight slip through the window.

For a long moment, Segrande says nothing. He stares down at Baltroit's still, still form.

"My son," he whispers, the sound gravel and air, pain and pleading. "Oh, my boy, what's happened to you?"

I step forward, considering what I might say, as Segrande collapses against the edge of the bed, throwing his arms over his boy's chest.

A keening wail rises up out of Segrande, anguished and raw, as if part of his own body has been severed.

And then he weeps.

If there were some way I could lessen his pain, I would. All I can do is stand beside him, offering little comfort, as he curls protectively over Baltroit and presses a kiss to his son's brow. Despair rattles Segrande's fingers as he sweeps his son's disheveled golden hair to the side, fixing it like he probably did when Baltroit was a young boy.

I see the depth of love a father should have for his child, and I know Segrande's loss is something I'll never forget.

His pain and grief are etched on my soul.

CHAPTER

26

LIRRA

SNEAKING INTO THE CASTLE HAS BECOME ALL too familiar, and yet I know this will not be the last time.

It took a while to help Orli feel safe and calm again. Death is never an easy thing to witness. For Orli, haunted by recent trauma, the scene in the market today was a debilitating portal into her terror-filled past. I don't think she noticed me or realized I was the one holding her tight until long after I got her home.

Now I'm headed to the last place I should be going. Perhaps I, too, am struggling with Baltroit's death more than I realize, because the only place I want to be is with Aodren.

The castle is eerily silent. No doubt, mourning customs have begun.

I wait for the change of guards. Since two

are always stationed in the corridor, the only way to reach Aodren's room is by taking the servants' passage. When the guard on the bottom floor switches shifts, I have a free minute to sneak into the passage. The rest of the way to Malam's corridor is clear.

I pick the lock on Aodren's door and slip in unnoticed. His head is in his hands; he could be asleep, sitting at his desk. But when the door swishes closed, he glances up, eyes red. He shifts his elbows, and I see a few pieces of parchment and a quill. Who could he be writing to at this late hour?

"Hullo, Aodren."

He scrubs his face, appearing confused, as if he cannot fathom my reason for being here. "Now . . . isn't a good time for me."

"I know. I came because I didn't want you to be alone."

His eyes flare for a split second before his attention skips to the window, to me, to his hands that are now pressed against the desk in front of him. And in the breath between seconds, I suddenly see another side of Aodren, one I hadn't noticed before. A lonely man who has known very few friendships. Where does he go when he needs safe harbor? A place of comfort? Love?

After witnessing Baltroit in the market, seeing his uncontrollable rage, I'm certain Sanguine had something to do with his death. I'll have to tell Aodren eventually, but now isn't the time to discuss it. Aodren needs emotional support. I didn't know Baltroit well, but I have experience with loss.

"Today was hard," I tell him. "Do you want to talk about it?"

"No. I . . . It's very late."

"I can leave if you want."

"No." His fingers rake through his hair, scratching his scalp and then stopping to comb his messy locks back into submission. "I mean, you don't have to go."

"All right." I walk deeper into his chamber and move to the chair nearest his desk.

Aodren picks up the quill and rolls it in his hand. He doesn't say anything for a few moments, and while I'm content to sit here in silence with him, I get the feeling he has no one to help ease his burden. Da, Astoria, and Orli have always been there for me to turn over all my worries, frustrations, and fears. Who has been here for Aodren?

"I know we do not know each other well, but if you need to talk, I'm here."

He drops the quill and stares blankly at the parchment on his desk, half-covered in swoopy handwriting, though I cannot read what's written.

"I knew him, but I wasn't . . . he and I weren't friends," Aodren says. "He was my guard, and I—I could've done more to know him."

"I suppose we can always do more for those around us. But don't discredit yourself. You gave him an opportunity he longed for. And even after the melee, I know you treated him with respect and provided him encouragement."

Aodren shuts his eyes and breathes through his nose. "His death is in my name . . . like so many others," he murmurs, and a fissure forms in my heart. His voice, raw and bereft, makes me want to cry because he sounds so lost. So alone. And filled with guilt.

"This isn't your fault."

He looks at me, unconvinced, and then reaches for the letter he's composed. He folds it and starts to pinch the edges flat.

"When my mother died, I was badly burned in the fire," I find myself admitting.

Aodren's head snaps up, his fingers stilling on the letter. His attention unleashes a bout of nerves. It's a silly reaction, really. I can see he wants me to continue, but I'm not used to being open with anyone except Orli.

"My father blames himself for not coming to save us faster, not stopping the men who did it. He even blames himself for speaking out . . ." I pause, not wanting to lead him down the dark tangent of Malam's past.

"Against the Purge?" he asks, filling in my blank space.

I chew my lip. "Yes."

Aodren sets the letter down. "He was right to stand up against the Purge. He was the only one brave enough to do so."

"Yes. But can you see, the fire that killed my mother and scarred me changed my father as well. The grief was too much to bear. He questioned his actions and blamed himself. It's not

his fault, though. I never blamed him, and yet his guilt wors-
ened when I started having nightmares as a young girl."

"What were they about?"

"Mostly about being trapped. Tight spaces have been a
problem for me ever since my da told me how my mother died.
When the Malamian guards set fire to the walls of our home,
my mother and I were trapped inside. I don't remember it, of
course, but there is a large scar across my back and side, and
knowledge of her death has planted seeds of fear in me. I know
it's irrational, but the moment I'm confined, logic fades. And
I know it's not my father's fault. It was just something terrible
that happened."

"I'm sorry, Lirra," he says.

I respond with a grim smile. "I didn't mean to tell this
story to draw your sympathy."

"I know." Aodren picks up the letter and runs his fingers
over the crease. "I understand what you're saying about guilt.
But it's difficult not to feel responsible. At least in some part."

"You know it's not your fault, right?" I ask, pleading.

Aodren holds the letter, hands no longer working at anything. "On some level, yes. But . . ."

"But?"

"There was more I could have done."

"Like what?"

"If I had paid more attention to the rumors about the
Channeler oil before we reached the summit . . . If I had talked
to Baltroit. There are people from the market saying he died

because of the oil. There are guards who say they saw him drink it. I didn't know he had access to it." He stares up at the ceiling. "If I had known . . ."

"You could've what?" I push him, and a scowl shifts over his face. "There's no way of knowing if you would've found answers or caused more problems."

He abandons his seat and tosses the letter to the desk as if the ink is laced with poison. "Problems are my specialty lately." He cracks a cheerless grin.

"What else is going on?"

"An old rule was uncovered about the jubilee. King Gorenza brought to my attention that members of the Channelers Guild cannot represent a kingdom."

Was it only yesterday that Aodren talked to me about Aunt Katallia? If she cannot perform for Malam at the jubilee, who else will stand up for Malam?

"What will you do?" I ache for him. He already has too much to bear.

"Find another Channeler. At least, that is my hope. Time is running out and there are few willing to expose themselves as a Channeler to a kingdom with a history of killing Channelers."

"That doesn't sound promising."

"There is one girl I might've asked. I considered it even, but . . ."

"But what?"

"But it would require asking her to announce allegiance

to a kingdom she doesn't currently claim as her own. Nor do I think it would be fair to ask so much of her, after all Malam has done to her and her family," he says in a subdued tone. My skin tingles all over. I think he's talking about me. "I wouldn't mind, however, if she wanted to move to my kingdom for a time. I've gotten to know her over the past week, and I'd like to know her better."

My mouth goes dry. I could never stand up for Malam. Considering it makes me feel like a traitor to my mother, my father, and Astoria. But, at the same time, his suggestion starts a thrumming in my veins.

Aodren must sense my hesitancy, because he gives me a rueful smile. "Though I might want to ask, I won't do so officially. It wouldn't be fair."

I see what he's doing. He's putting me before Malam. In all the time we've spent together, this is the first time he's not putting his kingdom first. And I'm not sure what to make of it. Part of me wants to help him.

I'm relieved he hasn't really asked. Da and I left too much behind there. I could never go back.

The guilt and pressure he feels, I'll never fully understand, because I'll never rule a kingdom. His eyes are still closed, so I eliminate the distance separating us and wrap my arms around him, hoping to take away even an ounce of his pain. Aodren jolts in my arms, not realizing at first my intention, and then his hands clutch my back and tug me tight to his body.

Aodren has taken on the responsibility for thousands and thousands. His countrymen see the distance between themselves and him, looking to their king as a figurehead instead of a person. Yet Aodren chooses to see his people, their needs, their pain, and their grief, and take them on as his own.

I turn my head to rest my cheek on his chest, and listen to his heartbeat.

If only he didn't have to stay this course alone.

The mourning custom in Malam is two months of silence. In Shaerdan and Akaria it's one week. In the Plovian Isles it's three days. And in Kolontia it's not clear they mourn their dead at all.

Deaths have happened at the All Kingdoms' Summit before. Because it's impossible to put the entire event on hold for the many travelers who have come to Shaerdan, the rule book states mourning will be observed for two days.

People grieving don't wander far from their lodgings during this time. Because Baltroit was one of the kingdom champions and his father is a dignitary, Judge Auberdeen and all the visiting leaders honor Baltroit by leaving the castle to travel to the cliffs where the funeral is held. Baltroit's body is cremated, and his ashes are scattered over the sea.

I spend the days visiting Orli and Astoria, and testing my glider. I try asking around about the oil, determined to finish this job for Aodren and to help Da, even if he didn't want my assistance. My searches turn up nothing about the maker or the supplier. However, talking to guards and the tournament healers verifies that Baltroit did, in fact, take Sanguine. I want to share this information with Aodren, but though I catch a few glimpses of him, he's always surrounded by his guards, so we're not able to talk.

The distant chime of the bells from the cathedral on the cliff signals the end of mourning. The Kingdoms' Market will be open again. Tonight is the joust, and in two days is the jubilee showcase.

After bathing and donning a simple frock, I snag a biscuit and an apple and head out to my shed.

Loren and Kiefer tag along, two shoulder-height squirrels that crawl all over the place and get into everything while I attempt to load the components of the glider into the carriage. They bounce with excitement in their shared enthusiasm for the joust. For me, though, Baltroit's death, along with Da's absence, has dimmed my anticipation of any more tournament events. All I want is for the showcase to come and for my performance to go well. Today I'll drop off my glider at the Elementiary. For safety and organization, Astoria and the showcase organizers require all equipment be turned in today. They'll ensure it's taken to the field for the performances.

The kitchen door scrapes open, and Eugenia steps out with Julisa on her hip. My youngest sister, a roly-poly babe, has a ribbon hanging from her drooly mouth. A wet mark stains the shoulder of Eugenia's eggplant dress.

"Off to see Astoria?"

"Yes." I gently push the wings a little farther into the carriage before shutting the door.

Her gaze zips to the twins, who are now chasing each other around the carriage. She tells them to carry on elsewhere. When they pay her no heed, she huffs and shifts Julisa higher. "You've been gone a lot."

I nod. Eugenia has never needed additional information before.

"The boys said there was a young man here a few days ago." I cannot tell what Eugenia is thinking.

"Oh." I flounder for an answer. "He's a friend." It occurs to me that Eugenia might be upset that I've brought someone home. Someone Da hasn't allowed into his circle of trust. "He's not from around here. He won't be able to find his way back."

Her face lights with a knowing smile, though I'm not quite sure what she knows. "You haven't brought a friend home before."

"It's never been allowed."

She untangles her hair from Julisa's wet fingers. "Your da wants to keep us safe. But since you share his work, I think you're old enough to decide who is trustworthy. And who is dangerous." Eugenia's expression softens.

"You've been so busy doing work for your da. You deserve to invite a friend over." Eugenia doesn't know exactly what I've been doing, but when I've been gone this much before, the reason always involved Da's work. For the most part, that is true now.

"Orli visits every week."

"I meant a *male* friend." She tsks as she walks across the grass toward me. Julisa babbles on her hip, swinging the slobbery ribbon. "Is he in town for the festivities? He's welcome to come by again. You could invite him to Monday dinner."

I step back and fake a coughing fit to hide my laughter. If only she understood who she was suggesting I invite to dinner. "I don't think he'd be able to get away."

"Just keep the offer in mind." Eugenia watches the boys. When she speaks again, her tone is subdued. "I know not much has happened in Celize with the mourning of that poor Malamian boy, but have you heard any word?"

Smudges darken under her eyes, and her shoulders curl forward. I see now that Eugenia is tired. Possibly lonely.

I know what it's like to wait for Da. Seems like most of my life I've been waiting for him to return. Eugenia needs someone to run after the boys, to feed and change Julisa, to talk with.

Aye, that person could be me.

But it should be Da.

"Not yet. But soon," I tell her, calculating what other rocks I can look under to find out more about Sanguine. If I can solve this puzzle, Da will see that he can trust me to take more of the workload. Then he can be home with his family.

. . .

At the Elementiary, Astoria is talking to the group of Channelers who have come to check in and receive the performance placement for the upcoming showcase. Usually, she wears bright-colored dresses, but today she looks official in a long black dress that must be sweltering. To drum up interest for the two nights of jubilee, Channelers are encouraged to show their talents at the Kingdoms' Market. Then, in two days' time, at dusk, the tournament field will come alive with magic from twenty women. It'll be a pale comparison to the grand finale, but it will be exciting. Participating in any night of the jubilee is a dream come true.

"Remember, women, we want them to see the strength of our magic," Astoria says, enlivened by her cause. I'm too distracted by her arms, flapping like sluggish bat wings, to be inspired. "Let's put on a show that reminds the audience why our abilities are to be respected and revered. Those who aim to harm us will see how powerful we are."

One by one, Astoria reads through the list of names. As each woman receives her performance order, the chatter in the Elementiary grows.

"Lirra," Astoria calls out, and I wedge between two fire Channelers to get closer. "Your glider performance will be the last one of the night."

My audition was terrible, so I know Astoria orchestrated this. I don't mind, however. Jitters turn me into one of my bouncing brothers. I shout my thanks over the noisy crowd and rush out the door to my carriage, withdraw my glider, and place it in the covered wagon that will be carting props and necessities to the tournament field.

A shadow moves behind me. It's Astoria hobbling out of the Elementiary. "I wanted to see your beautiful glider before you loaded it."

The wings have been folded down and wrapped in material. The bundle lies on the cart. "You'll have to wait two more days."

She leans both hands on her cane and smiles at me with rheumy eyes. "I've waited this long. A couple days more is manageable."

Astoria knows how I struggled against the guilt of wanting to help my father and at the same time wanting to explore where the wind could take me. But she encouraged me to use my magic to strengthen Channeler society. Each time Da left for business, she nudged me to build something new. I came up with gliders of all sizes. Large ones to carry people. Small models for delivering letters—those, of course, have to be controlled by wind Channelers.

But Astoria is my champion.

The next few days will be busy. Seizing my chance, I hug her, feeling her fragile bones beneath my hands. "Thank you for getting me here."

"I'm proud of you, my girl. You were always meant to perform in the jubilee."

Those words dry out my throat and leave it aching. They mean a lot, coming from her. But I'd always imagined my father saying them.

She studies my face. "He'd be here if he could."

"Of course." I turn away, the tightness in my chest choking me. I don't want her to read anything more into my expression and feel pity for me. "If he'd let me help him more, he wouldn't be gone so often. Da doesn't have to manage the workload on his own."

She doesn't say anything.

Her silence always has a way of uncorking my frustrations. "Eugenia needs him. The littleuns cannot grow up without a father. All this time he's gone, he's missing out on their lives. If he would see that I'm here, that I'm capable of helping him —"

"He knows you are." She thunks her cane on the cobblestone. "You don't have to prove yourself to him."

"Don't I? We are partners and yet he doesn't trust me with anything that would actually lighten his load."

Even though she asked me to avoid Sanguine, I admit that I'm working with Aodren to find the maker and the supplier of the oil. "Da would've been back for the jubilee if he'd accepted help. But he didn't ask me. I'm sorry I didn't tell you before."

Astoria's papery skin turns sallow and bunches into a frown. She reaches out and squeezes my arm with ink-smudged fingers. "Lirra, you said you'd leave the oil alone."

I nod, swallowing hard. The last thing I want is to disappoint Astoria.

"I'm sorry. But Da's family needs him. If this is what it takes to prove he can trust me and rely on me more, then it's what I have to do."

I look at the front of the building to a group of Channelers leaving the Elementiary. Another day, I might join in their light steps, exuberant voices, and laughter. It's been five years since the last jubilee. Happiness is expected.

But long after I say goodbye, all I feel is dismay.

CHAPTER

27

AODREN

SEGRANDE IS TOO DISTRAUGHT TO RETURN TO the summit meetings to finalize trade agreements, so Leif attends in his stead and sits by my side.

It has been two days since we've met as leaders and dignitaries. Judge Auberdeen stands at the head of the table. His spectacles hang from the pocket of his formal coat. He greets everyone with pleasantries and proceeds to open the meeting as he did before. Except, instead of recounting the events attended and agreements made the previous day, he refers to when last we met. The day Baltroit died.

His mention of Lord Segrande's son is followed by murmured condolences or silence. Even Gorenza has finally dammed the flow of verbal attacks.

Leif has been on edge since I informed him that he would be attending this meeting. I hoped by now he'd feel more comfortable conversing with others.

He drums his fingertips on the arm of the chair, his thigh, and then the table.

"Last we met, we were discussing north-to-south routes." Judge Auberdeen slips into the empty seat beside Judge Soma. "Shall we start there?"

Most nod or mutter an agreement.

"Lord Segrande had proposed a route from Akaria that would run through Shaerdan's southern end and wind up through Malam and into Kolontia." I stand and lean over the table to gesture to the map, pointing out the exact cities the route would touch. "This would be advantageous for all of us, because for the first time we'd have one route that winds through each of our kingdoms."

"What of Plovia?" Queen Isadora's fingers rest against the thick obsidian braid that coils over her shoulder and down the front of her yellow dress.

I extend my reach over the table and point at the largest port city in Akaria. "The route that runs north–south doesn't truly start or end here. I'd hoped for a regular shipping route from Plovia to Akaria. If we can align meeting times between ship merchants and traders on land, this route will link us all."

She glances to her dignitary, seeking confirmation. When he nods, she turns to me and lifts her dainty chin. "We're intrigued."

"As are we," says Fa Olema.

I sit in my chair, allowing others to examine the map.

Queen Isadora slides her hair over her shoulder and reaches for the parchment. But Gorenza's hand slams down on the table, stopping her from moving it.

"There's no point discussing shipping routes until we agree it's a favorable trade for the kingdoms on the continent."

The queen draws in a hiss of a breath. Her hands rest one on top of the other on the table. Long neck, flawless features, she is the picture of poise. But her eyes are clear and focused. Beneath the calm exterior she presents, a viper waits, ready to sink its fangs into Gorenza.

He stands, leaning his stocky weight on one hand. The man is oblivious to Isadora's fury. "We're hesitant to open a route through our southern mountains. These areas are a concern." His free hand sweeps over the map, encompassing nearly all of my kingdom. "How can we monitor the goods coming through, when anything can get into Malam?"

"What does that mean?" Leif balls up his fists in his lap.

Gorenza looks down his sharp beaklike nose. "Your fellow champion died so easily in that market brawl. It's suspect, no?"

"What have you heard?" I demand. How does Gorenza know about Baltroit? The circle of people who know about the oil is small.

He stares at me, giving nothing away with his flat expression. "I think we should be asking—what secrets are you hiding?"

In closed conversation this week with Ku Toa, Seeva, and Katallia, I confessed all I've learned about the Channeler oil and the effects it has on the takers. Based on the stories from the guards, I am almost certain Baltroit ingested Sanguine. This discussion, however, wasn't shared with anyone else. Not even Segrande or Leif. They were deep in mourning. I didn't want to stain their memories of Baltroit. Until more information can be found, I plan to keep quiet.

Gorenza pounds his fist on the table. "You want us to set up trade routes through your land, when there is no guarantee of safety."

"Traders have always been safe in Malam." Leif grips the chair arms.

Gorenza sits and shakes his head. "You are a foolish child, just like your boy king."

My captain whips to face me.

"Leif," I say, under my breath, warning him away from reacting.

"You're too young to know," Gorenza sneers. "Too young to remember the fear traders had of Malam. When Malam closed its borders before, it shut down all trade. And now you want it back?"

"We're moving on from the past," I say, but my comment falls on deaf ears.

Gorenza leans back in his chair and picks something out

of his teeth. "Like spoiled children, you want your routes back."

"Yer a bloody fool. You don't know what yer talking about." Leif shoves his chair away from the table and lurches to standing. "All yer interested in doing is holding back Malam."

"Leif." I stand. "Sit. Down."

Begrudgingly, he does, and goes right back to tapping his fingers. Across the table, Gorenza grinds his teeth, looking madder than a bull on stampede.

It matters not that Gorenza isn't Leif's king. It is still a requirement for respect to be shown to all leaders during the summit. While Leif's frustration is understandable, his verbal attack is not.

The meeting continues for a short time with no progress, until the tension in the room swells. It's then that Judge Soma suggests a break, since the second half of the joust has been rescheduled for this afternoon. Perhaps that's exactly what Leif needs.

The other tournament events were held in the evening. The joust, however, will begin midafternoon, to accommodate the mourning schedule changes.

The blue sky would be spotless if not for two slashes of dirty gray clouds. Unlike the soft golden glow of the tournament lanterns, the sun's harsh brightness exposes all the field's flaws. Mud, caked and dried, mats the grass. Divots give the field a pimpled appearance. Chipped paint flakes from the royal stands. Spectators press together, a sheen of perspiration glossing their unsmiling faces.

And from the east end, piles of horse dung give off a foul odor.

The announcer takes the stand across the field from where I sit in Malam's nobles' section. Lord Segrande is seated on my left-hand side. He's spoken few words since Baltroit's passing, and so I may as well be sitting alone. No other lord from Malam has come to sit with us. The Malamian fans nearby are subdued.

The announcer waves the black and silver banner for Kolontia as Hemmet rides onto the field. The clanking plated armor worn for the joust covers all of him. His horse wears the black and silver ribbons. And the pole he carries has been painted in matching colors. On the southeast side, the crowd cheers.

The announcer lifts Akaria's red and yellow banner and calls Fehana to the field. Her black armor gleams under the sun as she rides out on a raven black horse, a beast that stands a head taller than Hemmet's steed. A wind of whispers rolls through the crowd. Everyone is in awe of the southland horse. When Fehana loops the field, her appearance awakens the onlookers.

Before the event begins, as the riders move to opposite ends of the jousting field, the crowd rises, shouting and cheering.

A horn blares. Hoofs thud, armor clanks, lances crunch, and the crowd screams.

Fehana wins the first match.

The sounds repeat as each match is announced and those competitors enter the field. Leif must joust twice as many times to make up for Baltroit's absence.

In the third round, the announcer calls for Leif and Folger from Shaerdan. In silver armor, with Malam's colors hanging from his painted horse, Leif enters the field, and immediately the crowd cheers. People shout for the Channeler Defender, their enthusiasm reminding me why I needed Leif in this competition. In spite of this being his first time on the field, the support of the spectators proves he's a new crowd favorite. A Malamian favorite.

Their cheers buoy up my hope. Today's meeting made me realize the losses Leif has recently suffered. His predecessor was killed during the coup. His relationship with a woman in Malam ended. And now he's lost Baltroit, his co-competitor. It makes sense that he needs an outlet, somewhere to release his anger. I should've thought about that before bringing him into a trade meeting.

On this field is where he belongs.

The horn sounds, and all of Malam holds their breath as Leif gallops toward the Shaerdanian.

I'm suddenly nervous. If Folger hits him in the wrong spot, will Leif's wound reopen? Will it take him out of the competition for good?

Their clanking armor and the beat of the horses and the

screams of the crowd grow louder. And then Leif thrusts the lance at Folger's chest. The impact knocks the Shaerdanian from his horse.

Folger falls. Leif wins.

I clap and shout for the Channeler Defender. This is a man Malam can rally around.

Segrande and I are standing near the carriage, guards at our sides, when my eyes catch on Leif's red head. In the haze of dusk, I lost track of him moments ago. He's on the shoulders of the crowd, being carried toward the tavern tents. I hear him call out for Malam, and the people swarming his sides echo his cry. After the first match, Leif successfully unseated his following three opponents. Though Malam lost by one technical point to Kolontia, the Malamians didn't care. They hoisted him up and paraded him around.

He is their winner. And the sight couldn't make me happier.

They lower Leif to the ground. People flock around him, slap his back, laugh and talk and cheer their champion. Though dusk has fallen, I see how their faces shine with pride. The sight ignites a blaze of hope in my chest. This was what I'd hoped for when we came to the summit.

Musicians, standing in the open grassy area outside the tavern tents, play a boisterous tune with their fiddles and drums. As night deepens, lanterns start to blaze to life, emanating a soft golden glow that falls over the couples dancing. Partners swing each other around in circles, their laughter joining the night's music.

"Go with him," Segrande says. His dark mood hasn't broken since Baltroit's death. "Celebrate with Leif. We have no more meetings. Let me be alone today."

"Were we not going to discuss today's trade meeting?"

Segrande doesn't answer, but it's as if his desire to be alone conjured up a familiar brunette. She strolls to the tavern tents in a summer dress. The sight of Lirra beckons me forward. Perhaps it would be best if I celebrated with my countrymen and gave Segrande time alone. He needs time to grieve.

Lirra moves to Leif's side. He notices her, and his expression changes. It becomes more animated, more open. He dwarfs her, a fact made obvious by the placement of his arm around her narrow shoulders. Lirra leans into the embrace and lifts her mouth toward his ear. I pause, wondering if perhaps I might be interrupting a private moment. His arms wrap around her, closing their embrace, and then they're both spinning around, joining the dancers.

I watch her with Leif, seeing the way she dedicates all of her attention to whatever he's saying. The way laughter quakes through her entire body. The way she must make him feel like a king.

And I realize that I've allowed things to go on too long with Lirra.

Their friendship is easy and free. Easier than anything

Lirra and I could ever share. What Segrande said the day we were by the docks makes sense now. The price of actually being king is solitude. My life is for Malam, the very kingdom that destroyed Lirra's family. Killed her mother. Left scars on her body. It wouldn't be fair of me to expect Lirra to forget those transgressions and live in the kingdom that inflicted harm and destruction in her life.

She must already know that there could never be anything real between us. Perhaps she has already accepted that what we've been sharing is nothing more than a Summit dalliance.

My chest tightens and cracks.

The summit will be over soon, and yet there is much work left to be done. There isn't time left to further this relationship. Nor is there reason if we will never have a future together.

"Changed your mind?" Segrande asks, and I realize I've stopped walking. "Fine, let's go. You can catch me up on today's trade meeting, and we can discuss the jubilee. Have you found someone yet?"

"No, I haven't." I tear my gaze away and follow him into the carriage. In spite of the warm evening, my body goes cold.

CHAPTER

28

LIRRA

PRUDENCE MEETS ME AT THE JOUST. SHE SIdles up to me right as the winners are announced. The boom of celebration drowns out our voices, so we wait as the Kolontians and Malamians swarm the field. They lift their competitors and carry them out, singing their kingdom's praises. Prudence and I trudge slowly behind the mass exodus. If only I had my glider here, I could sail us right over the crowd.

When we finally break free, I accompany her to her family's merchant tent. We duck into the corner for privacy.

"I asked around." She tips her head so a wave of tawny hair keeps our conversation private from anyone who might pass by. "No one is talking."

"You mean, they might know something, but they're not talking?"

She nods.

"Who has enough power to silence every trader here?"

"I don't know," she whispers. "You said you're looking for the maker. The question is, what Channeler has that much power?"

Immediately, four women come to mind. The Channelers Guild. I know it's not them, but whomever it is has power that rivals theirs.

"I considered the Guild," she says.

"It's not them."

She shrugs. "Maybe not. But it's interesting your aunt Katallia cannot represent Malam in the jubilee. Everyone's talking about it, and it doesn't look good for Malam."

I don't like how her suggestion paints my aunt. Nor do I like that Aodren has no Channeler to represent Malam. I think of the conversation I had with Aodren the night Baltroit died and I wonder if I should've made a different decision. It worries me that he hasn't found someone yet. "What does that have to do with Sanguine?"

She waves her hand for me to lower my voice, and we edge closer to a table of quills. "All I'm saying is there's been a lot of talk about how Channelers are treated in Malam, and how it's only getting worse. When King Aodren has no Channeler willing to stand up for him, people might see that as the breaking point of their acceptance for Malam."

I rub my temples. "Yes, Malam has a terrible history. But Aodren wants to change that. The problem is, someone keeps sending fake Sanguine to Malam, and people are ingesting it, and it's harming them. So naturally, they blame the Channelers. Which makes things worse. It's a terrible cycle."

"Exactly my point."

I straighten and glance out the tent opening to the people passing by. The crowds that gathered for the joust filter down the aisles of the market. The day is shifting into night.

I am stuck on what she's said. Could it be that whoever is making Sanguine is doing so to cause disputes in Malam between Channelers and the giftless?

With a head full of questions and no answers, I bid Prudence goodbye and rush to the tavern tents. Da used to say that a pint of ale solves problems. Anywhere ale flows regularly, there is sure to be a fertile field of information ready for harvest. A little patience is all that's needed to overhear a few secrets.

I see Leif just outside the tent, surrounded by fans. They don't deter me. I rush to congratulate him.

Though there must be two dozen people wanting to shake his hand or pat his back, Leif sees me and smiles in relief.

"You did well," I say.

He cannot hear me over the clash of music and cheers. He steps closer and leans in.

I repeat myself, and he looks at me with so much gratitude. "You really think so?"

"Of course, you were amazing." I cannot understand how he would doubt himself, but the thought is gone as soon as Leif cries, "Let's dance."

He swings me around to the fiddler's tune until we're both dizzy and I can hardly breathe.

"Let me take a break," I say, and then because there are men and women lined up to congratulate him, I add, "Go, dance with another."

When we part ways, I go into a tent and order water. The barkeep gives me a hard time, but fills my request. Sipping water from a mug, I sit at a table near the rear. There I wait and listen.

It is at least an hour before Leif saunters into the tent. I lift my hand to wave him over so we can talk more about his jousts, but he doesn't notice me. He stalks to the makeshift bar, sits on a stool, and orders a drink.

My patience often wanes while waiting for information to land in my lap, so I pass the time by watching Leif. The way his foot repeats an impatient tap on the stool's rung amuses me. Leif glances at the barkeep, who has stopped to talk to another man. A flash of anger registers on Leif's face, an unusual expression for him. My curiosity is fully snagged now. I watch, rapt, as he reaches into his pocket and withdraws something small. I'm not sure what he's holding until his hand lifts, providing a glimpse of a bottle. Leif pops the cork and quickly tips it to his lips. In that brief second, the tent's lanterns illuminate the draining burgundy liquid.

No. It cannot be.

How can he drink Sanguine after Baltroit's death?

I'm on my feet and moving to his side in a blink, unable to sit back and watch my friend fall victim to its clutches just as Baltroit did.

"What was that?" I whisper by Leif's ear.

He jerks out of his chair, obviously startled to find me leaning over his shoulder. "Lirra, what are you doing here? Spying on me?"

"First, I told you I was coming in here an hour ago. Second, only a man with a guilty conscience would be worried about that. Third, if that was what I think it was, I'm glad I was here to spy on you. Tell me what's going on. Now."

Leif's gaze shifts around and then he's striding out of the tent and barking at me to follow. This man is not the Leif I know. This Leif stops in the small alley outside the tent, where the barkeeps toss their slop. It smells of fermented excrement. Here, the lantern light doesn't quite reach the ground. I refuse to walk any farther.

I gag, but Leif doesn't seem to notice the stench. He spins around to face me, finger pointed at my nose. "Don't be putting my business out there for everyone to hear. You've got a loud mouth."

"Me?" I ask, pierced by his unexpected words. They hurt more than I want to admit. This man isn't the kind cousin I've come to know and love. "No one overheard. Please, tell me what you drank."

People walk by, and Leif pops his neck. When more pass, he grips his shoulder. With each group that comes near to our secluded location, his signs of edginess increase.

I pray for a lull, and when it comes, I press him on the issue again. "Are you taking Sanguine?"

He lets out a quiet "aye."

"Why?" The question explodes out of me. Ku Toa's Sanguine helped Leif make a miraculous recovery. Why would he want the imposter? It has so many terrible side effects.

But then realization dawns . . . The shock of it hits like a slap across the cheek.

I cover my mouth.

When Aodren and I discovered the fake, dangerous oil, Leif was still unconscious. Since he's woken, he hasn't been around anytime Aodren and I discussed new information we'd uncovered. My guess is Aodren has been busy and overlooked explaining to Leif the difference.

"I don't see what you're all worked up over. It helped me heal," he says. "Figured more couldn't hurt."

Seeds. "Leif, you couldn't be more wrong." I launch into everything I know about the fake Sanguine. In spite of his short temper and harsh tone, at his core, this bear of a man is trustworthy, honorable, and good. His expression twists with conflict, and a flush rises to his freckles as he listens.

When I finish divulging all the details of the imposter oil and the role it likely played in Baltroit's death, Leif grips a handful of his auburn hair and stares off into the night.

"Ku Toa only had the one bottle," he says after a beat, his tone the gray blue of a stormy sea. "Bludger. I didn't know it was different. I swear it, Lir. Figured it'd get me into fighting shape faster. Get me off my duff so I wasn't a useless bludgering sack. Then I could help out the king like a bloody captain should." He kicks the grass, and whatever else might be on top.

"*Gods,* I didn't know." Remorse drags in his words, pulls down his shoulders, and cracks my heart open.

"You couldn't have known." I step backwards, slowly coaxing him out of the alley.

"Why didn't you tell me sooner?" he asks, the question simmering with aggravation.

"With everything that was going on, I suppose it was overlooked."

He lets out a dissatisfied grunt. And takes another step toward me.

"Where did you get the oil?"

"Baltroit."

"Who did he get it from?"

Leif stares up at the sky. "I think he said Otto. Baltroit knew some of the other champions had used it to give them an edge. Said it was only fair he used it too." He pulls the bottle out of his pocket and rolls it between his palms. "If I'd known . . . I thought it was more of the same. I just . . . didn't wanna let Aodren down."

When his gaze drops to my face, it's brimming with regret. "No more. I won't take any more."

"Good idea."

"Lirra" — my name is a question, one full of worry — "let me tell the king on my own, yeah? It should come from me."

"Of course." Leif has a good heart.

We leave the tavern tent. Leif trudges toward the carriages, his steps heavy and slow, while I dart toward the darkened field. Though on different paths, we have the same destination — the summer castle.

I sneak through the servants' passages, my steps quicker, more eager than they should be in light of the news I bear. Aodren has been on my mind for the last two days. Knowing I'm soon to see him makes my bones trill like I'm carrying a bolt of lightning.

Regardless of the late hour, celebrations echo from other kingdoms' corridors, clinking goblets, cheers, and boisterous voices. Malam's hall, however, is quiet. I watch Lord Segrande leave King Aodren's room, cross the hall, and enter his personal quarters. I check Leif's door and hear him snoring, then I move to Aodren's. I hear nothing, but since Segrande just left, I know Aodren must be there. Could he have fallen asleep already?

I pick the lock on his chamber and enter.

Aodren sits in a large chair beside the unlit fireplace, a book in hand, the weak light from the wall sconce casting shadows on half his face. The door snicks shut, and he looks up.

"The only person who would break into my room at this hour would be you, Lirra."

The way he speaks my name, a soft rasp, releases a flock of birds inside me. I feel the fluttering frenzy of their wings and the weightlessness of their flight. It makes me bold. "It was strange to not see you these past few days. Would you think me odd if I said I missed your company?"

A line trenches between his brows. He rises, and his hands fumble to button his gaping shirt. I stare at him, his odd reaction, and suddenly rethink my comment. Have I said too much? The unexpected awkwardness shoos the birds away.

"I was teasing," I say, wanting to erase the last minute. He knows I'm lying.

Aodren's hand flattens over his chest. He leaves the desk and sits by the fireplace. "Forgive me. My appearance is not appropriate for company."

"You're more dressed than the first time I snuck in." I try for lighthearted. It comes out stiff. "I can suffer your shocking state of undress."

"Lirra." This time my name has no soft corners. This time it's a warning.

The toe of my boot dips into the tight grooves of the stone floor. My insecurity rears up. Our meetings are usually easy. In a remarkably short time, Aodren has come to know me better than most. He's been privy to my secrets and fears. Have I done something wrong? Forgotten something?

The answer comes instantly— He's lost a man, and here I am showing no sympathy.

My head is too full of the jubilee, Aodren, the conversations with Prudence, and Leif's confession about Sanguine.

"I'm sorry." I rush forward and take the seat closest to his. "Baltroit's death must be difficult for you."

"It has been more so for Lord Segrande."

"Baltroit is actually the reason I came to talk to you tonight." I launch into the information that confirms the cause of Baltroit's death, while managing to keep Leif out of the discussion. I explain that Baltroit took the oil, thinking it would be beneficial. He had gotten some before the first night of melee. He didn't understand the dangers but liked his increased ability during the fight. He kept taking the Sanguine after that.

"Do you know who gave Baltroit Sanguine?"

"I think it was Otto." I scoot to the edge of the cushion. "Also, I met with someone today." I recount the story Prudence told me last week about Duff Baron, the oil, and the two men.

"She has no idea who it was?"

"Actually, I was thinking about what I know about Sanguine. And I realized that it would have to be made by someone who is quite powerful. Someone as powerful as a member of the Channelers Guild."

"Do you suspect one of them? They've pledged their support to Malam. I trust them."

"There has been disunity between the women before." I clutch my stomach, truly considering if it's a possibility. With results as dire as we've seen, it would be foolish to completely dismiss anyone as a suspect. "I don't like discussing the possibility of this any more than you, but it's something to consider."

He folds forward, elbows landing on knees. His face is drawn, disbelief and frustration muddying his unfocused stare at the fireplace. "You're suggesting that it could really be anyone. Even a Guild member. As long as that person has a reason to hate Malam."

I reach forward to twine my fingers through his like the time he took my hand in the tunnel under the summer castle.

He stands, moving away from me, every piece of him abruptly morphing into the cool, aloof king of Malam, a man I haven't seen since we first met. "I thought there was a chance the oil was being misused. That perhaps the maker didn't know. It's not possible. People are dying. The maker must know the dangers. Which means it is not Katallia or Seeva. Neither one of them has marks of dark magic on their hands, arms, or neck. For the amount of oil in Malam and Shaerdan, the sign of dark magic would be unmistakable."

He's right. In my shock of considering it might be one of the Guild members, I overlooked that fact.

"Is there anything more?"

"I — I don't think so."

"Thank you for delivering the information. I appreciate your time. As you can see, the hour is late, so . . ." He walks to the door, stride sharp and brusque, a clear sign he wants me to go.

I stand, but remain rooted to the floor, silence surrounding us, uncomfortable and itchy, like an ill-fitted starched shirt.

"Aodren." My tone is thin and uncertain.

His fingers hover on the door handle.

"Have I . . ." I fight down the overwhelming rush of vulnerability. "Have I offended you?"

"No, of course not."

"You seem upset. And if I caused it or did something wrong, I want you to tell me."

"My concern is with the late hour. It's not proper for you to be here." Aodren faces the door.

He showed no care for propriety last week when he asked me to stay. Or when he slept at my home. Is this a castoff? I tug at my commoner's dress, confusion, hurt, and anger prickling through me. Did I imagine something more between us? Not a true relationship, per se, since he is the king of Malam and I'm a Shaerdanian Channeler, but I thought there was a spark.

I think of our kiss, and the truths I told him in Da's cellar, and my eyes burn.

It hurts to look at him and see the cool, aloof profile. My dry throat clicks on each swallow as I pull a response together, trying to say something honest that won't make things worse. "I didn't like you much at first. I thought you were a copy of your father."

Aodren winces.

"You surprised me because you're nothing like him. You care about your people, and you care about Channelers. I saw the truth in you, and I let down my guard, which isn't something I usually do so quickly. But I enjoyed our time together. And, well . . . I thought you felt the same. A mistake, of course. Please, if I've acted too brazen or overstepped my bounds, tell me. I'd like to sort this out so we can keep working together."

He turns and stares at me as if I'm the puzzle that needs sorting out. "You wonder if you overstepped your bounds, but the truth is, I fear I've overstepped mine."

I bite down on my lip. "I don't understand."

"I saw you and Leif tonight. You were laughing with him. It reminded me that we never were supposed to become more than friends. I'm returning to Malam in a week. And you live here. That's a long distance to maintain a friendship . . . or something more. There's nothing that can become of us beyond this week."

Nothing can become of us.

He's explaining the reasons, but he is shifting from one point to the next too quickly. My brain doesn't have time to keep up with what he's saying. The hurt rolls through my body, finding all the corners and shadows.

"I've allowed things to go on too long," he says.

I squeeze my eyes shut, unable to look him in the eye while it feels like everything is crumbling on the inside. What he's said pierces me. But I cannot fault him, because he's right. He's leaving soon. I will not follow him. There isn't a future for me in Malam. And as king, he couldn't leave his kingdom to make regular visits to Shaerdan. There is no future for us.

CHAPTER

29

AODREN

AFTER THE NEXT DAY'S SUMMIT MEETING, I send a message to Segrande, Leif, the Channelers Guild, and the Akarian leadership, requesting a brief meeting in my chamber before the evening meal. When everyone arrives, there isn't much time to talk. But it would be unwise to put off discussing Sanguine any longer. Now that there have been two deaths —Baltroit and the man who attacked the Channeler in Malam—the efforts to stop the supplier must extend to someone other than Lirra. I have to start trusting other people to help me. To my chagrin, I haven't spoken with Leif and Segrande about the Channeler oil since our first conversation about the oil rumors. I've been too distracted with the melee, Baltroit's death, and Lirra.

At the thought of her, a dull ache awakens at the base of my skull.

I rub my neck. Once everyone is seated near the grand hearth in my room, I bring up the oil. "I've asked you all to come so we might discuss Sanguine."

Last week, Segrande sent the Guild a letter detailing the reports we'd received from the Malamian lords. Sanguine was mentioned, but I've learned so much more since the letter was penned. I quickly divulge most of what I know about the oil. I explain that there is a real oil and a fake oil.

"We received Lord Segrande's letter, though the information was a little late in coming." Seeva says with a piercing, scolding look. "When Channelers are in danger, we demand that the Guild be informed immediately. Luckily, we had already been looking into the oil. Months ago, we heard rumors in Malam of this oil, but thought they were mere misunderstandings linked to the new imports of Channeler remedies. After all, true Sanguine is legendary, and the older generations of Malamians have heard of it before. When one of our Channeler sisters was detained in Malam and accused of murder, we investigated further and discovered there is, in fact, another oil being referred to as Sanguine." Her gaze swings to me, punctuated by the pursing of her lips, as if to say, *You should have told us sooner.*

I blow out an irritated breath. I should be more sympathetic to their frustration. I could have told them sooner, but I didn't know what information to share. There was little I knew about the oil. What I know now was mostly handed to me by Lirra.

"It was not my intention to withhold information. I could have shared this information before now. However, I wasn't certain of the threat until after arriving in Shaerdan for the summit," I say needing her to understand deception wasn't my intent. "And even after arriving, I've had to sort between rumors and substance."

Leif cracks his knuckles, seeming irritated. "So, you've been gathering information, sir?"

"I have," say and continue, explaining the two different Sanguines and my belief that whoever is supplying the imposter oil to traders is doing so with the purpose of fooling buyers into believing they're purchasing the real Sanguine and attaining Channeler magic. Beside me, Leif shifts in his seat. He was restless during the summit meeting as well. Perhaps all this talk makes him feel uncomfortable since it is real Sanguine that saved his life. I sum up my information by explaining the hazards of ingesting the fake oil.

Katallia sends a warm, reassuring smile, but my comments draw frowns from Leif and Segrande. They aren't pleased to hear that I've been working on this without them. I have been remiss by focusing so much on Lirra. What happened last night is for the best.

"It seems we've come to similar conclusions." Seeva, who has been standing near the hearth, crosses to the open seat beside Fa Olema. "You didn't mention your source, though. Who gave you this information?"

I hesitate, not wanting to betray Lirra. Each person in this room, however, can be trusted with the Elementiary woman's name. "Astoria. She runs the Elementiary here."

"A credible source." Seeva says. "Did she mention anything about who is making the oil?"

I shake my head.

Fa Olema, who has sat mostly silent through our conversation, leans forward in his chair. "What are you doing to stop the trade?"

"I am working with another to identify the supplier," I say, though that search has been unfruitful.

"Why not start with the traders and work your way back to the supplier?" Seeva asks.

"The only way to prevent a weed from spreading is to tear out its root," Ku Toa answers before I can. She has been standing beside my window. She walks away from it, her robes sweeping the ground. The evening twinkles from the window behind her. "Alerting the traders might alert the creator."

She crosses to the chair beside the desk. The wood creaks as she sits down.

I draw strength from her unlikely alliance. "Exactly. If we can find who is making the oil, we can halt production. We will deal with the traders later."

"The analogy makes sense if you can find the creator

through other means," Seeva says. "What if the only way to find the root of this problem is by starting with the traders?"

I lean forward. "A valid concern. But one we shouldn't pursue until we've exhausted all other methods."

Seeva taps her finger on the folds of blue fabric hanging off her knee. Her cheeks are drawn down in a frown.

Fa Olema looks at Seeva. "What has you worried?" His ancient voice crawls out of him.

"Quietly seeking out the supplier could take time," she says and then, turning her attention to me, adds, "In the meantime, the damaging effects of the imposter oil will be blamed on Channelers. Your kingdom is already divided. What if old fears, spurred by this oil, begin to spread again? Your lords' letters prove it's already happening. Malam may return to old ways, and other kingdoms may go down the same path."

"You mean, a path we have already left." Segrande cuts into the conversation, the first he's spoken today. The lack of energy in his words softens their impact, and a moment passes before anyone in the room turns to look at him. He leans against the wall near the door. His arms are crossed. He looks haggard and ten-years older than the man who accompanied me into Shaerdan.

"Official treatment of Channelers in Malam may have changed, perhaps," says Seeva, her eyes seeming more lined and tired. The stress is taking a toll on her. "But there are leaps that need to be made before Channelers will feel safe and welcomed in your kingdom."

"Perhaps they should recognize the efforts that have already been made." Leif cuts in, his eyes darting between Seeva and his hands. He stands up and abandons his chair for a place beside the window. He looks in the direction of the city of tents, the tournament field, and the Kingdoms' Market. "If they still don't feel welcome, that's on them."

I have barely registered his callous, misrepresentative comment when Seeva rises. She yanks her flowing blue dress around the chair and points a long, straight finger at Leif. "You have been hailed as a champion for Channelers. And yet you think the rejection, the hatred, the harm, the killing is on us?" Her pitch peaks and then drops to a hiss. She is an ocean storm. "Your ignorance is fathomless."

Leif blinks, his expression switching from anger to one stricken with shame. Flush faced, he mutters an apology. What has gotten into him?

We spend the remaining time organizing a plan. We agree that we'll each seek out information identifying the supplier.

"Finding and stopping whoever is at the root of the oil trade is important," Seeva says. "But I fear it will be equally critical to quash the rumors. And if necessary, educate our kingdoms about the imposter Sanguine."

Everyone nods in agreement.

"The jubilee is the most attended event of all," Katallia supplies, her voice optimistic. "Thousands will come to the field to see the grand finale. If we need to spread word, perhaps we should do it there."

"If you spread word of Sanguine, won't it make Channelers look bad?" Leif asks.

The room's occupants face him with varying expressions of mild interest, scrutiny, and irritation.

He scratches his neck, leaving three angry red marks. "If you tell the crowd of a fake Channeler oil that kills, then you say the killer oil is being falsely sold as the real Sanguine, won't that make Channelers look bad?"

It takes a second to sort through his long, loaded question. "I agree," I say.

Olema straightens his robes. "An unfortunate risk. However, as you've made evident, eventually oil consumption results in death."

The grave understanding of what he's saying hits me. "It would be remiss of us not to share the truth."

"But it will divide Malam further," Segrande says.

Seeva nods. "And yet that is the risk you will have to take. The people must be told."

Segrande approaches the chairs. "You would support the spread of information that could possibly risk Channeler safety?"

"Channeler safety is our first concern." Seeva exchanges glances with Katallia. She digs her fingers into the chair back. Her eyes look tired. "We mentioned before that we would have to withdraw support if Channelers are being threatened. And it seems to me that is happening. I'm sorry to say that if you cannot catch the creator and the supplier of the false

Sanguine, we will have to formally withdraw our support of Channelers in Malam during the Jubilee."

I blanch. That would defeat everything I've worked for in the last year. It would destroy Malam, and possibly send us spiraling back to the horrific crimes that were seen during the Purge.

"You understand that naming the maker means we'll be naming a Channeler?"

Seeva stares at me. "We understand that. Channelers that have fallen into dark magic have been named before. You have till the night of the Jubilee finale to find the supplier."

CHAPTER

30

LIRRA

I SPEND THE DAY PRACTICING FOR THE JUBILEE showcase and trying to make a list of possible oil makers. No names come to mind. That's because my head is a mess. All I can think about is last night's conversation. Aodren made logical sense. There is no future for us, not when I won't go to Malam, and yet, I cannot stop the hurt flowing through my veins.

When the night settles over Malam, I decide to return to the castle.

It's a brash decision, but I'm not satisfied with last night's conversation. Aodren and I need to come to a better understanding. He may want to end this spark between us, but he can't put an end do our deal. We've agreed to exchange information. I need to get to the root of the imposter Sanguine to prove to my father that he can rely on me. That he can trust me. That I can be an asset to him.

Once I've snuck inside the castle, I stop at Leif's room. I'll check on him to see how he's dealing with the oil's affects. But my door is on the knob when I hear his loud snore sawing through his room. He needs rest. I'll visit him another time.

I leave and continue on to Aodren's quarters. I slip in with silent steps. He's hunched over his desk, head propped on his hand as he reads through a stack of letters. He glances up and pushes a chunk of golden hair off his face. His emerald gaze flickers with shock, before clearing into an unreadable mask. "You're back."

"I came to talk about the oil."

He frowns. "Is there not a better time we could discuss Sanguine? It's quite late, Lirra."

I hate the precise way he says my name.

"Aodren, can I ask you something?"

His mouth is slightly open, as if he's about to talk. But he closes his lips and nods.

"Did you . . . did you enjoy our time together?" I ask, the question tumbling out of me. I should be embarrassed by my inability to accept his rejection.

He blinks. "Yes."

My throat clicks as I try to swallow over my dry tongue. "I—I did too. We have a week left."

"Yes. But—"

"We don't have to waste the week," I say, hoping it comes across as bravery. Not desperation. But the aftertaste of last night's hurt is chalky in my mouth.

Aodren stands and walks around the side of his desk. "What are you suggesting, Lirra?"

I take a deep breath. "I like spending time with you. And you said you like spending time with me. It'll be easier to stay focused on the oil if . . ." My heart isn't hurting. "If we work together. Why waste the time we have left when we can spend it enjoying each other's company? We were working well as a team."

Aodren's brows dip together, and I notice a small scar slashed across the right one. "But what about when I must return to Malam?"

"It won't be any different from parting ways now," I say, though that is a lie. Every moment I spend with Aodren, deepens our connection. I don't want to think about walking away from him seven days from now. But I'd rather do it in a week, than now.

Aodren eliminates the distance between us and takes my fingers in his hand. "If you're sure. I could go for this plan you're suggesting. In fact, it sounds like the best plan I've heard at the summit." He smiles and I feel it down low in my stomach. "Perhaps I was too hasty last night."

"Perhaps you were jealous," I tease, changing the focus from serious to playful. If I keep things light with Aodren, I can avoid falling for him more than I already have.

"Jealous?" His shadow consumes me, and his finger guides a hair around the shell of my ear, drawing out my shiver. "Perhaps a little."

"Only a little?"

He grins the most blindingly handsome grin, and I have to lock my knees against its power. My heart tries to bang a path out of my body.

Those green, green eyes darken, flickering through all the shades of the skyward trees. And I think, *If only I could wander in this forest forever.*

But we don't have forever. I need to take charge of the time we have left, keeping things light and fun so when he returns to Malam, he won't have made a complete hash of my foolish heart.

I move first, leaning in, tipping my chin, and rising on my toes. Aodren's golden lashes flare as I stop just before my lips meet his. For a heartbeat, he doesn't respond; he stares at my face, as if he might be memorizing it. But the lingering insecurity from our talk roots deeper, uncertainty and embarrassment tangling like untended weeds around my assertiveness. I start to edge away. His hand slides around my cheek, stopping me. He kisses me lightly, gently, forcing my mouth to surrender to his with agonizing slowness.

"I was a lot jealous," he whispers some time later on a shared breath.

I cannot help but smile.

"You vex me, always. I'm jealous of anyone who gets time

with you. I want all your free moments. I cannot stop thinking of you, wanting to talk with you, searching for you when
we're apart. We'll have to make the most of our time together
because this is madness, Lirra."

Another fissure in my defenses. "Then we'll lose our minds
together."

The words seem to unlock something inside him, chasing away his sweetness. Aodren's fingers wind through
my hair, scattering pins. He tugs me closer. His stubble-
roughened chin scrapes my cheek, and a lash of frenetic energy, wild, charged, and free, snaps between us like lighting
cracks across the sky.

I'm lost in him.

In all the time Aodren and I have spent together, I didn't
realize a gale was burgeoning. But the winds were brewing,
churning, building into a terrible, overwhelming storm. And
though I have the ability to control the wind, I realize, all too
late, my walls are down and my heart would rather seek shel-
ter in the safety of Aodren's arms.

The next morning, in the early hour, a sliver of muted gray
light sneaks past the castle curtains. Aodren and I spent the
evening talking about the oil and the upcoming jubilee showcase. When we both started to yawn, Aodren asked me to stay.
His request was sweet and full of concern for my safety, so I
agreed. A rustling comes from the other side of the bed, where
Aodren slept on the floor.

Groggily, I slip out of bed and quickly pull on yesterday's dress over my chemise.

I hear a swift intake of air behind me. Aodren's gaze remains on my back, where hidden under my layers a large section of warped skin wraps my left side—an old, thick, puckered scar from the fire that killed my mother. He must've saw it before my dress was in place.

"Lirra..." His voice is somber and filled with an apology.

"It was a long time ago. I'm fine," I say, but the emotion in his expression doesn't fade.

"You've sacrificed a lot," he says after a long, silent moment in which his attention to me doesn't break. His narrowed focus makes my palms sweat. "You know, I see all that you do for your father and your friends. The weight of obligation you carry is similar to mine."

"That's kind of you to say, but I'm not that noble."

"No?"

"Your obligations are to a kingdom." I glance at the door and then turn back to face him. "Mine are to a few people. There is no comparison."

"I disagree." His mouth lifts into a sloppy and tired morning smile. "I think we have more in common than you think. We're both willing to sacrifice ourselves for the people we care about."

It's a kind sentiment, but if it were true, I would put more consideration into helping him out at the jubilee. Instead, I shoot him a smile, make a plan to meet him tonight at the showcase, and then slip out the door.

It isn't so easy to slip out of the castle. The halls are filled with servants making morning preparations. I manage to sneak into Leif's room to check on him, but he's sleeping like a hibernating bear. When I cannot wake him, I leave the castle and return home.

I spend the day preparing for this afternoon's showcase, the first part of the Channeler Jubilee. When the afternoon rolls around, I pack two outfits—a carriage driver's costume and my favorite dress, a pretty green and lace one for the show-case—and then go to see Orli. Tonight, before heading to the tournament field for the showcase, I must try to see Leif once more. There's no way of knowing if Leif has consumed as much oil as Baltroit. But I need to be sure he will make it through this. It's bold and daring to keep returning, but so far, the guards' schedule has been consistent with Da's notes. And this is a risk I must take because Leif was asleep the last two times I went by.

The showcase starts during daylight hours, and because it draws crowds even larger than the tournament events, there is a greater chance I could be seen walking away from the cathe-dral on the cliff. I want Orli to drive me away from the cathe-dral so no one knows I've been to visit Leif.

Only, when I get to her house and talk to her, Orli's answer is an emphatic no.

"I understand," I say. She's been struggling with leaving her home since we saw Baltroit die.

She unbraids and rebraids her hair three times while we sit in her pristine white room. She's fidgeting. I can see she wants to give me a reason, but I don't need an excuse. I never want to push her more than she can handle.

"I'm sorry I won't be there for your jubilee performance. I feel like I'm letting you down, just like your da. I don't want you to be alone for your big moment."

I squeeze her hand to show that I understand why she can't come and that I don't blame her. "You're not letting me down, and neither is Da."

"I thought we didn't lie to each other."

"It's silly to be hurt," I argue. "I know he's busy. I know he works hard."

Her fingers abandon her hair. "But so do you. And what you're doing is important too."

"I know. And you don't have to worry about me being alone. Aodren is meeting me before the showcase. Did I tell you he asked me to represent Malam in the jubilee?"

Her eyes widen. "What? Why didn't you mention this earlier?"

"I misspoke. He didn't ask, exactly. But Aunt Katallia can't do it because she's in the Guild, and he's desperate to find someone else. He wants me to offer to help, but I cannot do that. That would mean taking on Malam's name. After what they did to me . . . to you . . ." I lie back on her bed and stare at the white ceiling. If I squint, her room reminds me of a snowy winter in Malam. "It wouldn't be right."

Orli scoots off the bed and walks to the window. She pushes the curtain aside and peers out into the sunny morning. "Malam didn't do anything to me."

I almost miss what she's saying. But she turns around and repeats her words.

"It was a handful of deranged people. Not Malam. Not Aodren. And the same goes for you and your mum."

I roll to my side and prop my head on my hand. "What are you saying?"

"I was just thinking if that's your excuse, maybe you should rethink it."

My feet dangle as I maneuver off the bed. Frustration at her judgment kicks through me. "That's easy for you to say. What things are you not doing because you're stuck in the past?"

Orli's eyes widen with hurt, and instantly I wish I could pull the words back in.

"You're right," she says, abandoning the window. At one time, she would've hit back with harder punches. She would've made me look at the truth. Because that's what we used to do for each other. Always tell the truth. How is it we started skirting around the difficult issues? Why have we stopped asking hard questions? Is it because we'd have to answer them ourselves?

"Do you have your da's letter still?" Orli asks out of the blue.

"I do." It's been in the bottom of my boot since it came. I never follow his orders to burn them.

"I could try to locate where he was when he wrote the letter."

It's impossible not to stand there and gape. She hasn't used her Channeler magic since her return. She waited outside the showcase auditions because the number of Channelers there made her uneasy. Who is this girl, standing before me now?

"It takes too much energy," I say, immediately searching for ways to protect her. I realize what I'm doing and press my lips together. Since when did I become her guardian?

To be fair, my argument is valid. It takes an overwhelming amount of magic to locate a letter's origin. Also, it might not be that helpful because Da might have left the area. Still, it should be her decision, not mine.

"Seeing as I haven't been using much energy, I have some to spare. Besides, I want to help with the oil. There's no way to know where he is now, but the blood charm used on your letter is made from land magic. If there are any threads of energy left, I could locate where he was when he sent the letter. Maybe if you know where he was, it will help you find whoever is responsible for the oil."

I don't know why I didn't think of this before. It takes an incredibly powerful Channeler to perform a blood charm, and we know that a powerful Channeler is responsible for the oil. Could it be that it's the same person? Da always fulfills his side of a bargain, but what if he stopped looking into Sanguine because he didn't want to implicate a friend?

And even if it's not the same person, I haven't seen Orli this determined in months. She's finally willing to use her magic again. I don't want to stand in the way of that. I dig the letter out of my boot and hand it over.

When she apologizes again for not coming tonight, I nudge her shoulder. "You're already doing something to help me. I'm proud of you for taking this step. Don't worry about anything else. I like being a carriage driver."

"Then why'd you bring the dress?" She points at the green material poking out of my bag.

I shrug, and then blush. The truth is I'd hoped Aodren would see me in it, but all I tell her is, "In case a change was needed."

Orli snorts. "Sure. Tell your king hullo from me."

Your king. I like the sound of that too much.

I go to the cathedral on the cliff early, armed with ale, sweet cakes, and Beannach water. If Leif is suffering as Baz did, he'll need some distractions to take his mind off the Sanguine.

Sneaking into the castle at this hour is much more dangerous than early in the morning or late at night. The number of times I'm forced to slip behind a curtain or duck around a statue is twice that of other times I've roamed these halls.

When I reach Leif's room, however, it's obvious any risk taken to get here was worth it. He's a sweating, fidgety mess. Leif paces from one end of the room to the other. He doesn't even notice I'm here until he's walked past me a half dozen times. And then he startles and curses.

"Shhhh," I hiss, mindful of the guards who walk the castle corridors. It was difficult enough to maneuver around them. Drawing their attention now wouldn't be good.

I cross to the table and pull the items out of my satchel. "I don't know if these will help, but they might."

He holds up the ale and snorts. "Should I change one problem for another?"

I know he's never been much of an ale drinker, and I can see now ale isn't the best thing. "Don't be rude. I was only trying to help."

He rubs a hand over his ruddy cheeks and then flings away some sweat. "Thanks," he mutters, and paces away. "I wish I never had any of that damn oil."

"The first bottle saved your life."

Leif spins around and smacks the post of his bed. "I meant the bludgering fake stuff."

I don't respond. He's more volatile than the last time we spoke. It's clear by his bare feet and rolled trouser legs, he's staying in for the night. A good decision, all things considered.

"Why do you look like a scrawny boy?" he asks. His nostrils flare, and for a moment I think he's going to spout off something meaner, but he reins in the anger and takes a steadying breath. *It's the oil talking.*

"It made sneaking in easier." I shrug.

"Thank you. I'm sorry for acting like a massive scrant."

"It'll pass. Usually you're only a small one."

Leif smiles. It's warm and kind, a break in the storm clouds. Even if he is relaxed only for a minute, I'm grateful to have him back. The glimpse of the true Leif saddens me, though, because it proves how damaging the oil can be in such a short amount of time. "Good luck today, Lirra."

After saying goodbye, I take the servants' walk to sneak down to the lower floors, but I only make it one level before footsteps and clanks clatter ahead. The aromas of roasted duck and freshly baked bread hit my nose, and I know it must be servers approaching with a meal.

There's nowhere to hide. I go back up the steps and dart out of the passage into the grand hall, where I hide behind a pillar. But there are guards nearby, so when the servants pour out of the passage, I use their distraction to rush around the pillared rim of the room and lunge for the nearest open door.

Blue and gold flags, Shaerdan's colors, hang from the ceiling and drape the sides of the corridor. If the servants' entrance is in the same location as in Akaria's quarters, I know how to find my way out.

"Where are you going?"

My stomach leaps into my throat, and I slowly turn around to face whoever has discovered me.

No one is there. I spin around to check the empty hall and tiptoe forward a fraction of a step, testing to see if someone is watching me. *No one?* I huff out a soundless chuckle. I walk another couple of steps and see a door cracked open a sliver. The person who asked the question is in that room. I must've overheard part of a conversation.

Male voices rumble from the door. One sounds like Judge Soma. I turn and scurry away, but I pause. Judge Soma has secrets. I can tell by the way he watches others. This conversation might have some information I could use later. Da always said I should make the most of every listening situation.

I wedge behind the nearest draperies. That is when a man's voice — one I don't recognize — growls, "Sanguine's not gonna help with added skill."

I draw in a silent breath. *Sanguine.*

A third man's response sounds irritated. "Sod off, Folger."

Folger Falk, Otto Ellar, and Judge Soma?

A chair scrapes the floor and then the judge says, "Then don't take it for yourself. Give it to the Kolontians."

A man chuckles. "Eliminated Baltroit easy enough."

I swallow a gasp.

"I didn't know . . . It shouldn't have happened," a response comes, quieter than the others, stitched with remorse. Maybe Otto?

I need to flee this area and be gone long before they have a chance of finding me, but the need to know what's going on grounds me in place.

"He was a fool. How many bottles did he swallow?" This comes from Soma.

"Eight. Must've drank them all in one day. He was spun. I coulda told Baltroit that Judge Auberdeen had his sister the night before, and he would've attacked the chief judge."

Baltroit was set up on purpose. They meant for him to start a fight so he'd be eliminated. Otto might not have thought it would end in Baltroit's death, but what of the others? Did Folger and Soma mean for him to die? My chest somehow feels too tight and at the same time hollow, and my heart is banging so loudly.

"Keep it quiet, men," Soma says. A chair scrapes again, and the door hinges creak. I flatten myself against the stones. "Nothing comes back to me, understand? I don't want anyone knowing I'm feeding you oil."

They agree, their voices moving closer to my location, until footsteps clatter on the hall floor. They're leaving. I shrink even farther into the wall, not daring to breathe until the air shifts from the corridor's door swishing open and closed, and no more footsteps can be heard.

The roar of blood rushing through my veins is dizzying. I wait another minute or two, until I'm certain they've left.

This is proof Soma is the supplier. It makes sense. Prudence said one of the men was tall, and Soma certainly is that. He has a history in trading. And his position in the kingdom would make this dangerous enough for Da to not want to be involved. I have to tell Aodren. Once he knows, we can go together to the chief judge and stop the imposter Sanguine from ruining any more lives.

I dart into the empty hall and rush toward the servants' passage. My arm catches on something. I trip backwards, cap tumbling off my head, and slam into someone's body. It's Judge Soma. He has an iron hold on me. I yank away, trying to free my arm, and his fingers tighten, his grip bruising.

"Lirra Barrett, you aren't supposed to be here."

"Let me go." I thrash to free myself. He twists my arm behind my back until pain screeches through my shoulder and I stop.

"You shouldn't listen to private conversations." It's a deadly low whisper that sends a blast of alarm through me with hurricane force. "Guards!"

A sheen of nervous sweat dampens my tunic, as the guards drag me down to the holding chamber. I can barely breathe. I cannot go in the cell again. The darkness ahead reaches for me. It clogs my throat. We march closer, but the guards don't stop. We don't stop at the holding chamber. Why aren't we stopping? They're not going to free me.

Anxiety scuttles down my spine. Whispers across my neck.

"Where are you taking me?"

They don't bother to answer. Instead they open a door, wherein their lantern light falls on a half dozen torture devices. I start to kick and yank away, but their grip is too strong. I twist my hands, drawing on my Channeler magic. We're not ever supposed to use it to harm, but right now it's a necessity to protect myself. I conjure a wind, pulling it to me, and forcing the men to struggle against the gust. I jerk out of the guard's grip.

"Stop her," he shouts.

I change tactics, not wanting them to alert any other guards, and I call the air from the man, creating a vacuum so he struggles to breathe. His eyes widen, and he tries without success to suck in air. I won't do this too much longer. Just until he passes out.

A hand slams my face. My head whips to the side, and I stumble, pain bursting across my cheek.

"You scrant," the second guard curses.

Splotches blink across my vision. I clutch my face and groan.

"We're going to let you rot down there." His spittle wets my cheek. "You used your magic to hurt a man. That's against the law."

He drags me past the tables to a small door at the rear of the room. The guard I pulled the air away from pulls the door open, and light from his lantern spills into the space beyond.

He curses at me. "Get down there."

It's a narrow room; at least, from what I can see of the rounded walls, it doesn't seem as if it's more than a body's length in diameter. But it's deep. So deep I cannot see the floor. It could be three stories deep, or ten.

The guard chuckles darkly behind me, the sound echoing down into the hellish hole.

This is an oubliette.

This is the room in the castle, where criminals are left to rot. Every child in Shaerdan has been scared into finishing their chores by threat of the oubliette.

My legs lock up. I twist and try to jerk away while focusing my energy into my palms. But the guard smacks me again, and my lip splits. The metallic tang of blood coats my tongue.

The men shove me so that I stumble forward, falling halfway over the edge. I cry out. I scramble to grasp the rope ladder, and my heart turns frantic and tries to punch free. The guards laugh. One tells me to climb down before he loses patience and tosses me to the bottom.

Bastard.

The ladder twists and sways with my descent. The anticipation of being locked in here has me breathing like I've scaled a mountain. It saps my energy, making it feel like I've gone a league before I reach the bottom of the oubliette. I try to convince myself it's nothing to fear.

The moment the ladder is out of my hands, the guards tug it upward, leaving me no way to climb out. Then they slam the door.

I shudder and stare at the residual lantern glow peeking around the door's edges. A hand squeezes my lungs, and icy fingers walk across my neck.

I breathe in and out and in and out, keeping the rhythm the same until I'm calm. Calmer than the time I fell into the neighbor's dry well. In hindsight, the well wasn't frightening. I made it out alive. I tell myself that this oubliette is just like the well, so there's nothing to be panicked about. Nothing at all.

The light snuffs out.

An exhale rattles out of me. I suck in, but the air is too thin. It doesn't fill my lungs. I try again: in and out, in and out. Why is there not enough air?

I'm not afraid. I was fine in the dry well. I'm fine here. Finer than if they'd hung me. There's space to sit. Space to curl up and sleep. There's air to breath, I just need to slow down. I'm fine, really I am.

I sit down and pull my knees to my chest. My foot hits a stick. Were prisoners of old allowed to build fires? Any fire in as tight a space as the oubliette would have to be really small. My fingers grope around and find something hard and round and made with holes and teeth and—*ohgodsohgodsohgods*. The skull falls from my hands and clatters against other sticks. Sticks that are actually bones.

I prop my head on my legs and fight for a semblance of calm. Focus. Panic isn't going to help me escape the hell out of this hole.

CHAPTER
31

AODREN

SEGRANDE AND I GO TO THE KINGDOMS'
Market hours before the start of the
Channeler showcase. Leif stayed behind.
He didn't look well. I wonder if he pushed him-
self too hard after coming so close to death.

We wind through the crowds, guards at our
sides for protection. Picking up stray information is almost impossible with a group this size.
But since the meeting we had with the Guild and
the Akarians, Segrande has found a distraction
from the pain of his son's death. His desire to
catch the supplier has become his sole focus.

When we reach the north end of the market,
we pause by the tavern tent.

The Akarian, Kolontian, and Plovian competitors saunter off the tournament field, their

scuffed and sweaty attire attesting to the time they've spent sparring today. The swordfight takes place tomorrow, and two days after that, it will be the Channeler showcase. People cluster closer, until the crowd has grown so large the competitors cannot pass. Two of our guards rush ahead to help break up the crowd, but their efforts aren't needed after a carriage arrives. The crowd parts to make way.

Folger and Otto emerge from the carriage and follow the others into the champions' tent.

"Didn't you say Otto gave the oil to my boy?" Segrande's hunched shoulders might appear defeated to anyone else, but I see the way his chest moves up and down and the heavy blow of his breath parts his beard. He's barely containing his fury.

"That's what I heard."

He lunges forward, but my hand seizes his arm, halting his stride. If I let him go in the tent, he will kill Otto.

"Let me go," I tell Segrande. "He may know who the supplier is."

"He is the reason my son is dead." His voice sounds hoarse and out of breath as he says this.

"No," I tell him, lowering my voice so the guards don't hear. "We don't know if he knew the oil would kill Baltroit. For all we know, Otto may be just as misinformed. I will go and speak with him."

The fury Segrande showed a second ago is gone. Now he seems lost. "Go on," he says. "I'll wait."

The guards split, some remaining with Segrande and others trailing me to the tent. It takes some convincing, but I manage to get them to stay when I dart around the back side.

"You look like you could use something to pick you up." A voice comes from ahead. I peek around the corner, seeing Otto talking to Hemmet.

Hemmet snorts and props his hands on his hips, making himself even broader. "You're talking to the wrong man. I showed up to spar today. Where were you? Perhaps you should take your own pick-me-up and shove it—"

"I was busy. Other things going on. How's your head?" Otto asks, as if he and Hemmet are comrades. Which is a feeling obviously not shared by the other man.

Hemmet grunts.

"Look, I'm just trying to help a fellow competitor out. If you want something better than the Beannach water, something to get rid of the pain, come talk to me." Is he offering Sanguine?

Otto twists like he might walk away from the conversation, but stops when Hemmet asks, "What do you have?"

The question pulls Otto back. He reaches into the blue and gold pocket of his Shaerdanian uniform and pulls out a bottle. "Try this."

"I don't know if I trust anything from you." Hemmet eyes the bottle warily. Smart man. "What is this? Who gave it to you?"

Breath held, I'm on my toes, leaning forward to catch his answer.

Otto shakes his head and slips the bottle into his pocket. "Later," he says, and then disappears into the back side of the tent.

Should I say something to Hemmet? He didn't take the oil from Otto, a promising relief; however, that doesn't mean Hemmet will avoid it in the future. Otto will have more chances to convince Hemmet, and if that should happen, he may suffer the same fate as Baltroit. However, if I say something, my warning could get back to the supplier.

An image of Segrande, mourning Baltroit, comes to mind. The anguish of that night comes back so vividly, turning my mouth dry.

I lurch out of hiding. "Do not trust anything from Otto."

"Are you talking to me?" Hemmet points his thumb to his chest.

I move closer, my voice low. "Yes. I'm giving you friendly advice. Stay away from Otto. What he's trying to give you is harmful."

Eyes like narrowed slits, the champion puts his hands on his hips and steps in, as if to intimidate me. "You don't know what you're talking about."

The ferocity in his response is so much like his father's. They are both always on the ready to tear someone limb from limb.

"Do you think I would bother with this conversation if it wasn't a concern? I have taken a risk to talk to you, to warn you. If you don't want to know, then it's on you."

He cocks his head to the side. "What's in that bottle?"

Keeping one eye on the tent, I move in so no one can overhear. I explain Sanguine, the real version and the fake version, and the hazards of taking the latter.

He glances at the tent where Otto disappeared not long ago, and then shifts his attention back to me, with new curiosity. "Why are you telling me this?"

"I watched another man lose his son," I say, honestly. "While I have little love for your father, no man should have to suffer that way if it can be prevented."

It's one day away from the jubilee, when Seeva plans to make an announcement about Sanguine. I hadn't planned on confronting Otto to find out where he got the oil, but there is no way around it.

Trumpets play a song unlike any of the announcing tunes of the tournament. The chorus of horns creates a beautiful melody. When they end, the four women that lead the Channelers Guild walk out onto the field. Seeva takes the announcer's cone and welcomes the crowd. In the crush of people, I wasn't able to find Lirra before the start of the showcase. I imagined the field would be as full as it had been on the night of the joust or the melee. I was wrong. As I look down at the crowd from the nobility box, the number of spectators who have packed around the field far exceeds the size of other days.

Shouts and applause ring loud from one end of the field to the other. Unlike the Tournament of Champions, there are no discordant jeers mixed in. Maroon and gray flags dot the spectators, so I know my people are out there, watching the event.

Seeva talks openly about the Channelers' five powers: land, wind, fire, water, and spirit. Her explanation introduces the twenty women who will perform today by sharing their gifts with the audience. The crowd listens in reverence for the upcoming show, eagerly consuming Seeva's information. This showcase is much more than a talent event — it's educational for all in attendance.

Anxiety keeps me stitched tight as I listen to her talk. At some point, she will mention where each of the participating Channelers hails from. Everyone will know that there are no Malamian Channelers in the showcase, and they will know that Channelers do not feel safe in Malam. While their choice to stay away is one I fully understand, it also saddens me that the tide has been so slow to change in Malam. There are many in the crowd today. When they see Malam has no representative, how will they react?

But as the showcase begins and Channeler women enter the field, Seeva does not mention that none of them are from Malam.

A fire Channeler walks across the field, holding only a candle. When she reaches the center, she lifts her right hand, and the fire responds by expanding until the flame is taller than the woman. The spectators gasp in delight.

Two water Channelers throw small cups of water at each other, and before the droplets can soak the other, both raise their hands and the water sprays the crowd, igniting squeals of joy on this muggy day. Cheers come from men and women wearing Malamian maroon and gray. The sight of their delight and interest gives me hope.

The performances intensify as the show continues. I wait, anxious, to see Lirra take the field. Segrande arches one furry brow in my direction, noting my restlessness, but he doesn't say anything.

The announcer shouts Lirra's name, and when I hear it, my heart presses against my ribs with yearning. It's a need that has nothing to do with the kisses we've shared, but for more of her time, more of her laughter, more of *her*.

We wait, and my restlessness spreads to those around me. Segrande scoots forward in his seat and scans the women around the field.

"Where is she?" he asks.

She doesn't walk out onto the field. We wait, and Lirra never comes.

Where did she go?

When we return to the castle, I head to Leif's chambers. Lirra's absence doesn't sit right with me. But then, neither does

Leif's. I head to his room to check in with him first. Then I'll seek out Lirra. As eager as she was to participate in the showcase, I know very few obstacles would've prevented her from going.

Leif's hair is askew, and he's pacing his room like a caged animal. The sight of him, covered in perspiration and shaking with restlessness, is startling. My first concern is infection. I step inside ready to insist on seeing the knife wound.

He shoves a chair, knocking it to the ground. The force of his hit, his aggravation . . . I start to think about how edgy he was during the meeting with the Akarians and the Channelers Guild. The comment he made was callous, unlike Leif's usual kind manner. The answer comes to me rather quickly.

"You've been taking the oil," I say, after standing in his doorway long enough without him recognizing my presence.

The man nearly jumps out of his skin. He spins to me, the whites of his eyes showing, and I close the door.

There are few men left whom I trust. He is one of them. But the disappointment of this discovery punches me in the stomach and gives me cause to rethink my stance.

Some of the wildness clears from his eyes. "I was going to tell you," he says, remorse with no pretenses.

I gesture for him to continue. Leif launches into a story of how he caught Baltroit drinking Sanguine, and because he thought it sped up the healing process, Leif asked Baltroit to get some for him. Leif did not have the truth about the imposter oil, and for this, guilt rears up within me. I was too preoccupied with Lirra and the tournament to discuss the matter with him.

Leif scratches at his skin on his neck and then wipes sweat from his eyes. "I promised Lirra I wouldn't take any more, and I intend to keep my word."

The comment catches me unaware. "She knew?"

He pulls his shirt from his chest and fans at the perspiration. "Yeah, caught me the night of the joust."

Lirra and I have shared every detail about Sanguine since we agreed to work together. It matters not that Leif asked her to withhold the truth from me. The discovery that she kept his condition secret stings like a violation of trust. I could pick over the broken trust and withdraw, but then I consider Lirra and Leif's friendship. In all that's happened between me and Lirra, she's proven that she will always keep her word. I can accept that if she told Leif she wouldn't disclose this secret, it makes sense she wouldn't tell me. I dislike that she's done this, but I can appreciate her loyalty.

"I should've told you yesterday." His hands scratch his arms. "But I cannot even think straight. It's torture, feeling like I want to tear off my skin."

"How many bottles did you drink?" I ask, curious to determine how quickly the effects of the oil will show.

"Five."

An answering wave of alarm crashes over me swiftly. Five bottles are a pittance. The oil's hazards come on so quickly, more so than I understood. How many bottles did Baltroit drink before he died?

"Could you still be at risk of dying?"

"I don't think so." He blows out a frustrated breath and looks at his toes. "Though I'm weaker than before. Not taking the oil makes my body feel like it's been sparring all day long. I . . . I fear the outcome of tomorrow night."

"The sword fight of the tournament?"

He nods. "I knew it was going to be difficult to earn enough points to still be in the running for the cup. But now that my body is drained by the toll of the oil, I fear it will be impossible."

"You're unable?"

"I am able, but I don't have much energy. I don't know how long I'll last."

Leif is going to need my help. I wanted to stay out of the event and focus on the meeting, but the chance of victory calls to me. I see the benefit of having a win. Already I've seen the spectators pull together. That's the unity I need to promote and encourage once we've returned to Malam.

"I will fight with you," I tell him.

He lurches out of his chair, stepping into my space. He stops abruptly and juts a hand between us as if he wants me to shake it. I knock it aside and reach around to give him a quick embrace. I clap him on the back. "Tomorrow, you and I will win the cup."

. . .

After leaving Leif's room, I inform the guards that we'll be heading into Celize. Whatever they think about my choice to leave the castle at this late hour, they keep closed expressions, and ten minutes later we're riding for the Elementiary. If anyone knows what happened to Lirra, it'll be the older woman, Astoria.

The entire time the carriage rolls through the evening, a growing sense of unease tightens my gut. Lirra wouldn't have missed the showcase. Something is very wrong.

We arrive at the Elementiary. Despite the late hour, the streets are still lit with lanterns as people stroll between the shops. Sparks of light flicker from the smithy next to the Elementiary. A few children run around with small orbs, carrying flames just like the ones I saw at the showcase.

The excitement of the jubilee event is a current still running through the people passing by. But all I feel is something dark and full of dread.

The guards escort me to the Elementiary and bang on the door until the old woman opens it. Her eyes set on my face, without dipping in any show of respect. The men at my sides press closer. And I'm sure they want to punish her for her impudence. But I tell them to stay back so I may speak to her alone.

Astoria retreats into the Channeler school.

"Where is Lirra?" I ask as soon as the door snicks closed behind us.

"Why would I tell you?"

"I've extended patience to you out of respect for Lirra. I have done you no harm. And I only wish to repair the damages my kingdom has done. But I warn you, if your insolence does not end now and you do not yield the information I seek, I'll have my men detain you."

She stiffens, her nose flaring to the ring of steel in my voice. I can see the fight behind her eyes, wanting to cut me down with her words.

"My apologies, Your Highness." Disdain drips out of her. "Unfortunately, I don't know where Lirra is."

I stare at her for a long beat. There are probably a thousand reasons she would lie, but something tells me this is the truth. Which worries me even more.

I thank her for the information and then walk to the door. But before it opens, the noise from outside echoes into the Elementiary. Angry voices shouting, "Down with Malam!"

The clank of steel rings out.

"Channeler haters."

Someone screams.

I rush to the window. A view of the lantern-lit street shocks me. A swarm of people have surrounded the royal carriage. The guards, who were posted beside the door, have abandoned their stations to draw their swords and fight people away from the carriage. The driver has been pulled down from his seat and is barely fending off two men.

"They saw you had no Channeler at the showcase," Astoria says, her voice quiet and dark. "They know you have killed our mothers, daughters, and sisters. And they will not yield any longer."

I glance over my shoulder, seeing the hate born years ago.

Then I pull out my sword and rush into the fray.

CHAPTER
32

LIRRA

WHEN I OPEN MY EYES, THE WORLD IS black. What day is it?

The grit of the dirt on the floor digs into my palms, and I remember where I am. The oubliette. My lungs squeeze, and the blood whooshes through my ears, and there are no sounds except for my breaths.

I cannot have missed the showcase. The darkness is disorienting. *Maybe it's the same day,* I think to myself, even though my gut suspects an evening has passed. But I don't want to think about that. I haven't worked on my gliders for a year just to miss the showcase.

"Hello? Can anyone hear me?" I call out, trying not to feel discouraged when the sound echoes up and up and up.

I have to get out of here. I push myself to

stand. I don't think of the dark. No, I just reach out, stretching until I fall forward, hands landing against the jagged stone wall, stopping me from slamming my head.

My fingers skate over the rocks surrounding me. But as I move closer, I stumble on bones. Sticks. They're sticks.

In the dark, I walk the perimeter of the oubliette, tripping and falling and finding nothing helpful. No handholds. No rope. No spot to start climbing.

The base of this hellhole is too wide to reach if I extend hands and feet in opposite directions to climb out.

I stare at the top. It's too high to try to conjure a wind to lift me all the way up. I don't have the energy for it.

There's no way to escape.

"Hello! Help!" I cry, realizing that it doesn't matter what day it is. I'm going to miss the showcase, and the next one won't happen for another five years. That thought squeezes my lungs until I'm gasping, suffocating in this hole.

The only thing worse than missing the jubilee would be dying in here.

Somehow, it doesn't seem out of the realm of possibilities.

The creak of a door wakes me.

"Lirra?" Aodren's voice sounds oddly feminine, and when I blink my eyes open, he vanishes into the pitch-black.

The oubliette.

The last two days' nightmarish events return, making me wish I could bring back the dream of Aodren. Even if his voice had a womanly quality instead of the normal deep toe-curling tenor, I'd take an odd dream over this hell. I push off the floor, my fingers grazing bones as I sit up. A shiver skates up my spine. I lick the dried crust of blood from the corner of my mouth and blink, hoping my vision will adjust and give shape to this death pit. That doesn't happen. All I know is that it's dark, tight, filled with bones, and there is no way out.

I already tried to find a way to escape.

I suppose panic should be setting in about now. But after a night here, my stomach has hardened into a lump with no more allowance for fear.

"Lirra, are you there?"

Not a dream! "Orli?" I whisper, though I'm not sure why my voice is lowered. "What are you doing here?" If she's at the oubliette door, she must've found some way to deal with the guard.

"I came to help you out, unless you like being down there."

"Oh, Orli, I cannot believe you're here, I—I . . ." Gratitude wells up into a lump, clogging my throat. I have no idea how she found out I was here or what she went through to enter the castle and find me. "You are everything to me. Thank you. Thank you. Thank you."

"Stop thanking me. You would've done the same. We must hurry. The guards are unconscious, but they may wake soon."

"Did you make them a sleeping aid?"

A laugh. "I'm rusty, so I don't know how long it'll last." There is a current of strength in her voice that's been missing for months. After her ordeal in Malam, I never thought I'd hear it again.

"I'm going to throw down the rope," she says, and then I hear a rustling. *Thwack, thwack,* the rope ladder must be unrolling and falling against the stone wall. I try to listen to which side of the room it's falling down. It's close —

Thwack. It smacks my face.

"Stars!" I grab my cheek and rub the spot.

"Sorry."

I rub the sting out of my cheek and then reach for the ladder. My fingers grip the rough fibers, and I climb onto the first rung. The room bows out around the bottom of the oubliette, so I cannot use the wall for leverage. The climb is difficult as the rope swings from side to side.

"Lirra, be quick." I've only gone seven rungs.

"Are they waking?"

"No." She grunts. "It's ... the ... rope." She puffs out breaths in between each word. "It's breaking."

I scramble upward, climbing as fast as my fingers can grip the rough holds, but every few steps my foot slides through the rung, or my hands miss the grab. Not a speck can be seen in this black hole.

A crackling snap echoes through the oubliette.

"Lirrrraaaaaa!"

I throw myself off the rope as it slumps to the ground and thrust my palms out, calling on my Channeler energy as fast as I can to push the air below. Instantly, the force stirs the air, creating a wind that presses back. The more energy I can release, the farther the wind will send me upward.

But creating enough wind to lift me to the top of the oubliette is quickly draining my energy. A tingling sensation crawls through my limbs and splotches dance in my vision as my body bobs upward. My boots scrape the wall. I can hear Orli calling my name from above, which makes me think I'm a little more than halfway to the top. Exhaustion hits, and I'm lightheaded.

I push more energy out, ignoring how rapidly my body's stores are depleting from the exertion. Only a miracle will get me to the door.

My boots scrape the stone again. I reach out with a hand and realize the wall is two hand spans from my head. The room narrows at the top in a bell shape.

"Lirra? Are you okay?"

"Coming." It's the voice of an injured animal. I don't even know if Orli heard. My head is spinning. The vertigo increases, and I know I cannot make it.

I thrust both hands at the wall ahead and straighten my legs. When I have a firm press, one that will keep me from falling, I halt the outward flow of energy. The release kicks through me, and a spasm racks my body, nearly shaking my grip off the wall.

I've seen the twins climb the walls of the house this way. I just need to keep pressure on the wall, I tell myself. Hold it together, and get to the door.

"I can hear you. You must be close. Keep going, Lirra," Orli says.

I listen to her voice. The door isn't far. I can make it.

A tremor rattles me from shoulder blade to wrist. Fingers and toes slide upward, one small step at a time while I maintain even pressure between hands and feet. A fire burns through my lungs, the blaze heating every muscle in my body until sweat drips from the tip of my nose.

"You're close," Orli says.

Another hand. Another foot.

The pads of my fingers meet wood. The door! Gods of old, I've never been so happy to touch a door frame before. I edge up the walls of the oubliette, not realizing I'm holding my breath until my hand can wrap over the wood beam and all the air in my lungs whooshes out.

Orli seizes my wrist and instructs me to get a good hold with my other hand before shoving off with my feet. I do what she says, grasping the wood frame with both hands and then pushing off the opposite wall with the all the threads of energy left in me. At the same time, Orli yanks my body, and we go tumbling haphazardly though the doorway into the torture chamber.

I roll to my back and stare at the chains hanging from the ceiling, breath jerking through me. "You . . . freed . . . me . . . thank . . . you. How did you know I was here?"

Orli's arms wrap around my body, and she squeezes me in a tight hug. "When you didn't come to tell me about the showcase, I knew something was wrong," she says, explaining that she went looking for me and found the carriage outside the cathedral. "I went to the castle next. I pretended to be a Channeler assistant to the healer. After I was in, I just had to find Leif. He admitted he was the last person to see you. He interrogated a few guards, and discovered you'd been caught."

Too exhausted to laugh, I turn my head to face her and whisper, "Thank you."

The torture chamber door scrapes open.

I try to scramble up, but Orli pats my arm. "Don't worry. It's only Leif."

But the person who enters is not my cousin. It's one of the guards who works for Judge Soma. Orli cries out in shock as the man advances, his dagger extended.

"Both of you, get through that door." He points to the oubliette.

She shudders beside me, and I think she's afraid until I see her hand slide toward her boot.

The man moves closer and reaches for her, just as the door behind him bangs open. Leif stands there, breathing heavily. His face is cut and bruised like he just walked off the melee field.

"You got away," Leif says.

The guard spins and swings his dagger in a cutting arc. Leif scrambles back, barely saving his stomach from an eviscerating slice. The guard swings again, but he's smart and fast. He's not getting close enough for Leif to land a punch.

Leif lunges for the man, putting himself in line of the guard's weapon. It's a move of desperation, one that makes me think there's a reason Leif needs to end this fight.

Orli yanks her dagger free.

"Are more coming?" I cry out.

"Yes," Leif pants.

I take the blade from Orli, knowing my throwing skills are much better than hers. We may get only one clear shot. Leif's shout echoes through the torture chamber. The guard has sliced him across his left arm. I wait for them to circle, and as soon as the guard's back is to me, I lurch up and throw the dagger. It sinks into the man's upper right shoulder, catching him unaware. The impact most likely won't kill him, but it causes him to drop his blade. Leif jumps on him, tackling him to the ground and knocking him unconscious.

"We have to hurry," Leif says. He points an accusatory finger at Orli. "I told you to wait."

Orli sits up. "Yes, but that was ages ago. She wouldn't have lasted much longer."

Leif scrubs his hand over the back of his neck. "Sorry. I tried to hurry. I went for Aodren's help. Figured if he used his status to free Lirra, it would be better than knocking out the guards. Only he—he couldn't come." His eyes widen. "He was unable to talk . . . But then I ran into Judge Soma."

At the mention of the traitorous, deceiving man's name, my eye twitches.

"I mentioned I was looking for you, and the next thing I knew, five guards were trying to jump me."

"Did you beat them back?" I ask.

"Aye," Leif says wearily. He helps me stand, but now that he's not fighting, he seems weak and shaky.

"Soma is the reason I'm in here. He's the supplier," I tell Leif and Orli. I explain the conversation I overheard yesterday.

"Seeds." Leif blows out a low whistle. "We need to get you out of here."

Orli grasps my free arm and props it over her shoulders. My energy is spent. I used more than I should've to escape the oubliette. Using too much could've killed me. My vision fills with splotches, and Leif tells me to hold on. He and Orli help balance my weight as we trudge out of the torture chamber and through the belly of the summer castle. After we exit the cathedral on the cliff, Leif lifts me into the safety of my family's inconspicuous carriage. My legs and arms barely have energy to move.

Leif puts a bottle in my hand.

"What's this?" I ask.

"The real Sanguine."

I stare at him, confused.

"Some had been used on another . . . but the person didn't need it all, so the Ku gave the remainder to me to see if it would help curb the effects of the imposter Sanguine."

"And have you used it?" I ask, my thoughts even more tangled from his explanation. Who was the other person using the oil? And why?

"You need it more than me," Leif says, voice gentle. "Your legs can barely hold your weight. You used too much energy escaping. You need this to recover."

"I cannot take this from you," I start to say, and he holds up a hand, silencing me.

"You can. You found me and helped me out of a mess I didn't even know I was in. It's my turn to help you. There isn't a full bottle there, but you're not on your deathbed, so there should be enough for you to recover. And I can already tell that I'm going to make it. The other Sanguine got to me, but I'm not going down easy. Drink it, Lirra."

Leif waits while I swallow the sweet, thick liquid. The taste of it comes in hints of flavors that each only last a second. Cinnamon, sandalwood, an ocean breeze, a summer melon. Even before I lunge forward and give Leif a parting hug, I can feel the oil moving through me, filling my energy stores and enlivening my muscles. Leif promises to find Aodren and deliver the news about Judge Soma.

I fall asleep in the back of the carriage.

Orli nudges me awake. The carriage is no longer moving.

"How are you feeling?" she asks.

"Good," I say, stretching. "Really good. Why? Where are we? Why are we both sitting in the back of the carriage?" The windows covers have been drawn.

She holds up a finger. "Too many questions. Wait for me to explain."

I press my lips together and wave her on.

Orli twists the dust cover cloth between her hands. "There was another reason I waited for you to come see me after the showcase. Remember I said I could try to locate the blood charm?"

"Yes."

"Well, it worked."

She flattens the cloth on her leg and looks up at me. "The blood charm was activated at the Elementiary."

Why didn't Astoria tell me she'd seen Da when I asked? Was she helping him find the creator of Sanguine? I need to talk to her again, to see if she has more answers. "Let's go there next."

"I figured you'd say that after you woke from your nap." She pushes open the door. "We're already there."

Wind gusts through Celize's narrow roads, carrying the green scent of earth, crumbled rocks, and impending change. My gut tells me all the secrecy surrounding Sanguine is soon to be unearthed, and I'm itchy for the answers. It would be wonderful to have more information to help Aodren.

The Elementiary doors are locked. I'm not expecting that, considering the early hour. I walk around the back, to where Astoria's home is connected to the building. I'm barely raising my hand to knock on her door when the sound of someone coughing stops me.

"She has asked about you." I recognize Astoria's rumbly, old voice.

This is the woman I trust and love, so it makes no sense that my first reaction is to hide. But some instinct tells me to tiptoe over to the small flower garden and wedge myself beside the window. It's hard to hear over the crash of waves against the cliffs beyond her home. I can tell Astoria is talking to another person, but I cannot tell what they're saying. I move until my head is as close to the window as it can be without being visible to anyone inside.

The thump and scuff of Astoria's cane-assisted walk nears the window. "She's upset that you haven't returned yet." Astoria's voice is louder now, though still in a hushed, guarded tone. "Don't dismiss what I'm saying. She didn't tell you that she entered the showcase."

"Lirra entered the showcase?"

I'd recognize that voice anywhere. I grip the windowsill to stop myself from running inside the house and hugging him. Da is here? Has he just arrived?

Astoria says something I don't catch.

A gruff "you know that wasn't possible." And then, soft and reflective: "She never said anything."

His sadness triggers my own. I step away from the window, intending to walk inside and tell him everything about my gliders. I missed the showcase, but it will be enough to share them with Da.

"I have a meeting with Soma shortly about the oil," Da says, and I stop. *Sanguine?* Will Da confront him? The dust of the oubliette's bones still coats my skin. A sharp snap of anxiety for what Soma will do to Da whips through me. Da cannot go alone to meet with the judge. I have to tell him —

"Not the truth. It will devastate her, Millner." Astoria's warning breaks through my spiraling thoughts. I missed what was said before her somber comment. What has Da done?

"She is a clever girl. If she convinced King Aodren to share what was in his letter, I know she didn't stop there. Besides, all this time I've been talking to traders, threatening them even, and you go and tell her about Sanguine."

"I had to warn her away. What if she decided to use it?"

My father snorts, and it's more derisive than I thought possible from him. "Why stop there? You may as well have told her all I've done. I'm surprised she hasn't caught on to me already." The lash of anger subsides into remorse, both so unlike his usual cheer.

Surprised she hasn't caught on to me . . .

I stumble away from the window, a hand flattened to my stomach and a bitter tang in my saliva. Nonononono. I don't want to know the truth to this secret. And yet the cogs of my brain are twisting the pieces into place, and all I can think of is a memory from the past.

Da's dimpled rose-hued cheeks paired with a wide grin when he measured my height two years ago. "Beetle, any day now you're going to pass me up. What shall I call you then?"

I stretched onto my toes, laughing when I rose a fraction above him. "You mean today?"

Prudence's description of the two people who left the oil at Duff Baron's drop point could be anyone — one tall and one short and round through the middle.

Or, they could be Judge Soma and Da.

It doesn't matter that Aodren is leaving at the end of the All Kingdoms' Summit; there's no future for us now. Not when one of the men supplying the oil that's spurring Channeler rumors and discord in Malam is my father. For the first time, I think of Da by the name all of Malam knows — Archtraitor.

I stare at the window, turning over everything we've learned about the oil. We're still missing a piece of the puzzle. Da and Judge Soma couldn't make the oil themselves. There must be a Channeler involved.

Could it be . . . Astoria?

CHAPTER

33

AODREN

L EIF NEARLY KNOCKS ME OVER WHEN I WALK
out of the healer's room.

Margeria saved my driver's life and
tended to my bruises. The fight outside the Elementiary took only moments to double in size
as more Shaerdanians and Malamians rushed
to join. But a fire ignited in the smithy's shop,
and soon heat and flame were billowing from the
building. Everyone fighting was forced to stop
and put out the blaze. The last thing I remember
was rushing toward the flame.

When I woke in the healer's room, my head
felt as if it had been crushed. The truth was close:
the fire had set off an explosion. And I'd been hit
by debris.

"You're up and walking," Leif says, his gaze

skating over me. His face has taken a beating. He's out of breath and sweaty.

"Leif," I say in surprise, "I've been down for a day. I've had time to recover. But what happened to you?" I give him a sideways look, taking in the sweat running down his temples. Did he go out and get in a fight from the anger? This cannot just be a side effect of the oil.

"Don't look at me like that," he snaps, and then rubs his brow. "Sorry, sir. I—I didn't mean . . . You can look at me . . . I'm fine. It's not from the oil."

His disheveled state is a concern and draws the attention of Seeva and the other Guild members as they file out of the room.

Ku Toa stops and nods to him. "It did not work?"

He shakes his head. "I didn't take it."

My expression must be complete confusion, because she turns and explains to me that half a bottle of Sanguine was used to heal me. She gave him the remainder to help him overcome the effects of the imposter oil.

"And you didn't take it?" I turn to Leif, surprised that he didn't accept her generosity. "And . . . is that blood on your arm?"

He seems baffled about the last bit. He glances to where his shirt has been sliced and then side to side at the guards in the hall. "Right, yes. I was cut. Two nights ago, Lirra came to see me because . . . That doesn't matter. And when she left for the—"

"Did you say, *Lirra?*" Katallia breaks apart from the group and returns to my side. "I was worried when she missed the showcase. We haven't seen her since."

"She, uh, was sneaking out," Leif says, wincing as if Lirra's aunt will be shocked or dismayed. She is neither. "She ran into Judge Soma. Overheard him talking about the oil. He admitted to giving it to Otto and Folger, and he said something about giving it to Baltroit. Lirra said it was obvious he's the supplier."

Katallia sucks in sharply. "Seeva, come back!"

"But what of Lirra? Where is she now?" I ask, urgency screaming through my veins.

The other women return, and Leif continues. "He caught her and had her thrown in the oubliette."

The world stands still, and at the same time my head spins, imagining what Lirra must've gone through. If she could barely survive the confinement of the regular prison cells, how could she have survived even one minute in the oubliette, let alone an entire night? I never should have involved her in my search for the truth about the oil.

"I realized where she was with help from her friend Orli. I came down here to get help, but you were unconscious. So I went back. But not before running into Soma's guards." He gestures to his face.

"The supplier is Judge Soma," Seeva is saying to the other Guild members.

This news is a blessed relief that couldn't have come soon

enough, considering the tournament and the grand finale of the jubilee are tonight. If only Lirra weren't the cost.

"Where is she now?" I break into the conversation. It doesn't matter that I have finally secured a meeting to determine trade with the Kolontians. I have to go to Lirra.

"At her home."

"And what of Judge Soma? Has he been arrested?" I'm ready to hunt the bastard down right now.

"Guards will be sent to detain him," Seeva says. "He will be held in his quarters."

"He would be better detained in the oubliette."

Soma doesn't deserve the luxury and comfort of his quarters. Not when Lirra spent the night in the oubliette.

"Your Highness," Seeva holds up a hand. "I understand your concerns. However, Judge Soma is Judge Auberdeen's right-hand man. The law states that the evidence must be reviewed before he is convicted and punished."

"And what has Judge Auberdeen said about his right-hand man?"

"Only that he'll not pass judgement on his kinsmen until the evidence has been brought forth."

I grit my teeth, too furious to respond. What more does Auberdeen need?

"Judge Auberdeen has agreed to meet with us two hours before the tournament to hear all evidence," Seeva says, even though I'm already walking away from the group. "Then, we can officially have Judge Soma thrown in the cell and we can announce the truth to the crowd, bringing an end to the rumors."

Her plan sounds fair, even if I don't like it. At least the Sanguine nightmare is almost at an end. Any of the relief to be had is eclipsed by my anxiousness to see Lirra.

My guards fall into place behind me as I exit the hall. They will follow me all the way to Lirra's house if I don't stop them.

"I'm going alone" I say, regardless of the risks of traveling without their protection.

Both men stare at me. Lirra trusted me with the location of her home. I won't compromise her family's secrecy. "You won't follow me. That's a command. Do you understand?"

One nods, and the other's eyes widen. In spite of the danger of traveling unguarded, I've done it before and can do so again now so as not to lead anyone to Lirra's private home.

They agree to stay with Leif, and then I walk out of the castle and saddle up Gale. It's a relief to ride my horse for the first time since arriving at the summit, instead of being carted around. At my urging, Gale tears out of the stables and across the Shaerdanian countryside of rolling hills cloaked by low hanging clouds and patches of forests. We enter the secluded glade around Lirra's quaint home, and as I dismount, a few stray raindrops fall from the gray sky.

Leaving Gale to graze on the grass, I stride to the front door and knock.

"Aodren? What are you doing here?" Lirra's voice comes from behind me.

I spin around and find her walking toward me. Air rushes into my lungs at the sight of her.

"What are you doing here?" she repeats, the words brisk and prickly.

I leap off the door's stoop and meet her in the middle of the field. "I was worried. Leif told me what happened and I . . . I came as soon as I knew. Are you well?"

I have no doubt that the story Leif relayed, one told to him by Lirra, of Judge Soma and the Shaerdanian champions is true. And soon, all three will receive their due punishment. I'll make sure of it.

"Well enough." Her answer is tired and small. Her arms press tight to her body, and her gaze skitters around the clearing, lingering on the space separating us. Her eyes take in the smudges of soot on my tunic and my disheveled hair. "And you? Are you well?"

"I am. More so now than before. There was a fire, but I'm fine. And as for Soma, he'll be dealt with, for this and for the Sanguine. When I think of you in the oubliette—"

A shudder rolls from her shoulders to her toes, and I shut my lips, pressing them into a sealed line to keep from saying anything more that would bring her discomfort.

I step forward, opening my arms. "Lirra? Truly, I'm here if you need to talk."

She doesn't move forward, and I wonder if she realizes I have just repeated the same words she gave me when I was suffering. Lirra stares at my arms. One hard blink, and then: "I'm fine. I am."

If the dark smudges under her eyes and the unusual pallor of her skin are any indication, she is lying. To both of us.

"But I'm not," I say.

Her chin kicks up, a question forming on her mouth.

"I think of you stuck there, and it kills me. I should have known something was wrong when you didn't meet me before the showcase. I'll never forgive myself that I wasn't there for you."

Lirra draws in a stuttering breath.

It feels like we are two damaged ships at sea amidst a swell threatening to sink us, when all we really need to survive is each other. The provisions she's lacking I have in abundance, and what I need is simply her.

Her lips are sealed together tight. Her eyes stare at me with more sadness than I can handle.

My body lurches toward hers, and I pull her into my arms.

Lirra softens, her body slumping against mine, her curves the right fit to my hard angles as if we were made for each other. I breathe in her bright, sunshine scent, wanting to capture it. A quiet sob catches on my surcoat, and her shoulders tremble.

"Lirra," I whisper, tightening my arms around her. "Lirra,

I'm here." I run a soothing hand up and down her back and then hang my forehead beside her neck, wishing I could do more to return her light. "It must have been terrifying."

Her head bobs.

"I'm sorry." I run my fingers over her hair and drop a kiss onto her forehead. "I'm sorry you missed the showcase. You worked hard, and everyone would have loved your gliders."

She clutches me tighter, as if she'll never have the chance again. I have to swallow my chuckle, because I have no intention of ever letting go. "I wish I could take away your anguish. I would do anything for you." The firm truth in my words surprises me.

Lirra leans back to peer up at me with sad eyes, and then she's moving away, freeing herself from my arms and drying her face with the backs of her hands. Did I say something wrong?

She looks off at the gray horizon. "Is there another reason you came? Other than to check on me?"

I stare at her. She's using all my worst lines. Is she trying to push me away?

"You were my only reason," I admit.

Her hands flex. Shadows move over the ground we're standing on. Above us, clouds block the sun.

"Leif told me how you were caught," I say after a long pause, knowing at some point her testimony will be a key piece of evidence if the Channelers Guild cannot find anything else.

I explain what Leif told us about the conversation Lirra heard. "A meeting is set with the Akarians and the Channelers Guild for this afternoon. We will meet two hours before the start of the tournament and the jubilee. They need proof that Soma is supplying Sanguine. Your testimony would be enough. Will you come?"

"I . . . I could've been mistaken," Lirra says, as if she cannot believe it herself. "I'm not certain I heard him correctly."

"Pardon?" I'm shocked. Leif had seemed so sure of Lirra's story. And I've never known Lirra to lie, not about something as important as this.

"Soma may not be the supplier."

May not be? "You don't need to fear his reaction," I say, guessing the reason. "He will not be able to touch you again. As soon as I return to the castle, I'll use my authority to ensure he will not approach you, and neither will his guards. You won't have to look over your shoulder." She will have the protection of the alliance among Akaria, the Channelers Guild, and Malam. More than that, she'll have mine. I will never allow anyone to harm Lirra again.

"I'm not afraid of him." Her voice is stronger now. A raindrop hits her cheek, and she bats it away. "He might be giving Sanguine to his competitors—that's something he's already admitted to. But it doesn't mean he's broken the law. At least, not one that has been written in the big rule book."

Could Leif have misunderstood? No.

"Why would Judge Soma put you in the oubliette, then? There has to be more to this story," I say, my voice sharpening at the end.

Lirra jolts. She turns around, giving me her back. Dirt from the oubliette marks her clothing and hits me with new guilt. "There is nothing more."

She has no motivation to protect Judge Soma. I can fathom no other reason why she'd lie for him. This doesn't make sense.

"No new development? Anything to clarify what you first heard?"

She emphatically shakes her head. "No. I overheard him giving Sanguine to Otto and Folger, nothing more. It doesn't prove he's the supplier."

That much is true. During the first dinner the summit shared, Soma admitted he thought the oil was beneficial. If Lirra has nothing more incriminating to add, there isn't enough to prove Judge Soma is the supplier. The conversation Lirra overheard was all we needed, and now she's pulling it away. Why?

"You're certain?" I ask.

"I have already answered this, Aodren. Yes, I am certain. I have nothing more." Her voice is tight and angry.

I pace toward Gale, trying to get a hold on my thoughts. Lirra's posture is strung tight as a cistern's strings, and her hands are clenched in the loose material of her tunic. There is no reason she could possibly want to help Judge Soma after he threw her in the oubliette. But she's lying, I'm certain of it. I just don't know about what.

"I'll let Leif know," I say, my acceptance coming out gruffly. "Will you still come to the meeting?"

"I have nothing for them."

"Yes, I know, but you have been part of this search. I would like for you to give any input. We will meet two hours before the tournament, by the field."

She dips her chin in a small nod, and I take it to mean she will come. It's a relief. I stare up at the gray clouds slinking across the sky and darkening the horizon. A raindrop hits my nose, my shoulder, my chest, a warning of the downpour sure to come.

"The summit is almost over," I say, loathing the fact that I will be returning to Malam in a few short days. She turns around, and I take in the beautiful curves of her face, wanting to memorize them. There is so much left to learn about Lirra. Something tells me that I could spend a lifetime near her and still be entranced by her wit. If I thought there was even a sliver of a chance she'd consider living in Malam, I would ask her to come with me. Her family still has land there that is rightfully hers. But I know how she feels about Malam. She will never leave Shaerdan.

"Let's not waste what little time we have left talking about the oil," I say, wanting to stretch these last days until they last forever. I hate that today's reunion has already been damp-ened by Judge Soma. "You missed the showcase, but I am still eager to watch you fly your gliders. Will you show me?"

Lirra's gaze is caught on Gale, who has moved from her lawn to the edge of the clearing, where the grasses grow longer. More raindrops patter on the ground.

"Or we could go for a ride," I offer when she doesn't re-spond. "I know it's starting to rain, but what do you say?"

The edges of her mouth quirk upward.

A gust of wind blows between us. The almost smile flits away, and Lirra steps back. "You're leaving soon."

"I don't have to."

"Not today. I meant you're returning to Malam after the summit." Her hand waves in the air, as if adding a dozen more tasks to an invisible list. "There's no time left."

"We could make time." I don't care that I sound desperate.

"Do you not have a meeting today?" She wears a tight smile.

"I canceled it."

"You shouldn't have done that. Not for me," she says, and I want to yell. Can she not see how important she is to me?

"Lirra. Of course for you." I step forward. "I want to be here. I would do anything for —"

"Don't say it," she whispers. "The time we've spent together has been fun, but . . . I have other things that need my attention. My life is busy." She adds a light laugh that rings false in my ears.

There is so much wrong with what she's said, I don't know where to begin. I shudder against the forced happiness in her tone, because it mocks the depth of what I feel. Whatever has developed between us has completely entranced me. I know she feels similarly. She admitted as much the other night. *Fun,* she said. Yes, it has been that, and also so much more. I've given her my trust, and if I'm being honest, my heart as well.

Perhaps the approaching end has eclipsed her feelings. The summit is nearly over, and for that I have no solution. Regardless of my feelings for Lirra, I must return to my kingdom, and I know she will stay in hers.

"Meet me at the cathedral tomorrow before dawn," I implore. "This doesn't have to be the end. Let's not say goodbye now."

Her eyes sweep closed. Is she thinking of watching the sunrise with me? *Gods,* I hope so.

A rumble of thunder bellows above, and Lirra's eyes snap open. The clouds give up their fight, and the rain falls. Lirra raises her hand to keep droplets out of her eyes and glances to the house. "I cannot."

The rejection is a slap.

"Aodren," she says, and I think she's drumming up a response to soften the blow. "I don't think we should see each other again. It's best we part ways now."

Her words level me.

"Is that really what you want?" I croak. "Is this where we end?"

"Goodbye, Your Highness."

CHAPTER

34

LIRRA

THE RAIN SOAKS ME. I KEEP MY HEAD DOWN, eyes pinched closed, as Aodren's horse gallops out of the clearing, each hoofbeat a chisel to the fractures in my heart. When he's gone, all that remains is a mess of splintered, ugly pieces inside my hollow chest.

It's better this way. Da's knack for keeping secrets won't stand against the Channelers Guild and two kingdoms' determination to uncover the truth. From the little I overheard this morning, I know that when the entirety of Da's machinations comes to light, the devastation will be immense. All this time, as Aodren and I were searching for someone with Channeler knowledge and power in the trade industry, I never considered Da.

I still don't understand how he and Soma are

working together, or if Astoria is involved. I hope for the sake of my broken heart that she is not.

All I'm certain of is what I heard.

I'm surprised she hasn't caught on to me, Da said. But now that I have, I wish I'd never looked into Sanguine, never thought to prove myself to Da so he could spend more time at home. Of all the secrets I've kept for my father, this is the one that hurts the most. The Akarians and the Channelers Guild are all hunting down the truth alongside Aodren. It's not a matter of if he'll find out the truth, but when. He'll never look at me the same.

The thought is too much to bear, so I made the selfish choice. I picked facing his confusion and pain today rather than the loathing rejection that is sure to come.

"Lirra, you'll catch a cold," Eugenia shouts. The squeak of the door is barely audible over the downpour. She holds it open and waves at me. "Hurry in."

She doesn't complain when I step into the kitchen and a lake of water drips from my trousers. Eugenia wraps me in a blanket, the one from her bed. "What were you doing?"

A shiver racks my spine. I shake my head, mouth too chalky and bitter to talk.

"We came to the showcase." She waits, and when I don't respond, she adds, "The boys were so excited to see your gliders. But you didn't perform."

I think of my glider and wonder if it's still sitting on a Channeler cart at the tournament field. I spent months designing and building the wings. Performing in the showcase has been a secret dream of mine for so long. And now what? Do I wait another five years? The answer falls into the same gray obscurity that has become Da's future as well as my own.

"I decided not to," I say, voice wooden.

"Lirra." She touches my arm. "I was wrong to criticize you for not spending enough time helping your da. His business, that's his dream. And I know you try to help him because you love him. But his business isn't your dream. Let it be his, while you find yours."

"Is that all? I . . . I should go change."

"You must've had a long night," she says, not wanting to pry, and at the same time, her tone is tinged with curiosity. Again, I don't respond. Her hands are working the mess of hair off my drenched face. "You look weary. Which won't do for today's event. The boys have been looking forward to watching the last tournament event and then the grand finale of the jubilee. Everyone will be in their finest for tonight, so we need to get you dried, rested, and dressed in that pretty green gown you own."

Her tone is no different than usual, but today I hear a gentleness in her voice, a motherly sound. Has it always been there, and I never noticed?

"If only your father had returned in time," she sighs.

I tuck away the rise of hurt into the farthest corner of my heart and step out of her loose embrace. The little *clip-clap* of footsteps announces the twins. Julisa must be down for a nap.

"Why's Lirra all wet?" Loren kicks the puddle I've made.

"Don't spread the water," Eugenia scolds. "Go fetch a rag to help sop up the mess."

Of course he doesn't listen. Instead, Loren points at my clothing. "You been playing in the rain? Without us?"

I don't know why the question loosens a broken laugh. "Something like that."

"I like the rain, but I hope it clears before dusk," Loren says. "We're dying to see the jubilee."

"We're hoping they'll let you fly your gliders tonight, Lir," Kiefer admits. Hardly ever one to talk, his soft-spoken manner is the first spread of balm to the ache inside me. "Since you missed last night."

Eugenia rubs the blanket over my arms, adding more warmth to the ice under my skin. "After the excitement that's been building in this house, it would be a wonderful thing if the Guild allowed you to perform. Perhaps you can talk to your aunt Katallia and she can find some way for you to go on."

Her enthusiasm is echoed by the boys.

"Do you think?" Kiefer asks.

His hopeful face, so sweet and genuine and mirrored by the others, hurts my heart, because I know the answer will disappoint. "No, I've missed my chance. But . . . there is always next time."

Eugenia scoots the littleuns out of the kitchen. For once, I allow myself to lean on her, using her support to help me to my attic room, where I strip out of my wet clothes and find solace in the cocoon of my warm bed.

The lumps of the straw mattress dig into my hip. My blanket, well-worn and comfortable, itches my neck. I toss side to side, seeking rest.

It doesn't come until long after Aodren and the Guild have begun their meeting.

We reach the field, the twins winding around me. They're so excited, it takes time to navigate through the crowd. After we find a place with a decent view, I tell Eugenia that I'm going to check on my glider, to ensure that it's still here and no one has harmed it.

"The fight is soon to begin," she says, reminding me. The crowd is busy calling out for their champions. Each time I hear Leif's and Aodren's names, it spreads a seed of ache through me. I can't decide if seeing Aodren will hurt too much or if I need this final glimpse of him.

I rush to north side of the field where the Channelers were supposed to meet yesterday for the showcase. Hopefully all is well with my glider, and I can return to sit with Eugenia and the littleuns.

"You did well, Beetle."

I spin around to face Da. My heart is lodged so high in my throat, the ache makes it impossible to swallow. He stands at the edge of the tent, thinner than he was two months ago. Even the edges of his face are not quite so soft and round. The rosy glow that used to light his cheeks is gone. Any joy I feel at seeing him again is pierced by confusion and anger.

"You deceived me, Da," I say, direct as we've always been with each other, as he should have been with me from the start of his dealings with Aodren. "You sent me that letter and made me take one to Aodren. You acted as if you were helping him, as if you cared to find out the truth about Sanguine. But you already knew the truth, didn't you?"

He twists side to side, seeing who might be listening, and then moves closer. A frown turns his muddy brows into one furry slash. "Careful, Beetle. There are ears all around. Now what's this? You think I've done what?"

I prop fists on my hips and breathe out a puff of air from my nostrils. "Why don't you tell me?"

"We can talk about this later." He reaches out to guide me back toward the field, and I shrug away. Talking about this later isn't acceptable.

"I heard what you said to Astoria. I *heard* you."

And I tell him everything. From the fight at the fountain and my night in the cells to my search for the truth about Sanguine with Aodren to Judge Soma and the oubliette. The only thing I do not tell him is that saying goodbye to Aodren is the hardest thing I've ever had to do. And when I'm finished, he looks rattled to his core.

"Oh, Lirra. You were never meant to get involved. I didn't want this for you." His mouth gapes, and his neck wobbles.

"But you don't understand, not everything. I need you to let this go. Drop this matter. Please."

"Drop this?" My anger sparks. "Do you deny that you're working with Judge Soma on this?"

"I am not conspiring with Soma."

I arch a single brow, expecting an explanation, which he doesn't provide.

"Tell me the truth." The demand snaps out of me like a whip. Near the tent, people turn and look at us. Da sees them, and his lips pinch together. I no longer care if people hear us. I'm overfull of secrets.

"I cannot," he whispers. "This is why I asked King Aodren not to tell you anything."

I want to stomp away or hit something or shake him, but all I can do is stand here in frustration so thick it's nearly suffocating. "Why?"

"You're too clever and persistent for your own good, Beetle. Let this go."

"After everything I've told you, that's all you have to say? That you cannot tell me for my own good?" I spit out the questions, venom dripping from each word. "I have dedicated everything to you. I've set aside everything I've ever wanted so I could serve you, help you, be the partner you needed to make up for Mother's death and for all you lost because of me. I—I thought if I did enough, I would be worthy of your sacrifice. At least of your time. But—but . . ." The meanness subsides into all my hidden truths, spilling out so rapidly, it's as if one of my wings has broken and I'm falling to the earth at full speed.

"Oh, my girl," he says, unbearable sadness lacing his voice.

A hot tear streams down my cheek. I shove it away with the back of my hand. "I don't understand this. I don't understand why you've done this. Why you won't explain. Have I not done enough to deserve the truth?"

"You have." It comes out broken and sorrowful. "You've done more than I ever should've asked."

I feel like a deflated windbag. The carts carrying the Channeler items are close by. I trudge to the cart holding my glider. It's a relief to find my wings safely tucked under a tarp, hidden away. The cheers of the crowd increase and then fade, and the announcer calls out the name of the first competitor.

"I would've liked to see you fly," Da says behind me.

Me too.

CHAPTER

35

AODREN

I LEAVE THE CHAMPIONS' TENT AND WALK A wide berth around the tournament field, hoping to unburden my thoughts. Though the rain has taken a break, the grass is soggy underfoot. It sends a chill up through my legs that adds to my already dampened mood.

At the meeting with the Guild and the Akarians, it was decided that the break between the sword fight and the start of the jubilee will be when Seeva and I take the field and inform the crowd about Sanguine. The consequences will be devastating because without Lirra's story, Auberdeen won't detain or punish Judge Soma. Even if I explain to the crowd that there is likely one person with ill intent behind the trade, there is sure to be backlash. Already, I've had lords requesting all Channeler trade be ended because the goods cannot be trusted. Tonight's announcement will only add fodder to their fears. Then, when no Channeler stands up for Malam, everyone will conclude that Channelers are not welcome in Malam, no matter how many decrees I pass.

I walk behind the stands where the nobility sit. Judge Soma reclines in his seat, conversing with other noble kinsmen from Shaerdan. I want to tear him apart. It guts me to see him sitting here. He's guilty of the trade, I know it. But I'm left without proof and no time remaining to find it.

The tournament begins soon.

With a clear mind on what must happen tonight, I walk around the north end of the field, avoiding the large crowds on my way back to the champions' tent.

Carts and carriages of jubilee supplies clog this area. I wind through them and discover Lirra. Shock rocks through me when I realize she's conversing with Millner. He's a little worse for wear, but his appearance is a miracle. I can only hope he knows more than what he included in his letter.

The rumble of voices and cheers from the field drown out the sound of their conversation. I cannot hear what Millner and Lirra are discussing. However, I watch her beautiful face. Tonight it's an artist's canvas of shifting scenes. Anger fades into sadness, which settles into resolve. The sun slips down into the ocean, and the last bruised remnants of the sunset in shades of purple and yellow and orange light her face, and glint against the tear on her cheek. I want to be by her side, helping her through whatever is causing her so much pain. But she made it clear this afternoon that she wanted nothing more to do with me. I must respect her wishes.

People pass between us, blocking my view. When the crowd clears, Lirra is gone. However, Millner remains beside the carriage.

Instead of heading toward the tournament field, he walks to where a covered wagon is parked a little ways from the Channeler carts. Now that the sun has dipped below the horizon, it's difficult to see clearly. I think he lifts his hand, as if he's greeting someone.

It is not my usual method of operation to listen in on private conversations, but I'm certain Lirra knows more than she told me this morning. Secret or not, what Millner has to say may be the answer I need, that my kingdom needs. Considering how stingy he is with answers, and how Lirra is not willing to talk to me, my only option is take the information out of the air. I draw on every speck of sneaking skill I've learned from Lirra and maneuver until I'm within hearing range. It's a good thing I haven't donned any armor yet, or crouching silently beside the carriage wheel would be impossible.

Two people converse on the other side of the wagon, Millner and an older woman. The crackle in her aged voice sounds like the woman I met at the Elementiary, Astoria. But I'm not close enough to know for certain.

"She thinks I'm the one who is supplying the oil." Millner's voice crumbles around the words.

My intake of breath is swift. *Lirra believes Millner is guilty?* Why would she come to this conclusion? My confusion is only made worse when I think of the last twenty-four hours. Her belief that Millner is the supplier must be related to the reason she emphatically declared Soma was innocent. When I returned from Lirra's home, I assigned Leif to follow Soma everywhere, to make sure the man keeps far away from Lirra, and to report any suspicious activity. Even now, I have Segrande keeping an eye on Soma while Leif prepares to fight. Neither one of them has reported anything that raises suspicion. So is it possible Lirra is right about Millner?

I strain to listen.

"What did you tell her?" the woman asks.

"I asked her to let the topic go."

"And will she?"

Never. Even I know Lirra won't be deterred from seeking out something she wants. Our entire time together is proof of that.

"Let us hope," Millner says. The man is a fool.

"How much longer will it take?"

An aggravated sigh comes out of Millner. "It doesn't matter that I've informed the traders of the dangers of Sanguine;

the people they're selling it to only want more. I spent the last two months talking to every trader who has gotten the oil from Soma. Very few would relinquish their remaining stock to me. Those who did charged a small fortune. I've had my life threatened a dozen times for trying to stop the trade."

If he is trying to stop the trade, it doesn't make sense that he would be the supplier. So why is this information something he couldn't have shared with Lirra? What could be worse than Lirra thinking her father is the cause of so much destruction?

"It's time to approach the Guild, Astoria."

"You cannot." Her response is harsh and cold. It's a punch.

"Your oil has spread too far. Too many people are at risk. People have died. One of the champions has died."

"He deserved it," she says, and the malice in her tone shocks me. She wasn't a supporter of mine by any means, but this is more callous. "What does it matter if a few Malamians die? How many of my Channeler sisters perished in the Purge?"

"A life for a life? Is that what is this? You told me it was a mistake. That you had made an oil for trade and didn't realize the harm it would do."

A pause.

"You did realize," Millner says.

I lean against the carriages, the truth nearly knocking me off my feet. Lirra has told me that Astoria is like a grandmother to her. Astoria was there for Millner when he fled Malam with his baby daughter, helping him establish a new life in Shaerdan. Is this why Millner wouldn't tell Lirra the truth? To protect her from this betrayal? Gods, Lirra believes her father is guilty when really it is Astoria.

"They. Killed. My. Sister." Astoria's fury clips her words. Her tone is full of spikes and edges and venom. "She had a family and a small Elementiary in Malam, and they destroyed it! They killed your wife. They hunted thousands of Channelers over the last twenty years. Every single giftless citizen of Malam is culpable. All of them. The murders are on their heads, not mine. They wanted to pillage us and take our power. Well, I gave it to them. Every greedy Malamian can have a taste of Channeler power. And I hope it rots them from the inside out."

"No, Astoria. Listen to yourself. Those days are over," Millner argues with her, but she can no longer see reason.

"They will never be over, you fool. Their hatred and fear are a poison. It will seep into their soil and pass on to the next generation. That king thinks he can convince my sister Channelers to return. It is a trap. And I will do what I can to expose him."

"Astoria." Millner's voice cracks. "You shouldn't have done this."

"He wants us for our magic, so I'm giving him a bitter dose of what we can do." Her voice curls and snaps.

"You're blinded by your anger. Can you not see that your plan will hurt Channelers in the end?"

"You know that isn't my intention," she shrieks. "But there are always casualties in a war. If one of us should fall for the rest of us to recognize the dangers, then that is what must happen. Those Channelers that moved to Malam were foolish. That land is festering with fear and hate. Channelers will never be safe there."

"And Soma?" Millner asks.

"He had the most access to traders in Malam. He knew it was dangerous but wanted to make himself into a wealthy man."

"He hurt my girl," Millner roars.

His shout is overwhelmed by the boom of applause and rhythmic stomping. The fight is starting. Hand on my sword, I step out of hiding to confront Millner and Astoria.

"Been looking for you." Leif is rushing in my direction, hands full of armor, two swords strapped to his back, and a third holstered at his waist. "Seeds, this is heavy. You're next. If you don't come right away, Malam will be disqualified."

I rush to suit up in armor. I don't want to leave the matter of Astoria unattended. I must inform the Guild.

"I need to send a message to Seeva," I tell Leif.

"It'll have to wait till after," he says, and hands me a second sword. We hurry onto the field and join the other competitors.

Our names are shouted, the cheers of the crowd surge, and

maroon and gray flags are waved. The blare of trumpets starts the final event of the tournament.

In order to win the cup, we must win the sword fight flag. Unlike the melee, only two competitors enter the center of the field at a time. Points are earned by hits garnered during the timed bouts. Each champion will fight two different bouts against competitors whose names will be chosen at random. At the end of the evening, points will be tallied, the victor of the night declared, and a flag awarded.

The sound of a distant storm crackles in the background as Leif steps up for his first fight. It is against Fehana, the Akarian warrior. Leif's sword starts off fast, but as she rains strike after strike down on him, he cannot keep up. His energy is lower than it was two weeks ago, and his body weaker from trying to recover. It isn't long before she overwhelms him and wins the match.

He shakes her hand and trudges back to my side.

I'm called up next. From the start of the sword fight, fortune is finally in my corner. I duel one of the Plovians. His swordsmanship is no better than I expected after seeing him and his fellow champion in the other events. He is no match for my years of trained skill, and I accumulate many points before my first bout is over.

Shaerdan wins a match when Otto beats Hemmet, then the Akarians score a win over Kolontia. They're followed by a

Plovian facing off against Shaerdan's other competitor, Folger. Shaerdan wins.

Then Leif is called up to fight the Kolontian. I can tell he's tired, and his body strains to block and parry. He struggles to move through drills we have done a hundred times, but Leif is full of grit. His muscles flex and shift as he gives everything to the bout.

"Leif O'Floinn of Malam" is called as the match's winner, and the crowd booms their approval. People cheer for him, the Channeler Defender of Malam. The support of the audience is so strong, it gives me hope that when Malam doesn't have a Channeler stand up at the jubilee, they will be forgiving. Perhaps they will understand that change takes time.

I'm called up next for my second bout. This time, my name flits around the tournament field as a light patter of rain plinks against my plate armor. The crowd's support only increases the pressure. Hemmet, the Kolontian, raises his sword against mine. He just lost to the Akarian warrior, and anger blazes hot in his eyes. He will be a formidable opponent.

He proves as much the moment our swords clash. If I hadn't seen the man fight the first night of the melee and I hadn't warned him away from the fake Sanguine, I'd be tempted to think he's taken the imposter oil. He is a blaze of speed. Our battle sends a constant ring of steel into the wind and rain. I land a hit, only to feel the sting of his moments later. Between clashes, we circle each other, avoiding the muddy puddles that have formed on the field. I know to win this match I must dig deeper, draw up strength from the years of training, and sharpen my strikes.

On his next swing, I parry and twist. The movement gives me enough space to slam the blunt of my blade against his ribs. He grunts. I hear the sound echoing from the mouth hole in his helmet. Hemmet tries to defend against my attack. I lunge, cut, strike, twist, hit, faster and faster, drawing on every ounce of strength to gain a strong lead. I only need to keep it up until the rule makers blow the horn.

The crowd is louder than the waves that crash against Celize's cliffs.

Hemmet blocks my swing and thrusts his sword against my shoulder. The injury from the melee screams to life. I shuffle back, putting distance between us to catch my breath. My feet slip out from beneath me. I tumble into the mud.

Hemmet raises his sword.

I roll to escape his swing, and suddenly I can't breathe. My lungs stop working. No air comes in or out. *What's happening?*

I grasp my neck. Why can I not breathe? I roll my head to the side, looking for Hemmet, and his blade, which should've dropped already. I tear at my armor, trying to pull oxygen into my body. Hemmet watches me, not understanding my actions. He lowers his blade.

I open my mouth, futilely attempting to suck in air.

From what I see of Hemmet's eyes, he appears equally confused. The ground beside me thuds. He has dropped his sword. His hands are on my helmet, yanking it off.

My vision fades into spots, and then darkness.

CHAPTER
36

LIRRA

ODREN DOESN'T INSTANTLY GET BACK ON his feet, and I know something is wrong.

Hemmet's hit wasn't hard enough to have Aodren writhing, or grasping for his neck. What could be the problem?

I push my way through the crowd to get closer, worry building with each step.

Hemmet's sword drops to the ground, and then he's on his knees, reaching for Aodren's helmet. After he yanks it off and tosses it to the side, I can see Aodren's wide eyes, and the sight of his frantic movement hits me like arrows of fiery panic.

He cannot breathe! Realization whips through me that this isn't because the air has been knocked out of him.

Someone has created a vacuum, drawing Aodren's air.

My gaze ricochets in every direction in search of the Channeler and lands on Astoria, not even a dozen paces away, her hands subtly turned toward the field. The world grinds to a halt and at the same time spirals out of control. Astoria is the woman who taught me how to pull air from someone. I see her concentration and know with dizzying certainty what she's doing. A voice in my head screams, *This cannot be true,* so emphatically, so shrilly, I wince.

"No!" I shout.

And then my feet are moving, I'm running, shoving people out of my way, and slamming into Astoria, knocking her to the ground. She yelps and gapes up at me, eyes wide with guilt and at the same time wounded.

I scramble to my feet and look to the field, to Aodren. It's as if every particle in me once belonged to him and is now vying to return. I want to rush to his side. The only thing that keeps me in place is knowing Astoria didn't have enough time to completely suffocate him.

He'll be fine.

"What. Have. You. Done?" I look down at her.

Astoria presses herself up into a seated position and gasps. Her face crumples in pain, and her body shudders. Instinct has me reaching for her. When our palms connect, the warmth of her touch is dulled by the wind and rain and deception. But still, because of our history and who she is to me, I hold her quivering hand in mine and hate myself for doing it.

Her head sweeps side to side in a listless movement. "He was going to tell you."

"Tell me what?" I try to sound harsh, and yet, even though I know she has done something unforgivable, it hurts me to see her this way. Tears start to leak down her papery cheeks, mixing with the steady flow of rain, and my emotions almost spill over too. Astoria, who helped my father raise me from when I was a baby, tried to kill Aodren.

And then I think of Da's sadness, his plea for me to stop looking into Sanguine. I had already suspected Astoria's participation. But, to my own shame, I put more blame on my da, not wanting to believe Astoria would use her magic to cause so much harm.

"Tell me." I lurch forward and grasp her arm, yanking up her sleeve. Black veins twist over her age-spotted skin. A sign of dark magic.

I know the truth now, but I need to hear it from her.

"He overheard me talking. He knows I made the imposter Sanguine."

"Why, Astoria? How could you do such a thing?"

"I wanted to teach them to fear us. They've abused us for so long, Lirra. And now they want us back. They want our magic. So I gave them a terrible taste of our power. I showed them how dangerous it could be. Malam took everything from me." Her body trembles. "Just like they took everything from you. I wanted them to know that they are right to fear us."

The venom she spits shouldn't surprise me. All along, Astoria has been outspoken about her hatred for the Malamians who persecuted Channelers.

"Men have died," I cry, trying to get a hold on what enrages me most.

"Not as many as our sister Channelers. Do not feel sympathy for them," Astoria says, her voice turning more bitter. "They got what they deserved."

My limbs shake so violently with fury and remorse that her hand falls from mine. "And Da? How was he involved?"

"It didn't take him long to uncover my secrets once the bloody king of Malam sent him hunting. So I pretended I'd made the oil by accident. I sent your father to gather it up for me." She grits her teeth and shivers from the falling rain. She looks like a wild beast. "Your father deserved to be sent on a wild goose chase. He should never have agreed to work for that murdering bastard."

"Don't call him that," I say. "Aodren is a good man."

Da rushes over and crouches down beside me and Astoria. Shame at the realization that I've just given Astoria patience and love in light of her obvious betrayal and yet couldn't spare Da anything more than an angry word overwhelms me.

"Da, I'm sorry, so sorry." He pulls me into his arms. "I should never have doubted you."

Da strokes my hair and pats my back. "No, it is I who haven't been here for you."

The movement of people behind us catches my attention. Seeva, Katallia, and Judge Auberdeen approach us. Judge

Soma follows behind them with an uneasy look on his face. I jolt at the sight of him, but my father stands beside me, keeping his arms around my shoulders, lending his support. Support I'm not sure I even deserve.

I am not the only one who realizes Aodren was targeted by a wind Channeler. Judge Auberdeen demands an explanation.

Da recounts the day, months ago, that the king of Malam hired him to look into Sanguine. It didn't take him long to find his way back to Astoria. She convinced him that she'd created an oil, hoping it would have the benefits of the real Sanguine. But to her dismay, the oil harmed the giftless. He didn't know she was lying. He didn't realize that she wanted him out of the way so she could keep making the oil and giving it to Judge Soma to distribute. After all the abuse and pain, Astoria was certain Malam wanted to enslave and abuse Channelers for their power. Rage for every Channeler that had been killed fueled her.

Da spent two months tracking down each trader that sold the Sanguine. He bought batches of the imposter oil, only to discover more had flooded the market.

"I didn't know it could kill people," Judge Soma interrupts, eager to clear his name.

"A liar till the end." Astoria looks at him and sneers. "You're no better than any Malamian. I warned you of the consequences, but as soon as you saw that you could make money, you started shipping the oil as quickly as I could make it. And then you gave it to your fighters. I warned you it would kill them." Astoria slowly rises to her feet with the help of my aunt Katallia.

The chief judge turns to Soma and Astoria. The rain is light now, only a drop here and there. "What I've heard tonight and the information given to me by Millner is enough to have you executed."

Soma starts to deny the claims, but Judge Auberdeen silences him by beckoning the guards forward. "Seize them, and have them put in the holding cell."

I look to the far side where Aodren now stands beside Leif. Since the crowd was unaware of what happened off the field with Astoria and Judge Soma, they accepted the match as being over. The announcer declared Hemmet the winner of the bout, and the crowd's mixed reception to the news fills the night. A horn blares, signaling the end of the matches. Absorbed in Astoria's revelations, I had forgotten that the world around me did not stand still.

The yells of the spectators fall silent, and the announcer takes a minute to tally up the points earned. A collective breath is held as people wait to find out who will take home the sword fight banner.

"And the winner of the sword fight is . . . Akaria."

Stomping and cheering thunder through the crowd. The champions shake hands, and the two women warriors stride to the center of the field to accept the crowd's approval. I watch them out of the corner of my eye, but mostly my focus remains on Aodren. Leif leans over to him, and moves his fingers as if counting and then a disappointed frown cuts a deep line between Aodren's brows. I wonder what they're talking about.

My answer comes right away, when the official tournament horns are blown and two men carry the emerald-encrusted gold cup to the field.

"The tournament has been a great show of strength and skill," the announcer says, recounting moments of the melee, the joust, and tonight's sword fight. One at a time he calls forward each competitor, congratulating them on a job well done. My hope soars for Aodren as applause rings out when he steps forward.

"Now, let us announce the team that rose above the rest. The winning champions of the All Kingdoms' Cup are Akaria's woman warriors."

Everyone around the field surges to their feet, and applause fills the air as the two women walk forward to accept the cup. My eyes are on Aodren. He is gracious and kind to clap for them, his applause boisterous and genuine. Only those who know him well would see his lingering disappointment, and I want to go to him and say something that will bring back his smile. But after the secrets I've kept and the horrible way I treated him today . . .

"You want to go to him," Da says, always good at reading my thoughts. Besides Orli and Aodren, no one knows me better. "Did you think I missed the way you called him Aodren earlier?" He smiles. "I've never heard you refer to him as anything other than the bloody king of Malam before."

I do want to go to Aodren. But first I have to fix a wrong. "I'm sorry for not believing you. Everything I said wasn't fair. I love you, Da. I was angry with you for being gone and not including me. I took it to mean that you didn't rely on me. It hurts that you witheld inforrmation from me. But I can accept that you can manage your business how you want. I should've been patient and waited for you to tell me the truth when the time was right."

I feel the weight of his arm around my shoulders. "I love you too, Lirra. But if we're here to shed our lies, you need to be honest as well. I have spent too many days away from my family. I keep trying to save the world to save you. When, really, I'm losing you. I'm losing my family. I didn't need you to prove that you could manage that dangerous task. I knew you could. I just wanted to keep you safe and protected. And that's wrong of me. Because the more I try to keep you safe, the more I end up hurting you."

"But I want to help you. It's because of me that you had to give up your entire life in Malam."

He shakes his head. "No, it is because of me that your life was changed. You don't have to prove yourself to me. Lirra, you are one of the best parts of my life. You owe me nothing. If anything, I want you to take this time for you. What would make me happy is to see you live the life you've dreamed of."

I try to talk, but a soft sob comes out.

"I want you to know I'm here for you, so you have freedom and time to create your wings."

I've resisted allowing myself to really think about this for so long.

Before I can say anything more, Da nudges me forward. "Go on," he says, because he knows I cannot keep myself out of it. "Go brave one more storm tonight."

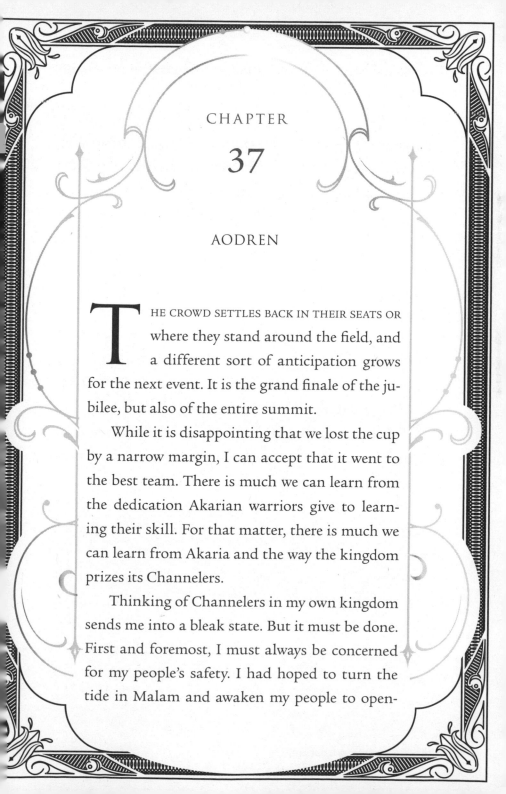

CHAPTER

37

AODREN

THE CROWD SETTLES BACK IN THEIR SEATS OR where they stand around the field, and a different sort of anticipation grows for the next event. It is the grand finale of the jubilee, but also of the entire summit.

While it is disappointing that we lost the cup by a narrow margin, I can accept that it went to the best team. There is much we can learn from the dedication Akarian warriors give to learning their skill. For that matter, there is much we can learn from Akaria and the way the kingdom prizes its Channelers.

Thinking of Channelers in my own kingdom sends me into a bleak state. But it must be done. First and foremost, I must always be concerned for my people's safety. I had hoped to turn the tide in Malam and awaken my people to openness when it comes to those who are different from them. But it has been an uphill battle, one only made worse by the spread of the terrible oil.

It galls me to have only Astoria's name to give Seeva as I leave Leif's side and stride to the center of the field. The operation seems too big for the older woman to run on her own.

Seeva comes from the opposite direction. We meet in the center, and I tell her what I overheard beside the Channeler carriages.

"I know," she whispers.

She does? When did she find out? And how? I would ask, but the announcer approaches us and holds a cone for Seeva to talk through so her voice will be amplified. She spreads her arms wide. "Welcome to the final event of our great summit, the jubilee grand finale!"

If I thought the spectators were loud before, it is nothing compared to the thunderous boom that shakes the ground I'm standing on. I have never seen so genuine a smile on Seeva's face. She explains the power of Channelers, and how their gifts enrich our world but should never be taken for granted or misused.

"Recently, we have heard word of a Channeler remedy that is being sold in our kingdoms called Sanguine. This oil, however, is not the same miraculous healing oil from Akaria that is also called Sanguine." Her blunt truthfulness takes me off-guard. A gasp rolls around the field as Seeva explains the difference between the Akarian Sanguine and the new, fake Sanguine. Disapproval sounds like a low thunder.

Someone cries, "The Channeler oil killed our champion!" More shouts follow.

The crowd shifts with uneasiness, like a beast rearing up to bellow. It isn't Seeva's responsibility to face them alone. I should be the one talking about Sanguine to my people.

My insides are made of Segrande's rocks.

"Let me finish," I tell Seeva, sick with how Malamians may take the rest of the news, and yet knowing it must be done. Seeva gives me a surprised look, and then steps away. There are few times I have felt this alone against the world. Suddenly the weight of my words carries them down so deep inside me, it's almost impossible to find them.

"If you will allow me to address my fellow Malamians. What Seeva has spoken is true." I confirm her findings on the two oils and then explain the truth of Baltroit's death. "He fell victim to the oil because he didn't know the grave consequences. But use of this oil can result in death." Murmurs grow louder and louder, and the very shaky hold I have over the crowd is moments from being lost.

"But we have arrested the people responsible for this oil," Seeva says, and my jaw unhinges so quickly, I almost look at the ground to see if it's there.

Seeva catches my eye and nods. "We have detained Judge Soma and Astoria Jarom of Celize for their roles in creating and supplying oil for the trade that has caused harm to citizens of Malam and Shaerdan." Her declaration unleashes a torrent of gasps and chatter. No one seems to believe what has been said, least of all me. And at the same time, a thrill of relief goes through me.

Only, it doesn't seem as though people are pleased with the explanation. The animosity grows. In the wall of angry people, there are some who stand out. Their actions are different from the crowd's.

A mother rocking her babe, a father with his small son sitting atop his shoulders, a little girl waving a Malamian flag. I hold to those sights and remind myself that these are my people. This news cannot divide them.

All you need to be is a voice. Lirra's advice comes back to me, and I clutch it like a lifeline. Be the voice that starts the change. It must begin somewhere.

"I have told you this news so you will be aware. Whoever is supplying this oil has no regard and no respect for Channeler magic and Channeler culture. Whoever is supplying this oil does not value life, whether Channeler or giftless. All of us are important. All of us deserve a place to live where we can feel a part of the community, where we can raise our families in safety, and we can learn and celebrate the differences in others." My voice cracks from shouting.

The world seems to pause.

"We are a nation that has been divided, torn apart by our

past," I say. "But it doesn't have to define us. I plead for unity in Malam, between all the people who live there. Our differences are what make us strong and valuable and important. We can be strong together, and face the future as a united people."

I wait, as silence falls over the faces across from me.

To my left, Seeva clutches her robes, and the sight rattles me, because I know everything depends on this moment, this speech. If I cannot convince the Guild that Malam is changing for the better, it will be that much harder to convince Channelers to return to Malam. It will be that much harder to move on from the past.

Start a storm. "I ask you now, who of you will stand up with me? Who will set aside the past and stand up for unity in Malam?"

"I will."

The small voice at my rear startles me. I turn around.

"Lirra?"

She grins. Her smile nearly knocks me off my feet. Then she edges to the cone and shouts, "I am Lirra Barrett, daughter of Millner Barrett. Some of you know him as the Archtraitor of Malam." Gasps spread. "Nearly eighteen years ago, my mother was killed after my father publicly spoke out against the Purge. Since that terrible time, my father and I have been living in Shaerdan. But I stand before you now and announce myself as a supporter of Malam. I have talked with King Aodren. He is a good man who has a vision for a better future. He cares about each citizen, giftless or Channeler. I pledge now to stand with him. Tonight, I will stand for Malam at the jubilee."

The reactions vary throughout the crowd, but they're silenced when Leif ambles to my side, his steps stiff from tonight's fight.

"I will stand with King Aodren, and I will stand for Malam."

Next comes Lord Segrande.

And from there, one by one, Malamians stand in the crowd. Emotion blazes in my eyes and shakes me to my core as I look out to an entire tournament field of people on their feet. At the south side, I spot Lirra's friend Orli. She waves, and shouts her allegiance along with hundreds of other voices, all pledging to stand united with me and with Malam.

LIRRA

I CAN SEE AODREN WANTS TO TALK, BUT I GIVE his hand one quick squeeze and rush off the field to prepare for the jubilee finale. We have so many things to say to each other, but they will have to wait a little longer. The announcer takes back the amplifying cone and calls out the performances of the grand finale. It is the perfect ending for the crowds that have flocked here tonight.

Seeva rushes around, assuring each woman from the five kingdoms that water Channelers will combine their efforts to hold back the rain from destroying any presentation that would be ruined otherwise. Aodren is escorted to the stand where Malam's nobility sit, and I cannot help but notice with glee the many back pats he receives and hands he shakes. For a man who once thought no one truly saw him, now he holds the eyes of all five kingdoms.

I stand beside my aunt Katallia and Da. My hands twist through my gown.

I worry that my presentation will not be as grand or glorious as the four other kingdoms', but I decided to make this choice only moments ago. Da encouraged me to seek out what I want. And what that is combines gliders and Aodren.

When Seeva is done giving directions, the women separate with a final few minutes remaining before the jubilee begins.

I go to where my wings have been kept dry in Astoria's carriage. A bittersweet feeling spreads through me as I check the knots a dozen times and test the flexibility and strength of each joint. The bottom straps have been adjusted many times to fit my arms and torso, so when I lie beneath the wings, I will resemble a bird.

"You were meant to fly." Orli shoves the hood off her cloak and approaches the carriage.

"You came." I stand and smile, happy to see her emerge from the press of people.

Her eyes roll upward. "If I can rouse enough courage to track down a blood charm, break into the summer castle, and sneak you out, I think I can manage attending the jubilee to support my best friend."

"But you didn't know I was going to perform," I say.

"I know. I was prepared to sit in the crowd beside you." Orli's hand squeezes mine.

She would make the effort to battle back her fears for our friendship and the simple act of sitting beside me—the fact nearly chases away all the ache left by Astoria's betrayal.

She points to my wings. "When you fly over the field, I will cheer the loudest. But I want you to remember that the truth can be your wings as well. Don't let your flight stop tonight. It's time to follow your heart, follow your truth to new adventures and new lands."

The call of the trumpets announces the show's start. Orli hugs me goodbye and rushes to the spectators' section.

The first woman steps onto the field. I'm too nervous to watch the performances, but if the thunderous applause that follows each Channeler is any indication, they are all spectacular.

"And now for the final presentation of the night, Lirra Barrett, Channeler of Malam."

I step forward, my heart beating like a hammer against my ribs. Katallia and Seeva are standing at the side of the field. They check my wings and send me off on my own. The organizers roll out a tall platform to the center of the field that was here as part of the showcase events.

The weight of the audience's rapt attention follows my climb to the top. Looking down on everyone, I hold my hands out, calling on my influencing power over the wind. But my nerves scatter my energy. I think of what happened to my smaller glider in the preliminary meeting, and my knees knock like two woodpeckers fighting to the death.

I cannot seem to gather more than a light breeze. If I were to jump off the platform, the weight of the wings wouldn't catch the air. They'd send me straight to the ground.

People squirm with impatience. Whispers wind around below me. *What's she wearing? What is she waiting for?* A fire of embarrassment licks over my skin, and my eyes burn. Somewhere below, Aodren is watching me choke.

I press my eyes shut, willing myself to focus like Astoria once taught me, but then her image thwarts my effort. The weight of the wings presses against my back.

A voice rises from the crowd. "Fly, Lirra."

Leaning from Malam's nobility platform is Aodren, cleaned up from the fight, in all his kingly garb. He wants me to *fly*. My blood sings in my veins. I rally my energy and extend my palms, reaching for the wind overhead. A surge answers, a warm plume of air shifting over the field.

I leap off the platform. A collective gasp sucks through the crowd as the wings take me down before finding the rising pressure of air needed to sustain flight. Applause echoes around me like thunder. Pulling the ropes fastened to the wings, I glide around the field, weightless, happy, and free.

He shakes hands with people for what seems like hours. I watch from the opposite end of the field, where Da talks to Aunt Katallia. Eugenia stands beside me with the littleuns scampering around us, their arms outstretched like wings.

I apologize for not telling Orli what I overheard at the Elementiary, but she brushes away the apology. "It's understandable," she says. Astoria made her choices, and I will have to accept that her absence will hurt for a long time.

When Orli leaves, Da moves into her spot. He stands beside me and follows the line of my attention. "If we are to have no secrets, Lirra, you should tell me more about your king."

I watch Aodren. Tomorrow is the final day of the summit, when the meetings wrap up and the retinues pack to return to their kingdoms. I have stood for Malam tonight, but I don't know exactly what that means. Seeva said that declaring my allegiance to Malam tonight only recognizes it as my homeland. There are no other obligations concerning the neighboring kingdom.

It breaks me to think that tonight or tomorrow may be the last time I see Aodren. So much so that I utter, "He is their king. I have no claim to him." The admission makes me unbearably sad, and at the same time, I couldn't be prouder of his actions.

"Is he the man who came to our home?" Eugenia asks, stepping up to Da and dipping her shoulder beneath his, so she is safely tucked into his side. Sweet Julisa sleeps in Eugenia's arms.

No more secrets. "Aye."

Eugenia's eyes flare, and I can tell she wants to say more, but she doesn't want to risk waking Julisa. "On Monday, the littleuns and I will add your name to our prayers when we go to the cathedral. It seems you will need prayers for the safekeeping of your heart as much as your father needs them to keep his nose out of trouble and to continue bringing him safely home."

My head cocks to the side. Is that what Eugenia does at the cathedral on the cliff each Monday? She prays for safety? I always thought she was making penance. This night is one of endless surprises.

"You know, I knew his father," Da says.

My nose wrinkles as it always does when he brings up the horrors of his past.

"No, no. Before the dark times. Leon and I were friends."

I listen to Da tell of a boy who looked similar to Aodren but was anxious and fearful. As the years passed, his fears bled into his leadership and eventually took over his kingdom. "That man may look like his father, but I can tell you now, he's nothing like Leon. I think his people are starting to see that as well."

His admission is something Aodren would appreciate hearing. Though I watch the king of Malam, a smile wide across his face, and I think he already knows.

I walk over to the carriage and grab my wings. "Ready?"

"Time to go already, Lir?" Loren complains.

"It's late."

He crosses his arms and pouts. "But what of Aodren, the bloody king o' Malam?"

Eugenia gasps. "Loren, what did you just say?"

My laugh echoes over Loren's excuse. "I think he'll be all

right," I say about Aodren. Though I cannot say the same about myself.

The next day I wake to the twins poking my back.

"Whaaa?" I roll to face them.

"Why do you always grumble in the morning?" Loren's face is a knuckle's distance from mine, his eyes wide and scrutinizing.

"Why do you always have to wake me?" I ask.

"You said you would let us play with the gliders."

That is true. After the nonstop business of the last two weeks, it's hardly believable that there is nothing left to be done today. It takes time to load up the carriage with the gliders, but once I'm done, we wave goodbye to Da and Eugenia. The boys sit beside me as I roll the carriage out of our family's secret patch of forest and up to the highest hill.

From there, our view stretches from the Skyward Forest to the south to the All Kingdoms' tents to the northwest. The bangs and shouts of people packing up camp come from the city of canvas. Already, many tents have been taken down.

Aodren may still be at the summer castle. The traveling parties headed east haven't been swathed in Malam's royal colors, and none have toted the mark of royalty. He is probably busy preparing to leave.

My interruption would be just that, an interruption.

I work on strapping the twins to the glider. I give them a quick lesson on how to steer, one they've already had from me a dozen times over. But I can never be too cautious with my brothers. If needed, I'll guide them on the wind back to me, though I don't tell them that. Instead, I wish them luck and send them off the steep edge of the hill.

Their squeals peal out, their happiness and glee masking the sounds of the summit's end.

I watch them fly and see what Orli saw when she said my gliders could change Channeler society. My imagination takes in a sky of gliders, or other inventions that could be used by both giftless and Channelers. It's a beautiful dream, one that I hope to have a part in. Even if I don't know when, I know change is on the horizon for my kingdom and for Malam. Maybe the future is closer than I think.

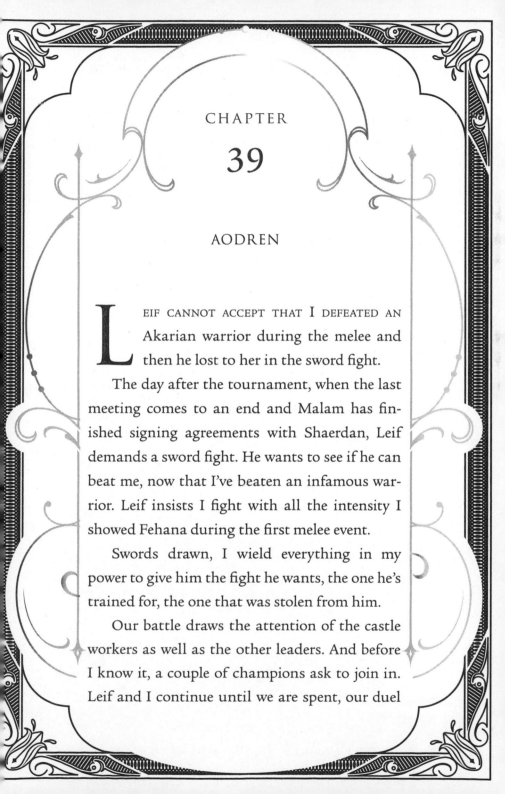

CHAPTER

39

AODREN

L EIF CANNOT ACCEPT THAT I DEFEATED AN Akarian warrior during the melee and then he lost to her in the sword fight.

The day after the tournament, when the last meeting comes to an end and Malam has finished signing agreements with Shaerdan, Leif demands a sword fight. He wants to see if he can beat me, now that I've beaten an infamous warrior. Leif insists I fight with all the intensity I showed Fehana during the first melee event.

Swords drawn, I wield everything in my power to give him the fight he wants, the one he's trained for, the one that was stolen from him.

Our battle draws the attention of the castle workers as well as the other leaders. And before I know it, a couple of champions ask to join in. Leif and I continue until we are spent, our duel ending in a tie. Given some time to recuperate, Leif then challenges Fehana. In the time I've spent with Leif, I haven't seen him as happy as he is while fighting the warrior.

The next day, the carriages are packed and ready to go. Our traveling party is scheduled to leave for Malam.

I've shaken hands with each leader, even Gorenza, who managed to address me as King Aodren when he said goodbye. Segrande joins me where I stand beside the carriage.

"You truly proved yourself," Segrande says. "I'll admit, I had my doubts. But your speech the night before last showed your true colors. You're the rock Malam needs to lean on."

Segrande and his rock metaphors. "Thank you."

The older dignitary climbs aboard while I wait outside the carriage for Leif. He finally emerges from the stables with Gale trotting behind him.

"You're certain you want us to go ahead?" he asks.

"I am."

"If you've not caught up by tomorrow, we'll turn back."

"The carriage travels much slower than me. Keep on the path. I'll reach you before you cross the border."

He grinds his teeth, and I can tell he doesn't like the plan. But I need to do this next thing alone.

The clearing outside Lirra's home is empty. This time, to avoid drawing notice, I'm wearing the hat she lent me and the tunic. I leave Gale to graze as I gather the nerve to approach the house.

Before I can reach the front door, it swings open and Lirra's two brothers come tearing out. The first stumbles to a stop when he sees me. "Oi! It's the bloody King o' Malam."

"Loren!" A woman's voice comes from inside. "I told you not to use that language."

Loren looks over his shoulder and then winks at me before he and Kiefer scurry out of sight.

A woman appears in the door, dark brown hair the same deepness as her eyes that flare when they see me.

I slide the hat off my head. "Good afternoon, Mrs. Barrett. I came hoping to talk to your—"

"My daughter?" Millner shuffles up the stairs of his cellar, the boys following him. Once he's on the lawn, it takes him only two seconds to reach my side. For a portly man, he is incredibly nimble.

"Your High—"

"Aodren," I interrupt. "How are you, sir? I wished to see Lirra."

Millner's assessing eyes roam over me. "What's this? You've decided to be a commoner?"

"I may be the king of Malam, but I'm also just a man, one who is quite taken with your daughter."

"Is that so?" Millner's cheeks ball into fall apples, and his eyes twinkle. "And what do you have to say to her?"

I clear my throat. "I—I was hoping, that is . . ." I clear my throat. "Seeds, this is harder than I thought." I wipe my brow. If he's the gatekeeper, the only option I have is to be honest so he'll fetch her. "She pledged herself to be Malam's Channeler the night before last. And I was hoping, well, wondering if she wanted to spend time in Malam to assist in setting up an Elementiary in the royal city."

A snort sounds behind me, and Millner chuckles.

I turn to find Lirra standing in her family's doorway. The seams of the green dress she wears make trails across her lovely curves.

"I like your outfit," she says, stealing the words off my tongue.

"Not more than I like yours," I say, and my response is rewarded with a twitch of a smile.

"Please, Your Highness, don't let me interrupt. You were saying you want to steal me away to Malam."

Her father coughs. "Lirra."

At the same time, I jump in and explain, "It was more of an official request. The last thing I want is for your father to think I am a thief come to sneak you away."

"But you've gotten so good at sneaking."

The pressure of her father's gaze on me makes me want to sink into the ground. I would rather face Hemmet again than this. I step closer to Lirra, eliminating the space between us. "If you would be so kind, my lady, I've come to ask you to return to Malam with me."

Her smile fades now, and her eyes shift around the clearing.

It takes only one word from her stepmother to empty the

clearing. After bowing and blushing, Lirra's stepmother waves and drags her husband into the home. Now Lirra and I stand outside alone.

Her teeth press down into her lip.

"Will you consider it?" I ask. "I feel like the tides have finally turned. But I need you at my side. We have worked well together, and I would like your help in moving Malam forward."

"Is that the only reason you want me to come?"

I study her face, unsure if she can handle what I truly want from her. Because I've learned that honesty is best, I simply say, "No."

My fingers wind around hers, seeking contact like gravity exists for only our hands. Lirra stares down at our entwined fingers and then her blue eyes lift to mine. They are the sky I want to spend my days under for the rest of my life. Of course, I don't tell her this. I can see making the move to Malam will be a frightening enough change for this brilliant girl.

"The other day, you said you were busy with life," I say, reminding her.

Sadness spreads over her face. I cannot allow it to linger for more than a moment.

"I was hoping that's a burden we could share in Malam." I slide my free hand into the thick length of her hair, knowing I will never get enough of the silky strands. Her chin, ever so slightly tips up. I need no more invitation to drop my mouth to her soft lips.

Just as I lose myself in her sunshine, she moves back and reaches for my hand.

"Well, we make a great team," she says. "Look at all we've done. And even more has happened in the past week."

She's right. After the grand finale, there were meetings to finalize trade, discussions between leaders for how to proceed with Sanguine, and talks with my men to take the unity and pride we've established here back to Malam.

Change is on the horizon for Malam, but this time, I can see the valley beyond. Not all my people were here for the All Kingdoms' Summit, but there were enough to start a change. As Lirra said, it takes one voice.

Thankfully, I'm returning to Malam with a chorus.

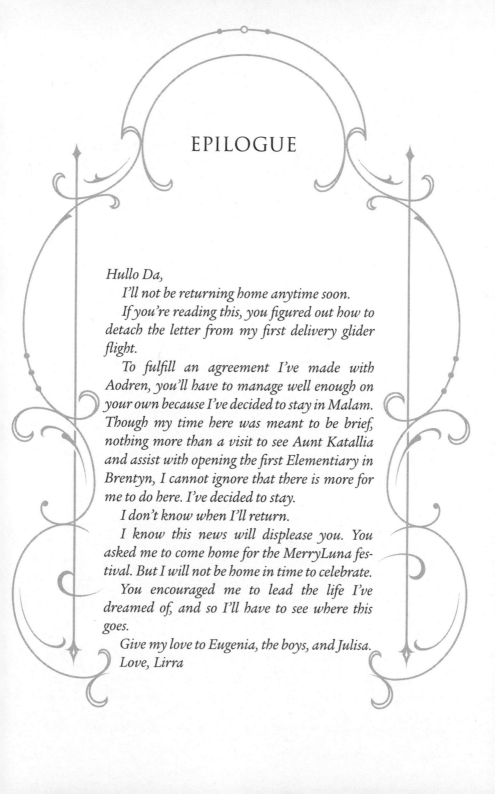

EPILOGUE

Hullo Da,

I'll not be returning home anytime soon.

If you're reading this, you figured out how to detach the letter from my first delivery glider flight.

To fulfill an agreement I've made with Aodren, you'll have to manage well enough on your own because I've decided to stay in Malam. Though my time here was meant to be brief, nothing more than a visit to see Aunt Katallia and assist with opening the first Elementiary in Brentyn, I cannot ignore that there is more for me to do here. I've decided to stay.

I don't know when I'll return.

I know this news will displease you. You asked me to come home for the MerryLuna festival. But I will not be home in time to celebrate.

You encouraged me to lead the life I've dreamed of, and so I'll have to see where this goes.

Give my love to Eugenia, the boys, and Julisa.

Love, Lirra

ACKNOWLEDGMENTS

Each time I write a book, I think, this will be a breeze to write. After all, I've written a few novels and it stands to reason that I've mastered the skill of novel writing. But it doesn't take long to realize I'm wrong. I get lost in the words and can't remember how to write a book at all. Without the following people, my champions, critics, and creative coaches, this book might still be stuck on my hard drive, in literary limbo. I owe them my gratitude for helping me remember how to write.

First and always, my thanks to my family for their patience, encouragement and faith. To my husband, my children, my parents, and my siblings, your support always has a way of lighting the darkness. You're there when I need you most. I love you all.

No show of gratitude could ever be enough for Caitlyn McFarland, who helped me take the seed of an idea and mold it into a flushed-out story. Thank you, Caitlyn, for being my sounding board, my first reader, and my friend when I was sleep deprived and whiny. My heartfelt thanks go to Lindsey Leavitt, who took my plot crises and showed me a smorgasbord of possibilities. When I started to lose my way, Charlie Holmberg, Kathryn Purdie, and Pintip Dunn helped draw more emotion into the story by giving invaluable romance advice.

To Rahul Kanakia who is brilliant and knows exactly when to call me and share anecdotal humorous advice. My gratitude to Veeda Bybee for writing on my couch when I needed a friend and nudging me to continue learning and growing. And the hugest huggy thanks to Jodi Meadows and C. J. Redwine who are practically shoe-ins for Buffy the Vampire Slayer because they saved me from a rabid bat attack and became my go-to cheerleader support when I wanted to give up.

I would be utterly adrift without my agent, Josh Adams, who always manages to steer me in the right direction. Thank you for being my champion on this literary journey. I am ever grateful that you found value in that first manuscript I sent your way.

My heartfelt thanks goes to Nicole Sclama, who found the heart of my story and helped it to beat through the pages. And to my wonderful team at Houghton Mifflin Harcourt—Tara Shanahan, Tara Sonin, Alia Almeida, and Emma Gordon —you have provided wonderful support, creative marketing ideas, and stunning books. You are a joy to work with.

While writing *Once A King,* I found friends in the blogger/ Instagram community that inspired me and encouraged my love of reading and writing. Thanks to Christine Manzari for supporting me and offering friendship. Many thanks to the wonderful Bookstagrammers that have welcomed me and of- fered wonderful advice—Bridget Howard, Kristen Williams, Kayla Cercone, Erin Fehres, Cait Herold, Brittney Singleton, Brie Wood, Tara Hansen, Christy Mullins, Fallon Vaughn,

Kristina Selby, Rebecca Longi, Joanna Garcia, Dina Dennaoui, Meredith Mara, Sara from @novel.novice, Lori from @Lori-imagination, Lisa from @lifeinlit, Nicole from @fearyourex, Christy from @cbookaddiction, Anna from @thecityofdark-clockwork, Mariana from @bookisglee, and Mai from @book-ish_mai.

My warmest thanks goes to those that have been willing to hear my ideas and give feedback and friendship over the years—Peggy Eddleman, Jessie Humphries, Emily King, Tricia Levenseller, Elana Johnson, Adam Johnson, Sara Larson, Rosalyn Eves, Brekke Felt, Taffy Lovell, Erik and Shanelle Bayles, and Rob and Karly Code.

And last but not least, to all the readers. I'm ever grateful for your kind words and willingness to read my stories. Your continued support and pre-orders always humble me.